GRAND PASSION

Also by Jayne Ann Krentz
in Thorndike Large Print ®

Family Man
Perfect Partners

This Large Print Book carries the
Seal of Approval of N.A.V.H.

GRAND PASSION

JAYNE ANN KRENTZ

Thorndike Press • Thorndike, Maine

Published in 1994 by arrangement with Pocket Books,
a division of Simon & Schuster, Inc.

Throndike Large Print ® Romance Series.

The tree indicium is a trademark of Thorndike Press.

The text of this Large Print edition is unabridged.
Other aspects of the book may vary froom the original edition.

Set in 16 pt. News Plantin by Juanita Macdonald.

Printed in the United States on acid-free, high opacity paper ∞

Library of Congress Cataloging in Publication Data

Krentz, Jayne Ann.
    Grand passion / Jayne Ann Krentz.
      p.   cm.
    ISBN 0-7862-0162-2 (alk. paper : lg. print)
    ISBN 0-7862-0183-5 (alk. paper : lg. print : pbk)
    1. Large type books. I. Title.
  [PS3561.R44G7 1994b]
  813'.54—dc20   93-49684

For Claire Zion, editor and friend:
You believed in me from the beginning —
My thanks.

Prologue

Max Fortune sat alone in the hidden chamber of the cold brick mansion and contemplated his collection. It was something he did frequently. He had learned long ago that his paintings and books were the only things that truly belonged to him, the only things that no one could take away from him.

Most of the masterpieces that hung on the walls of the secured, climate-controlled vault had been created by modern artists who were only just beginning to achieve the recognition they deserved. A few paintings were already acknowledged as works of genius. Some of the artists were still undiscovered, except by Max.

Although he knew their present and future value, Max had not collected the paintings as an investment. Savage, bleak, and technically brilliant, the canvases reflected something inside himself that he could not put into words. Many were the stuff of the old nightmares that he had had as a child.

He had no doubt that one day every painting in his possession would be acclaimed as the unique creation it was. His instincts were unerring when it came to art. He had the inner eye.

With the exception of the complete works of Dr. Seuss and several tattered volumes of The Hardy Boys series, the rare books in the glass cases would have fetched enormous sums at any auction. Max coveted books almost as much as he coveted paintings.

He especially valued old and rare books, books that had a history, books that had meant something to someone. When he held an old book in his hands, Max knew a fleeting sense of connection with people who had lived before him. He felt as though he shared a small part of someone else's past. It was as close as he got to feeling like a member of a family.

The elegant old house, which Max occupied alone, sat on Seattle's Queen Anne Hill. It commanded a sweeping view of the city and Elliott Bay and was considered a prime piece of real estate. Everything in the mansion, from the 1978 California Cabernet Sauvignon that Max was drinking to the exquisite Oriental rugs on the polished hardwood floors, had been chosen with great care.

But Max knew better than anyone that all the money he had lavished on the great brick structure had not accomplished the impossible. It had not turned his house into a home.

Max had not had a home since the age of

six. He was fairly certain now that he would never have one. He accepted that stark fact. He had long ago learned that the secret of surviving was not to want the things he could not have.

Max's philosophy of life worked quite well for the most part because there were very few things he wanted that he could not have.

Among the many things that Max had acquired for himself was a formidable reputation.

People described his reputation in different ways. Some said he was dangerous. Others said he was brilliant and ruthless, utterly unrelenting in his pursuit of a goal. Everyone agreed on one thing, which was that when Max Fortune set out to do a job, the job got done.

Max knew that his legendary reputation was based on one very simple fact: He never screwed up.

Or, almost never.

1

It had taken Max Fortune nearly a month to locate Jason Curzon's mistress. Now that he had found her, he didn't know what to make of her. Cleopatra Robbins was definitely not the sort of woman he had been expecting to find.

Max stood quietly near the roaring fire and surveyed the chaos that filled the cozy lobby of the Robbins' Nest Inn. In spite of her evocative first name, Ms. Robbins certainly did not look like a sultry charmer who made her living by seducing wealthy men old enough to be her grandfather.

She looked exactly like what she purported to be a cheerfully harried innkeeper trying to deal with a flood of new arrivals.

Max glanced at the series of insipid seascapes hanging on the walls as he listened to the hubbub going on around him. He smiled with faint derision. It was obvious that Cleopatra Robbins was not only not a typical seductress, she was not much of a connoisseur of art. Anyone who would hang those bland views of storm-tossed seas would be incapable of appreciating the five Amos Luttrell paintings that had been left in her care.

It was just as well she preferred the seascapes, because Max intended to take the Luttrells from her. They belonged to him. They constituted his inheritance from Jason Curzon, and Max had every intention of claiming them.

He was prepared to use whatever tactics were necessary to recover the legacy. Having to fight for what was his would be nothing new for Max. Since the age of six, he had done battle for everything he had ever wanted in life. Sometimes he lost, but more often he won.

Max rested both hands on the intricately carved hawk that formed the grip of his cane. With an effort of will that was second nature to him, he ignored the persistent ache in his leg. The old wound was acting up again tonight, bringing back memories he had no intention of indulging.

He concentrated instead on Cleopatra Robbins as she bustled about behind the front desk.

Max remembered that Jason had called her Cleo. The nickname suited her much better than the more dramatic Cleopatra.

Trust Jason to choose a mistress who did not fit the stereotype. But, then, Jason had always had a gift for looking beneath the surface. He'd had the discerning eye of an intuitive collector, a man who trusted his own instincts rather than the opinion of others. The stunning array of paintings he had bequeathed to his favorite art museum in Seattle bore testimony to his unerring taste. But the five Amos Luttrells had formed the centerpiece of his collection.

Curzon had owned close to two hundred paintings at the time of his death. As far as Max knew, Cleopatra Robbins was the only mistress Jason had ever collected.

An unexpected sense of wrongness rippled through Max as he tried to envision the woman behind the desk in bed with Jason Curzon. Jason was the closest thing Max had ever had to a father. He told himself he should have been glad that the old man had had some feminine companionship during the last year and a half of his life. God knew, Jason had had many lonely years after the death of his wife.

But for some reason Max didn't like the idea that the female providing that companionship had been Cleo Robbins.

Max concluded that she was somewhere in her late twenties, perhaps twenty-seven or twenty-eight. He studied her precariously listing topknot of thick, dark, auburn hair and found himself wondering what it would look like tumbled down around her shoulders. There was no particular style to the design of the topknot. The rich mass of hair had obviously been twisted into position in a hurry, anchored with a clip, and left to flounder under its own weight.

Instead of the exotic kohl her namesake might have used to outline her eyes, Cleo Robbins wore a pair of round, gold-framed glasses. Max realized that in an odd way they served the same purpose as elaborate makeup, concealing the real expression in her wide, hazel green eyes.

The lady he had been hunting for the past month looked out at the world with the professionally friendly gaze of a successful innkeeper, but he sensed something deeper and more compelling about her.

Max had an inexplicable urge to try something that he knew from experience rarely worked. He looked into Cleo Robbins the way he looked into a painting.

To his surprise, the commotion and noise around him receded, just as it did when he was transfixed by a work of art. The world and his focus narrowed to include only Cleo Robbins. He felt the familiar stirring deep inside himself almost immediately. It made him uneasy. He was accustomed to feeling this sense of fascination and longing only when he was in the presence of the things he collected.

Jason had told Max that the talent could be applied to people as well as art and books. But Max had discovered the hard way that the ability to see beneath the surface had its limits when it came to dealing with other human beings. People were more complex than art, and all too often they had an ability to hide the deeper truths about themselves.

Nevertheless, there was no denying the kick-in-the-gut feeling he was getting now as he studied Cleo with what Jason had called his inner eye.

"Just one moment, Mr. Partridge. I'll have someone take your luggage up to your room." Cleo gave the irritable-looking Mr. Partridge a spectacular smile as she banged the silver bell on the desk.

"About time," Partridge muttered. "Took me nearly three hours to get here from Seattle. Don't know why in hell the company had to pick an inn way out here on the coast for this damn fool motivational seminar. Could have held it at one of the big hotels in the city."

"I'm sure you'll find that at this time of year the Washington coast provides a wonderful setting for an educational retreat." Cleo glanced anxiously toward the staircase. "I'm afraid my bellhop is busy at the moment. I'll give you your key, and you can go on up to your room. I'll have the luggage brought up to you later, if you don't mind."

"Forget it. I'll carry it myself." Partridge snatched up the suitcase at his feet. "Can I at least get a drink somewhere around here?"

"An excellent selection of Northwest wines and beers is available in the lounge, Mr. Partridge."

"Damn. What I really need is a martini." Partridge snatched up his key and stalked toward the staircase. The next three people in line behind him surged forward in a wave.

Max watched as Cleo braced herself for the onslaught. He saw her glance again at the stairs. When the missing bellhop did not materialize there, she turned back to face the wave with a warm smile of welcome.

The lobby door slammed open with a crash. Max saw lightning crackle across the night sky. Rain, wind, and two more drenched inn patrons blew into the hall. They joined the crowd milling around in front of the hearth.

"Lucky Ducky go swimming."

Startled by the high, squeaky voice that came out of nowhere, Max looked down. A small boy with a head full of blond curls looked up at him. He was dressed in a miniature pair of jeans and a striped shirt. He appeared to be no more than five years old, and he had

16

a thumb stuck in his mouth.

"I beg your pardon?" Max could not recall the last time he had conversed with a child.

The small boy yanked his thumb out of his mouth long enough to repeat his statement. "Lucky Ducky go swimming." Jamming his thumb back into his mouth, he gave Max an expectant look.

"I see." Max sought for a suitable response. "It's a cold night for swimming, isn't it?"

"Uncle Jason said ducks can swim anytime, anywhere."

Max's hands tightened around the hawk-headed grip of the cane. "Uncle Jason?"

"Uncle Jason's gone," the child confided with a wistful expression. "Cleo says he's in heaven."

"Jason Curzon in heaven?" Max contemplated that. "Well, anything's possible, I suppose."

"Did you know Uncle Jason?"

"Yes."

The boy took his thumb out of his mouth again and gave Max a bright, toothless smile. "My name is Sammy Gordon. Did you know my daddy, too?"

"I don't think so." A staggering thought occurred to Max. "Not unless your daddy was Uncle Jason?"

"No, no, no," the child said, clearly impatient. "My daddy isn't in heaven like Uncle Jason. My daddy's lost."

Max realized he was beginning to lose the thread of the conversation. "Lost?"

Sammy nodded quickly. "I heard Mommy tell Cleo that he had to go find himself."

"I see."

"He never did, I guess."

Max did not know what to say to that. He glanced across the crowded room and saw a pretty woman with short, honey-blond hair emerge from the office behind the front desk. She went to give Cleo a hand.

"That's my mommy," Sammy volunteered.

"What's her name?"

"Sylvia Gordon." Sammy eyed Max's cane with deep interest. "Why do you have to lean on that? Did you hurt yourself?"

"Yes."

"Will you be all better soon?"

"I hurt myself a long time ago," Max said. "This is as good as I'm going to get."

"Oh." Sammy was intrigued.

"Sammy?" Cleo came around from behind the desk. "Where are you?"

Max's head came up swiftly. Jason's mistress had a rich honey-and-cream sort of voice, perfectly suited to a Cleopatra. Another jolt of awareness went through him. He could almost hear that warm, sensual voice in bed.

18

"Here I am, Cleo." Sammy waved a wet thumb at her.

Max's eye was caught by a glimpse of silver as Cleo emerged from the crowd. He glanced down and frowned when he saw that Jason's mistress favored shiny, silver-toned sneakers with glittering, metallic laces. The rest of her attire was not nearly as tasteless, but it wasn't particularly inspiring, either. It consisted of a yellow oxford cloth button-down shirt and a pair of faded jeans.

"I wondered where you were, Sammy." Cleo smiled at the boy, and then her eyes met Max's.

He saw the startled expression that appeared in her soft hazel gaze. For a few seconds her gold-framed glasses afforded her no protection at all. In that brief moment she was as open to him as a work of art, and he knew that she was as aware of him as he was of her.

The impact of the flash of raw intimacy stunned Max. It was a dangerously disturbing experience, completely unlike anything he had ever known with another human being. Until now the only things that had had a similar effect on him were extraordinarily fine paintings and very old books. Desire, fierce and completely unexpected, swept through him. He fought it with all the willpower at his command.

Cleo's gaze slipped briefly to Max's cane, breaking the spell. When she looked up again, she had her professionally hospitable expression firmly in place. Her eyes were still very lovely, but they were no longer as clear and readable as they had been a few seconds earlier. The lady had stepped back behind her veil, and Max had himself under control once more.

"We'll be right with you, sir," she said to Max. "As you can see, we're a little busy at the moment."

"He's a friend of Uncle Jason's," Sammy volunteered.

Cleo's eyes widened. The professional politeness in her expression disappeared. It was replaced by a brilliant, welcoming warmth that made Max's insides tighten.

"You're a friend of Jason's?" Cleo asked eagerly.

"Yes."

"That's *wonderful*. Don't worry, I'm sure we can find room for you. Make yourself comfortable while Sylvia and I finish the check-in. I didn't catch your name."

"Max Fortune."

"Right. Sammy, show him into the solarium. He can wait there."

"Okay." Sammy looked up at Jason. "You can follow me."

Max kept his eyes on Cleo. "If you don't mind, I believe I'll wait here. I wanted to speak with you."

"Of course," Cleo said easily. "Just as soon as I have a free minute." She glanced down at Sammy. "Honey, do you know where Benjy is?"

"Benjy's gone."

Cleo was clearly nonplussed. "Gone?"

Sammy nodded. "That's what Trisha says."

"She must have meant he was busy," Cleo said.

"Nope." Sammy shook his head with grave certainty. "He's gone."

"Good grief. He can't be gone," Cleo said. "He's supposed to be here tonight. He knew we had this group arriving."

"Cleo? Where are you?" A young woman who appeared to be no more than nineteen or twenty approached with a stack of towels in her arms. She, too, was wearing jeans. She also had on a loose-fitting plaid flannel shirt. Her light brown hair was tied back in a ponytail, and her attractive features were marked with fine lines of tension.

"Right here." Cleo frowned in concern. "Are you okay, Trisha?"

"Sure, just real busy."

"Where's Benjy?"

"I don't know." Trisha's eyes slid away

from Cleo's. "We've got a problem in two-ten. The toilet's stopped up."

"Just what I needed," Cleo muttered. "Benjy's the master plumber around here. Where is he when I need him?"

"Want me to work on it?" Trisha asked.

"No, you finish making up the rooms. I'll get someone else on it." Cleo swung back around and pinned Max with a hopeful look. "What did you say your name was?"

"Max Fortune."

"And you were a friend of Jason's?"

"Yes."

"A good friend?"

"Yes."

Cleo gave him a dazzling smile. "Then that makes you practically one of the family, doesn't it?"

"I don't know," Max said. "Does it?"

"Of course it does. Jason would never have sent you out here to meet us unless he considered you family. At times like this, family pitches in around here. Jason always did his share when he was staying with us. Do you mind?"

"I'm afraid I don't quite follow, Ms. Robbins."

"No problem. I'm sure you'll figure it out soon enough. This way."

"Ms. Robbins, I'm here to talk to you."

"Later. Like I said, I'm really swamped right now." Cleo led the way down a short hall.

A strange sense of disorientation gripped Max. "Ms. Robbins, if you don't mind, I'd rather wait out here."

"Everyone helps," Sammy said. He took his thumb out of his mouth again and grabbed a fistful of Max's Italian-designed, hand-tailored jacket. The fine silk-and-wool-blend fabric crumpled beneath the devastating assault of the little fingers.

Max gave up trying to argue and allowed himself to be tugged down the hall. Cleo was already well ahead of him. She had a closet door open at the end of a corridor and was peering inside.

"Aha. Here we go." She reached into the closet, hauled out a plunger, and held it triumphantly aloft. "Trisha said it was room number two-ten. Sammy can show you the way, can't you, Sammy?"

"Okay," Sammy said happily.

Max eyed the plunger. It dawned on him just what was expected of him. "I think there is a misunderstanding here, Ms. Robbins."

She gave him an inquiring look. "You did say you were a friend of Jason's, didn't you?"

"That's what I said." Max eyed the plunger grimly.

23

"Jason was always terrific about lending a hand when one was needed," Cleo said encouragingly.

Max looked at her. He didn't know what to make of Jason's mistress, but he knew that until he found the five Amos Luttrell paintings, he was going to have to bide his time. "I'll see what I can do."

"Wonderful. I really appreciate this." Cleo thrust the plunger into his hand and gave him a smile of deep gratitude. "Run along with Sammy, now. I've got to get back to the front desk." She turned and hurried down the hall without a backward glance.

"This way." Sammy yanked on Max's jacket. "There's stairs in the back."

Max set his teeth and allowed himself to be dragged off, plunger in hand, toward an unknown destiny. He felt as if he'd accidentally stepped into another world, where the laws of nature were slightly altered. *Jason, what the hell were you doing out here,* he asked silently as Sammy led him up the back stairs to the second floor.

"In here." Sammy pushed open the door marked two-ten.

The room was empty. Max swept the frilly, fussy, overstuffed furnishings with a single glance and dismissed everything, including the picture of the spaniels that hung over the bed.

It was a classic example of Victorian sentimentalism and extravagance at its worst.

Max walked across the ugly flower-pattern carpet and glanced warily into the white-tiled bath. He was willing to acknowledge that the Victorians had known how to do bathrooms. He approved of the huge, white, claw-footed tub.

He did not, however, like the way water lapped at the edge of the toilet bowl, threatening to spill over onto the floor. At least it appeared to be clean water, he thought. He supposed he should be grateful for that much.

"Lucky Ducky go swimming," Sammy reminded him again.

Realization dawned on Max. "In this particular toilet?"

"Ducks can swim anywhere."

Max resigned himself to the inevitable. He leaned his cane and the plunger against the wall while he shrugged out of his expensive jacket. He hung the jacket carefully on the hook behind the door. Then he unfastened his gold cuff links, put them in his pocket, and rolled up the sleeves of his handmade white silk shirt.

Family pitches in at times like this.

It was an odd thing to say to a man who had not been part of a real family since the age of six. As far as Max was concerned, the series of foster homes he had lived in after his mother was killed in a car accident did not count.

He had never known his father, a faceless figure who had walked out of his life before he was even born. Max had never bothered to search for him. He had no interest in locating a father who did not want to claim him.

It was after he had been shunted off to the second foster home that Max had begun collecting things. *Things* didn't reject you, he had discovered. *Things* didn't walk away from you. *Things* didn't tell you in a thousand subtle ways that you weren't good enough to be a member of the family. *Things* could be taken with you when you moved on to the next temporary location.

It had been books at first. Surprisingly enough it was easy to collect books, even if you couldn't afford them. People were astonishingly eager to give them to you. Teachers, social workers, librarians, foster mothers — they had all been delighted to give books to young Max.

For a long while he had worried that someone would eventually ask for them back. But no one ever did. Not even the librarian who had given Max his very first volume of Dr. Seuss.

Most of the other children had quickly

grown bored with their free books and had traded them to Max for what seemed to him like ridiculously low prices: a candy bar, a toy, a couple of quarters. Each book had been a rare bargain as far as Max was concerned. It was something that belonged to him. Something he could keep forever.

When he was young he had hoarded his treasures in his suitcase. They were always packed and ready for the next, inevitable move. He had asked his social worker for a lock and key for the dilapidated piece of luggage. She had smiled an odd, sad smile and given him one without question.

Max was sixteen when he discovered what was to become the grand passion of his life: modern art. He had skipped school one afternoon to wander through Seattle's Pioneer Square. For no particular reason he had walked into several of the galleries. In two of them he had seen paintings that had reached straight into the secret center of his being. For the first time he understood that there were others in the world who had nightmares and dreams that resembled his own. He had never forgotten the experience.

When he was in the presence of paintings that touched the raw core inside himself, Max did not feel quite so alone.

Max had been twenty-three when he and

Curzon had met. That had been twelve years ago. Max had just gotten out of the Army and had taken the first job he had found. It was manual labor for the most part, but Max had liked it right from the start. The work consisted primarily of crating, transporting, and hanging the paintings that an art dealer named Garrison Spark sold to his clients.

Max hadn't particularly liked Spark, whose ethics were questionable at best, but he had been transfixed by some of the art he was allowed to handle. Spark, in turn, found Max's unerring eye for art extremely useful. The two made a pact. In exchange for the job, Max promised not to voice his opinions on the authenticity of certain paintings that Spark sold unless the client asked for that opinion.

Max had delivered two paintings, both genuine, to Jason Curzon before the event occurred that had changed his life. The moment was still crystal clear in his mind.

He had just uncrated a large canvas, a dark, abstract picture purported to be the work of a new and rising artist whose paintings Jason had been eager to collect. Max had stood politely aside, allowing Jason to examine the picture in silence.

Jason had gazed into the painting for a long time before he had turned to Max with an enigmatic expression.

"What do you think?" Jason asked.

Max hid his surprise. In his experience clients never solicited the artistic opinion of the man who delivered their purchases.

Max looked at the painting. He had seen three other works that had been created by the same artist. He had been immediately compelled by the others. This one left him unmoved. He weighed his answer carefully. He knew Jason had paid a huge sum for the picture.

"I think it's a fake," Max finally said.

Jason gave him an appraising look. "So do I."

"A very good fake," Max said quickly, mindful of his treasured job. "After all, it fooled Mr. Spark."

Jason had merely arched his brows at that remark. He sent the painting back to Spark with no explanation other than that he had changed his mind. But the following month he had invited Max to view his private collection.

Max had been enthralled by the visions that hung on Jason's walls. At the end of the tour Jason had turned to him.

"You're smart and you think fast on your feet. Most important, I think you've got the inner eye," Jason said. "You ever think of doing something a little more intellectually demanding than crating and uncrating art for Garrison Spark."

"Like what?" Max asked.

"Like coming to work for me. I'll put you in charge of buying art for Curzon hotels. You'll report directly to me, and you'll answer only to me. It will mean travel, an excellent salary, bonuses, and mingling with the corporate hierarchy. Interested?"

"Why not?" Max said. He knew a turning point in his life when he saw one, and as usual he had nothing better waiting for him in the other direction.

Jason surveyed Max's cheap brown suit, permanent-press shirt, and frayed tie. "First we're going to have to polish you up a bit.

Jason was as good as his word. He taught Max everything he needed to know in order to move in the rarefied circles of the international hotel business. Max learned quickly. He copied Jason's exquisitely polished manners and wore his expensive new clothes with natural ease.

After having fought his way through the foster care system and the Army, he was not intimidated by the high-powered corporate types with whom he came in contact. Jason wryly observed that the situation was just the opposite. Most people were intimidated by Max.

"An extremely useful talent," Jason said a year after Max had been on the job. "I think we should make use of it."

Max knew how to make himself useful when it suited him. It suited him to please Jason Curzon.

Within six months he had become much more than the curator of Curzon International's art collection. He had become Jason's right-hand man.

His responsibilities had evolved swiftly. Someone else was eventually appointed to manage the art collection. Max was put in charge of gathering intelligence on the competition and reporting on the suitability of potential hotel sites. From the beginning he made it his goal to learn in advance everything Jason needed in order to make far-reaching decisions regarding potential acquisitions: local politics in foreign locations, including the names of the specific officials who expected to be bribed before construction could begin on a new hotel; the reliability, or lack thereof, of certain members of Curzon management; sites that were ripe for development or, conversely, needed to be abandoned before they started losing money. Max had made himself an indispensable authority on all of those things.

For all intents and purposes, he had been

second-in-command at Curzon.

In the process he had learned the correct way to drink tea in Japan, coffee in the Middle East, and champagne in France. He bought his shirts in London, his suits and shoes in Rome, and his ties in Paris. And he bought art and books wherever he found them.

Curzon Hotels was a family-owned business that had been bequeathed to Jason and his brother, Dennison, by their father. Jason had always held the reins of the company, not only because he was the elder brother, but because he had the savvy intelligence required to manage the business. Dennison had not liked being relegated to second place, but he had tolerated it because there was no doubt that Jason was the natural leader in the family.

Now, with Jason gone, Dennison was determined to demonstrate that he had as much business acumen as his brother.

While he was alive, Jason had given Max the illusion that he was almost a member of the Curzon family. Three years ago Max had made the mistake of thinking he was going to become a real member, but that promise had dissolved in the ruins of his relationship with Kimberly Curzon, Dennison's daughter.

Six weeks into the engagement, Kimberly had come to her senses and realized she could not marry a man with no background or family connections. She had married Roarke Winston, instead, the heir to a large industrial empire.

Max had realized then that he would never be a member of the family.

He had handed in his resignation the day after Jason had died of a massive heart attack. A week later he had set out to find the legacy Jason had spoken of on his deathbed.

"Five Amos Luttrell paintings," Jason had whispered after ordering his brother's family from the hospital room for a few minutes. "They're yours, Max. They don't go to the museum with the others. I wanted you to have them. Your inheritance from me. You understand? It's in my Will."

Max had gripped the old man's hand, hanging on to him as if he could draw him back from the brink. "Forget the Luttrells. You're going to pull through this, Jason. You're going to be okay."

"Bullshit. I'm eighty-three years old, and this is it. Better to go out this way than some of the ways a lot of my friends have gone. Been a good life for the most part. I had a fine wife for forty years, and I had a son I could be proud of."

"A son?" Max had been startled by the revelation. He had been told that Jason and his wife had never had children.

"You, Max. You were the son I never had. And you're a damned good one." Jason's gnarled fingers bit into Max's hand. "Those paintings and everything else you find out there on the coast with them are yours. Promise me you'll go get them."

"Take it easy, Jason." Max could feel the unfamiliar dampness in his eyes. It was the first time he had cried since his mother had died. "You've got to rest."

"Left 'em with Cleo."

"What? The paintings? Who's Cleo?"

Jason's answer had been lost in a wracking, wheezing cough. "Met her a year and a half ago. Amazing woman." His frail fingers grasped Max's with unnatural strength. "Been meaning to introduce you. Never had a chance. You were always off somewhere. Europe, the islands. Always busy. Too late now. Time goes by so fast, doesn't it?"

"Jason, try to get some rest."

"You find her, Max. You find her and you'll find the paintings and everything else."

"Jason, for God's sake. . . ."

"Promise me you'll go after them."

"I promise. But don't worry about that now. You're going to be all right."

But Max had no longer been able to keep Jason back from the edge. Jason's hand had gone limp then, and the ghastly wheezing had finally stopped.

Max pushed aside the memories. He had found the mysterious Cleo, and soon he would find his Luttrells. He picked up the plunger and took aim at the toilet bowl.

"I'll help," Sammy said.

"I think it would be best if you supervised."

"Okay. I'm good at that. Cleo lets me supervise a lot."

Max went to work. Five minutes later, amid a great deal of gurgling, a yellow plastic duck popped to the surface.

"Lucky Ducky," Sammy exclaimed in delight.

Max eyed the plastic duck. "Very lucky. From now on Lucky Ducky had better do his swimming somewhere else."

"Okay."

Cleo appeared in the doorway, breathless and more disheveled than ever. She was heavily burdened with luggage in both hands. Several tendrils of hair had escaped the topknot and were hanging down in front of her eyes. She blew them out of her way. "How's it going in here?"

"Max saved Lucky Ducky," Sammy said.

"My hero," Cleo murmured.

"I believe the toilet will flush properly now," Max said coldly.

The bathroom light sparkled on the lenses of Cleo's glasses as she grinned at him. "I'm really very grateful to you. This is Mr. Valence's regular room, and I was afraid I'd have to shift him to another one. He doesn't like to be shifted around. He's kind of fussy. Tends to get upset when things deviate from the usual routine."

Max held the dripping plunger over the toilet. "Look, if you don't mind, Ms. Robbins, I would very much like to speak with you now."

"Just as soon as I've got this lot settled and dinner has been served. In the meantime, I seem to have lost my bellhop. Any chance you could lend a hand?"

"He hurt himself." Sammy pointed to the cane leaning against the wall.

Cleo's gaze darted to the cane. A deep, embarrassed blush rose in her cheeks. "Oh, sorry, I forgot. Never mind. I'll get someone from the kitchen staff."

For some reason that rankled. "I can handle a few suitcases, Ms. Robbins."

She looked skeptical. "Are you sure?"

"Yes, Ms. Robbins, I'm sure."

Her smile was brighter than the fluorescent light over the mirror and infinitely warmer. "Terrific. By the way, please call me Cleo. I like to be on a first-name basis with anyone who can unstop a clogged toilet in a pinch."

"Thank you," Max said through his teeth.

Cleo looked at Sammy. "Maybe you'd better see if they need any help in the kitchen, dear."

Sammy assumed an air of grave importance. "Okay, Cleo." He looked up at Max. "Family always pitches in at times like this."

"Well, I'm off," Cleo announced. "Got to get this luggage to the right room. See you later, Max. Grab dinner in the kitchen when you get a chance." She whirled about and disappeared around the edge of the door.

"Bye, Max. Thanks for finding Lucky Ducky." Sammy dashed out of the room in Cleo's wake.

Alone in the bathroom, plunger in hand, Max looked down at the plastic duck floating in the toilet bowl. "What the hell have you gotten me into, Jason?"

For the next three hours, Max was fully occupied. He carried countless suitcases, straightened out a logistics problem in the tiny parking lot, poured after-dinner coffee and sherry for guests in the lounge, and replaced a burned-out bulb in one of the rooms.

He didn't get a chance to go in search of Cleo until after eleven o'clock. When he finally tracked her down, she was alone in the small office behind the front desk.

She was seated with her back to him at a table that held a computer and several piles of miscellaneous papers and notes. His trained eye skimmed appreciatively over her. It was not the first time that evening that he had found himself intrigued by the subtly graceful line of her spine and the sweet, vulnerable curve of her neck. Her feet, still clad in the silver athletic shoes, were tucked under her, toes resting on the chrome base of the swivel chair.

He stood silently in the doorway for a moment, watching Cleo as she concentrated intently on a printout spread out on the desk. Without taking her eyes off the figures, she absently reached up to unfasten her hair clip. The simple feminine gesture triggered a heavy, pooling sensation in Max's lower body.

He stared, enthralled, as Cleo's hair fell free around her shoulders. The glow of the desk lamp highlighted the red fire that shimmered in the depths of the thick, dark stuff. Max had a sudden, urgent need to warm his fingers in the flames. Unconsciously he took a step forward. His cane thudded awkwardly on the floor.

"What?" Startled, Cleo spun around in her chair. She relaxed when she saw Max. "Oh, there you are. Come on in. Have a seat. I thought you were George."

"Who's George?" Max regained his self-control in a heartbeat.

"My night desk man. He phoned and said he'd be a little late tonight."

"I see." Max moved across the small space and lowered himself onto the chair near the window. With cool precision he positioned the cane in front of himself and rested his hands on the hawk. "I think it's time we talked, Ms. Robbins."

"Cleo."

"Cleo," he repeated.

She smiled. "I suppose you're wondering if you can have the same arrangement that Jason had."

Max gazed at her uncomprehendingly. "I beg your pardon?"

"It's okay. I don't mind. You're a friend of his, after all. Heck, it's the least I can do. I'm sure Jason would have wanted you to enjoy what he enjoyed here."

Max wondered if he was hallucinating. He could not believe that Cleo was offering to let him take Jason's place in her bed. "I am overwhelmed by your generosity, Ms. Robbins. But I'm not sure Jason would have wanted that."

"Why would he object?"

"Jason was a good friend," Max said. "But there are limits to any friendship."

Cleo looked briefly bewildered. "You're an artist, just as Jason was, aren't you?"

Max lowered his lashes slowly, veiling his gaze while he digested that comment. Jason had freely admitted he could not draw a straight line, let alone paint. He had collected art, not created it.

"Not exactly," Max finally said carefully.

Cleo gave him a sympathetic, knowing look. "Say no more. I understand completely. You haven't been able to sell yet, so you're reluctant to call yourself an artist. I know know you feel." She hesitated. "I'm a writer."

"You are?"

She blushed. "I've got a book coming out this spring. It's called *A Fine Vengeance*. It's a sort of woman-in-jeopardy thing. Suspense and romance."

Max eyed her thoughtfully. "That's very interesting, Ms. Robbins."

"I haven't told anyone except the family about it," Cleo said quickly. "I'm waiting until it actually shows up in the stores, so I'd appreciate it if you wouldn't mention it."

"I won't say a word about it," Max promised.

"Jason knew about it, of course. So I don't mind if you know, too. The point I was trying to make is that it isn't whether or not you sell your work that makes you an artist not a writer. It's whether or not you work at your craft."

"That is a point of view, I suppose."

"Sometimes a person can be very good and still not sell. Take Jason, for instance. He never sold a single painting;, and he was a wonderful painter."

"He was?"

"Certainly." Cleo tilted her head to one side and gave Max a curious look. "You must have seen his work. Those are his paintings hanging out there in the lobby. Didn't you recognize his style?"

Max turned his head sharply and stared through the doorway at the series of uninspired seascapes. "I didn't recognize them."

"Didn't you?" Cleo looked briefly disappointed. Then she smiled again. "I love those paintings. They'll always remind me of Jason. In a way they're his legacy to all of us here at Robbins' Nest Inn. Who knows? Maybe one day they'll be worth a fortune."

Never in a million years, Max thought. "And if they do turn out to be quite valuable," he asked softly, "what will you do? Sell them?"

"Good heavens, no. I could never bring myself to sell Jason's work. It belongs here at the inn."

Max cleared his throat cautiously. "Ms. Robbins . . ."

"Cleo."

He ignored the interruption. "Jason owned five Amos Luttrell paintings. Before he died he told me that he had left them here at the inn."

"Who's Amos Luttrell? Another friend of Jason's?"

She was either the most accomplished liar he had encountered in years, or she was a naive idiot, Max decided. His money was on the former. He could not imagine Jason having an idiot for a mistress. In which case he was up against an extremely clever opponent.

"Luttrell was a master of neo-expressionism," Max said blandly.

"Expressionism? That's modern art, isn't it?" Cleo wrinkled her nose. "I've never really liked modern art. I prefer pictures that make sense. Dogs, horses, seascapes. That kind of thing. I don't have any modern art hanging here at the inn. It wouldn't fit in at all."

A cold anger raged through Max. There was only one conclusion. Cleo was obviously aware of the true value of the Luttrells and had decided to play dumb. She was going to pretend she knew nothing about them. She must have realized that Max had no proof she had them in her possession.

It was a clever tactic, he admitted to himself. And one he had not expected to encounter. But, then, nothing was going quite as he had anticipated here at Robbins' Nest Inn.

"Now, then, as I was saying," Cleo continued blithely, "if you're an artist like Jason, you'll probably enjoy the arrangement I had with him."

Max raised one brow. "What, exactly, are you offering?"

"The same salary I gave Jason plus room and board any time you're staying with us in exchange for the kind of odd-job work you were doing tonight. I promise you'll get plenty of time to yourself to paint. You can have Jason's old room in the attic. It's quiet and comfortable. Jason liked it."

Room and board but not her bed, then. At least not yet. "I'm not exactly a starving artist, Ms. Robbins."

"I know that." Cleo smiled gently. "But there are a lot of different ways to starve, aren't there? You're a friend of Jason's, and that's all that matters."

"I'm not sure I would make a good Antony," Max said dryly.

"Huh?" A second later Cleo's face turned a charming shade of warm pink. "Oh, I get it. I'd better warn you that we have one iron-clad rule around here. No Cleopatra cracks and absolutely no asp jokes."

"I'll try to remember that."

"So? Are you interested?" Cleo gave him an inquiring look.

The sense of unreality that had gripped Max earlier returned. He stared at Cleo for a long while, and then he made his decision.

What the hell, he thought. He had to find out what had happened to his Luttrells, and it wasn't like he had anything or anyone waiting for him in Seattle. Jason had sent him in this direction for a reason. Max decided he might as well follow the yellow brick road to the end.

Another turning point, he thought. And as usual, he had no reason to go back.

"As it happens," Max said, "I've just lost a job. I'll take the deal you gave Jason."

2

"Andromeda, these muffins are out of this world." Cleo popped the last of the hot muffin into her mouth and chewed happily. "As usual."

Andromeda, the head chef of the Robbins' Nest Inn, smiled serenely. All of Andromeda's smiles were serene. She was heavily into metaphysical studies. "I'm glad you like them, dear. It's a variation on the corn bread recipe Daystar's been using for the past few months. You know Daystar. She can't stop experimenting."

"The old recipe was terrific, too, but this one is even better. The guests are going to love these little suckers." Cleo scooped up another corn bread muffin and slathered it with honey.

She hastily devoured it as she surveyed the busy kitchen. Andromeda's staff, all middle-aged and all members of the Cosmic Harmony Women's Retreat, were an industrious crew.

The arrangement between the inn and Cosmic Harmony was simple and lucrative for both sides. Andromeda and her team provided first-rate seafood and vegetarian cuisine for the inn's guests that was unmatched anywhere else on the coast. In return Cleo paid the Retreat a portion of the inn's profits and agreed not to force the women into standard white kitchen uniforms.

Andromeda and her friend, Daystar, were the cornerstones of the inn's kitchen staff. Other members of Cosmic Harmony came in at varying times, depending on who was available and what skills were needed. This morning Cleo recognized Nebula and Constellation hard at work. One was preparing muesli, and the other was slicing sourdough whole wheat bread. The women at Cosmic Harmony generally adopted new names when they came to the Retreat. Some stayed for a few days, weeks, or months. Others, like Andromeda and Daystar, were permanent residents.

All of the women at work this morning had the sleeves of their long, jewel-colored gowns secured above their elbows. Their bright head scarves and strange bronze and silver necklaces added an exotic touch to the kitchen.

The latest edition of the guidebooks had recently begun citing the cuisine at the Robbins' Nest Inn as one of the best reasons to visit the Washington coast in winter or any other time of the year.

For Cleo, the women from Cosmic Harmony provided something much more important than a money-making restaurant; they provided friendship and a place to go when she needed peace and serenity. She often went to the Cosmic Harmony meditation center after one of the recurring nightmares that plagued her from time to time.

The Retreat, situated on a magnificent stretch of land overlooking the ocean, had once been an exclusive golf resort. The resort had failed years earlier and had slowly rotted into the ground.

Five years ago Andromeda and Daystar had conceived the notion of turning the abandoned site into a commune for women. Initially they had leased the grounds and buildings. But three years ago, together with Cleo's assistance, they had pooled their limited resources and purchased the old resort at a foreclosure sale.

Andromeda and Daystar, who formed the core of Cosmic Harmony, had not always been involved in metaphysics and philosophies of self-realization. They had, in fact, started out as members of a Seattle bridge club that had met every Tuesday for years. As time went past, each had found herself on her own due to divorce. The bridge club had been the only thing that had remained stable in their lives.

Andromeda's name in her former life had been Mrs. Hamilton R. Galsworthy III. She had helped create Cosmic Harmony six months after her husband, a doctor who was Board Certified in Gynecology, had run off with his aerobics instructor. Mr. Galsworthy had had an extremely capable lawyer who had managed to ensure that Andromeda did not get more than a token amount in the divorce settlement.

Andromeda had explained to Cleo that she bore no ill will toward her ex-husband, who wound up being divorced by the aerobics instructor within a year. "It was really very sad, dear," Andromeda had once explained. "The poor man was sixty at the time, and they say she had him doing an hour of high-impact aerobics twice a day. With ankle weights, no less. He hasn't been the same since, I'm told. One assumes his karma finally caught up with him."

But there was no going back for Andromeda, not even when Hamilton R. Galsworthy III, M.D., showed up at her door, a broken man, offering to come home. Andromeda had already launched herself on a new path of cosmic enlightenment. In addition, she and her bridge partner, also recently divorced, had discovered that their friendship for each other was a stronger, more enduring bond than the relationship either had had with her ex-husband.

Andromeda sipped a cup of herbal tea in a slow, ceremonial manner. "I wanted to speak to you about one of your new guests," she said to Cleo. She was nearly sixty, a cheerful elf of a woman with a halo of curly gray hair and bright, inquiring eyes. When she moved, the small bells attached to the hem of her gown tinkled merrily.

Lately, every move Andromeda made had an air of carefully cultivated grace and ritual about it. She was currently studying the traditional Japanese tea ceremony and its implications for daily living. It was the latest in a never-ending series of such philosophical explorations for Andromeda.

"We got twenty-five new arrivals last night," Cleo responded. "Another Seattle company is sending some of its employees through one of Herbert T. Valence's three-day motivational seminars."

"Oh, dear. Another one of those, eh?" Andromeda shook her head. "Hard to imagine that anyone really believes there are five easy steps to wealth, power, and unlimited success."

Cleo grinned. "I get the feeling good old Herbert does. The guy must be making money hand-over-fist with these seminars."

"True. He does seem to be doing rather well, doesn't he? This is the third seminar he's booked in here this winter," Andromeda observed.

Cleo laughed. "Just be grateful he's decided the inn makes a suitable setting for his uplifting and inspiring messages."

"I am, dear. I am well aware that the inn is doing very nicely this winter because of Mr. Valence. However, when I mentioned the new guest, I was not referring to one of the seminar attendees."

Cleo smiled wryly. "Let me guess. You're

49

talking about Jason's friend, right?"

"Yes. Are you certain he was a friend of Jason's?"

Cleo glanced at Andromeda in surprise. "He says he is. He certainly knew about Jason having stayed with us from time to time during the past eighteen months. And he knew about the arrangement Jason and I had worked out." Cleo wolfed down the last of the muffin. "At least I think he did. I offered him the same deal, and he took it."

"He's working for you now?"

"Uh-huh."

Andromeda frowned delicately. "I told you when Jason first started to show up around here on the weekends that he was not exactly what he seemed."

"I know, but I liked him. You said you liked him, too. We both agreed we could trust him."

"Well, I knew he was not a threat, of course. In his own way Jason needed us. I am not so certain about this other man."

"You only met him briefly last night."

Daystar swooped down on Cleo before Andromeda could respond. "Saw his car in the parking lot." She hoisted a spatula in a warning manner. "My ex-husband bought a Jaguar like that right before he married his secretary. Your Mr. Fortune is no starving artist, Cleo."

Cleo smiled at her. Daystar was a sturdy,

competent-looking woman whose shrewd, no-nonsense eyes reflected her assertive, inquisitive attitude toward everything and everyone. She was the airy, ethereal Andromeda's natural opposite. Cleo had often thought the two made a perfect pair.

"Jason wasn't exactly starving either," Cleo pointed out. "At least not in the literal sense. But he needed a place like Robbins' Nest Inn in order to paint. And he wanted to help out around here."

Andromeda gave her a gentle smile. "You mean he wanted to be part of our extended family."

Cleo shrugged. "Maybe Max Fortune wants the same thing."

"Or perhaps he wants something else," Daystar said darkly.

"I doubt it," Cleo murmured. "Don't forget, I saw him with a toilet plunger in his hand. You learn a lot about a man when you see him in action like that." She popped the last bite of muffin into her mouth. "Besides, what else is there for him around here except the same kind of family thing that Jason found?"

"I don't know," Daystar said. "I'm just suggesting that you be cautious. The fact that he knew Jason does not automatically make Mr. Fortune a member of the family."

Andromeda nodded in agreement. "Daystar is right, dear."

"Don't worry, I'll be careful," Cleo promised.

She was about to pick up the teapot when a flash of awareness made her pause. There had been no telltale sound above the clatter of pans and the hum of conversation that filled the kitchen, but Cleo knew without turning around who was standing in the doorway. A small thrill shot through her, leaving her tingling from head to foot.

Apparently her strange reaction to Max Fortune last night had not been just a curious by-product of the stress she had been under at the time. She was perfectly relaxed this morning, and yet she was experiencing the same unsettling sensation. She took a deep breath and braced herself.

"Good morning, Max." Cleo swung around, pot in hand, and smiled at him. She would not make a fool of herself, she vowed silently. She would be calm and dignified. She struggled to keep her expression limited to one of polite welcome, but inside she was bubbling with the delicious, unfamiliar excitement.

It was clear in the light of the new day that her imagination had not been playing tricks on her. Max Fortune's impact on her senses was devastating. She found herself staring in spite of her determination to be casual and cool.

He was the man in the mirror. She had never seen his face clearly in her dreams, but the moment he had materialized, she had recognized him.

Cleo gave herself a small, imperceptible shake in an effort to free herself from the disorienting sensation that was sweeping through her. She forced herself to concentrate on facts, not fantasy.

Max was obviously in his mid-thirties but definitely not in any danger of going soft. There was a lean, hard quality to his body. His boldly carved face bore a disquieting similarity to the hawk on the handle of his cane.

The subtle fierceness that marked him gleamed clearly in his gray eyes. There was an air of unrelenting watchfulness about Max Fortune, as if he trusted no one and depended on no one. Cleo sensed that this was a man who took nothing for granted. He looked as though he expected to have to fight for whatever he wanted in life.

But the hard-edged, potentially ruthless element in him was overlaid with a tantalizing air of polished civility. It was a powerful, compelling image for Cleo; one that was straight out of the deepest, most secret recesses of her imagination. There was no doubt about it; the well-hidden, carefully contained, very sensual aspect of her nature recognized Max Fortune.

He was the man who lived in the shadows of her secret fantasies.

Perhaps it was not so strange that she knew him on sight, she thought ruefully. After all, she had written a book about him. She just hadn't known his name at the time.

The cane should have had the effect of making Max look at least somewhat vulnerable. Instead it only served to reveal another hard edge. It hinted at pain that had been subdued by the force of sheer willpower and self-control. Cleo found herself wanting to touch and soothe that old anguish in him.

She gripped the handle of the teapot, completely at a loss to explain her reaction to this stranger who had walked in out of the storm last night and made a place for himself near her hearth.

"Good morning." Max examined the kitchen and its unusually garbed staff. His expression showed no particular reaction except mild interest. "Is this where I get breakfast?"

"Definitely." Cleo jerked herself out of the thrall that had enveloped her. "Andromeda can fix you up, can't you, Andromeda?"

"Of course." The tiny bells on the hem of Andromeda's gown chimed as she turned away to put two corn bread muffins on a plate.

"There is also muesli with fresh fruit and yogurt over on the counter. Take whatever you want."

Max's gaze was on Cleo. "I'll do that."

Cleo felt a tremor go through her. "Tea?" she asked quickly.

He glanced at the pot in her hand. "Any coffee available?"

"Right over there." Cleo nodded toward the freshly brewed coffee that was sitting on the counter. "Have a seat at the table, and I'll get you a cup."

"Thanks."

Cleo ignored Daystar's speculative frown. She scooped up the coffee pot and another muffin for herself and hurried to follow Max to the nook where the staff of the inn grabbed meals during busy times.

"Don't expect service like this every day," Cleo said lightly as she slid onto the bench on the other side of the table. She poured coffee into a cup. "Around here, everyone fends for himself when the inn is full."

"I'll remember that."

"We're going to be swamped for the next three days with this motivational seminar crowd," Cleo observed.

"I saw the audiovisual equipment being set up in the parlor. What's this seminar stuff all about?"

"Herbert T. Valence's Five Easy Steps to Wealth, Power, and Unlimited Success," Cleo explained.

Max looked up. "There aren't five easy steps to all that."

"No?"

"There's only one step."

Cleo was intrigued. "What's that?"

Max shrugged. "You fight for it. And when you've got what you want, you fight again to defend it."

"Not according to Herbert T. Valence. He says the trick is to think positive and affirm your goals every day. I gather he started giving these seminars a couple of years ago. He's got quite a reputation."

"The man's either a fool or a con artist."

"Mind your tongue." Cleo chuckled. "Thanks to Mr. Valence, I have a full inn. Try a muffin." She tore hers apart, heedless of crumbs. "I've had two already, and I swear this is going to be my last one."

Max picked up a knife and went to work on one of his muffins as if it were an uncut diamond.

Cleo stopped chewing and watched in fascination as he methodically split the muffin in half. Next, he cut off a quarter of the muffin with grave precision.

He put down the knife, picked up a spoon,

and dipped it into the honey pot. When he had collected a quantity of the thick, golden stuff, he gave the spoon a deft twist. Not a single drop of honey fell back into the pot or onto the table as he gracefully transferred it to the muffin on his plate.

It was like watching a Borgia or a Medici eat, Cleo thought. One had the feeling that behind the polished manners, there was a sheathed sword tucked politely out of sight.

Max's eyes met Cleo's just as he was about to take a bite. He stopped with the muffin section halfway to his mouth. "Something wrong?"

"No, not at all." Cleo grinned. "It's just that Jason was the only person I ever saw who ate Daystar's muffins so neatly. Most people inhale them."

"I'm sure they're excellent." Max glanced at the women who were preparing breakfast. "Your kitchen staff is a little out of the ordinary."

"I'll say. They're fantastic." Cleo leaned forward and lowered her voice. "Someone's always trying to steal Andromeda and Daystar. Every restaurant owner and inn manager on the coast would kill to get them."

"Where did you find them?"

"I didn't. They found me." Cleo sat back. "They're from the Cosmic Harmony Women's Retreat. The Retreat is about a mile and a half from here, on the other side of the cove. You can see it from your window."

Max looked up from his muffin. "I saw something that looked like an old resort."

"It was at one time. The resort folded. It wasn't the right kind of establishment for this section of the coast. At any rate, after I opened the inn, Andromeda and Daystar decided I needed a first-rate kitchen to attract business. They, on the other hand, needed a stable source of income to run the Retreat. They waved a contract in my face, and I signed."

"Just like that?"

"Sure. I tend to make most decisions on the spur of the moment. For instance, I bought this place within twenty-four hours of looking at it. Of course, if I'd gotten a good look at the antique plumbing I might have hesitated a bit. It gave me nothing but trouble for the first two years. But Benjy wandered into my office one day a year and a half ago looking for a job, and my maintenance problems were solved."

"Until Benjy disappeared last night?"

Cleo frowned. "I wonder where he is. I'm getting a little worried. It's not like him to just up and vanish like this. He and Trisha . . ." The phone rang before Cleo could finish the sentence. She snatched up the kitchen extension that hung on the wall of the nook. "Robbins' Nest Inn."

"Cleo? Thank God. This is Nolan."

" 'Morning, Nolan. A little early for you to be calling, isn't it?" Cleo relaxed back against the wall and braced one foot on the bench. She saw Max's gaze go to her bright, gold-toned sneakers. She thought she detected disapproval in his cold gray eyes.

"Sorry." Nolan's voice was uncharacteristically sharp. "Cleo, I need to see you as soon as possible."

She groaned. "I told you I couldn't have dinner with you until the weekend. I've got an inn full of guests."

"Forget dinner. I want to talk to you right away. This is important."

Cleo took her foot down off the bench and straightened. She had never heard this particular edge in Nolan's voice. "Is something wrong?"

"You tell me."

"You're not making a whole lot of sense, here, Nolan."

"Damn it, Cleo, I have to talk to you."

"Take it easy," Cleo said soothingly. "We'll talk. Do you want to come by the inn now?"

"No," he said swiftly. "I can't do that. Look, can you meet me down at the beach?"

"Nolan, this is February, not August. It's

59

cold outside. Why do you want to meet at the beach?" Cleo was acutely aware that Max was listening to every word.

"The beach, Cleo. Fifteen minutes. You owe me that much, at least."

"I *owe* you? Nolan, have you gone nuts? I don't owe you a thing."

"You do now. I'll see you in a few minutes."

"Wait a second, I've got the breakfast crowd to deal with. I can't just dash out of here."

"This won't take long," Nolan said. "And it's really important. It affects both our futures." He hung up the phone.

Cleo made a face as she replaced the receiver. "He sounds a trifle upset. Guess I'd better go see what he wants."

"Who's Nolan?" Max picked up the knife again and started in on the second muffin.

"Nolan Hildebrand is the part-time mayor of Harmony Cove. I think he has bigger political aspirations, but I try not to hold that against him. I mean, somebody has to go into politics, right? At any rate, I've been sort of seeing him for about five months."

Max's gaze was hooded. "Sort of seeing him?"

Cleo blushed. "You know. Dating him. It's not like either one of us has a lot of choice around Harmony Cove. It's a very small town, in case you didn't notice."

"I noticed."

"Well, anyhow, Nolan and I go out to dinner a couple of times a week when I'm not too busy here at the inn." Cleo didn't know why she was feeling awkward. Perhaps it was because Nolan was one of only a tiny handful of men she had dated since the death of her parents four years earlier.

It had taken a long time to get over the searing trauma that had shattered her life the day she had walked into the bloodspattered living room of her parents' home. It was that same terrible room that she still saw in the occasional nightmares that brought her awake in a cold sweat.

The authorities had called it a case of murder-suicide. For some reason no one could explain, perhaps in the heat of a passionate quarrel, successful businessman Edward Robbins had killed his wife and then turned the gun on himself.

Cleo had never been able to accept the reality of it. Six months of therapy had done little to help. She was gradually able to deal with the loss, but not the reasons behind it. They made no sense to her and never would.

She had been an only child, and she alone knew how deep the bond had been between her parents. It was not inconceivable to her that one might have chosen to follow the other into the grave, but it was impossible to believe that one would have murdered the other. The authorities had explained that such things happened, even in the best of families.

When she had eventually surfaced from the state of numbed shock into which she had been plunged on that day of horror, Cleo had found herself alone in the world. She had been twenty-three at the time.

Slowly, painfully, she had begun putting her life back together. She had gone to the coast frequently during that period, drawn by the eternal, soul-soothing appeal of the ocean. It was there she had discovered the Cosmic Harmony Women's Retreat and the strength to rebuild her world.

With the money left from the trust fund her parents had established for her, Cleo had purchased the old Victorian inn that sat on the bluff high above Harmony Cove. Slowly, but surely, she had gathered a clan of friends around her.

It was a loose-knit group, and some of the members changed from time to time, but there was a central core that consisted of Cleo, Andromeda, Daystar, Sylvia Gordon, and her son, Sammy. Trisha Briggs and Benjy Atkins had both been added to the clan somewhere along the line. So had Jason Curzon. An extended family had been created, albeit a non-traditional one.

Although she had needed the closeness of her friends, Cleo had felt no need for a lover. She did not think she was cold or frigid, but there was no denying that a part of her seemed to have gone into hibernation somewhere deep inside her. Her therapist had suggested that Cleo had become deeply wary of intimacy because of the manner in which the close bond between her parents had been so shockingly severed.

On the one hand Cleo longed for the sort of relationship her parents had enjoyed, the therapist explained, but on the other hand, she was fearful of what might lie at the heart of it. Only a dark sickness of the mind could have made Edward Robbins turn the gun on his beloved wife. The therapist was convinced that Cleo now feared that such a powerful love might be based on an equally powerful and very dangerous obsession.

The only thing Cleo knew for certain was that she could not give herself to a man unless she loved him the way her mother had loved her father. Cleo understood that for her it would have to be a grand passion or nothing at all.

She had been dating Nolan Hildebrand for some time now on a casual basis, but she had not gone to bed with him. She knew she never would.

Max watched her intently. "Did Jason know about Hildebrand?"

Cleo was surprised by the question. "Of course. I told you, Nolan and I have been seeing each other for quite a while."

Max put down the last, unfinished bit of muffin and folded his arms on the table. He leaned forward, his eyes cold. "Are you telling me that Jason didn't mind sharing you with the mayor of Harmony Cove?"

"Sharing me?" Cleo blinked, astonished. "What on earth are you talking about?"

"You know damn well what I'm talking about. I knew Jason for twelve years, and I know that he was not the kind of man who would share his woman with another man."

A warm tide of embarrassment flooded through Cleo as she finally understood what he was talking about. "Are you crazy? Jason and I were friends."

"I know."

"Good friends. Not lovers. For heaven's sake, Max, he was old enough to be my grandfather."

"So? You wouldn't be the first woman to latch onto an older man in hopes of getting your hands on some of his money."

"So that's what this is all about." Anger

64

surged through her, driving out the embarrassment. "For your information, Jason didn't have much money. He never even managed to sell one of his paintings. He was an old man who was living on a pension and Social Security."

"Is that right?"

Cleo slid out of the booth and got to her feet. "I don't believe this. I thought you were a friend of Jason's. I thought you knew all about him and about his family here at the inn."

"Are you telling me you weren't Jason's mistress?"

"I don't think I'm going to tell you a damn thing, Mr. Fortune. I'm afraid you'll have to excuse me. I've got to race off and meet another one of my many lovers. When I get back, I'll expect to find you checked out." Cleo spun around on her heel and stalked out of the kitchen.

She refused to glance back over her shoulder as she left the room. But she could feel Max's cold eyes on her all the way to the door.

Fifteen minutes later, still seething from the small but extremely unpleasant scene in the kitchen, Cleo parked her car in the unpaved lot above the beach. Nolan Hildebrand's Jeep was the only other vehicle in sight. Few people

65

came to the beach at this time of year.

A cold, rain-soaked blast of wind struck Cleo as she got out of her car. It tore her hair free from its precarious moorings and whipped it into a froth around her face. There was a storm boiling out over the ocean. It would arrive within the hour. She intended to be back at the inn by the time it hit shore.

And Max Fortune had better be gone when she got there, she told herself. She shook her head in disgust, unable to believe that she had misjudged him so badly. Usually her instincts about people were highly accurate.

The Jeep door opened, and Nolan climbed out. He hurried toward her, the collar of his leather jacket turned up to shield his neck from the wind. The brisk breeze ruffled his light brown hair, accenting his handsome features. He carried a brown paper sack in one hand.

Cleo contemplated him with a sense of affection. She had known from the beginning that Nolan was not fated to be the great love of her life. At the start of their relationship, he had made a few determined attempts to seduce her, but when she had declined the invitations to his bed, he had seemed oddly content.

Nolan was a pleasant dinner companion, and Cleo genuinely admired his efforts as town mayor. He worked hard at the part-time position while practicing law at the small firm his father had established.

"I was afraid you wouldn't show up." Nolan came to a halt in front of her. He jammed one hand into the pocket of his jacket and regarded her with troubled eyes.

A flicker of real concern went through Cleo. Something was obviously very wrong. "What's this all about, Nolan?"

"I just want to know one thing." Nolan thrust the paper sack at her. "Did you write this?"

"What in the world?" But Cleo could feel the familiar shape of a book inside the sack. Her blood stilled.

She opened the bag and glanced inside. She found herself gazing at a familiar stark white cover. The title, *The Mirror*, was embossed on it in the same shade of white. A length of scarlet ribbon curling evocatively across the bottom of the white cover was the only note of color.

"Oh, dear," Cleo murmured.

"Did you write that?" Nolan bit out.

"Well, yes. Yes, I did, as a matter of fact. It was published a couple of months ago." She smiled tentatively. "My first book, you know."

"You published it under a pen name?"

Nolan asked, sounding as though he wanted to be very certain of his facts.

"Yes." Cleo gingerly reclosed the bag. She cleared her throat. "It's, uh, considered a rather fine example of women's erotica, you know."

"Erotica."

"It actually got very well reviewed in several literary magazines and one or two feminist journals."

Nolan gave her an outraged look of disbelief. "It's porn, that's what it is."

"Oh, no, definitely not." Cleo clutched the book protectively to her breast. "I told you, it's erotica. There's a big difference."

"Not to the media, damn it. Not to every right-wing newspaper columnist who decides I'm too liberal on First Amendment issues. Not to the conservative, small-town voters of Harmony Cove."

Cleo bit her lip. "I don't understand."

"Christ, Cleo." Nolan ran an exasperated hand through his wind-tossed hair. "I'm starting to build a political career. Don't you know what this kind of thing could do to me?"

"I wrote the book, not you."

"Don't you see? It's bad enough that I've been dating you. What if we'd gotten married? I'd have been ripped to shreds as the husband of a porn queen."

Cleo stared at him. "You never said any-thing about marriage."

Nolan scowled. "Well, I was starting to think about it."

"Nolan, that's ridiculous. We're not in love, and you know it."

"I was beginning to think we would have made a good team." Nolan gave her an ag-grieved look. "You know what it's like for a politician these days. The media dissects ev-erything under a microscope. Your back-ground seemed perfect for a wife."

"Perfect?"

"No scandals, no radical politics, no pre-vious marriages."

"And a nice income of my own from the inn?" Cleo suggested dryly.

"Money had nothing to do with it," he said with righteous indignation. "It was your char-acter that attracted me. Hell, I even know for a fact that you don't sleep around. The only thing that bothered me a bit was your friend-ship with those weird women at Cosmic Har-mony."

"My friends are not weird." Anger flared inside Cleo. "You think I've got a pristine past? What about my parents?"

"What about them? I know they're dead."

"But you don't know how they died, do you? I never told you that."

Nolan scowled. "I got the impression they were in a car accident."

"That's the impression I've let most of the people around here have. It's easier to explain than the truth."

Nolan looked wary. "What the hell's the truth?"

Cleo lifted her chin. "They say my father shot my mother and then killed himself. How's that for a skeleton in the closet? Do you think the media would have ignored a juicy tidbit like that?"

Nolan's shock was obvious. "Are you serious? You should have told me."

"Why? I have a right to my privacy. Besides, it's hardly the sort of thing one discusses over dinner at the Crab Pot Restaurant." Cleo pushed her glasses higher up on her nose and took a steadying breath.

She was furious with herself for having allowed Nolan to goad her into telling him the painful facts of her parents' death. It was something she rarely talked about with anyone.

"We might have been able to finesse the stuff about your parents, although it would have been difficult. But we'd never have been able to explain that damn book you wrote." Nolan's gaze turned bitter. "You really had me fooled."

"Sorry about that. I didn't know you were considering me for a position as a politician's wife. You might have mentioned it earlier. I would have told you all the lurid details of my past right up front."

"Is that right?"

"Damn right." She widened her eyes in mocking derision. "You don't think I'd actually want to be a politician's wife, do you?"

Nolan's face reddened. "Look, I'm sorry about this, Cleo. And about your folks. About everything. Hell, I know I'm not handling this very well. It's just that the business with that damned book came as a shock."

"I can see that."

"Look at it from my point of view," Nolan pleaded. "I didn't know you'd actually published anything, let alone a book like *that*." He looked at the paper sack she was holding as if it contained a snake.

"I didn't tell you about *The Mirror* because I didn't want anyone outside the family to know that I'd written it."

He snorted. "I'm not surprised."

"I'm not ashamed of it," she stormed. "It's just that this book was a very personal thing for me. I knew no one around here would understand. I didn't want the kid who works at Bennington's Drug Store leering at me every time I went in to buy shampoo. I didn't need the attendant at the gas station making snide remarks. I didn't want to have to explain it to Patty Loftins down at the beauty shop."

"I can sure as hell understand that." Nolan turned away to gaze out over the choppy ocean. "Patty's got a mouth the size of the Grand Canyon."

Cleo looked down at the brown paper sack she was clutching. It was impossible to explain *The Mirror* to anyone. It was too intimate. Too much a part of her most secret self. She had poured all her most private fantasies into the book, baring her deeply sensual soul.

The passion that was trapped inside her had combined with the aching loneliness to form a searing account of a woman on a quest for emotional intimacy and physical release. The tale had literally cascaded out of her a year and a half earlier. The book had been published a month ago.

The critics had, generally speaking, responded very favorably to *The Mirror*. Only Cleo knew that none of them had really understood it. They had thought the book was a work of autoeroticism; that the female narrator was locked in a fantasy of startling intimacy with the masculine elements of her own nature.

They did not comprehend the significance of the man in the mirror.

72

Writing *The Mirror* had been a cathartic experience for Cleo. It had also taught her that she wanted to keep on writing, although she knew she would never again need to write a book like *The Mirror*.

"I wish I could explain this to you," she said quietly. "*The Mirror* was a one-of-a-kind thing for me."

"I should hope so. I read some of that stuff last night. I couldn't believe you'd written it. You wouldn't even go to bed with me." He shot her a fulminating look. "Just as well, I guess. I'd never have been able to compete with the fantasy in that damned book. No man could. That woman in the book is making love to herself. She doesn't need a man, does she?"

"Nolan, you don't understand."

"Sure I do. Now I know why you wouldn't sleep with me. It wasn't because you were so damned pure, was it? It was because you've decided no mere male can give you what you can get from your own imagination and a good vibrator."

"Stop it right now." Cleo took a step back. "I don't want to hear another word about this. I told you, you don't understand."

"I understand what that book could have done to my chances for getting elected to the state legislature next fall. it would have turned me into a laughingstock in the press."

Cleo had had enough. "Relax. You're saved. As far as I'm concerned, we never have to see each other again unless our shopping carts collide in the aisles of the grocery store."

"Damn it, Cleo, I didn't mean to have it end this way. It's just that I was really getting serious about our relationship."

"Don't worry. You've had the good sense to break things off before I could do any damage to your brilliant political career."

"It wasn't just that," he muttered. "I liked you, Cleo. I mean, I really liked you."

Cleo sighed. "I liked you too, Nolan. Believe it or not, I still do. Heck, I'll probably even vote for you when you run for office next fall."

"Thanks." He suddenly seemed at a loss for words. "Look, I won't say anything about that book to anyone else."

"I'd appreciate that."

"Well, I guess that's that, then. No hard feelings, huh?"

"Sure. Right. No hard feelings." Cleo turned around and started toward her car. Halfway there, a thought struck her. She turned back. "There's just one thing I'd like to know."

"What's that?"

"How did you find out about *The Mirror*?"

74

His mouth thinned. "Someone left it in my mailbox along with a note."

A chill went through Cleo. "A note?"

"Yeah. I left it in the book."

Cleo nodded and walked on to her car. She opened the door and got inside. For a moment she sat behind the wheel, watching as Nolan started up his Jeep and took off down the narrow road toward town.

When the other vehicle was out of sight, Cleo slowly opened the paper sack. She gazed at the cover of *The Mirror* for a long time, and then she opened the book and took out the folded sheet of paper inside. The note was brief and to the point.

The Queen of the Nile is The Queen of Filth. A man with an important future ahead of him cannot afford to be seen with a whore.

The tone of the note was uncomfortably familiar. It bore a remarkable resemblance to the anonymous letter Cleo had received last month.

After the initial shock of receiving it, Cleo had dismissed the letter. It had been forwarded through her publisher, after all, and she had assured herself that the sender had no way of knowing her real identity.

But now she had to confront the fact that someone not only knew her identity as the author of *The Mirror*, he or she was apparently determined to punish her for having written it. And that person knew who she was and where she was.

Cleo's hand shook as she turned the key in the ignition. She suddenly wanted to get back to the safety of the inn as quickly as possible.

3

Max paused beside the open door of the large parlor. The quaintly furnished room was filled with seminar attendees. At the front of the parlor a man with silver, blow-dried hair, a chunky gold watch, and a massive diamond ring held forth. He was wearing a jacket and a pair of handmade leather shoes that Max knew had cost at least as much as the ones he, himself, owned. There was obviously money to be made in the motivational seminar business, Max decided.

"My name is Herbert T. Valence, and you know something? I am incredible." Valence radiated intensity. He practically bounced on his toes as he gazed expectantly around the room. "I am amazing. I can do anything I want to do. And you know what? So can you. Say it after me, everyone. *I am incredible.*"

"*I am incredible,*" the audience repeated as one.

"I am amazing," Valence said. He looked as if he were about to burst with excitement and enthusiasm.

"*I am amazing.*"

"I can do anything I want to do," Valence prompted.

"*I can do anything I want to do.*"

"The power of positive thinking is literally out of this world," Valence announced with a triumphant smile. "It's pure energy. It's raw fuel, waiting to be poured into your creative engines."

Max watched with interest as Valence seemed to levitate back across the room to his wall chart.

"I am here to teach you the secret of having it all," Valence told the audience. "Money, power, success, and self-esteem. They can be yours by following my simple Five-Step Program. You want to wear clothes like mine? Drive a Porsche like mine? You'll be able to do just that when you've finished my program. I guarantee it."

Max lost interest and walked on toward the

lobby. He stopped in front of the first of the series of seascapes that hung there and stood looking into it for a while.

There was nothing to see beyond the surface image of a storm-tossed sea. The technique was poor, the design was static, and the colors were dull. It was the work of an amateur. Jason had been right in his own estimate of himself as a painter.

"There you are, Max. I've been looking for you." Sylvia Gordon waved from the office doorway. "There was a phone call for you a few minutes ago. I rang your room, but there was no answer so I took a message."

Max turned away from the seascape he had been studying and walked over to the front desk. "Thank you."

"No problem." Sylvia smiled. "Sorry I couldn't find you when the call came through." She handed him a piece of paper. "Whoever she is, she sounded very anxious to get hold of you."

Max glanced at the note. *Kimberly called. She wants you to return her call as soon as possible. Very important.* The *very important* had been underlined three times.

"Just a business matter," Max said. "It's not really important."

He crumpled up the note and tossed it in the wastebasket, just as he had the half dozen other urgent messages he had received from Kimberly Curzon during the past month. He wondered absently how she had managed to track him down here at the coast.

"Is Cleo back yet?" he asked.

"No." Sylvia glanced at the wastebasket where the note had disappeared. When she looked at Max again there was speculation in her eyes. "But I expect her any minute. She won't be away long. Not with this crowd filling up the inn."

A roll of thunder drew Max's attention to the window. It had grown dark outside. The blustery wind was howling beneath the eaves. The rain would hit at any minute. Even as Max watched, a shaft of lightning arced across the sky.

"Another storm," he said.

Sylvia shrugged. "It's that time of year. Listen, I wanted to thank you for finding Sammy's duck last night. He really treasures that thing."

"It was no problem."

"Lucky Ducky means a lot to him because Jason gave it to him." Sylvia smiled tremulously. "Sammy's at that age when he's looking for a male role model. You know how it is."

"Sammy said his father's lost. He says he went off to look for himself."

Sylvia grimaced. "Children take things so literally, don't they? But he's not entirely wrong. Doug came home from the office one day and announced that he couldn't handle the responsibility of a wife and child. He said our marriage had been a terrible mistake. He packed up his things and left. Sammy was only a year old at the time."

"I take it your ex doesn't come around to visit Sammy?"

Sylvia shook her head. "Doug went back east, where he apparently decided he was ready for responsibility after all. The last I heard he had married again and started a new family. He's never contacted Sammy and me since, except through his attorney. He does occasionally remember to pay child support."

The lights went out just as another flash of lightning lit up the darkened sky.

"Darn," Sylvia muttered. "There goes the power again. I hope it's just a blown fuse this time. Last month a tree went down across the lines, and we were without electricity for hours."

Max seized the opportunity. "I'll check the fuse box, if you like."

Sylvia gave him a grateful look. "Thanks. Hang on a second." She reached under the front desk and produced a flashlight. "We keep one handy, as you can see. This sort of thing happens a lot around here."

Herbert T. Valence stormed out of the parlor just as Sylvia handed the large flashlight to Max. His expression of intense enthusiasm had been replaced by a look of intense agitation.

"What is going on around here?" Valence demanded. "I'm trying to run a video in there. What's happened to the power?"

"I'm going to check on it," Max said mildly. He took the flashlight from Sylvia.

Valence scowled. "Well, hurry up about it, will you? I've got a seminar to teach. I've got a reputation to maintain, you know. I can't do my best work without my audiovisual equipment."

"Try being creative," Max said. "Just think positive. Positive thinking is the fuel that runs the engine of creativity, remember?"

Sylvia turned away, but not before Max saw that she was struggling to bite back a laugh. Valence's face tightened with outrage.

"Is that supposed to be funny?" Valence asked coldly.

"I'm just giving you some of your own advice." Max stepped around him, heading for the basement stairs. "And I'm not even going to charge you for it."

"Now see here," Valence sputtered, "I don't

have to put up with that sort of rudeness.

The lobby door opened at that moment. Max glanced back over his shoulder as wet wind and a disheveled-looking Cleo swept into the room.

Cleo was clutching a brown paper sack protectively under one arm. He saw the strained expression on her face as she swung around to close the door. Apparently the meeting with Hildebrand had not gone well.

"Whew." Cleo shut the door and ran her fingers through her wet hair. "It's pouring out there. Everything all right in here, Sylvia?"

"No, everything is not all right," Valence said before Sylvia could respond. "The power is off. I want it fixed immediately. I'm trying to run a seminar, as you well know, Ms. Robbins. I've got a reputation for flawless performance, and I simply cannot work without electricity."

Max watched as Cleo summoned up her innkeeper's soothing smile. "Yes, of course, Mr. Valence. We'll get someone on it right away."

"I'm already on it." Max held up the flashlight.

Cleo's gaze flashed to his face. "I thought you'd be gone by now.

"Whatever gave you that idea? You just hired me."

Cleo looked as if she badly wanted to respond to that, but Valence's presence forced her to restrain herself. "What do you think you're doing?"

"I'm going down to the basement to check the fuse box. Any objections?" Max waited politely.

Cleo set her jaw. "I'll come with you."

"I think I can handle this on my own," Max said.

"I said I'll come with you." Cleo managed another serene smile for Valence. "Just give us a few minutes, Mr. Valence. I'm sure we'll have everything back under control very soon."

"I should hope so," Valence muttered. "My time is extremely valuable. I can't afford to waste it sitting around waiting for someone to turn on the electricity." He shot one last annoyed glance at Max as he stalked back down the hall to the parlor.

Max watched Valence disappear. "Did you know he's incredible?" he said to Cleo. "Also amazing."

"What on earth are you talking about? Here, give me that." She snatched the flashlight out of his hand and strode down the hall to the door that opened on to the basement stairs. "Why aren't you gone?"

"There are a number of reasons." Max opened the door and surveyed the inky depths

83

of a vast basement. "One of which is that I haven't apologized for the small misunderstanding we had at breakfast."

"It was not a small misunderstanding." Cleo switched on the flashlight and started down the basement stairs. She still had the paper sack tucked under her arm. "You were rude, crude, and obnoxious."

"You may be right." Max's cane tapped softly on each step as he followed Cleo downstairs. "However, I'd like the chance to apologize for assuming you were Jason's mistress."

"A *gold-digging* mistress." Cleo reached the foot of the stairs and swept the beam of light around the crowded basement.

"All right," Max said patiently. "I apologize for assuming you were his *gold-digging* mistress."

"Okay, you've apologized. Now you can leave."

Max took a tight grip on his hawk-headed cane. She was not going to get rid of him this easily. She still had his Amos Luttrells. "I'm afraid I can't leave just yet."

Cleo crossed the room to the circuit-breaker panel. "Why not?"

"I told you last night. I need the arrangement you're offering. I don't have another job."

She turned away and concentrated on opening the panel cover. "That's not my problem."

Max could tell that she was wavering. He decided to change tactics. "What happened with Hildebrand?"

Cleo flipped a switch, and the overhead light came on. Her smile was grim. "Nolan came to the same conclusion about me that you did. He thinks I'm a fallen woman. As a budding politician with a career in the White House ahead of him, he can't afford to be associated with the likes of me."

Max was surprised by the jolt of anger that went through him. He studied Cleo's set face. "This was a sudden conclusion on Hildebrand's part?"

"Very sudden."

"What prompted it?"

"I can't imagine." Cleo closed the panel door and switched off the flashlight. "You'll have to excuse me. I've got a lot of things to do, and you've got a long drive ahead of you."

Max positioned himself directly in her path. "Cleo, wait. I meant what I said. I'm sorry about the misunderstanding, and I don't have anywhere else to go. I'd appreciate it if you'd let me stay for a while. I'll earn my keep."

She hesitated. The uncertainty was plain in her eyes. "Look, I'm sorry about your situation, but you really can't expect me to give you the same arrangement I gave Jason. Not after what you said this morning."

"Jason was your friend," Max said quietly. "He was my friend, too. What did you expect me to think when he talked about a mysterious woman named Cleo? He was on his deathbed. He didn't have the strength to give me a detailed explanation of just how you fit into his life. All I knew was that he —" Max broke off, searching for the right words. "Cared for you."

Cleo's expression softened. She lowered her eyes and was silent for a long minute. Finally, she met his gaze and said, "All right. For the sake of our mutual friendship with Jason, I'll let you stay."

"Thanks," Max said. It had been easier than he'd anticipated. The lady was obviously a sucker for a hard luck story.

"But only through this long weekend," Cleo added, just as if she'd read his mind and suspected she'd been had. "There's still no sign of Benjy, and I could use an extra hand around here for the next three days. But I'll expect you to leave on Tuesday. Understood?"

"I understand."

Three days was a long time, Max thought. A lot could happen. He'd been known to make and break multimillion-dollar deals in a period of three days. He'd once orchestrated in less than three days the ransom and rescue of an entire contingent of Curzon executives who had been kidnapped by terrorists. With any luck he would find his Luttrells in the next three days.

And if not, he'd find a way to stay on longer at Robbins' Nest Inn.

Herbert T. Valence was right. The trick was to think positive.

Cleo glanced into the lounge around nine o'clock that evening. Max and Sylvia were pouring after-dinner coffee and sherry for the inn guests. A pleasant fire blazed on the hearth, creating a scene of warm contentment. A low murmur of conversation wafted across the room.

Cleo had been chiding herself for her lack of willpower all afternoon. She knew she should have sent Max packing as soon as she returned from the meeting with Nolan. She had told herself she would kick him out if he was still hanging around the place. But somehow Max had managed to make her feel sorry for him.

She could not escape the feeling that she had been manipulated.

"You'll have to admit that Max adds a certain style to the place," Sylvia observed as she paused beside Cleo. "Jason used to have that same aristocratic air when he poured coffee and sherry. The guests love it."

"He acts like he owns the place," Cleo muttered. "Look at him. Every inch the gracious lord of the manor."

"Face it, Cleo. Put a man like Max to digging a ditch, and he'd manage to make it look like he owned the ditch and a hundred thousand acres surrounding it."

"Maybe he does. He drives a Jaguar. And those clothes he's wearing didn't come from any bargain basement."

"He's trying to be helpful," Sylvia said. "He's done everything you asked him to do this afternoon. He even hauled logs in for the fire, which was probably not an easy task with that cane of his."

Cleo winced as a shaft of guilt lanced through her. She sincerely regretted having asked Max to fetch the firewood. The truth was, she hadn't even considered his bad leg when she'd issued the order. Something about Max made it all too easy to forget his cane and everything it implied. Max simply did not look like he had any weaknesses.

"There's something about him that bothers me," Cleo grumbled.

"Like what?"

"I'm not sure," Cleo admitted. She hesitated. "He thought I was Jason's mistress."

Sylvia glanced at her in surprise and then grinned. "No kidding?"

"It's not funny."

"Yes it is. Do you know what your problem is? You've been in a lousy mood ever since you returned from seeing Nolan."

"Nolan thinks I'm a porn queen."

Sylvia's mouth fell open. "What?"

He found out that I wrote *The Mirror.*"

Sylvia stared at her. "No one knows you wrote it except members of the family. I didn't tell a soul, I swear it, Cleo. I can't believe anyone else did, either."

"I know. Don't worry about it. I guess the secret was bound to leak out sooner or later."

Sylvia frowned. "I know how important it was to you to maintain your anonymity with that book."

"It's such a personal thing," Cleo said. "I won't mind people knowing I wrote *A Fine Vengeance*. But *The Mirror* has too much of me inside it."

"I understand," Sylvia said gently.

Cleo shifted restlessly. "I told Nolan that I don't want to deal with the snide remarks people will make, but the truth is, I don't want to deal with their rude curiosity. I had too much of that kind of thing after my parents died. People asked me the most awful, personal questions about what it had been like to find them —" Cleo broke off abruptly. "There's no telling what kind of questions they'd ask about *The Mirror*."

Sylvia put a comforting arm around her. "It's all right, Cleo. Take it easy. The most important question at the moment is, who told Nolan?"

"I don't know," Cleo admitted. "Someone put a copy of the book into his mailbox, along with a note saying I'd written *The Mirror*. The note also said that I'd make a very unsuitable wife for a man with political ambitions."

"My God, that's downright weird. No wonder you've been upset all afternoon. What did Nolan say?"

Cleo smiled wryly. "He said I was no longer a viable candidate for the position of Mrs. Nolan Hildebrand. Said my pornographic past could seriously jeopardize his political career. He hoped I'd understand why he was dumping me."

"Why, that little slimeball," Sylvia muttered. "I trust you told him to take a long walk off a short pier?"

"It's over, and it really doesn't matter. My relationship with Nolan never amounted to much in the first place." Cleo met Sylvia's worried gaze. "I don't want the rest of the family to know about the note. It would only upset everyone."

Sylvia nodded in agreement. "All right. I won't mention it. But what about Nolan? Won't he tell everyone you wrote that book?"

Cleo smiled wryly. "I doubt it. He doesn't want anyone to know he associated, however briefly, with a woman of doubtful virtue."

"No offense, Cleo, because I know you liked him, but the guy's a jerk. He's probably got a brilliant political career ahead of him."

Cleo started to respond and stopped short when she saw Sammy running toward them down the hall. The little boy was dressed in his pajamas. He grasped Lucky Ducky firmly in one small fist.

"What are you doing up, honey?" Sylvia asked in concern. "You're supposed to be asleep."

"Can't sleep." Sammy clung to his mother's hand and pressed close to her leg.

"A bad dream?" Cleo asked gently.

"No." Sammy hugged Lucky Ducky close. "Trisha's crying."

"She is?" Cleo frowned. Trisha slept in the room next to Sammy's.

"Won't stop." Sammy turned his face into Sylvia's skirt.

"I'll go up and see what's wrong," Cleo said. "Don't worry about her, Sammy. I'm sure she'll be fine."

Sammy nodded but did not raise his head.

Sylvia picked him up and hugged him tightly. "Cleo will talk to her, honey. Everything will be okay."

"Trisha's probably unhappy because Benjy's gone," Cleo said. She exchanged a glance with Sylvia. "Keep an eye on things here."

"Right," Sylvia said. "Max and I can handle the lounge crowd."

Sammy brightened suddenly as he caught sight of Max behind the bar. "There's Max. Hi, Max." He waved Lucky Ducky in greeting.

Max glanced toward the door. His gaze went to Sammy and then to Cleo. He put down the bottle of sherry he had been wielding and walked over to join the small group in the doorway.

"Something wrong?" he asked quietly.

"Trisha's crying," Sammy explained. "Cleo's going to go make her feel better."

"I see." Max watched Cleo intently. "Do you think it's serious?"

"From Trisha's point of view, yes," Cleo said. "She's worried about Benjy. There's been no word from him. I'll be right back."

Cleo turned away and hurried toward the back stairs. She was not surprised by the announcement that Trisha was in tears. She had been concerned about her since last night, when they had all discovered that Benjy had vanished.

Trisha's room was on the third floor. She had moved in two years earlier when she had taken the job at Robbins' Nest Inn. Trisha and Benjy had been drawn together from the moment they had met. Cleo knew they had a lot in common. Too much, perhaps. Both came from badly mangled, nonsupportive families. They had become close friends within the framework of Cleo's extended clan. About six months ago, Cleo knew, they had become lovers.

Cleo had watched the inevitable romance spring up between Trisha and Benjy with some misgivings. She was not at all certain that either of them could cope with the responsibilities of a committed relationship, yet she knew that was exactly what both desperately wanted. There had been an odd sense of fate about the pair. It was as if they were two lost waifs clinging to each other in a storm.

Cleo stopped in front of Trisha's door and knocked softly. "Trisha? It's me, Cleo."

"Cleo?" Trisha's voice was muffled. "I'm in bed. Please go away."

"Trisha, you know I can't do that. Sammy says you've been crying. Let me in. We'll talk."

"I don't want to talk."

"Not even about Benjy?"

"Especially not about Benjy." Trisha suddenly burst into wracking sobs.

Cleo couldn't stand it any longer. "Let me in, Trisha, or I'll use the master key."

There was a moment of painful silence. Then the door opened slowly to reveal Trisha's tear-blotched face.

"Oh, Trisha," Cleo whispered. She opened her arms.

"I know why he left," Trisha wailed. She flung herself into Cleo's comforting arms. "It was because of me."

"Of course it wasn't because of you." Cleo patted Trisha's shoulder. "Benjy's got problems of his own, you know that. He's got a lot to deal with."

"I know," Trisha sobbed. "And I gave him one problem too many."

"Trisha, it's not your fault that Benjy left."

"Yes, it is," Trisha said in a choked voice. "I'm pregnant."

Cleo closed her eyes briefly, her worst fears confirmed. "Oh, Lord."

"I told Benjy, and he couldn't handle it. That's why he left. Cleo, what am I going to do? I'm so scared."

"It's all right," Cleo said quietly. "Everything's going to be all right. You've got family now, remember? You're not alone."

★ ★ ★

It was nearly midnight before Cleo wearily made her way to the tower room on the third floor. She had chosen her small sanctuary with care immediately after she had moved in to the inn.

Her private quarters were tucked away out of sight of the guests' rooms. Her small suite in the tower afforded privacy and a view of the sea. There were times when Cleo badly needed both. Being surrounded by family and inn guests was all very well most of the time, but there were occasions when Cleo needed the protective solitude of her own rooms.

She unlocked the door, her mind still on Trisha's unhappy situation, and let herself into the lovingly overstuffed domicile. It was furnished, as was the rest of the inn, in the most flowery expression of Victorian style. Every item, from the chintz wallpaper and the canopied bed to the ceramic clock on the table, had been carefully chosen by Cleo.

She flipped the switch on the wall, leaving the door still open behind her. The bedside lamp cast a warm glow over the frilly white pillows arranged on the bed.

The light revealed something else on the bed: a length of red satin ribbon curled like a scarlet snake on one pillow.

Cleo stared at the ribbon in stunned shock.

95

She suddenly felt light-headed. Her fingers, still clutching the doorknob, started to shake.

"Cleo?" Max materialized behind her in the open doorway, looming over her. "I've been looking for you. I wanted to talk to you before you went to bed."

"Not now," she got out in a hoarse whisper. She could not take her eyes off the red satin ribbon.

"What the hell?" Without apology, Max shouldered his way past her into the room. He swept the surroundings with a single glance and then swung around to face her. "What's wrong?"

"Please," she whispered. "Go away."

"You look like you've just seen a ghost."

"Go away," she hissed.

Max ignored the command. Instead he calmly closed the door. "Don't faint. I'm no good with fainting women." He put an arm around Cleo and pulled her tightly against his chest.

"I'm not going to faint. I've never fainted in my life." Cleo wanted to resist the compelling heat of his body, but it was soaking into her, driving out the chill that had gripped her a moment earlier. She stood there, leaning against him for a few minutes.

The man in the mirror.

Eventually she started to relax. Max felt solid and strong and he smelled good. Cleo

96

inhaled the enticing combination of soap and maleness. She had never before found herself captivated by a man's scent, but Max's fascinated her. Surreptitiously she tried to bury her nose against his chest.

"Are you okay?" Max asked.

The question broke the delicate thrall that had begun to form around Cleo. Embarrassed, she raised her head, straightened her glasses, and pushed herself away from him. "I think so. Sorry about this. I was a little startled by something. I'm okay now."

Slowly he released her. His eyes never left her face. "What was that all about?"

Cleo knew she should keep her mouth shut. But her defenses were down because of the shock of seeing the ribbon on the pillow and because of the way Max had held her. She knew she owed him absolutely no explanations. But she suddenly needed to talk to someone. If Jason had been there, she would have told him the whole story.

Max had been Jason's friend. Max was not a stranger. Not really.

"That ribbon shouldn't be there." Cleo didn't know where to start. She went over to the bed and stood looking down at the coiled length of satin. "Someone put it there."

"A gift from Sammy?"

"No." Cleo hugged herself. "God, no.

Sammy wouldn't know anything about the significance of a red satin ribbon left on a pillow."

"But you do?" Max did not move.

"It's a scene out of a book I wrote." Cleo shivered. Then she spun around and went to the bookshelf. She took clown the copy of *The Mirror* that Nolan had given to her that morning. "It's from this. Chapter three."

Max took the book and glanced at the cover. "You wrote this? It says the author's name is Elizabeth Bird."

"That's me. Elizabeth Bird is a pen name. Until recently it's been a deep, dark secret known only to members of the family. But today it has become painfully obvious that someone else knows it."

"Why did you try to keep yourself anonymous?"

Cleo watched his face. "Take a look at the book."

Max flipped open the cover and scanned the inside flap. He looked up after a moment, his eyes unreadable. "You write women's erotica? I thought you wrote romantic-suspense."

Cleo lifted her chin. "I wrote one book of erotica before I started writing romantic-suspense. *The Mirror* is that book." She bit her lip and could not resist adding, "It was actually rather well received. Even got some good reviews." Of course, Max wouldn't believe that, Cleo thought. She wished she hadn't sounded defensive. She wished she'd kept her mouth shut.

"I see," Max said. There was absolutely no inflection in his voice.

For the life of her Cleo could not tell what his reaction was to the news that she had written *The Mirror*. "That book you're holding in your hand is the chief reason Nolan decided I was unsuitable company for a rising politician."

"Ah, well. Politicians tend to be a rather dull bunch, don't they? No imagination."

Cleo smiled dangerously. "I suppose it confirms your earlier opinion of me as a loose woman."

"It confirms my impression that you are a very unpredictable woman." Max sat down on a small, chintz-covered chair without waiting for an invitation. He leaned his cane against a table and started to massage his thigh with an absent movement of his hand. "Why don't you tell me what this is all about?"

Cleo sighed and flopped down into a wingback chair. She stretched her legs out in front of her, shoved her hands into her pockets, and eyed Max thoughtfully. She was already regretting her impulse to confide in him.

"There's not much to it, objectively speaking," she admitted. "All I know is that some disgruntled reader has apparently decided to punish me for writing that book. He or she sent a really nasty letter to me last month."

"What did you do about it?" Max asked.

"Nothing. What could I do? There was no signature. It was forwarded from my publishers, so I assumed the person who wrote it didn't have my real name and address. But this morning Nolan told me that someone left a copy of my book in his mailbox."

"Anonymously, I assume?"

"Yes. Along with the warning that I wouldn't make a good date for a politician. And tonight I walk in here and find that ribbon on my pillow."

"You suspect you're being pestered by an outraged reader?"

"Who else could it be?" Cleo shuddered. "Some weirdo is out to harass me, I guess. And he or she was right here in my bedroom tonight. It's creepy." It was more than that; it was frightening. But Cleo was not about to admit it. Not yet, at any rate.

"I might be able to help," Max said quietly.

Cleo stared at him. "How?"

"I know a man who runs a firm that specializes in corporate security and investigations. If you like, I can ask him to check out a few things."

"Forget it. I don't want to get involved with a private investigator."

"Why not?"

Cleo set her teeth. She'd been burned once by a private investigator who had taken her money and done nothing for her. She didn't intend to get conned again. "It's not worth it. I don't want to blow this up out of all proportion. Whoever it is will get tired of the game after a while and go away."

"You think so?"

"This sort of thing happens to writers sometimes," Cleo said defensively. "There's not much a person can do."

"I'm not so sure about that. Look, I can at least have O'Reilly check out the guests who are staying here this weekend. We can find out if any of them have a reputation for being rabid censors."

"I told you, I'm not going to pay a private investigator to look into this."

"You won't have to pay him," Max said softly. "O'Reilly is a friend of mine. He owes me a couple of favors. He'll be glad to do this for me."

Cleo hesitated. "You think so?"

"Yes. There's no harm in running a quick check." Max looked thoughtful. "It will take some time, though. I doubt if I can get O'Reilly to do it in just two days."

Cleo eyed him with instant suspicion. "Is this a pitch designed to convince me not to kick you out on Tuesday?"

"Yes." Max shrugged. "I don't have anywhere else to go. Jobs are hard to get these days.

She groaned. "I knew it wasn't going to be easy to get rid of you.

4

I recognize him even though I cannot see his face clearly in the mirror. He's a phantom in the glass, confined forever in a silvery world, but I know him instantly when he touches me.

His fingers are warm, not cold, although he is locked away in that frozen place behind the mirror. He wants me as no one else has ever wanted me. I want him. In some way I cannot explain, I know that he is a part of me. Yet he is as trapped in his prison as I am in mine.

When he comes to me tonight he will put his hands on my breasts, and I will shudder in response. The heat will rise within me. He will watch my face and see the desire in me. I do not have to hide it from him. He alone will understand the need and the longing and the passion inside me that no one else has ever seen. In his arms I will be free.

But what about him? Will I ever be able to release him from the mirror?

Max closed *The Mirror* and put the book down on the small nightstand beside the bed. He took a slow breath and concentrated on controlling the deep, sexual ache that had settled into his groin. He should have had enough sense to stop reading after he'd finished chapter one.

But he had been unable to resist continuing on to chapter two, even though the sensual fantasies in the book were so vibrantly female in nature that they felt alien. The fact that they were Cleo's fantasies was what had compelled him, seduced him, captivated him. In *The Mirror*, Max knew he had found another window through which he could view her.

The glimpses he'd gotten tonight were going to keep him awake for a long time.

He pushed back the covers and swung his legs over the edge of the bed. Old pain, familiar and unpleasant, lanced through his left thigh when he got to his feet. Automatically he glanced down at the scar. It looked as ugly as it always did, and it called up the usual memories.

Memories of one of the few times that he had screwed up royally.

Max reached for his cane to steady himself. He waited a minute, and gradually the pain eased. He made his way over to the window and looked out across the night-shrouded cove. Through the steady fall of rain he could see the lights of the Cosmic Harmony Women's Retreat winking in the distance.

Max gazed at them for a long while, and then he glanced back over his shoulder at his newest temporary home. He had stayed in a lot of places over the years, from cheap, thin-walled trailers to European castles, but this was the first time he had lived in an attic.

The large room under the eaves of the old inn was surprisingly cozy. It was also comfortable, so long as he remembered to duck the steeply sloped roof beams near the walls. Luckily there had apparently not been enough frilly Victoriana left over to waste on this portion of the inn. To his infinite relief, the furnishings up here were worn, rustic pieces that suited his taste for clean, straightforward shapes and forms.

Max envisioned Cleo asleep in her canopied bed one floor below and immediately regretted it. The image only served to intensify the heavy feeling in his lower body. It was going to be a long night.

His gaze fell on the coil of red ribbon lying on the desk, and his mouth tightened.

He'd made a tactical error this morning when he had confronted Cleo with his assumptions about her role in Jason's life. He was rarely so clumsy.

Having neatly wrecked his chances for insinuating himself easily into her odd household, Max had realized immediately that he'd needed a new pressure point. He'd had to find a way to convince Cleo to let him stay on at the inn. The incident with the red ribbon had provided him with a perfect excuse for hanging around.

He had told her he'd have O'Reilly check out the guests who were staying at the inn, and he fully intended to do just that. But he was going to tell O'Reilly not to rush the check. Max needed time to search for the Luttrells.

He scooped up the scarlet satin ribbon and let the ends trail through his fingers. The realization that someone had invaded Cleo's bedroom in order to deliberately frighten her sent a frisson of cold anger through him. Literary criticism had its place, but this particular critic had gone too far.

He was definitely not in a mood to sleep, Max decided. It sounded quiet downstairs. This would be a good opportunity to take a look around the inn's basement. He'd already prowled through several upstairs rooms and found nothing. The basement was the sort of place someone like Cleo might have chosen to conceal five valuable paintings.

Max shook his head in disgust at the thought of the magnificent Luttrells stashed in a damp basement.

He crossed the room to the closet. As usual, he had brought a fully packed carryall with him. The habit of being ready to leave at a moment's notice had been formed when he was a boy and was too well entrenched to be broken now.

Max tugged on a pair of dark trousers and one of the new white shirts he had recently received from his London tailor. For no good reason that he could think of, he stuffed the scarlet ribbon into his pocket. Then he headed downstairs.

The inn was quiet. Each floor was well lighted, but no one was about. Herbert T. Valence's intensive training in motivational techniques had apparently exhausted the seminar attendees.

Max saw the light on in the small office behind the front desk as soon as he walked into the lobby. He paused, listening intently for a moment. Then he went forward sound-lessly, careful to keep the tip of the cane on the carpet so that it would not announce his arrival. He expected to find George, the inn's night desk man, at work.

A loud snore rumbled through the lobby. It emanated from the inner office. Max's brows rose. He took another few steps and glanced through the open doorway of the inner office. A thin, bald man somewhere in his mid-sixties was seated in Cleo's chair. He was fast asleep, his head down on his folded arms.

So much for night security at Robbins' Nest Inn.

But what was bad for security created a con-venient situation for Max. He could take his time exploring the basement. He started down the hall that led to the basement stairs.

When he went past the glass-walled solar-ium, a tingle of awareness made him hesitate. He stopped in the doorway. The lights were off inside the room, but there was enough of a glow from the hall to reveal a familiar, grace-ful figure lounging in one of the regal fanback wicker chairs.

She sat alone in the shadows, gazing pen-sively out into the rain-soaked darkness. Cleopatra contemplating the fate of Egypt.

The throbbing sense of urgency that still

swirled deep within Max flared back into life once more. Instinctively he brushed his hand across the pocket that contained the length of red satin.

"Hello," Max said quietly. "I take it you couldn't sleep either?"

Cleo's head came around very swiftly. She blinked at Max's backlit figure, as if trying to make out who had invaded her private realm. He could see that the soft, dark cloud of her hair had worked its way free of the clip that was supposed to keep it in place. She was wearing her usual uniform of snug, faded jeans and an oxford cloth button-down shirt. Her gold sneakers gleamed in the shadows.

The faint hall light revealed Cleo's wary, shuttered expression. An emotion other than desire stirred inside of Max. He recognized it vaguely as concern. He had not seen that particular look on Cleo's face before, not even when they had discussed the significance of the red ribbon on her pillow.

"I had an unpleasant dream," Cleo said quietly. "I get them sometimes. I thought I'd come down here for a few minutes to get rid of the cobwebs. What are you doing up?"

Max wondered what sort of dreams it took to awaken Cleo and cause her to seek refuge in the solarium.

He walked into the darkened room and sat down in the wicker chair across from her. For a moment he said nothing. He could hear the burbling of the water in the shallow, tiled fountain that was the centerpiece of the room.

"I had nothing better to do, so I decided I'd come down and see how easy it was to get hold of a master key or the key to your room," Max improvised carefully.

"The key to my room?" Cleo looked briefly startled.

"Someone must have used one or the other to open your door earlier tonight."

"Oh, I see." Her fingers clenched around the arms of the wicker chair. "It wouldn't have been that hard to get hold of a key, I'm afraid. I suppose you saw George?"

"He's asleep."

Cleo wrinkled her nose. "He usually is. The thing is, we've never had much of a security problem here at the inn."

"I noticed that the front desk is frequently unattended for several minutes at a time during the day, too," Max pointed out.

"Yes. We're always a little short of staff. Everyone pitches in when we're full. Sometimes that means whoever is at the front desk has to help out in the kitchen or check on a problem in one of the rooms."

Max gingerly stretched out his leg and absently massaged his aching thigh. "The bottom line here is that almost anyone could have entered the inn sometime today, swiped a key for a few minutes, used it to unlock your door, and left the ribbon on your pillow."

"Yes." Cleo's brows drew together. "Believe me, from here on out, we'll make certain we keep a much closer eye on the keys."

"I think that would be a good idea," Max said dryly. "For openers, the keys should be kept inside the office at all times, not left on the hooks behind the front desk. No one but members of your staff should be allowed into the office, and the door should be locked if the front desk is unattended, even for five minutes."

"I'd already figured that out for myself," Cleo muttered.

"Tomorrow morning you can get me a complete list of everyone who is staying at the inn this weekend," Max continued.

Cleo leaned back in her chair, rested her elbows on the arms, and steepled her fingers. She gazed at him, brooding. "You're serious about having your friend O'Reilly check out my guests, aren't you?"

He was surprised by the question. "Did you get the impression that I wasn't serious about it?"

"Not exactly. You look like the type who

takes most things seriously."

"In my experience it's the things which don't get taken seriously that cause the most problems," he said.

"So you take everything seriously," Cleo concluded. "Sounds like a rather grim way to go through life."

"It's the way I am."

"I'll bet you're a real fun date."

The flash of humor in her eyes disconcerted him. Max forgot about his aching leg for a moment as it struck him that she was laughing at him. It was an odd experience. People reacted to him in a variety of ways, but virtually no one found hint amusing. "I've never had anyone comment on that."

"You're a strange man." The amusement faded from Cleo's eyes. "I don't know what to make of you, Max. I thought I did when you arrived, but now I'm not so sure."

"I can prove that I was a friend of Jason's, if that will make you feel more comfortable around me."

Her eyes widened. "I believe you were Jason's friend."

"And I apologized for thinking you were Jason's mistress."

"Yes, I know." She waved a hand in a magnanimous gesture. "I've decided not to hold that against you any longer, by the way."

"Thank you," Max said humbly.

"I mean, I can sort of see where you might have gotten the impression that Jason and I were . . . well, never mind." Cleo blushed. "I can see where you got the idea."

"When you decide what it is that's still bothering you about me," Max said gently, "let me know."

"I'll do that." She watched intently as he rubbed his thigh. "What's wrong with your leg?"

"It aches a little sometimes. Especially after a long day."

"How did you hurt it?" Cleo asked. "Were you in an accident?"

"You could say that."

"How long ago did it happen?"

He was amused by her sudden fascination with the topic. "Three years ago."

"It looks painful."

"Occasionally it is."

She bit her lip. "I suppose it's bothering you tonight because of all that firewood you lugged into the lobby this afternoon. You should have said something when I asked you to do that."

"It's got nothing to do with hauling firewood around. Sometimes it just aches, that's all."

"Does massage help?"

Max shrugged. "I don't know. I've never tried professional massage.

"I give a good therapeutic massage." Cleo's smile was tentative. "I learned how to do it when Andromeda hired a massage therapist to teach the women of Cosmic Harmony. Andromeda's into holistic medicine, you know."

"I'm not surprised."

"Want me to work on that leg?"

Max abruptly stopped rubbing his thigh. He flexed his fingers slowly as he imagined what it would feel like to have Cleo's hands on his leg.

"All right," Max said. He was going to regret this, he was certain of it. But he seemed to be lacking in willpower tonight.

Cleo got slowly to her feet. She took two steps to close the distance between them and knelt on the floor beside his chair. Her eyes were huge and luminous behind the lenses of her glasses.

"Tell me if I hurt you," she whispered.

"I will." Max took a deep breath and waited for the exquisite torture to begin.

Cleo put her hands on his thigh. For a while she did not move at all. She simply let the warmth of her palms soak through his trousers into his skin.

Max was startled by the amount of soothing

heat she was generating. He looked down at Cleo's bent head. She was concentrating intently on her task. The delicate, sensual curve of her neck was within reach. All he had to do was move his hand a scant six inches or so, and he would be touching her. Max gripped the arms of the chair.

"You're very tense." Cleo frowned as she pressed her fingertips gently into his hard, muscled flesh. "Try to relax. According to the massage therapist who taught me how to do this, the chief cause of soreness in the muscles is tension."

"I'll try to remember that."

She began to knead his thigh with long, smooth strokes. "How does that feel?"

"Good." It was true, Max realized, surprised. No one had ever offered to massage his leg for him since his "accident." He hadn't realized how soothing it would feel to have someone else work on the knotted muscles of his thigh.

"Andromeda is very good with herbs. I'll ask her to mix up something you can use as a muscle relaxant," Cleo said.

Max winced at the thought. "Never mind. I generally use brandy when things get bad."

"I think you'll find one of Cosmic Harmony's herbal teas will work just as well. The guests love them."

Max didn't feel like arguing. He closed his eyes and focused on the sensual touch of Cleo's hands. Another window, he thought. Another glimpse into the intriguing depths of Cleopatra Robbins.

Long minutes passed during which Max's leg began to feel infinitely better. But the massage did nothing to diminish the driving need inside him. The sense of urgency was growing beyond control.

"Cleo, I've been reading *The Mirror*," Max said.

Her hands stilled. Max swore silently, wishing he'd kept his mouth shut.

"I suppose you think it's pornography, just like Nolan did."

"No," Max said. "I think it's beautiful."

"Beautiful?" Her voice was little more than a whisper.

"More than beautiful. It's fascinating."

Cleo's hands began to move again on his thigh. "Really?"

Max opened his eyes and looked down at her averted face. "Reading it is like looking into a fine painting. There are hundreds of layers to see. Some are obvious, others aren't. Some can be described, but the most important ones can't be put into words at all. You have to feel them."

Cleo flashed him a misty smile. "You sound

like Jason when you talk like that. He said some people see art with another eye.

"He called it the inner eye."

"That's right." She tilted her head a little to one side. "Is that how you see art?"

"Yes."

"It sounds strange. Can you see into people the same way?"

"Not usually," Max admitted. But I'm learning to see you that way, he thought. The knowledge went through him like wildfire. The more he knew about Cleo, the more he wanted her. This was exactly how he felt when he was in the presence of a fine painting that spoke directly to him.

He wanted her.

"You're lucky you can't see into people the way you do art." Cleo continued to stroke his leg. "I can sometimes, and it's very frustrating for the most part."

He studied the sweet, vulnerable line at the nape of her neck. "Why do you say that?"

"Because it doesn't do much good. Even when you can see things about people, you usually can't change them."

"You sound like you're talking from experience."

"I am." Cleo looked up, her eyes troubled. "The reason Trisha was sobbing her heart out tonight is because she just found out she's pregnant. She says Benjy left because she told him about the baby."

"I see. I'm sorry about Trisha, she seems like a nice enough kid. But what does her situation have to do with what we were talking about?"

Cleo's shoulder rose and fell in a small shrug. "I knew the first time I saw Trisha and Benjy together that they would cling to each other. They're two of a kind. Two orphans in a storm. I wasn't surprised when their friendship turned into a romance. But I also knew it could lead to disaster."

"Why?"

"Because both Benjy and Trisha have had to be so strong in order to just survive, that they're both very fragile when it comes to dealing with other people. Does that make sense?"

"I don't know," Max said.

"Take my word for it. Adding a baby to the equation was just too much stress. Especially for Benjy. He's never had a father of his own, and I imagine the thought of becoming one himself terrified him. No wonder he disappeared for a while."

Max touched a stray lock of Cleo's hair. She did not seem to notice. "You're not to blame for Trisha's situation."

"My point is that I could see deeply enough

into both Trisha and Benjy to know that this mess Trisha's in was almost bound to happen. But I couldn't do a thing to stop it. Knowing what was coming didn't do any good, did it? I couldn't avert the catastrophe."

"It wasn't your responsibility to avert it," Max said.

Cleo smiled wryly. "Trisha and Benjy are both part of the family. I should have been able to do something about the situation before it got out of hand."

"I thought I was the one who took things too seriously."

Her smile faded. "This is serious. Trisha and Benjy are both family. I care about them."

He couldn't think of anything to say to that. Cleo obviously had an odd definition of family. On the other hand, Max thought, he couldn't think of a better one. He decided not to comment.

Cleo worked for a while in silence. Her fingers probed gently, seeking the depths of his taut muscles. "I'm glad you didn't think *The Mirror* was pornographic," she said after a moment.

"It's just the opposite." Max closed his eyes.

"You sound very certain of that."

"You know what they say about pornography." Max smiled faintly. "You know it when you see it. *The Mirror* isn't it."

"What makes you so sure?"

He searched for a way to put his inner knowledge into words. "*The Mirror* is alive. It generates a variety of responses, not just a sexual reaction. It's an affirmation of life and the future. Pornography is static."

"Static?"

He spread the fingers of one hand wide and then let them relax. "It's one-dimensional. No past, no future, no depth, no emotion, except for a short-term sexual response which wears off very fast. I'm not saying it's good or bad; it's just boring after about ten minutes."

"Ten minutes?" Cleo repeated very innocently.

Max heard the laughter in her voice. He raised his lashes and gazed at her through narrowed eyes. "Okay, fifteen, if it's really well-done pornography."

She laughed softly. Her fingers continued to move on his thigh. "How is your leg feeling now?"

"Much better." It was the truth.

"You're not an artist, are you, Max?"

"No."

"So what did you do for a living before you came here?"

"This and that," Max said. "Odd jobs for the most part."

"What kind of odd jobs?"

He hesitated, uncertain of how much to tell her. If she knew he had worked for Jason she might think that he had merely been an employee and therefore had no real claim to the Luttrells. She might even conclude that she had more of a right to them than he did. Max preferred her to know only part of the truth, that he had been Jason's friend. It put him on an even footing with her. After all, Cleo had been no more and no less than Jason's friend, too. She would not be able to salve her conscience by telling herself that her relationship with Jason was closer than Max's had been and that therefore she had more of a right to the Luttrells.

Max realized at that moment that somewhere along the line he had decided that Cleo did have a conscience.

"I worked for an art dealer once," Max offered as an example of the odd jobs he had performed.

"It must have paid very well," Cleo said.

"Yes." He knew she was thinking about the Jaguar and probably about his expensive clothes. He decided it was time to change the topic. "But I'm not in that line of work anymore."

"How did you meet Jason?"

"We shared a mutual interest," Max said.

"Art?"

"Yes." He hoped she would stop there.

Cleo paused. "Max, were you telling me the truth when you said that Jason was rich?"

"Yes." He wished he could read her mind. For the life of him he could not tell if she was playing the innocent brilliantly or if she really was innocent. He'd had very little experience with innocence of any kind. He didn't trust himself to recognize it on sight.

Cleo pursed her lips in a thoughtful expression. "I always sensed that there were a lot of things we didn't know about Jason. But he didn't seem to want us to know them, so I never asked. I figured he'd get around to telling us in his own good time."

"Perhaps he would have. But time ran out for him." Maybe she really was what she seemed to be, Max thought, irritated at not being able to decide.

It was then that he realized with stunning clarity that he wanted her to be as innocent as she appeared. He did not want to discover she was nothing more than the conniving little art thief that all the available evidence indicated she was.

He wanted something more, too. He wanted her to want him.

Max had been certain last night that Cleo was aware of him in a deeply sensual way, just as he was aware of her. He had seen the unguarded reaction in her eyes during those first, fleeting moments. But he detected nothing overtly sensual in the way she touched his thigh tonight. Her fingers were gentle and soothing, not deliberately seductive.

He tried to reconcile the picture of the woman who knelt beside him with the image he had of the woman who had written *The Mirror*. There was a paradox involved here, and it fascinated him. Max had a mental vision of fire frozen in ice.

All his male instincts told him that Cleo Robbins was not very experienced, and yet *The Mirror* had burned with a searing, passionate sensuality.

Max was suddenly, intensely aware of the length of satin stuffed into his pocket.

"Cleo?"

"Yes?"

Max could not think of a way to put the question he wanted to ask into words. Instead he reached into his pocket and slowly drew out the length of scarlet ribbon.

Cleo's hands stopped moving on his leg. She stared, transfixed, at the ribbon in his hand. Max saw the sudden, deep stillness in her. He wondered if she was afraid of him.

The abrupt need to protect her was so strong, it caused his hand to shake. "Don't be frightened."

She looked up at him, her eyes filled with silent questions. "I'm not afraid of you."

"I'm glad." The ribbon dangled from his fingers, almost touching the floor. He caught hold of the loose end with his other hand. The satin gleamed softly as he stretched it out to form a gentle loop. "I told you I'm reading *The Mirror*."

"Yes." Her voice was only a whisper.

"I'm on chapter two."

"Are you?" Cleo touched the tip of her tongue to the corner of her mouth. She glanced at the ribbon again.

"I know that the woman in *The Mirror* thinks she will recognize her phantom lover when she sees him, even though she has never seen his face clearly in the glass."

"Yes, she'll know him." Cleo's eyes were deep, fathomless pools of uncertainty and yearning behind the lenses of her glasses.

"What I don't know yet is how she will let him know that she recognizes him," Max said softly.

"She won't have to tell him. Not with words, at any rate."

"But he'll know that she knows?"

"Yes," Cleo breathed.

The blood roared, wild and hot, through Max's veins. He could not recall feeling so intensely alive in his entire life, not even when he contemplated his magnificent collection of books and art. He was balanced on the dangerous edge between joy and agony.

Without a word, because there were no words, Max raised the loop of red satin. He slipped it slowly down over Cleo's head.

She did not move. *Fire frozen in ice waiting to be freed.*

Max settled the length of inexpensive scarlet ribbon around Cleo's throat as if it were a necklace composed of priceless rubies. He tugged gently on the ends of the ribbon, drawing her to him. Cleo leaned forward as if caught in a spell.

Max released the ends of the ribbon and plucked Cleo's glasses from her nose. He set them down on the floor beside his chair. His eyes never left hers.

Cleo blinked once or twice as if she were inside a cave gazing out into bright sunlight. With a soft, low groan, Max lowered his mouth to hers.

Cleo shuddered at the first touch of his lips, but she did not pull away. She tasted him as if sampling a new, exotic wine. The nibbling sensation at the edge of his lips nearly sent Max beyond the reach of his self-control.

He brushed his mouth lightly across hers, teasing forth a tentative response. There was feminine eagerness shimmering just beneath the surface. He could feel it.

But he could also feel the hesitation in her. She wanted him, he realized, but something was holding her back. It was as if she was not quite certain how far she wanted to go down this particular road.

He also sensed that there was an awful lot of ice between him and the flame that burned inside Cleo. But the fire was there, waiting to be set free.

He opened his mouth on hers. Cleo hesitated a moment longer, and then she gave a small, murmuring sigh and put her arms around his neck.

Max suddenly realized that he had been ravenous for a very long time. Cleo's mouth was sweet and ripe, incredibly fresh. After the first taste, he wanted to devour the fruit. Never had anything tasted so exquisitely good.

He urged her lips apart. She followed his lead, allowing him into her moist warmth.

There were two ways to deal with ice, Max reminded himself. One could melt it or one could chop through it with an axe. The latter was far and away the fastest method, and he was in a hurry.

He started to haul Cleo up off the floor and into his lap.

She gasped softly under the assault. Max felt the incipient panic in her. So much for the fast approach. He took a deep breath and kept a savage grip on his clamoring need.

He lifted his mouth from Cleo's reluctantly and looked down into her bemused eyes.

"I'm sorry," Cleo whispered.

He smiled slightly. "I'm the one who probably should be saying that." Except that the only thing he was sorry about was that she had drawn back before he could finish what he had started.

She smiled tremulously. "Don't apologize. It's just that I wasn't prepared to have a very private fantasy come to life."

"Fantasy?"

Cleo eyed him warily. "Don't pretend that you haven't read chapter three."

"Chapter three?" Max was getting confused.

"That's the chapter in my book in which the man in the mirror puts a red ribbon around the woman's throat and draws her into the glass. She steps into his world, and he makes love to her there."

"Just as I did to you?" Max was pleased with himself.

"Yes. Just as you did to me. Except that you didn't exactly make love to me, did you?" She touched her full, soft mouth. "You only kissed me." Cleo scowled briefly. "Are you sure you didn't read chapter three?"

"Very sure. But I will definitely read it before I go to bed tonight," Max promised. "And possibly chapter four as well."

Cleo's cheeks burned a brilliant shade of pink. "Maybe it would be better if you didn't. I think you've read far enough to get an idea of what *The Mirror* is all about."

Max held her eyes. "There's no way I can stop now."

Cleo gazed at him with a disturbingly serious expression. "Maybe we'd better get something clear here. If you're looking for an entertaining interlude out here on the coast, forget it. I don't do entertaining interludes."

"Neither do I," Max said.

She picked up her glasses and pushed them firmly onto her nose. Her face was flushed, but her eyes were steady and clear. "To be perfectly blunt, I don't do interludes at all, entertaining or otherwise."

"Not at all?"

"No."

"Never?" Max persisted, curious.

Cleo got to her feet and retreated to the shadows of her fanback chair. She gazed out into the night for a long while.

"Once, a long time ago, when I was twenty-three, there was a man. But we broke up after my . . . after my parents died. There hasn't been anyone since."

"Why not?" Max asked, greedy for every scrap of information he could collect. He wanted to learn everything there was to learn about her, he realized. He had to dig down through the layers and find all the closely guarded secrets.

"I don't know why not." Cleo's eyes flashed with a sudden shower of angry sparks. An instant later the fireworks vanished as quickly as they had appeared. "That's not entirely true. A therapist told me that I've never been able to cope with the way my parents died."

"How did they die?"

Cleo looked down at her clasped hands as if debating how much to tell him. She appeared to come to some sort of decision. "They say my father shot my mother and then turned the gun on himself."

"Jesus," Max muttered.

"The theory is that I can't reconcile the fact that they loved each other with the way they died. It's impossible for me to believe that the bond my parents shared was tainted by some sick obsession of my father's."

"There's a certain logic to that," Max said quietly. "Look, Cleo, I'm sorry I pushed for so many answers. I had no right to do that."

"Damn." Cleo shot to her feet and walked to the glass wall. "I don't know why I'm telling you all this. You're the second man I've confided in today. I guess this business with the anonymous notes and the ribbons has me more rattled than I thought."

Max narrowed his eyes. "You told Hildebrand about your parents?"

"He made me mad when he said I wasn't pure enough to be a politician's wife." Cleo sighed. "I got kind of mouthy, I guess. Told him I had another skeleton in the closet besides *The Mirror*. I couldn't resist pointing out that the press would probably have a field day with the facts surrounding my parents' death."

"I see. How did he take it?"

Cleo shrugged. "Oh, he was well and truly shocked. Max, I'm sorry I got into all this with you tonight. It's a very private matter. Until today no one but the family has known what happened to my folks."

"I don't intend to discuss it with anyone else."

"I didn't think you did." She bit her lip. "I just wanted you to realize that I'm not a good candidate for a quick fling or even a long-term affair."

Max reached for his cane and got slowly to his feet. He folded his hands on the hawk and stood watching Cleo. "I won't push you into anything you don't want."

Her answering smile held a curious blend of uncertainty and relief. "Thanks for understanding. I'm sorry about what happened here tonight. It was my fault."

Max smiled to himself and headed for the door. "Don't be too sure of that. See you in the morning."

"Max?"

"Don't worry, Cleo. From here on out, we'll do it by the book. Your book."

5

Shortly before dawn the next morning Cleo gave up trying to sleep. She pushed aside the quilt, got out of bed, and crossed the room to cast an appraising eye at the weather.

The dark sky was overcast, but it was not yet raining. There would be plenty of time to get in a brisk walk along the top of the bluffs before the next storm struck.

After the restless night she'd just spent, she needed to clear her head with the crisp, cold sea air. Perhaps later in the day she would go to the meditation center at Cosmic Harmony. Unfortunately there wasn't time to do that this morning. Cleo wanted to be at the inn when the morning rush started in the kitchen. As Jason had once observed, there was no substitute for close supervision in a small operation such as the Robbins' Nest Inn.

Cleo felt a twist of sorrow at the memory of her friend. She eased it aside as she stepped into a pair of jeans and put on a blue oxford cloth shirt. Jason would not have wanted her to dwell too long on his passing, she reminded herself as she laced up her gold sneakers. Jason Curzon had believed in living for the future, not the past.

She grabbed her hunter green down parka on the way out the door. She made her way downstairs and walked through the still slumbering inn. Gentle snores from the vicinity of the office told her George was still on duty and as alert as ever.

She let herself out through the door at the back of the kitchen. Andromeda, Daystar, and the morning crew from Cosmic Harmony had not yet arrived. And the guests would certainly not be stirring for a while.

The chilled air hit her like a tonic when she stepped outside. The night was giving way slowly to the gray light of the new day. The biting cold made Cleo abruptly aware of the fact that she had forgotten her gloves. She stuffed her hands into her jacket pockets and started off along the bluff overlooking the sea.

She wanted to think about a lot of things this morning: the dream, Benjy's disappearance, Trisha's problems. She needed to deal with all of them. But her mind resisted her efforts to concentrate on any of those issues. No matter what she did, it kept spinning back to the one, single event that had dominated her thoughts for most of the night: Max's kiss.

It was the first time she had kissed a man since her parents' death and not felt the subtle sense of wrongness that had tainted every other relationship she'd had.

All she had experienced with Max last night was a wondrous sensation of exultant joy. She had wanted him, *really* wanted him.

The passion that she had known lay buried inside her had awakened and responded to the touch of a real man at last. Relief soared through her at the realization that she had found the one who could help her free herself.

The man in the mirror had finally walked into her life.

But to Cleo's chagrin, things were not as clear as she had expected them to be if and when she found the right man. There were so many unknowns about Max Fortune, so many uncertainties.

One of the factors that troubled her the most was that he did not seem to be responding to her in the same way that she was responding to him. She had been so sure that if she ever encountered the man in the mirror in the real world, she would not only recognize him immediately; he would also recognize her. She knew from the things her mother and father had said that they had known they were meant for each other from the first moment they met.

But when Cleo had looked into Max's eyes last night, she had seen not just sexual desire, but a disturbing element of calculating control. She sighed unhappily at the thought. She had to face the fact that although her response to him had been instantaneous, pure and unfettered, Max Fortune apparently had his own agenda.

That made him dangerous. Theoretically it should have set off her finely tuned alarm system.

So why wasn't she getting that old, familiar feeling of wrongness about him? she wondered.

She recalled the way he had put the red satin ribbon around her throat and drawn her to him in a perfect imitation of a scene in chapter three of *The Mirror*.

A little too perfect, she thought wryly. She'd be willing to bet that Max actually had read that chapter before seeking her out last night.

The feeling that she no longer had the dawn to herself made Cleo turn her head and glance back over her shoulder. She managed a polite smile of greeting for Herbert T. Valence, who was striding briskly along behind her.

Valence was nattily dressed as always in an expensive-looking camel coat, paisley print silk scarf, and a pair of taupe leather shoes. Whatever brand of mousse or spray he had used to anchor his silver locks into place was impervious to the snapping breeze. Not a single hair was moving in the brisk breeze. The diamond on his pinky sparkled in the early light.

She appeared to be inundated with spiffy dressers these days, Cleo reflected, amused. The combined sartorial elegance of Max and Herbert T. Valence was definitely elevating the inn's image this weekend.

"Good morning, Ms. Robbins." Valence bobbed his head with birdlike speed.

"Good morning," Cleo said. "I didn't hear you coming up behind me. Out for a morning walk before your next seminar session?"

"I make it a point to walk one mile every day," Valence informed her. "Proper aerobic exercise is essential to a successful attitude."

"It's always nice to meet someone who practices what they preach."

"I have a reputation to maintain, Ms. Robbins. I can only do that if I live by my own five basic rules of success."

"What are your five rules, Mr. Valence?"

Cleo asked curiously. "Or don't you hand those out for free?"

"As we have a professional relationship, I don't mind giving you my five rules."

"How kind of you." Cleo wondered if the list would include clicking his pen exactly five times before replacing it in his coat pocket and always staying in the same room at the inn. During the course of her so-called professional relationship with him, Cleo had had occasion to observe a long list of such eccentricities in Valence.

Valence held up his hand and pointed to his thumb. "The first rule is to concentrate on the objective." He pointed to the next finger. "The second rule is to prepare a plan to meet that objective. The third rule is to resist the impulse to deviate from the plan. The fourth rule is to pay attention to every detail and to make certain it is covered before proceeding with the plan."

"And the fifth rule?" Cleo asked.

"The fifth rule is to always think in terms of success, never in terms of failure."

Cleo considered that. "But what happens if one does fail, Mr. Valence?"

Valence tilted his chin at a proud angle. "Failure is not an acceptable outcome for those who orient their lives toward success. I assure you that I did not acquire my reputation by making mistakes, Ms. Robbins."

"Must be kind of tough having to live up to that kind of reputation," Cleo mused.

"The rewards more than outweigh the effort involved," Valence said. "You should know what I'm talking about, Ms. Robbins. Look at what you've accomplished at your age. You're the owner and proprietor of one of the most successful inns on the Washington coast. How did you talk a bank into loaning you the kind of money it must have taken to open Robbins' Nest?"

Cleo looked out over the steel gray sea. "I had some money of my own."

"Ah, I see. Family money, then."

Cleo thought of the trust fund she had inherited after her parents' death. "Yes."

"I apologize for my questions," Valence said a bit gruffly, as if he had suddenly realized he might have intruded on Cleo's privacy. "Didn't mean to pry. The thing is, I'm always interested in success stories. I guess you could say I collect them."

"You collect them?"

"Yes, indeed. Whenever I find an interesting one, I like to dissect it. Find out how it happened. I learn things from it that I then incorporate into my seminars."

"Well, there's not much to my story, Mr. Valence," Cleo said. "I bought the inn with my inheritance. With the help of some good friends, I've made it work. That's all there is to my tale."

Valence bobbed his head again. "You've certainly got an unusual group of employees. Your kitchen staff all look like they're from some New Age commune, and that new one, the man with the cane, doesn't dress or act like hired help."

"Well, he is hired help," Cleo said shortly. "But I don't know how long he'll be staying." That realization made her catch her breath. The thought of Max leaving sent a flash of pain through her. She realized she did not want to lose the man in the mirror now that she had finally found him.

"In my opinion, his manner is far too arrogant for his position."

Cleo smiled to herself. "I'll speak to him about it."

"I suggest you do that." Valence glanced at his chunky gold watch. "I should be getting back to my room, I suppose. I want to go over my notes. Before I bid you good day, however, Ms. Robbins, there is something I wish to discuss."

Cleo stifled a groan. "What's that, Mr. Valence?"

Valence gave her a disapproving look. "I trust there will be no more upsetting occurrences such as the loss of electrical power that I was obliged to endure yesterday afternoon."

Cleo smiled wryly. "I'm afraid that sort of thing is beyond my ability to control, Mr. Valence. We'll do our best, but I can't guarantee anything, especially during a storm."

"If you cannot promise a reliable power source, I may be forced to select another location for my seminars," Valence warned.

"As I said, Mr. Valence, we'll do our best to keep you up and running."

Valence grunted a rather dissatisfied response. "Well, that's that, then. We shall just have to see, won't we?"

"I guess so," Cleo said. "Have a good day, Mr. Valence."

"Thank you. Same to you."

Valence stopped, made a neat one hundred and eighty degree turn, and started back toward the inn.

Cleo watched as he tucked his chin into the warmth of his expensive coat and leaned resolutely into the crisp breeze. Then she continued on her way along the bluffs. She thought about what she had just told Valence about Max. *I don't know how long he'll be staying.*

An excellent reason for being extremely cautious, Cleo thought. Max was definitely an unknown quantity, even if she did have the distinct sensation that she had been waiting for him all of her life.

Cleo delayed the family meeting on Trisha until after the last of the crowd of seminar attendees had checked out the following day. She held it during the lull that ensued in the afternoon before preparations began for the evening meal.

Andromeda, Daystar, Trisha, Sylvia, and Cleo sat down on the benches of the kitchen nook. Trisha looked at the others and burst into tears.

"There now, dear, don't fuss so." Andromeda handed her a napkin to blot her eyes. "You aren't the first woman to find herself in this sort of situation, and you won't be the last. The important thing to remember is that you aren't alone."

"I thought he loved me," Trisha whispered.

"I think he does," Cleo said gently. "But Benjy's confused about a lot of things."

"Too confused to use any birth control, apparently," Daystar muttered. She gave Trisha a severe look. "I seem to recall mentioning the subject to you a while back, young lady. What went wrong?"

Trisha started to sob heavily. "I'm sorry. I just wasn't thinking. You don't know what it's like."

"Don't I?" Daystar snorted. "I'm sixty-two years old, my girl, and I didn't spend those years in a box. Believe me, I know what it's like. Passion is no excuse for stupidity. A woman has to use her head. She has to stay in control of the situation."

Trisha cried louder.

Cleo glared at Daystar. "For heaven's sake, this is getting us nowhere."

Andromeda gave her friend a scolding look. "Cleo's right. There's no point lecturing poor Trisha now. The damage is done. We have to go forth from here. As that Mr. Valence has been telling everyone all weekend, we have to think positive. Problems should be looked upon as opportunities."

"You're right. I'm sorry." Daystar patted Trisha with gruff affection. "Don't worry, Trisha. We're going to survive this."

"It was all my fault," Trisha wailed.

"It takes two," Cleo said firmly. "Benjy had just as much to do with this as you did."

"The difference is that Benjy can walk away from it," Daystar said bluntly. "Trisha can't."

"You know," Andromeda mused, "I'm surprised that Benjy did walk away. I thought that boy was finally getting his act together, as they say. He was working hard here, attending classes at the community college part-time. He was even starting to talk about the

140

future in a positive manner. I really believed he was going to make it."

"He was trying," Trisha said loyally. "I know he was."

"I agree," Cleo said. "And I know he cares for Trisha. I imagine he's feeling pretty scared at the moment."

"Maybe we should have gotten some professional counseling for the boy," Andromeda said.

Daystar shrugged. "Don't know if that would have done any good."

Cleo decided to take charge before the discussion degenerated into a what-went-wrong-with-Benjy session. "I've been doing some thinking. We've known Benjy for a year and a half. He's a good kid, and I can't believe he's really run out on his responsibilities. I'll bet he's just gone off someplace to think for a while."

Trisha looked up from the napkin. There was a tiny flicker of hope in her eyes. "Do you really believe he'll come back?"

Cleo pursed her lips in thought. "I'm sure Benjy is very confused and shaken at the moment. He probably needs someone to talk to."

"Well, why didn't he talk to one of us?" Daystar demanded. "We're his family."

Cleo grimaced. "Have you noticed that with the exception of Sammy, we're all female?

Poor Benjy probably felt we'd be so busy sympathizing with Trisha that we wouldn't understand what he was going through."

Sylvia's brows rose. "That's a possibility, I suppose."

"It's important to remember that Benjy does have a responsibility in this, whether he wants it now or not," Daystar said. "A financial responsibility."

"I agree," Sylvia said. "Benjy may not be able to handle his moral and emotional commitments yet, but he can and should be required to handle his financial responsibilities. At least Doug still sends some child support once in a while. Benjy should do the same."

Cleo held up her hand. "Before we start pressuring Benjy to honor his financial obligations, I think we should try another tactic. I think we should convince him to come home where he belongs."

Trisha gave her another desperate look. "But he's gone. I don't know where he is. How can we find him?"

"Maybe Max can find him," Cleo said slowly.

"Max?" Trisha stared at her. "But how can Max find him?"

"Max says he has a friend who runs an investigation firm," Cleo said. "I don't have much faith in private investigators, but Max seems to think his friend is very good. Benjy hasn't been gone long, and he probably isn't trying to hide."

Trisha bit her lip. "Do you think Max's friend can find Benjy?"

"I suggest we find out." Cleo got to her feet with sudden resolve. As soon as the idea had occurred to her, she had sensed it was the right approach to the problem. "Stay here, I'll be right back."

She whirled around and headed for the door. She did not look back, although she was aware of the others staring after her in bemusement.

Cleo went down the hall to the lobby. There was no sign of Max. She tried the parlor next. It was empty except for three guests who were reading quietly in front of the fire. In the hallway she encountered one of the maids who came in on busy days and was helping clean up after the seminar guests.

"Darleen, have you seen Max?"

"I think he's in the solarium with Sammy," Darleen said.

Cleo changed direction and went down another hall. A moment later she walked into the solarium. Rain was beating pleasantly on the glass roof. The steady patter and the gurgle of the fountain were the only sounds in the room.

Max was seated in a fanback wicker chair,

his left leg propped on a matching wicker foot-stool. His cane was leaning against the wide arm of the chair.

It struck Cleo that Max looked oddly at home in the exotic surroundings. Something about the scene made her think of an elegant pirate who had retired to a South Pacific island. She winced when she saw that he was reading *The Mirror*.

Sammy was seated beside Max in the miniature wicker chair that Cleo had bought him for Christmas. He had Lucky Ducky and a picture book in his lap. He had his thumb stuffed contentedly in his mouth and seemed as intent on his reading as Max was on his.

"Hi," Cleo said softly.

Sammy took his thumb out of his mouth. "Hi, Cleo. Me and Max are reading."

"So I see."

"Max says books are special. He's got lots and lots of 'em. He keeps 'em in a secret room in his house where no one can see 'em except him."

"Is that right?" Cleo wondered what else he kept in that secret room. His heart, perhaps. She crossed the tiled floor. "Max, I wondered if you would mind joining me and the others in the kitchen."

Max looked up warily from *The Mirror*. "Why?"

Cleo cleared her throat cautiously. "We, uh, wanted to ask you to help us."

He gazed at her with a brooding stare. "Help you do what?"

"Find Benjy."

"Damn," Max said very softly.

Sammy yanked his thumb out of his mouth again. "You're not supposed to say words like that around me."

Max looked down at him. "I apologize. I don't know what came over me."

Sammy nodded. "It's okay. Just don't tell Mommy."

"I won't," Max promised.

Cleo waited hopefully. "Do you think you could find him, Max?"

"Max can find anything," Sammy announced. "He even found Lucky Ducky."

"O'Reilly might be able to locate him," Max said carefully. "What do you intend to do with Benjy if you do find him?"

"I'm not sure," Cleo said. She gave him her most winning smile. "But I think I'd like you to talk to him."

Max looked completely taken aback. "You want *me* to talk to him? I don't even know the guy."

"I realize that," Cleo said earnestly, "but you're a man, and I think Benjy will feel more comfortable talking to a man at this stage."

"What the hell do you expect me to talk to him about?"

"Not supposed to say hell either," Sammy said.

"Sorry," Max said brusquely.

Cleo kept what she hoped was a persuasive smile in place. "Ideally I'd like you to talk him into coming home. I want him to shoulder his responsibilities toward Trisha. But at the very least he needs to realize he has a financial obligation to her."

"You don't ask much, do you?" Max said grimly.

"What's an obligation?" Sammy asked.

"That's what people say a person has when they want that person to do something." Max didn't take his eyes off Cleo.

"Oh." Sammy appeared placated by the answer.

Max studied Cleo. "This is way outside my area of expertise. I am definitely not a social worker."

"But you said your friend O'Reilly was good at tracking down people," Cleo reminded him.

"Finding Benjy is one thing," Max said. "Talking him into coming back here is another."

"We've got to try."

Max looked at her. "I'd rather you left me out of this."

Sammy took his thumb out of his mouth. "I bet you could make Benjy come home, Max."

Cleo gave Max a searching glance. "Would you mind if we finished this discussion in the kitchen?"

"Something tells me I can't avoid it." Max took his foot down off the stool.

He started to reach for his cane, but Sammy jumped to his feet, picked it up, and handed it to him.

"Thank you." Max took the cane politely. He tucked *The Mirror* under his arm and looked at Cleo. "All right. Let's go."

Sammy sat down in his small fanback chair. "Are you going to come back and read some more with me, Max?"

Max glanced down at the boy. "Maybe."

"Okay. I'll wait here for you."

Cleo smiled ruefully as she led the way out of the solarium. "Sammy has really glommed on to you, hasn't he?"

"He does seem to be underfoot every time I turn around."

"I think he's trying to turn you into a sort of honorary uncle, just as he did Jason," she explained.

"It's okay," Max said. "I'm getting used to it."

Cleo pushed open the kitchen door. Trisha,

147

Sylvia, Andromeda, and Daystar turned to stare at them. The expressions on their faces ranged from anxious and hopeful to grim and determined.

"Well?" Daystar beetled her brows at Max. "Are you going to help us locate Benjy?"

Andromeda and Sylvia watched Max with an ill-concealed expression of appeal. Trisha sniffed into her napkin and gazed at him uncertainly.

Max surveyed the group sitting in the nook. His face was unreadable. "I can probably find Benjy for you."

The women traded relieved glances.

"That's wonderful," Andromeda said. "Will you talk to him? Try to get him to come home?"

Max's jaw tightened. "I'll talk to him for you, but I'm not making any promises."

"We understand," Cleo said quickly.

Trisha stirred uneasily. "I'm not sure this is a good idea. I mean, I don't know if Benjy can handle this kind of pressure. What will I say to him if Max does find him and bring him home?"

"For one thing," Max said, "you will stop calling him Benjy."

A startled silence fell on the group. Cleo and the others gazed at him in mute astonishment.

Cleo got her mouth closed first. "What are

you talking about? Benjy is his name. Benjy Atkins."

"Not if he comes back here willingly and shoulders his responsibilities," Max said. "If you're going to ask good old Benjy to become a man, the least you can do is to treat him like one. From now on, his name is Ben."

"Sure, Max, I can run that list of names through the computers," Compton O'Reilly said on the other end of the phone. "But what the hell's going on? Is it true you've left Curzon International?"

O'Reilly sounded amused, but that was nothing new, Max thought. He always sounded that way. Max was one of the few people who understood that O'Reilly's humorous approach to life was a facade. Since the death of his beloved wife and daughter in a plane accident five years ago, O'Reilly had retreated into a place where nothing seemed to bother him. Max would have envied him if he hadn't sensed that, for O'Reilly, the relentless amusement was a way to cover up the pain that still burned hot inside him.

"I'm through with Curzon." Max cradled the phone between his shoulder and his ear as he reached for a pen. "I've got a new position."

"No kidding?" O'Reilly said. "There've

been some rumors, but I didn't believe them. Thought sure the Curzons would make you an offer you couldn't refuse after the old man died."

"I'm not open to offers from Curzon." Max winced as he leaned back in his chair. He rubbed his leg and gazed out the window of his room. It occurred to him that he was starting to enjoy the view from the attic.

"I can't say I'm totally surprised to hear that some other big chain got you. Was it Global Village Properties? They've been after you for a long time."

"I didn't go with Global Village or any of the other big chains." Max tapped the pen idly against the pad of yellow paper sitting on the desk. The names of all the guests who had stayed at the inn that weekend were listed alphabetically on the first page of the pad. He had noted addresses and phone numbers beside each name.

"Picked a small independent, huh?" O'Reilly sounded briefly thoughtful. "What's up? Looking for a challenge? Going to buy out a small operation and start your own hotel chain? I can see you doing that. You're the one person who could give the Curzons a run for their money. Should be fun to watch."

"It's just a small inn on the coast, and I don't have any plans to buy it out and turn it into a chain."

O'Reilly chuckled. "Come off it, Max, I can't see you running a folksy little bed-and-breakfast place on the coast."

"You don't understand. I'm not running the place at all. I'm working for the owner."

"Doing what?" O'Reilly demanded.

"Odd jobs. Unclogging toilets, hauling firewood, tending bar. At the moment I'm trying to handle a small security problem," Max said. "Do you think you can stop laughing long enough to check out that list of names I just gave you, or shall I call Brindle Investigations?"

"Hey, no need to call the competition. I can handle this. Who do I bill?"

"Send the bill to me."

"Something I don't understand here," O'Reilly said. "You've already got the addresses for those people. What, exactly, do you want me to look for?"

"I'm not sure." Max scanned the page of names. "See if anyone on that list has connections with ultraconservative groups or off-the-wall religious organizations. You might also check on whether or not any of them have a record for getting arrested for making right-wing social protests or causing disturbances over First Amendment issues. That kind of thing."

"You think you're dealing with some morally outraged fanatic?"

"It feels like that," Max said. "My employer wrote a book that's just been published. I think what we've got here is a self-appointed censor who's decided to mete out his own brand of literary criticism to an author."

"Sounds like a guy who's got a couple of screws loose, is that it?"

"Whoever he is, he's the type who would go out of his way to frighten an innocent writer."

"There's no shortage of people who feel called upon to censor what other people read, Max, you know that."

"I know, but I'm hoping that the number of people who would take the trouble to track down an anonymous author and leave weird warnings around will make a much shorter list."

"I'll see what I can do," O'Reilly said. "I should have the info in a few days."

Max eyed the storm that was forming out over the sea. "There's one other name I want you to check out for me, while you're at it. I want to find a young man named Benjamin Atkins."

"Is he connected to your security problem?"

"No, I don't think so. Separate issue. He's

a former employee of the inn. Left in the middle of the night with no forwarding address."

"I get the picture. What did he take with him?"

"It's not what he took, it's what he left behind," Max said.

"Okay, be cryptic. What do I care? Give me what you've got on Atkins."

Max read off the few meager facts Cleo had given him. Ben's young life was all too easily summarized. Parts of it reminded Max of his own past. At least he hadn't gotten a young woman pregnant when he was barely twenty-three, Max reflected. He'd always been very careful not to get any woman pregnant.

That thought brought to mind a strangely tantalizing image of how Cleo would look ripe and round with his baby. A surge of possessiveness and wonder twisted Max's insides. *His baby.* It struck him that this was the first time he had actually thought about having a kid of his own.

"I'll get back to you as soon as I've got something," O'Reilly said.

"Thanks." Max hesitated. "By the way, there's no great rush on that Atkins situation."

"What the hell's that supposed to mean?"

Max kneaded his left leg and studied the sea. "It means that I'm in no great rush to get answers. Take your time." He hung up the phone.

The reason he was in no hurry to locate Atkins was because once he did he would have to carry out the mission that Cleo and the others had assigned him. It was almost certainly going to be Mission Impossible. Max was ninety-nine percent sure he wouldn't be able to talk Atkins into returning to the inn's odd family.

Hell, Max thought, he didn't have the slightest idea of how to go about convincing a young man to accept his responsibilities.

The Atkins situation was shaping up to be one of those exceedingly rare, but very memorable, occasions when Max knew he was almost bound to screw up. He hated failure, hated it with a passion. The price was too damn high.

When he failed to talk Atkins into coming back, Max knew he would not find a warm welcome waiting for him back at Robbins' Nest Inn. People treated you differently when you didn't give them what they wanted. An outsider was welcome only as long as he was useful.

It was a pragmatic issue, Max told himself, not an emotional one. Being edged out of the inn's cozy family would make it difficult to continue searching for the Luttrells. That meant he had to find the paintings before he left in search of Ben Atkins.

Max continued to massage his aching thigh. The answer was obvious. He would have to seduce Cleo. That would be the fastest, easiest way to get the answers he wanted.

Cleo was the key to recovering his inheritance. She had to know more than she'd admitted. There was no reason for Jason to have lied to Max on his deathbed.

Cleo knew where the paintings were, and Max knew from reading *The Mirror* that she was vulnerable to passion. Now that he had discovered the fire in her, he was almost certain he could make her want him.

Max stopped rubbing his thigh and contemplated the pot of herbal tea Andromeda had sent upstairs with him earlier.

"Cleo says you're having a bit of trouble with that leg of yours," Andromeda had said as she'd bustled about the kitchen, preparing the concoction. "Try a cup or two of this and see if it doesn't help."

"Does wonders for my arthritis," Daystar had volunteered.

"Try it, Max," Cleo had insisted. "Andromeda's teas are great for headaches and sore muscles."

The stuff tasted like essence of weeds, as far as Max was concerned. But the novelty of having Cleo and the rest of her "family" fuss over him had proved irresistible for some reason. He'd already gotten one full cup of the stuff down. Maybe it was his imagination, but his leg did seem to feel better, just as it had last night when Cleo had massaged it. He decided to try a second cup.

Hot images of the previous night flooded back, sending another rush of desire through his veins. Max sipped the tea as he allowed himself to savor the memory of Cleo's mouth under his. Sweet, fresh, and trembling with a shy eagerness.

His instincts told him that he could satiate himself with the warmth of her body as he had never been satiated before in his life. All he had to do was unlock the flame inside the ice.

But time was running out. O'Reilly was good. Max knew that even taking his time about it, his friend would come up with the answers he had been sent after fairly quickly. At that point Max would be forced to track down Atkins and talk to him. He had given his word.

That meant he had to find the Luttrells before he left in search of Atkins. Max knew that after he'd had his little man-to-man chat with Atkins, things would never be the same for him here at the inn. He would be an outsider once more.

No big deal, Max thought. He was used to the role of outsider. But he wanted those Luttrells.

Two days later Cleo popped into the kitchen to check on dinner preparations. She saw Daystar hovering over a large pot of what looked like Cosmic Harmony's very special bean and vegetable soup.

"Have you seen Andromeda?" Cleo asked.

"She'll be here any minute." Daystar added fresh basil to the pot. "Got delayed at the Retreat."

"Did something happen?" Cleo sniffed the soup appreciatively.

"Some man in a gray suit and a silk tie drove up just as we were leaving. He insisted on talking to her. Said it was important. I came on ahead to get dinner started." Daystar ground some pepper into the soup. "Any word yet on the whereabouts of Benjy?"

Cleo arched her brows. "You mean Mr. Ben Atkins?"

Daystar chuckled. "Oh, that's right. We're supposed to start calling the boy by his new name, aren't we?"

"Max says if we don't, he won't bother to even try to bring Ben back. And, no, as far as I know, there's been no word on his whereabouts."

"Trisha doesn't think Max can find him," Daystar said. "Or that Ben will agree to come back even if Max does locate him."

"We'll see." Cleo turned her head as the back door opened and Andromeda bustled into the room. Water drops sparkled on her iridescent blue rain cape.

"It's pouring out there." Andromeda peeled off the shimmering cape and hung it in a closet. "Thought I'd never get rid of that silly man. What a waste of time. He simply wouldn't take no for an answer."

Daystar closed an oven door. "Salesman?"

"You could say that." Andromeda frowned. "Except that he wanted to buy, not sell. His name was Garrison Spark."

"Hah. I knew it," Cleo muttered. "He was probably trying to steal you and the others for his own restaurant, wasn't he?"

"Not exactly, dear." Andromeda tied her apron around her waist. "He said he was an art dealer. He's looking for some paintings by a man named Luttrell."

Cleo widened her eyes. "Amos Luttrell?"

"Yes, I believe that was it. Why? Have you heard of him?"

"Uh, yes. As a matter of fact, I have." Cleo frowned. "Max mentioned him."

Andromeda picked up a knife and went to work slicing red peppers. "Mr. Spark claims there are five paintings by this Luttrell person floating around out here on the coast somewhere. Says they're worth a fortune."

Daystar glanced at her. "How much is a fortune?"

Andromeda shrugged. "Fifty thousand dollars."

Cleo's mouth dropped open. "*Fifty thousand dollars.* Are you kidding?"

The kitchen door swung open at that moment. Max loomed in the doorway. Sammy was right beside him, Lucky Ducky in hand.

"We need another tray of hors d'oeuvres in the lounge," Max said.

"With olives," Sammy said with an air of grave importance. "All the olives are gone."

Max glanced down at him. "That's because you ate them."

Sammy giggled. "Lucky Ducky ate them."

"I've got another tray ready to go," Daystar said. "I'll send it right out."

Max glanced at Cleo. "Something wrong?"

"Someone named Garrison Spark is looking for those paintings you mentioned the first night you arrived."

Max went utterly still. "Spark is here?"

"Not here," Cleo said. "He went to Cosmic Harmony. Andromeda talked to him. Max, Mr. Spark says those paintings are worth fifty thousand dollars."

"He lied," Max said quietly. "They're worth a quarter of a million. In five years' time they'll be worth a million."

"Good lord," Daystar breathed.

Cleo was dazed. "A quarter of a million?"

"Yes," Max said. He looked at Andromeda. "What did you tell Spark?"

Andromeda looked surprised by the edge in his voice. "I told him I had never heard of Amos Luttrell, let alone the paintings."

Cleo scowled at Max. "What's going on, Max? How could anyone think that Jason owned such valuable paintings?"

His eyes met hers. "I think it's time I explained a few of the facts of life as they relate to Jason Curzon. I told you he was not a poor man. That's putting it mildly. He was Jason Curzon of Curzon International."

"The hotel chain?" Cleo was stunned. "Are you certain of that?"

"Yes," said Max. "I should know. I used to work for him."

6

"So our Jason Curzon was really one of those Curzons? The head of the big hotel chain?" Cleo asked again later that night.

She was perched on a stool at the bar, a cup of Andromeda's herbal tea in front of her. It was a typical, slow, midweek night in winter. It was late, and the low hum of conversation in the shadowed lounge had a relaxed, sleepy quality.

Max was behind the bar, looking as professional as if he had spent his entire working life making espresso drinks and serving after-dinner sherry. He was, Cleo reflected, an amazingly adaptable man. He'd handled every task he'd been given with a calm, totally unruffled aplomb.

"That's probably the twentieth time you've asked me that question." Max picked up a newly washed glass and dried it with a white linen towel. "For the twentieth time, the answer is yes."

"He never said a word. Guess he didn't want us to know." Cleo shook her head in silent amazement. "We always knew his last name was Curzon, but we never dreamed he was connected to the hotel family."

"He obviously liked being treated as just another member of your family," Max said quietly. "He was apparently living out a pleasant little fantasy here on the coast. There was no harm in it."

"Of course not, it's just that it's so hard to believe that the head of one of the world's biggest hotel chains spent his weekends here at Robbins' Nest Inn. Sheesh." Cleo made a face. "I had him unclogging toilets, too. He used to help Benjy — excuse me, I mean, *Ben* — with the plumbing all the time."

Max slanted her a strange glance. "You really didn't know who he was, did you?"

"Never had a clue. Not even when we got the letter from a Mrs. Singleton telling us he had died."

"Roberta Singleton was his secretary. Knowing Jason, he had probably left her a list of people to notify in the event something happened to him."

"And we were on the list." Cleo recalled the many long talks she'd had with Jason here in the lounge. "At least I know now why he had so many good suggestions about running this place. I nearly doubled my profit this past year, thanks to him. It was Jason's idea to put in the computerized billing system."

"Jason knew what he was doing when it came to running hotels." Max picked up another glass. "He was the best in the business."

Cleo watched him closely. "No wonder you thought I was some kind of gold-digger when you first got here."

"Let's not reopen that subject."

"Suits me." Cleo took a sip of her tea and frowned as she remembered another topic he had brought up that first night. "So you worked for him?"

"Yes."

Cleo studied his expressionless face and knew intuitively that the single-word answer covered a lot of territory. "What exactly did you do for him?"

"Odd jobs. Same as I do for you."

"Somehow I can't envision you tending bar and handling luggage for Curzon International," Cleo said.

"Why not? I do it here."

"You do have a knack for making yourself useful." Cleo decided to abandon that subject. "What about those paintings you mentioned? Those Artie Lutefisks or whatever you called them."

Max gave her a pained look. "Luttrells. Amos Luttrells."

"Right. Luttrells. The night you arrived you

163

seemed to think Jason might have left them here."

"That's what he told me." Max's eyes were completely shuttered now. It was impossible to tell what he was thinking.

Cleo tilted her head to one side. "Now this Garrison Spark person is looking for them. He must think they're here, too. Know anything about him?"

"He owns a gallery in Seattle. Very exclusive. I worked for him for a while."

"Him too?" Cleo elevated one brow. "You do get around, don't you? What did you do for Mr. Spark?"

"Crated paintings. Transported them. Delivered them to their owners. Strictly manual labor. I didn't work for Spark very long." Max studied the reflection in the glass he was polishing. "He and I had a few differences of opinion on a couple of matters."

"What matters?"

Max looked at her, his gaze steady. "Spark is very smart, and he knows a great deal about contemporary art. But he's not bothered by pesky little nuisances such as honesty and integrity. If he thinks he can pass off a fake to a client and get away with it, he'll do it."

"Really?" Cleo was fascinated. "I've never met a crooked art dealer. He sounds kind of exotic."

"He's got all the ethics of a snake." There was a rough edge to Max's voice. "You heard what Andromeda said. He claimed the Luttrells were only worth fifty thousand."

"You're sure they're worth more?"

Max's mouth tightened. "A lot more."

"And you're sure they belong to you?"

"I'm damn sure they belong to me," Max said very softly.

"Did Jason actually *give* them to you?"

"Yes."

"He just up and gave you a bunch of very valuable paintings?" Cleo persisted.

"Yes."

"The two of you must have been awfully good friends," she observed.

"You could say that." Max stacked the dried glasses in precise rows on the counter. "On his deathbed he said —" Max broke off abruptly and concentrated on arranging the glasses. "Forget it."

Cleo nearly lost her balance on the stool as the deep emotions emanating from Max washed over her. She could also feel the equally powerful waves of the self-control he was exerting.

"Max?" she prodded gently. "What did he say to you?"

Max's eyes were stark when they met hers, but his voice was perfectly neutral. "He said something about me being the son he'd never had."

Cleo looked at him and knew beyond a shadow of a doubt that Jason's dying words constituted the most important words Max had ever heard in his life. "Oh, Max. . . ."

Max's mouth curved with cool self-mockery, but his eyes did not change. "I knew at the time that Jason was exaggerating. Hell, I was his employee, not blood kin. Nobody knew that better than me."

"Yes, but if he called you his son he must have cared for you a great deal."

Max's smile vanished. He concentrated on polishing another glass. "He was dying. Deathbed conversations are probably always a little melodramatic. I'm sure he didn't expect me to take him literally." He paused briefly, his gaze hardening. "But he did give me the Luttrells. There was no mistake about that."

She knew then that it had been a very, very long time since anyone other than Jason had told Max even indirectly that he was loved. She thought about the great love of her parents, which had bonded her small family together, and knew a searing sense of sorrow for all that Max had missed.

"Those Luttrell paintings are more than just a valuable gift, aren't they? They're your inheritance from Jason," Cleo said. "He wanted you to have them."

"He sent me out here to find them," Max said in the same dangerously neutral tone. "He said he'd left them in your care."

"Hmm. I wonder what he meant by that." Clec glanced at the paintings of English hunt scenes that decorated the walls of the lounge. "Jason never even mentioned them to me."

"Is that right?"

Cleo glowered at him. "What's that supposed to mean?"

"Nothing." Max smiled coolly, his expression speculative. "I'm just wondering what he meant, that's all."

"Well, I haven't got the foggiest idea," Cleo said. She was about to pursue the point when she realized that Max's attention had shifted to the door of the lounge. Cleo turned her head to see what he was looking at.

A man with the sharp, angular features of a tormented poet sauntered into the room. He was wearing a black pullover, black jeans, and black boots. His dark brown hair was swept straight back from his forehead and hung down to his shoulders. There was a distinctly smoldering quality to his heavy-lidded gaze.

Cleo smiled at him.

"Friend of yours?" Max asked softly.

She leaned slightly across the bar. "That's Adrian Forrester. Harmony Cove's great unpublished writer. He arrived in town a year ago and told everyone he was an author, but so far he hasn't made a single sale. He comes in here once or twice a week."

Max's brows rose. "I take it you haven't told him about your success?"

"Are you kidding? I seriously doubt that he would want to hear about it. I think it would depress him." She sat back as Adrian approached.

Adrian reached the bar and took the stool next to Cleo's with languid grace. He gave her the world-weary smile he had practiced to the point of perfection. A jaded Lord Byron consumed by ennui.

"I thought I'd drop in for an espresso," Adrian drawled. "I've been doing battle with a crucial scene in my book all day. Can't seem to get it the way I want it. Thought some caffeine and a change of atmosphere would help."

Cleo smiled consolingly. "Sure. Max, here, makes great espresso."

Adrian flicked Max a brief, dismissive glance. "Make it a double, pal. I need a jolt."

"I'll see what I can do," Max said. "But I'm warning you, if you say 'Play it again, Sam,' I won't be responsible for the results."

"Huh?" Adrian's brow furrowed in confusion.

"Forget it." Max went to work at the gleaming espresso machine. Steam hissed.

Adrian swung around on his stool to face Cleo. He nodded toward Max without much interest. "Someone new on staff?"

"Yes," Cleo said. She knew from experience that the only thing Adrian really liked to talk about was himself, so she changed the topic. "How's the writing going?"

Adrian gave an eloquent shrug. "I've got a proposal out to a couple of major publishers. I'm expecting to hear from one of them soon. They're going to go wild for it. I'll probably find myself in the middle of an auction. I suppose I'll have to see about getting an agent one of these days."

"Another mystery?"

"Yeah. It's called *Dead End*. Classic, hard-boiled detective fiction. It's the purest form of the genre, you know. Very few people are doing it these days." Adrian's mouth twisted in disgust. "Too many women writers out there doing romantic suspense."

"Is that right?" Cleo asked.

"Yeah. They're ruining the genre with a bunch of female detectives. Even in the books where the protagonist is a man, they give him a female companion." Adrian grimaced. "Everybody's doing *relationships*."

"What's wrong with that?" Cleo asked, thinking about the very romantic relationship

169

she had put into *A Fine Vengeance*. "I like some romance in a story."

"Give me a break, Cleo. Romance is women's stuff. I'm writing real books."

"Are you implying there's something wrong with what women like to read?" Cleo asked very politely. She tried to be patient with Adrian, but there was no getting around the fact that he could be a real pain.

"I'm saying that the modern mystery novel has been ruined by female writers who have insisted on making the relationships in the story more important than solving the crime," Adrian stated grandly. "Who the hell wants a relationship in a mystery?"

"Women readers, maybe?" Cleo suggested.

"Who cares about them?" Adrian gave her a dark, brooding look. "I'm writing classic mystery. Lean and mean. The tough stuff. My work is pared down to the essentials."

"The essentials, hmm?"

"I'm creating something important, something that will endure, something that the critics will love. I'll be damned if I'll cater to a bunch of women readers who are looking for *relationships* in a story."

Max set the espresso down in front of him. "I'm not so sure that's a smart move, Forrester. People have always read for character rather than plot. And good characterization requires a relationship of some kind."

Cleo smiled approvingly.

Adrian gave Max an annoyed look. "What are you? Some kind of literary critic?"

"Not tonight. Tonight I'm a bartender."

"Take some advice and stick with that job. Something tells me you aren't going to make it in a more demanding field." Adrian picked up the small cup of espresso, took a deep swallow, and promptly choked.

"Aaargh!" He sputtered wildly and grabbed a napkin.

Alarmed, Cleo reached over to pound him on the back. "Are you all right, Adrian?"

Adrian glowered furiously at Max. "What the hell did you put in this espresso?"

"I used French roast and doubled the shot." Max looked innocent. "You said you wanted it strong."

"Damn it to hell, that's downright lethal," Adrian growled.

Max smiled politely. "I make coffee the way you write mysteries. Lean and mean. The tough stuff."

Max was deliberately seducing her.

The day after the scene with Adrian, Cleo sat quietly on the mat in Cosmic Harmony's spare, tranquil meditation center and absorbed the full impact of what was happening.

171

Max was making it clear that he wanted to take her to bed.

It was a subtle form of seduction. Since that one kiss in the solarium, there had been no overt moves from Max. But Cleo could feel the mesmerizing desire in him whenever he was in the same room. It flowed over her and around her, enthralling her as nothing else had ever done.

Usually Cleo sought out the calm of the meditation center after one of the unpleasant dreams, but this afternoon she had come here to think about Max.

She gazed into the large yellow crystal that was the only object in the room and knew that she had reached a turning point in her life.

The crystal caught the pale light of the cloudy day and glowed a soft, warm gold. Cleo stared into the amber depths and thought about the past and the future.

She had always been very certain that if and when the right man showed up in her life, he would fall in love with her just as she would fall in love with him. She had been sure that the bond would be there between them from the moment their eyes met.

But Max Fortune knew very little about love and probably trusted the emotion even less.

He did, however, know a great deal about desire.

Soon, Cleo knew, she would have to make a choice. She could either surrender to the powerful sensual thrall of desire that Max was forging, or she could draw back to the safe place within herself.

She could draw back and wait.

Wait for what? she wondered. There would be no other man like Max. He was the man in the mirror.

But she had created the mirror, she reminded herself. The only things she saw in the glass were the things she, herself, projected into it.

The truth was that when she looked into the mirror of her mind and heart, she never saw a clear reflection of the man for whom she waited. Yet she was sure that Max was that man.

Earlier this afternoon she had confronted the fact that she was very probably in love with him.

The incident that had triggered the knowledge was a small one, but it had had a devastating impact on Cleo. It had made her realize that she had reached a point of no return.

It had all come about innocently enough. Sylvia had been busy when the time came to pick Sammy up from kindergarten. Max had offered to fetch him. Cleo had invited herself along for the trip because she had wanted to pick up some things at the drugstore in town.

She and Max arrived at Sammy's school a few minutes early and sat in the Jaguar in the parking lot, waiting for the children to come pouring out of the gate.

"One of us is always very careful to be here when Sammy gets out of school," Cleo had explained. "He gets very anxious if there's no one waiting."

"I see," Max said. He rested one arm on the wheel and watched the school entrance.

At that moment the door opened, and a dozen screaming kindergarteners dressed in rain coats and hoods raced out onto the sidewalk. Cleo spotted Sammy in his little yellow slicker. The boy was scanning the cluster of waiting vehicles, searching for his mother's car or, perhaps, Cleo's familiar red Toyota. He didn't recognize the green Jaguar immediately. His small face crumpled with alarm.

"He doesn't see us," Cleo said. She reached for the door handle.

"I'll let him know we're here." Max opened his door and got out.

Sammy saw him at once and broke into a happy, relieved grin. He dashed toward the Jaguar, heedless of the rain puddles. Max opened the back door.

"Hi, Max," Sammy said as he scrambled into the back seat.

"Hi, Sammy."

Sammy looked at Cleo. "Hi, Cleo."

"Hi, kid." Cleo turned in the front seat to smile at him. "How was school?"

"It was okay." Sammy opened a folder. "We made pictures. I did one for you, Max. Here." He removed a crayon drawing and held it out to Max.

Cleo realized that she was holding her breath. She knew in a moment of stunning clarity that if Max failed to properly appreciate Sammy's picture, he was the wrong man for her. It was that simple.

Max eased himself slowly back behind the wheel and closed his door. He took the crayon drawing without comment and examined it for a long moment.

Silence filled the Jaguar.

Then Max looked up, his gaze gravely serious. He turned in the seat to face Sammy. "This is one of the most beautiful pictures I have ever seen, Sammy. Thank you."

Sammy glowed. "Are you going to put it on the wall in your room?"

"Yes. Just as soon as we get home," Max said.

Cleo let out the breath she had been holding.

She knew then that her fate was probably sealed. She had fallen in love with Max Fortune.

Cleo felt another presence in the meditation room at the same moment that a shadow fell on the yellow crystal. She pulled her mind back to the present and waited.

"Andromeda said I would find you here." Max's cane thudded softly on the hardwood floor.

Cleo looked up at him. His eyes held the same shimmering intensity that she had seen in them when he had examined Sammy's drawing that afternoon. He held a single red rose in his right hand.

"Hello, Max." Cleo did not dare look at the rose. "What are you doing here?"

"I came to give you this." He dropped the rose lightly into her lap.

Cleo picked it up as if it might explode in her hands. Chapter five, she thought. The man had, indeed, been studying *The Mirror.*

The red rose in chapter five had symbolized seduction. Cleo wondered what Max would think when he got to the last chapter in the book. That chapter featured a white rose as a symbol of love.

Cleo wondered if Max could only go as far as the red rose. "I don't know what to say," she whispered.

Max smiled. "You don't have to say anything."

Her eyes met his, and she knew that he spoke the truth. There was no need to say anything, because Max knew exactly how close she was to falling into his arms.

The inn's lounge was quiet again that evening. The handful of guests were clustered around the hearth sipping espressos, lattes, and sherry. Cleo sat on her favorite stool and watched Max wash and dry glasses. Neither of them had referred to the small scene in the meditation center that afternoon.

"You know, you're really good at that," she said as Max rinsed another glass and set it on the tray. "You're good at everything around here. Remind me to have you take a look at one of the water pipes in the basement tomorrow. It's leaking."

"Something is always leaking around this place," Max said. "One of these days you're going to have to put in new plumbing."

Cleo sighed. "That will cost a fortune."

"You can't run a place like this without making occasional capital investments."

"Easy for you to say," she grumbled. "You're not the one who has to come up with the money. I wish Benjy would come back."

"Ben."

"Right, Ben. He had a knack for handling the plumbing."

Max seemed to hesitate. "Speaking of Ben —" He broke off abruptly and glanced toward the door. "Ah, I see we are about to entertain another one of your gentlemen callers."

"My what?" Cleo glanced around in surprise. "Oh, that's Nolan."

"The budding politician?"

"Yes. I wonder what he wants."

Nolan walked purposefully toward the bar. He was wearing a handsome leather jacket, a discreetly striped shirt, and a pair of dark slacks. His light brown hair was attractively ruffled and slightly damp from the rain. He smiled broadly at Cleo, just as if he hadn't labeled her book pornography a few days ago.

"Hello, Nolan." Cleo peered at him warily. "What brings you here?"

"I wanted to talk to you." Nolan sat down on the stool next to Cleo's. He glanced briefly at Max. "You're new here, aren't you?"

Cleo stepped in to make introductions. "Nolan, this is Max Fortune. He's a new employee. Max, this is Nolan Hildebrand."

"Hildebrand." Max inclined his head and continued drying glasses.

"Fortune. I'll have a double decaf nonfat grande latte," Nolan said.

Max elevated one brow, but he did not respond. He turned to the espresso machine and went to work preparing the coffee drink.

Cleo idly stirred her tea. "Gosh, Nolan, I hope you're not jeopardizing your chances of getting elected next fall by being seen here with me tonight. I'd really hate to have that on my conscience."

Nolan had the grace to look abashed. "You've got a right to be annoyed with me, Cleo. I handled that scene at the cove very badly."

"Was there a good way to handle it?" Cleo asked. She was aware that Max was listening to every word.

"I shouldn't have come unglued just because you wrote that book," Nolan muttered. "It wasn't that big a deal. I want to apologize."

Cleo widened her eyes in surprise. "You do?"

Nolan nodded his head with sober humiliation. "Yeah. I behaved like an ass. Will you forgive me?"

Cleo relented instantly. "Sure. Don't worry about it. I know it must have been a shock to find *The Mirror* stuffed into your mailbox along with that note."

"You can say that again." Nolan gave her a rueful smile. "It's still hard for me to believe you wrote something like that. I mean, it just seemed so unlike you, Cleo. All that stuff

179

about ribbons and mirrors and scarves and so on."

Max put a small paper napkin down in front of Nolan and positioned the latte glass in the center. "A fascinating tour de force in the neoromantic style, don't you think?"

"Huh?" Nolan blinked and turned to scowl at Max.

Max picked up another wet glass and went back to work with the dish towel. "I think *The Mirror* offers a unique and insightful perspective on the interior landscape of female sexuality."

Nolan scowled. "Who the hell did you say you were?"

"It varies. Tonight I'm the bartender," Max said. "But getting back to *The Mirror*; I have to say that I was very impressed by the intricately layered depths of many of the scenes. Weren't you?"

Nolan stared at Cleo. "You said no one else around there knew you'd written that book."

"Excepting family, of course," Max murmured.

"Family? What family?" Nolan demanded.

"Never mind," Max said. "Didn't you find that there was extraordinary shape and substance to the eroticism in the book? It goes far beyond the overtly sensual and into the realm of the philosophical."

"Look, I didn't come here tonight to talk about Cleo's book," Nolan ground out through set teeth.

"A definite sense of far-flung resonance pervades every chapter, every scene of the book," Max continued. "The fluent narrative voice conjures up an alternative reality that takes on a life of its own. For the male reader, it creates an alien world, a distinctly female world, and yet I'm sure you found that there was a strange sense of familiarity about it."

"Christ, I don't believe this," Nolan muttered. "Cleo, I wanted to talk to you about something very important."

Cleo gulped the last of her tea, nearly choking on her own laughter. "Sure, Nolan," she sputtered. "What's on your mind?"

Nolan shot a wary glance at Max and lowered his voice. "This is sort of personal."

"The portrayal of a female view of sexuality in *The Mirror* was nothing short of riveting," Max offered as he poured more tea into Cleo's cup. "The reader has the sense that the narrator is both the seducer and the one who is seduced. It brings up several interesting questions about the matter of reader identification, as far as I'm concerned. What was your conclusion?"

"Can't you shut him up?" Nolan asked Cleo.

Cleo looked at Max and saw the gleam in

his eyes. "Probably not."

"The reader must ask himself, for example," Max said in measured, pedantic tones, "just who is the seducer in *The Mirror*? Is it a work of autoeroticism? Is the narrator actually seducing herself when she looks into the mirror?"

That was certainly what the reviewers had believed, Cleo thought. She waited with a sense of impending fate to hear what Max had to say about it.

"I'm trying to have a private conversation here," Nolan said in a tight voice.

Max ignored him. "Personally, I think something far more complex is going on. Women writers, after all, are interested in relationships. I believe that the figure in the mirror is the *other*, and that, initially, at least, he is actually the seducer. But there's another problem in the book. I think the man in the mirror is just as trapped in his world as the narrator is in hers."

Cleo froze. None of the reviews that had appeared on *The Mirror* had understood that fundamental fact. Her eyes met Max's, and she nearly fell off the bar stool when she saw the deep, sensual understanding in his gaze.

She gripped the edge of the bar and held on for dear life. That shattering moment of silent communication did more to melt her insides than anything her imagination had conjured up when she wrote *The Mirror*.

Max smiled slowly at her. Instead of giving her a fresh napkin to accompany her second cup of tea, he put a playing card down beside the saucer. He reached into his pocket, removed a small object, and set it down on top of the card.

Cleo was afraid to glance at the face of the card. But in the end she was unable to resist.

When she looked down her worst fears were confirmed. The card was a queen of hearts. Lying on top of the card was a small, familiar key. She knew it was the key to the attic room. Cleo jerked her eyes back up to meet Max's. What she saw there stole her breath.

"What's going on here, Cleo?" Nolan glared at the card and the key. "What's this all about?"

"I don't know," Cleo admitted. But the admission was made to Max, not to Nolan. Nolan seemed to have faded somewhere into the distance. Max was the only person who mattered.

"There's only one way to find out, isn't there?" Max said softly. "You'll have to use the key."

It was a scene straight out of her book. Like the red rose, the key had been another symbol of seduction. Cleo was light-headed. It was as if she had stepped into a dream that she, herself, had fashioned but that Max now controlled. Nothing felt quite real. She wondered if Andromeda had been experimenting lately with the formulas of her herbal teas.

Nolan was looking confused and angry. He scowled at Max. "What's with that key and the card?"

"Cleo's been looking for them for a long time," Max said gently. "I found them for her."

Nolan turned back to Cleo. "Damn it, I'm trying to talk to you about something that involves a lot of money. I don't know who this guy is" — he jerked a thumb at Max — "but I've had about enough of his interference."

Max smiled dangerously. His eyes gleamed.

Cleo wrenched herself momentarily free of the silken web of sensual promise that was swirling around her. She tried to concentrate on Nolan's annoyed face. "What did you say about a great deal of money?"

Nolan apparently decided that he finally had her full attention. He leaned forward intently. "A man named Garrison Spark came by my office today. He's looking for some very valuable paintings that he thinks may have been left here in Harmony Cove. He says that old guy who used to stay here at the inn was actually a very wealthy member of the Curzon family."

"I know."

"Spark says Curzon owned the paintings but that he had sold them to Spark just before he died."

Cleo stared. "Mr. Spark told you that Jason sold him the Luttrells?"

Nolan leaned closer. "You know about them?"

"I know that the Luttrells, if they're ever found, belong to Max, here."

Nolan's knuckles were white. His eyes narrowed. "The hell they do. Spark said Fortune might try to claim them, but he says Fortune has no proof of ownership."

"And Spark does?" Cleo asked.

Nolan nodded quickly. "Spark can produce a bill of sale."

Max set a glass down very casually and picked up another. "Spark is very good at producing forgeries of all kinds."

Nolan ignored him. "Cleo, the paintings belong to Spark. What's more, he's got a client who will pay fifty thousand dollars for them. Spark says he'll pay a finder's fee if we can figure out where Curzon stashed the paintings."

"A finder's fee?" Cleo repeated. "You mean a commission?"

"He'll go fifty-fifty." Nolan was barely able to contain his excitement. "Whoever finds those paintings and turns them over to Spark will collect twenty-five thousand dollars. I could really use that kind of money for my campaign fund."

"I could use it to fix the plumbing here at the inn," Cleo mused.

Nolan's smile held a hint of satisfaction. "We'll split the twenty-five grand, Cleo. Deal?"

"Afraid not," Cleo said. "For openers, I have no idea where the paintings are."

"They've got to be around here somewhere," Nolan insisted. "Spark is convinced that Curzon hid them here in Harmony Cove. He talked to someone at Cosmic Harmony first because he'd heard that Curzon was friends with some of the women there. But I know how much Curzon liked you."

"Jason was my friend."

"Right," Nolan agreed swiftly. "And I'll bet that if he left those paintings anywhere, he left them here at the inn. Level with me. Do you know where they are?"

"No."

"Are you sure? Because there's a lot of money involved here. I know how sentimental you are. You're the type who would hang on to those Luttrells just because they reminded you of an old friend. But they're too valuable to be kept around as mementos."

"I'm not keeping them around as mementos," Cleo said patiently. "I have no idea where they are. And if they do turn up, Max has first claim to them."

"Not according to Garrison Spark." Nolan shot Max a disgusted glance. "According to Spark, Fortune was just a professional gofer. He did odd jobs for Spark for a while. Then he quit without any notice to do odd jobs for Curzon International, where he apparently managed to ingratiate himself with Jason Curzon. He says Fortune is an opportunist who always has an eye out for the main chance."

"A man's got to make a living," Max said.

Cleo stirred uneasily on the bar stool. She was still feeling disoriented. Out of the corner of her eye she saw the key to the attic room glinting in the soft light. "Nolan, I don't know anything about the paintings. You're wasting your time."

"Okay, so maybe you don't know where they are," Nolan said quickly. "But Spark thinks they're around here somewhere, either at the inn or at Cosmic Harmony. I propose we join forces to find them."

"Forget it," Cleo said.

"You heard the lady," Max said.

"Why don't you just shut up and tend bar?" Nolan muttered.

Max's smile was dangerously benign. "If

you don't want to talk business, I suppose we could go back to *The Mirror*. Did you notice the allusions and metaphors that permeate the book? The use of the scarlet ribbon was especially interesting. It creates both a threat and a bond. A brilliant commentary on the different ways in which men and women view sex and sensuality, don't you think?"

"Goddammit, I've had enough of this." Nolan got to his feet and turned to Cleo. "I'll talk to you some other time when he isn't around."

"I'm sorry." Cleo felt a pang of regret. Until the other morning at the cove, Nolan had been a friend. She jumped down off the stool and took his arm. "I'll walk you out to the lobby."

Nolan was immediately mollified. "This business with the Luttrells is important, Cleo. There's a lot of money involved."

"I understand." Cleo refused to look back at Max as she guided Nolan out of the lounge. "But I really don't know where the paintings are. Jason never said a word to me about them."

"You're sure?"

"Absolutely certain."

"They've got to be around here somewhere. Spark is sure of it." Nolan's mouth thinned in frustration. "Listen, Cleo, Spark says Fortune is a two-bit con man. He says the guy has no legal claim to those paintings."

"I think Max does have a claim to them," Cleo said quietly.

"Don't be a fool. Spark has a bill of sale. Damn it, it's obvious Fortune is trying to charm you into telling him where the paintings are. I don't want to see you get hurt, Cleo."

"Thoughtful of you."

"I mean it," Nolan said. "Cleo, in spite of what happened, we're old friends. I only want what's best for you."

"Thanks for coming by, Nolan." Cleo opened the front door. "I accept your apology. I'm glad we're still friends."

"Sure." Nolan came to a halt at the door. His brows drew together in a frown. "Why the hell did you let Fortune read your book? You said you didn't want anyone to know you'd written it."

"It's okay, Nolan. Max is one of the family." Cleo shut the door gently in his face and leaned back against it with a long sigh.

Max had behaved outrageously. She would have to speak to him. The trouble was, she wasn't sure quite what to say. All she could think about was the key to the attic room that he had given to her.

Cleo took a moment to regroup her forces. Then she straightened away from the door and stalked back into the lounge. The last of the guests were leaving to go upstairs to their rooms. Max was busy closing down the bar.

"I want to talk to you," Cleo said.

"Watch out for Hildebrand," Max said coolly as he shut off the lights behind the bar. "Spark has obviously gotten to him."

Cleo frowned, distracted. "What are you talking about?"

"You heard me." Max came around from behind the bar. He was leaning more heavily than usual on his cane. "Spark has convinced Hildebrand that it will be worth his while to find the paintings. Hildebrand has decided you can help him collect the twenty-five grand. That's the only reason he showed up here tonight."

"It wasn't the only reason. Nolan apologized to me," Cleo said stubbornly.

"Don't be a fool, Cleo."

"Funny, that's what Nolan just said. I'm getting all kinds of good advice tonight."

Max gave her a strange look. "Maybe you ought to take some of it."

Cleo took a deep breath. "Max, I'd like to talk to you about something important."

"I've got something I want to talk to you about, too," Max said. "O'Reilly phoned this afternoon. None of the guests who stayed here at the inn the night the ribbon was left on your pillow checks out as obviously weird."

Cleo was disconcerted. "I'd almost forgotten that your friend was running a check on those people."

"It doesn't mean one of them didn't do it, only that there's no obvious suspect."

"I see."

Max slanted her a brooding glance. "O'Reilly thinks the best way to handle the situation is to ignore it. He says whoever is behind the incidents will grow bored with them if you don't give him the response he wants."

Cleo thought about it. "Do you agree with Mr. O'Reilly?"

Max shrugged. "I'm not sure. But he's the expert on this kind of thing, not me. He says that, based on his experience, he thinks it's most likely someone from the local area who found out about *The Mirror* has decided to play some bad practical jokes on you."

"Some sour-minded malcontent who has nothing better to do, I suppose."

"His advice is to go to your local police chief if there are any more incidents."

"All right." Cleo made a face. "I told you private investigators weren't very useful."

Max paused. "I wouldn't say that. O'Reilly also told me that he found Ben Atkins for you."

That stopped Cleo in her tracks. She smiled

at Max in delight. "He did? Where is Benjy? I mean, where is *Ben?* Is he all right?"

"As far as I know. According to O'Reilly, Atkins is working at a gas station in a little town south of here." Max walked toward the door.

Cleo hurried after him, bemused by Max's strange, new mood. It was as if he regretted the fact that his friend had found Ben. "Did he contact him?"

"No." Max went through the door and started toward the stairs. "I thought I'd drive down and see him in person."

"Yes, of course." Cleo climbed the stairs beside him. "That would probably be best. It's really nice of you to do this, Max."

"Don't get your hopes up, Cleo. If he doesn't want to come back to Trisha and the baby, I can't force him."

"I know. But I really think Ben will want to come back home once he's had a chance to get over being scared. He just needs someone he can talk to, Max."

"Maybe." Max halted on the third-floor landing and turned to walk Cleo to her room.

Cleo glanced down at his cane. "Your leg is bothering you tonight, isn't it? We should have taken the elevator."

"I'm fine, Cleo."

"I could make you a batch of Andromeda's

special tea. I know the recipe."

"I've got some pills I can take." Max halted in front of her door and held out his hand.

Cleo reached into her pocket for her room key. Her fingers closed first around the key to Max's room. It burned her hand. She quickly dropped it back into her pocket and yanked out the right key.

Max said nothing. He simply took the key from her and unlocked the door.

Cleo stepped into the cozy safety of her room and turned to say good-night. "Max . . ."

His mouth curved faintly. "If you want to talk to me any more tonight, you know where to find me. All you have to do is use the key."

He turned and walked toward the narrow door that opened onto the attic stairs. He did not look back.

Cleo stood in the doorway of her room and watched until Max vanished. Then she slowly closed her door and went to stand in front of the window.

Beneath the scattered clouds, the ocean was a black silk cape that stretched out to the horizon. Moonlight gleamed on its folds as it shifted gently over the mysteries below. Cleo gazed out over the surface of the dark sea, trying to imagine what it concealed.

All you have to do is use the key.

It was another line from her book, of course.

Max was apparently memorizing every chapter.

She thought about the way he had been leaning on the hawk-headed cane as he went up the stairs. Her instincts had told her from the start that the recurrent ache in Max's leg mirrored the darker, deeper wound in his soul. He was a man who had survived without much love, and he had found ways to do without. But that did not mean he wasn't hurting.

Five Amos Luttrell paintings, no matter how beautiful or how valuable, were never going to fill the empty places in Max's life. She knew what Max needed, even if he didn't. He needed a home, just as she had needed one after her family had been destroyed.

Cleo opened her fingers slowly and looked down at the key and the card he had put into her hand.

She dropped both into her pocket and went to the door. She let herself out into the hall and went downstairs.

When she reached the kitchen she found a stainless steel kettle, filled it with cold water, and set it on the stove.

A few minutes later Cleo poured the boiling water over the herbs she had placed in a ceramic pot. She put the lid on the pot and added a cup and saucer to the tray.

She carried the tray down the hall and took

the small elevator to the third floor. Then she walked to the attic staircase door.

She climbed the darkened stairs to the attic and paused in front of Max's door. The floorboard in front of Max's room squeaked. She knew he could hear the sound from inside the room. Cleo put the tray on the floor and knocked hesitantly.

"Max?"

There was silence for a moment. Then Max's voice came softly from inside the room. "What is it, Cleo?"

"Open the door. I brought you some of Andromeda's tea."

"Use the key that I gave you."

Cleo took a step back as if the door had suddenly become red-hot. "Max, I didn't come up here to play fantasy games with you. I brought you something for your leg."

"I don't need anything for my leg."

"Yes, you do. Don't be so darn stubborn." Cleo dug the key out of her pocket, shoved it into the lock, and opened the door before she lost her nerve.

The only light on in the vast room beneath the eaves was from the small lamp beside the bed. It revealed Sammy's crayon drawing neatly pinned to the wall beside the desk. It also played over Max's dark, shadowed figure near the window.

Cleo saw that he had taken off his shirt and shoes. The only clothing he had on was a pair of trousers.

There was power in the smooth, muscled contours of Max's shoulders. Cleo stared at the dark, curling hair on his chest, fascinated by the way it formed a vee that plummeted beneath the waistband of his pants.

Max's eyes met hers. "The riddle of *The Mirror* is who is the seducer and who is the seduced."

Cleo's fingers trembled as she dropped the key back into her pocket and reached down to pick up the tray. "I didn't come up here to be seduced."

"Did you come up here to seduce me?"

"No."

"Then what are we going to do?"

"Drink tea. At least you are." Cleo kicked the door shut behind her and marched into the room. She put the tea tray down on the desk and poured a cup of the herbal brew. She held the cup out to Max. "Here, have some of this. It will make you feel much better."

"Will it?" Max's gaze was filled with a dangerously disturbing sensuality as he obediently took the cup from her hand. His fingers brushed hers.

"Yes." Cleo rubbed her damp palms on her

jeans. "At least I hope it will. You're in a strange mood tonight, aren't you?"

"Am I?" Max took a long swallow of the tea. Then he put the cup down on the desk. "The only mirror in this room is that one over there. I wonder what we'll see in it when we look into it together."

Cleo's gaze went to the old-fashioned full-length mirror on the wooden stand. A shiver of excitement stirred the hair on her neck. As if he knew exactly what she was feeling, Max reached out and took her by the hand. He led her toward the mirror.

Cleo couldn't speak. She waited one last time for the crashing tide of uncertainty and wrongness to wash over her, but nothing happened. There was no fear with Max, no desire to pull back from the brink. She floated across the room as if she were a balloon on the end of a string that he held in his hand.

Max drew her to a halt in front of the mirror. He stood behind her, his hands on her shoulders. His eyes met hers in the silvered glass.

Cleo felt the heat in him. A gathering sense of urgency welled up inside her in response. She was shaken to the core by the force of her own desire. She had not felt this way since she had written *The Mirror*.

"I'm glad you used the key tonight, Cleo." Max unfastened the clip that bound her hair.

She watched the thick mass of her hair tumble down around her shoulders. Then she felt Max's thumbs slide beneath the weight of it. His fingers touched sensitive skin at the nape of her neck.

"Max?"

"Beautiful," he whispered. He bent his head and dropped a kiss into her hair.

Cleo looked into the mirror and saw the face of the man inside the glass. For the first time the reflection was crystal clear.

The man inside the mirror was Max.

7

Max removed Cleo's glasses and set them down on a small table. He managed to invest the small action with a startling degree of intimacy. It was as if he had just removed a protective veil. She felt naked and vulnerable.

She could still see well enough to make out her own reflection and that of Max looming behind her, but the images were gently blurred. It was like looking at figures trapped in a silvery mist.

Max's eyes met Cleo's in the mirror. His mouth curved slightly. "Who is the seducer and who is the one who is seduced?"

Cleo shivered. The reflection in the mirror allowed her to see Max's hands move on her shoulders even as she felt the weight of them. The sensual power in him captivated all her senses. "I don't know. I never knew."

"Maybe there isn't an answer." Max flexed his fingers gently. He watched her face. "Maybe it's supposed to be like this."

"Like what?" Cleo could not tear her eyes away from the mirror.

"Like looking into a spectacular painting. Becoming a part of it. Seeing some of the layers and knowing that there will be no peace until you've seen them all."

"What happens when you've seen them all?" Cleo watched his hands slip slowly down her arms. "Do you grow bored with the painting?"

"No. It's impossible to see all the layers. So you keep looking, reexamining the ones you've already seen and searching out new ones. The hunger is always there."

Cleo touched one of his hands with her own. "Hunger?"

"You can satisfy it temporarily, but you know it will return, and you know you will need to look into the painting again. And again." He lifted the heavy weight of her hair aside, bowed his head, and kissed the side of her throat. "And again."

"It sounds painful." But the urgency in her that was generated by his warm, tantalizing kiss was not painful at all. It was exquisitely exciting.

Max's eyes gleamed in the shadows. "The hunger is part of the pleasure. But you know all about that, don't you?"

"No. Yes." She trembled as he traced the line of her jaw with his fingers. "I don't know." The eyes of the woman in the mirror were still veiled in mystery, even though she no longer wore the protective glasses.

"You described the sensation in *The Mirror*," Max said. He threaded his fingers through her hair as if it were so much precious silk. "There is hunger on every page. The book is filled with it. It's a hunger so deep it has the power to make the reader hungry, too."

"*The Mirror* is a fantasy," Cleo said breathlessly.

Max reached around from behind and started to unbutton her oxford cloth shirt. "A fantasy like the fantasy we're watching in the mirror. A fantasy which is also reality."

"No." But she was no longer certain of that. He was right, the fantasy was rapidly becoming a reality. Max was making it happen. It was disorienting and disquieting. It was also incredibly thrilling.

"You're the woman in the book, and you're the woman we're watching in the mirror, aren't you, Cleo?"

A light-headed sensation swept through her, leaving her a little dizzy. "If I'm her, who are you?"

"You know who I am. I'm the man in the mirror. And I'm the man who's touching you. The brilliance of *The Mirror* is that in it seducer and seduced become one."

She wanted to explain just how much of a fantasy *The Mirror* really was, but she could not find the words. He would never believe that she had an extremely limited acquaintance with the kind of sensuality she had described in her book. No man would believe that *The Mirror* had been created almost entirely from her imagination.

Cleo watched the image in the mirror as Max slowly and steadily undid the buttons of her shirt. She was riveted by the sight of his fingers as they slipped into the shadowed valley between her breasts.

The woman in the glass could not really be her, Cleo thought. She looked mysterious and exotic and sensual; she looked like a Cleopatra, not a Cleo.

Max's fingers touched her bare skin, and she sensed herself start to merge with the woman in the mirror. The man in the misty reflection looked at her with knowing eyes, eyes that saw the many layers waiting to be revealed. Eyes that were filled with a hunger that matched and perhaps exceeded her own. That knowledge shook her.

"Max, I think I'm getting a little scared," Cleo said.

"Of me?"

She looked into the mirror and saw the stark need etched into every line of his face. She also saw the control and self-discipline that governed that need, and she knew that she was safe.

"No," Cleo said softly. "I'm not frightened of you."

"Of yourself?" He had the shirt undone now. Slowly he parted it, revealing her breasts.

"Of the unknown, I think."

"But you know what's waiting for us, Cleo. You wrote a whole book about it." Max eased the shirt off her shoulders and let it fall to the floor. He circled her waist with his hands and slid his palms upward to cup her breasts. "I'm the one who's going into the unknown."

He meant it, Cleo thought, deeply intrigued. Not in the literal sense, of course, but she knew that in some way tonight would be a new experience for Max, too. The knowledge touched her deeply.

Wordlessly she lifted her fingertips to the side of his face. The movement caused her breast to glide upward. Max's thumb skimmed across her nipple, sending a searing jolt of sensation through her.

Cleo cried out softly and closed her eyes for a brief moment. She leaned back against Max, seeking the heat and strength of his body. He was as solid as a rock behind her. The heaviness of his arousal pressed into her buttocks.

Cleo opened her eyes when she felt Max's fingers go to the button of her jeans. He dropped soft, persuasive kisses into her hair as he slid the zipper downward. Cleo stared into the mirror as he eased the jeans and her panties down over her hips. It was like watching a dream unfold. She was part of it and yet still apart from it. The real Cleo was still hovering uncertainly between the image in the mirror and the woman who stood in front of it.

"Look at you." There was primitive male awe in Max's voice. "You're beautiful."

She wasn't, and she knew it, but part of the magic of the night was that Max could make her feel beautiful. Cleo smiled dreamily and put her hands on top of Max's.

He eased his fingers downward into the dark

triangle of curls that concealed Cleo's most secret places. She leaned her head back against his shoulder. When he slid one finger into the liquid warmth that had gathered in the folds between her legs, she moaned.

The right man.

Cleo turned abruptly within the circle of Max's arms and splayed her fingers across his chest. Without any hesitation she lifted her face, offering him her mouth.

Max groaned and crushed her lips beneath his. The full force of his own hunger broke over her. Cleo felt like a small, supple tree in a gale.

This kiss was not like the other one that Max had given her that night in the solarium. It was darker, more demanding, and far more blatantly erotic.

Cleo shuddered beneath the sensual onslaught, but she had no wish to pull back from it. Instead, she craved more of Max's brand of hunger. It was, in turn, making her insatiable.

Max cupped her buttocks in his hands and pressed her against his aroused body. She tasted his mouth with her tongue, and he, in turn, shuddered.

"I don't know if I'm going to live through this." Max covered her lips once more with his own and drew her back toward the bed.

"And I don't care so long as I have you tonight."

Cleo pressed herself closer. She felt Max stagger a little as he worked to balance her weight as well as his own without the aid of his cane. Cleo heard his sudden, sharp intake of breath and knew that his leg was protesting the added burden. She started to draw back.

"No." Max caught her hands and put them firmly around his neck. His eyes gleamed with passion. "Forget the damned leg. Hold on to me. Tight."

She clung to him and felt the heat that was radiating from his skin. Max was burning up with desire. She wondered if she felt as warm to him.

He collapsed back onto the quilt, dragging Cleo down on top of him. Cleo sprawled across his chest and burrowed into his warmth. She couldn't seem to stop kissing him. She wanted to touch him everywhere.

She showered him with kisses as he lay beneath her. His throat, his chest, his belly; she savored every inch of him. He was so beautifully, powerfully, inexpressibly *male*. The potential they shared was so vast that it almost frightened her. He was the exciting *other*, the one who would set her free and whom she, in turn, would free.

Max sucked in his breath again, but this

time, Cleo knew, it wasn't because of the pain in his leg. He wrapped one hand around her head and gently pushed her mouth against the skin of his flat stomach. "Yes," he muttered. "So good."

He reached out, captured her hand in his, and settled her palm over the fierce bulge in his trousers.

Cleo stilled as she cautiously explored the size of his erection. She forced her head up against the weight of his hand. "Max?"

His fingers trembled as he touched her breast. His eyes were shadowed with dark excitement. "I want you."

Cleo smiled tremulously. "I want you, too."

"Then there isn't any reason to stop now, is there?" He searched her face.

Cleo took a deep breath. "No. There isn't any reason to stop."

Max moved, turning onto his side and easing Cleo onto her back. He covered her body with his own and kissed her.

Cleo speared her fingers through his hair and arched herself against him. The reality of what she was experiencing transcended everything she had imagined when she wrote *The Mirror*.

Max tore his mouth free from hers and sat up reluctantly. He unfastened his pants and worked them off. Then he leaned over to open the small drawer in the nightstand. Cleo heard the rustle of a foil wrapper. When he was finished, he turned out the lamp and came back to Cleo.

"You're more beautiful then I had imagined," Cleo whispered. "And bigger." She blushed furiously. "I mean all over. What I meant to say was . . ."

Max smiled slightly as he fitted himself between her legs. "Yes? What did you mean to say?"

Cleo saw the humor in his gaze and shook her head impatiently. She reached up and caught his face between her palms. "Max, what I'm trying to say is that although in some ways you're different than what I expected, in other ways I know you in a way I can't explain. It was you I fantasized about when I wrote *The Mirror*. I don't understand it. How could I have known about you?"

"There's no need to understand it." He brushed his mouth across hers. "You seduced me the first time I saw you. Open for me, Cleo. God knows I need you."

She felt him probing gently, dampening himself in the moisture between her legs. She gripped his shoulders very tightly and braced herself. She was not quite certain what to expect, but the anticipation was threatening to overwhelm her.

Max raised his brows as her nails bit into his skin. "Don't worry, I'm not going anywhere tonight."

"I know." Cleo tried to unlock her fingers. "I'm sorry, I can't help it."

His soft laugh held a world of masculine satisfaction. It also held a tenderness that made Cleo feel safer than she had at any point since the death of her parents. She was in good hands, she told herself.

"It's all right," Max said. "I'm not complaining. It's just that no one's ever held on to me the way you're holding on to me."

"How am I holding you?"

"As if you'll never let go." Max took her mouth again. At the same moment he drove into her swiftly, filling her completely with one long, powerful stroke.

Cleo closed her eyes and gasped in astonishment.

Max went completely still, his entire body suddenly rigid.

Cleo cautiously opened her eyes and found him staring down at her with an expression of stunned shock on his face. Neither of them moved.

Max recovered first. "Don't tell me this was —" He broke off, struggling for words. "Was this your first . . . ?"

"Yes." She smiled up at him, aware that

her body was rapidly adjusting to the strangeness of having him lodged within her. "Remind me to drop a note to my therapist in the morning. I want to tell her that it was worth waiting for. I think she thought I was just being picky."

"Damn." Max rested his damp forehead on hers. "I didn't realize."

"I know." Cleo tightened her already fierce grip on his shoulders. She was acutely aware of the aching fullness inside her. "Do you think we could get on with it now?"

"I don't think we could stop it now."

"Good."

Max started to move within her. He was slow and careful and very, very thorough. He made love to her until his back was slick with sweat and his muscles trembled beneath his skin. Cleo felt her body clench around his with each stroke. She could not seem to get enough of the hot, thick feel of him inside her. She lifted her hips off the bed.

"My God, Cleo." He reached down and touched her with slow, knowing fingers.

"*Max.*" Cleo surrendered to the climax with a small, startled shriek.

"Don't be afraid. It's all right. This is how it's supposed to be." Max surged into her one last time on a ragged groan that signaled a surrender as great as her own.

Max was silent for a long time. He lay sprawled on the pillows, his arm around Cleo.

"Why didn't you say something?" he finally asked.

"What was there to say?" Cleo snuggled closer. She was feeling incredibly content and a little sleepy. All she wanted to do was close her eyes and glue herself to Max's warm strength. Unfortunately she was going to have to get dressed and traipse back to her tower room in a few minutes.

"How about, 'Say, Max, I've never done this before, and I'd appreciate it if you'd take your time and do it right,' " Max muttered.

Cleo smiled against his chest. "You didn't seem to need instructions or advice. You did it just right. By the book, as a matter of fact." She paused, remembering his words the night he had put the scarlet ribbon around her and kissed her. "As promised."

Max winced. "About that book," he said ominously. "Do you mind telling me how someone who is, uh . . ."

"Handicapped by the lack of personal experience?" Cleo offered helpfully.

"Let's call it romantically challenged," Max said diplomatically.

Cleo raised her head to look down at him. "Romantically challenged?"

"I was searching for the, uh, politically correct phrase."

Cleo started to grin. "Romantically challenged? *Romantically challenged?*"

"If you don't like that phrase, think of another."

"Let's see." Cleo considered carefully. "What about *relationship deprived?*"

"All right."

"No, no, wait. I've got a better one." Cleo sat up, holding the sheet to her breast. "How about *sexually impoverished?*"

"Whatever. Cleo, what I'm trying to ask is . . ."

"Hold it." Cleo held up a hand. "I've got a better one. *Differently experienced.*"

"Damn it, Cleo . . ."

"Wait, wait, I've got an even better one. How about *sensually impaired?*"

"Enough with the political correctness jokes," Max said. "I'm trying to carry on a serious conversation here."

"You started it. *Romantically challenged.* I love it." Cleo started to laugh.

"So how about answering the question?"

"*Romantically challenged.*" Cleo laughed harder.

"It's not that funny," Max said grimly.

"Yes, it is." Cleo was giggling so much now she could barely speak. "Especially coming from you."

Max gave her a quelling look. "Do you mind telling me how you managed to impart such an interesting note of realism to *The Mirror*?"

Cleo doubled over in another fit of giggles. "I relied entirely on my imagination."

He stared at her in disbelief. "Imagination?"

"If you think about it, you'll recall that most of *The Mirror* is taken up with the feeling of anticipation, not the actual experience."

"The hunger," Max said softly.

"Exactly. The hunger." Cleo savored the rich, warm feeling that filled her. More laughter bubbled within her. "Believe me, I understood that part very well."

Max's expression was bemused. "I won't argue with that. All the same . . ."

"For crying out loud, Max, you don't have to jump out of a plane to guess what it would do to your insides."

"You said that just before your parents died there was a man," Max said carefully.

"There was. Actually there were two or three. Not at the same time, of course. But I never went to bed with any of them."

"Why not?" Max persisted.

Cleo shrugged. "None of them was Mr. Right, even though I have to say that numbers two and three were really terrific kissers. Then, after my parents died, my therapist said

212

I developed that psychological block or whatever it was I told you about."

Max stared at her and slowly shook his head. "It's incredible."

"What is?"

"That you wrote *The Mirror* using just your imagination."

"Talent," Cleo said without a shred of modesty. "Pure talent."

"I've always had a lot of respect for the creative imagination," Max said.

"I'm not surprised. You are, after all, a connoisseur of fine art." Cleo's joy was threatening to explode in another burst of laughter. She didn't know if she would be able to contain it. "Tell me, oh, great expert, how do I compare to the average Van Gogh?"

Max narrowed his eyes. "More colorful."

"*Colorful.*" The laughter overcame her again. She thrashed about in the throes of it and managed to tumble over the edge of the bed. She landed softly on the carpet and burst into a fresh peal of giggles. "How about Picasso?"

"You're a little more unpredictable than Picasso." Max propped himself on his elbow and looked over the side of the bed. His gaze was enigmatic. "You seem to be in an unusually good mood tonight."

Cleo widened her eyes. "Gee, Max, do you

really think my mood is unusual under the circumstances?"

"Let's just say I've never heard of anyone who fell out of bed laughing after having sex."

"How many people do you know who waited this long to experience sex?" Cleo countered.

"You have a point." Max paused. "Forget what your therapist said. Tell me what you think you were waiting for all these years."

"The right man, of course."

Max stilled. "The right man?"

"Uh-huh." Cleo's giggles faded at last into a smug smile. She folded her hands behind her head and gazed happily at the ceiling. "My therapist said he'd never come along. That I was using the fantasy as an excuse not to get involved."

"What did you say?"

"I said I sure hoped he wandered into my life sooner or later, because I didn't have any choice in the matter. I *had* to wait for him. All the others felt *wrong*. She didn't understand that, and I couldn't explain it to her. It was one of the reasons why we parted company. That and the fact that she cost a fortune."

"Cleo," Max asked very softly, "how did you know I was the right man?"

She looked up at him from the floor and realized that he was deadly serious. She stopped chuckling. "I don't know. The same way you know a fine painting when you see one, I guess. Some sort of inner eye."

Max gazed down at her for a long while. Then his mouth quirked in a strange fashion. "Speaking of paintings, you really don't know where my Luttrells are, do you?"

"Nope." Cleo sat up. "I'm sorry, Max, but Jason never said a word about them to me."

"I believe you."

"Good, because it's the truth." Cleo smiled as she got to her feet. She found her glasses and pushed them onto her nose. "Holy cow, look at the time. I'd better get dressed and get to my room."

"Stay here with me tonight."

She gave him a wistful look as she pulled on her shirt. "I wish I could, but I can't. George might need to get in touch with me for some reason. He'd call my room, not yours."

"Call him now and let him know you're here with me."

Cleo blushed as she tugged on her jeans. "That would be a little awkward, don't you think?"

"No," Max said. "It would be honest."

"It isn't a matter of honesty, it's a matter of privacy." Cleo stepped into her silver sneakers and leaned down to tie the laces.

"And it isn't just him. Anyone else who needs me would look for me in my own room, too. People would worry if they couldn't find me."

Max sat up slowly. "If that's the way you want it, I'll walk you to your room."

"You don't have to do that." Cleo glanced up as Max shoved the sheet aside. The light of the bedside lamp revealed the jagged white scar on his thigh. "Oh, Max," she whispered.

He looked at her and saw the expression on her face. His eyes hardened as he reached for his trousers. "Sorry. I know it's not a pretty sight."

"Don't be ridiculous." Cleo hastened over to him and knelt beside the bed. She touched his leg with light, questing fingers. "No wonder it bothers you so much of the time. Does Andromeda's tea help?"

Max looked at her hands on his thigh. "Surprisingly enough, it does. But not as much as your massage technique."

Cleo stroked and squeezed gently. "My God, when I think about how much it must have hurt. . . ."

"Don't think about it," Max said dryly. "I don't."

"It must have been a terrible accident."

"It was my fault," Max said. "I screwed up."

Cleo studied the odd, puckered scar. "Were you driving?"

He smiled faintly. "Yes." He pulled on his trousers and levered himself to his feet. "Sure you don't want to stay?"

Cleo stood. "I'd love to stay. But I don't think it would be a good idea." She glanced at the tea tray. "Promise me you'll drink the tea before you go to bed."

"It'll be cold."

"It doesn't matter," Cleo insisted. "Drink it anyway."

"All right." He traced the outline of her mouth with his finger. "I promise. Come on. We'd better get you to your room. You've got an inn to run, and I've got a long drive ahead of me in the morning. We both need some rest."

She closed her fingers around his wrist. "Thank you for finding Ben for us."

Max's jaw tightened. "You're welcome. But you do understand that I can't guarantee I'll be able to talk him into returning, Cleo."

"I know." She smiled. "But somehow I think it will all work out. I'm sure that deep down Ben wants to come back to Trisha and the baby."

"I wish you and the others weren't so damn optimistic about it." Max picked up his cane and started for the door. His hand closed almost violently around the knob. "What happens if I can't convince him to come back here?"

"He'll come back with you," Cleo said, feeling extraordinarily confident.

Max said nothing in response. He walked her down the attic stairs and along the corridor to the tower room. When they reached her door he stopped and turned to face her. He tipped her chin up with his finger.

"Cleo," he said slowly, "about tonight. I'm not quite sure what to say."

"It's all right, Max." Cleo stood on tiptoe and brushed her lips across his cheek. "You don't have to say anything." She opened the door to her room and stepped inside. "Good night."

Max examined her in silence for a long moment, as if memorizing every detail of her face. "Good night, Cleo."

He turned and went down the hall to the attic stairs.

Cleo closed the door and leaned back against it. The glorious euphoria was still flowing in her veins. The whole world looked warm and rosy tonight. The future had never seemed so bright and full of promise.

She raised her eyes heavenward and smiled. "Jason Curzon, I don't know what you did with those paintings Max wants so badly, but thanks for sending him out here to look for them."

Everyone gathered in the kitchen the next morning to say good-bye to Max.

"Another stack of buckwheat pancakes?" Daystar asked when she saw that Max's plate was empty.

"No, thank you." Max folded his napkin with great precision and placed it on the table beside the plate.

"More coffee?" Sylvia hovered over him with the pot. "You've got a long drive ahead of you."

"I think I've had enough." Max glanced at his watch. "I'd better be on my way."

Cleo smiled at him from the other side of the table. "Promise you'll drive carefully."

He looked at her with the same unreadable expression that had been in his eyes last night. "I promise."

"We'll be waiting for you," Cleo said softly.

"Will you?" he asked.

Before Cleo could respond, Sammy darted forward and grabbed a fistful of Max's trousers. He tugged on the expensive fabric to get his attention. "Remember to fasten your seatbelt," he said earnestly.

Max glanced down at him. "I'll remember."

Sammy was clearly delighted that his instructions would be followed. He giggled, turned, and dashed out of the kitchen.

Sylvia smiled as the door swung shut behind her son. "You've been good for him, Max."

"We have mutual interests in common," Max said. "We both like books and fine art."

"Take your time driving back tonight," Andromeda advised. "There's another storm on the way. We'll hold dinner for you."

Max looked at her. "I might be very late."

Andromeda smiled serenely. "That doesn't matter. Dinner will be waiting."

Trisha gave Max a misty smile. "Tell Ben I love him," she whispered.

Max got to his feet. "I'll tell him."

"Thank you, Max," Trisha said.

He glanced at the ring of expectant faces that surrounded him. "I'll talk to Ben if I can find him. But there are no guarantees. Do all of you understand that?"

Cleo and the others nodded obediently, if impatiently.

"We understand," Cleo said cheerfully.

Max's mouth twisted. "Like hell you do," he muttered. "You all think I'm going to pull this off, don't you?"

"Nothing is for certain," Andromeda said. "But I think Cleo's right. You're the best man for the job."

"I'll walk you outside to your car." Cleo

fell into step beside him. "What time do you think you'll be back?"

"I don't know."

"Well, it doesn't matter." Cleo opened the front door. "We'll be waiting for you."

Max said nothing. When they reached the Jaguar, he took his keys out of his pocket and opened the door. He hesitated before he got behind the wheel.

"Are you okay, Cleo?"

She stared at him curiously. "Sure. Why do you ask?"

He glanced past her toward the others who were standing in the doorway, ready to wave farewell. "You waited a long time for last night. You must have had a lot of unrealistic expectations. I just wondered if you had any regrets this morning."

Cleo smiled slowly. "As it turns out," she murmured, "my expectations weren't unrealistic in the least. In fact, the actual experience far exceeded the most creative flights of my imagination."

Max looked as if he didn't know what to say next. "I, well, I just wondered."

Cleo batted her lashes outrageously. "Was it good for you, too?"

A dull red blush stained Max's high cheekbones. He fumbled briefly with his keys and dropped them on the seat. "Damn." He leaned down quickly to retrieve them. Then he straightened again. "Yes," he said. "It was very good. The best it's ever been."

Cleo grinned. "Right. Well, that's settled."

"I'd better be on my way."

She waited until he got behind the wheel. "Remember what Sammy said. Be sure to fasten your seatbelt."

Max buckled the belt and shoved the key into the ignition. His eyes met hers. "Good-bye, Cleo."

"Good-bye." She bent down to kiss him quickly on the mouth. "Hurry home." She closed the car door.

The Jaguar's engine purred behind her as she walked back to the lobby entrance where Andromeda, Daystar, Sylvia, and Trisha were gathered in the doorway. They all waved at Max.

Cleo turned to wave, too. Max did not wave back. She couldn't tell if he saw them in his rearview mirror or not. "Well, he's off."

Trisha dragged a hankie out of her pocket and blew into it. "Do you really think he'll bring Benjy — I mean, Ben — back?"

Cleo smiled at her reassuringly. "I think if anyone can do it, Max can."

"Cleo's right," Andromeda said. "Max seems very competent."

They all watched in silence as the Jaguar

disappeared from sight.

"He's gone." Sammy came running down the hall into the lobby. He was clutching Lucky Ducky, and his eyes were huge.

Cleo and the others looked at him in concern.

"What's wrong, darling?" Sylvia asked gently.

"Max went away for good." Tears formed in Sammy's eyes.

"No, dear, he just went to look for Benjy." Sylvia grimaced. "I mean, Ben. He'll be back tonight."

Sammy shook his head with solemn despair. "He went away for ever."

Cleo went down on one knee beside him. "How do you know that, Sammy?"

" 'Cause he took everything with him," Sammy sobbed. "I went upstairs to his room, and all his stuff is gone. Even the picture I gave him."

"You must be mistaken, honey." Cleo stood up quickly. "I'm sure his things are all there."

"They're gone," Sammy whispered. "His door was unlocked, and everything's gone."

"I'll go check," Cleo said.

She dashed up the three flights of stairs to the third floor and paused to catch her breath before she went down the hall to the attic stairs.

Sammy had to be wrong. Max was coming back. He'd said so.

Or had he? Cleo tried to recall his exact words. But the more she thought about it, the more she realized that although Max had implied he would return that evening, he hadn't actually promised to do so.

Cleo opened the narrow door at the end of the hall and took the attic stairs two at a time.

The door to Max's room was unlocked, just as Sammy had said.

Cleo opened it cautiously, aware of a cold feeling in the pit of her stomach.

The room was as neat and orderly as it had been the day Max had moved in. Cleo went through it methodically. Not a single one of Max's expensive white shirts hung in the closet. The dresser was empty. The black leather carryall was gone. So was Sammy's picture, and the copy of *The Mirror* that Cleo had given to Max.

It was as if Max had never been there.

Cleo sank slowly down onto the bed and clasped her hands very tightly in her lap. She remembered the question Max had asked her last night after he had seduced her.

Speaking of paintings, you really don't know where my Luttrells are, do you?

8

He would remember her joyous laughter for the rest of his life. Max could still see Cleo clearly in his mind, shimmering first with passion and then with delight. And he had been the one responsible for giving her both.

Max savored the unfamiliar pleasure that coursed through him. Even the pouring rain that partially obscured the highway and the knowledge of what lay ahead could not dim the warmth that welled up inside. He was not accustomed to being viewed as a man who could make someone else happy. He certainly had never seen himself in such a light.

But last night he, Max Fortune, had made Cleo Robbins happy.

She said she had waited all her life for the right man, *for him,* and she claimed she had not been disappointed. Last night, for the first time in his entire life, he, Max Fortune, had been someone's Mr. Right.

And this morning the bizarre little circle of friends that orbited around Cleo had treated him like an important member of the family. To them he had been a hero setting forth on a quest. Everyone had fussed over him, fed him homemade buckwheat pancakes, urged him to drive carefully, told him to hurry home, reminded him that dinner would be waiting.

Dinner would be waiting.

Max contemplated that notion for a long time. He could not remember anyone ever holding dinner for him. The closest he ever came to the experience was when he ordered room service at a Curzon hotel. Max decided that room service definitely didn't count.

Too bad he would not be able to enjoy arriving late at Robbins' Nest Inn to find a hot meal and a family waiting this evening. But he had known from the start that his odds of returning to a warm welcome were vanishingly small. After all, everyone would be waiting for a hero, and Max knew he probably would not qualify for the role.

Returning to Cleo and her family as a hero tonight meant returning with Ben Atkins in tow. There was little chance of that.

He had known the quest was doomed from the start. He should have refused it. But somehow, what with everyone from Cleo to Sammy expecting him to do something, he had been unable to say no.

After a long, sleepless night he had made his decision. He would go back to Harmony Cove this evening because he had to face Cleo and the others. He had to see their faces when he acknowledged that he had failed them.

When he saw the disappointment and the rejection in Cleo's eyes and in the eyes of her friends, he would leave. He had learned a long time ago that people only wanted him around as long as he was useful.

He wouldn't even have to waste time packing, he thought as he glanced at a road sign. Knowing what lay ahead, he had risen at dawn this morning, folded his belongings into the carryall, and stowed the bag in the Jaguar's trunk. Being packed and ready to leave was an old habit. He had picked it up at the age of six, and he had never really lost it.

It was easier, somehow, to have one foot already out the door when someone was about to tell you that you would have to leave, anyway.

Max slowed for the exit ramp marked Garnly. According to O'Reilly there were only three gas stations in Garnly. Ben Atkins was reportedly working at one of them.

Max cruised slowly through the drab little town. The rain was still falling steadily, a wet, gray veil that managed to conceal some of Garnly's less attractive aspects. He glanced down at the address he had written on a sheet of paper.

It was the second gas station on the left.

Max eased the Jaguar into the small parking area and switched off the engine. He sat quietly for a moment, staring through the rain at the figure working in the service bay.

The young man moved with a quiet certainty, as if he had been working on cars all his life. He appeared tall and thin in the stained gray coveralls. His lanky blond hair needed a trim. He seemed huddled in on himself, a man who communicated better with mechanical things than he did with human beings.

Max opened the door and got out of the Jaguar. He walked through the rain to the shelter of the service bay and waited until the mechanic noticed him.

"Be with you in a minute." The mechanic hunched over an alternator.

"I'm looking for a man named Ben Atkins," Max said.

"Huh?" The mechanic looked up with a wary expression. His face was like the rest of him, thin and closed in on itself.

"Ben Atkins," Max repeated.

The mechanic frowned in confusion. "I'm Benjy. Benjy Atkins."

"Guess I made a mistake," Max said. He turned to walk back to the Jaguar.

"Wait." Metal clattered on metal as Ben tossed aside his tools. "I told you, I'm Benjy

Atkins. What's this all about? Who are you?"

Max halted and turned around again. "Like I said, I'm looking for a man named Ben Atkins."

Ben stared at him as he wiped his hands on a dirty rag. "That's me. I mean, I'm Ben Atkins. But everyone calls me Benjy."

"Not any more," Max said. "I hear you're going to be a father. In my book that makes you Ben, not Benjy."

Ben looked stunned. "You know Trisha?"

"Yes."

"Is she okay?"

"No. She's scared to death."

Ben's face tightened into a sullen mask. "Who are you, mister?"

"My name is Max Fortune."

"Yeah, but who are you? How do you know about me? And about the baby."

"Let's just say I'm a friend of the family."

"I ain't got a family."

"That's not the way I heard it." Max glanced at his watch. "It's almost noon. You plan on eating lunch?"

Ben blinked. "Well, yeah. Sure."

"You're in luck. I'm buying."

"He'll be back," Cleo said with a stubborn confidence that she was not really feeling.

"If he planned on returning," Sylvia said

patiently, "why did he pack his things?"

"I don't know." Cleo propped her silver sneakers on top of her desk and glowered down into the dregs of her coffee. "I think he's used to being packed and ready to go. I have a feeling it's second nature for him. An instinct or something."

"Instinct?" Sylvia asked dryly.

"You saw how easy it was for him to move in here when he arrived. Max obviously travels light."

Sylvia wrinkled her nose. "You think he just sort of instinctively put his bag in the trunk of his car this morning?"

"Yes."

"Before anyone else was up and about?"

"Yes."

Sylvia lounged on the edge of the desk and sipped her own coffee. "Cleo, my friend, you might as well face facts. He's gone."

Cleo closed her eyes. "God, I hope not."

Sylvia was silent for about three full seconds, during which she examined Cleo's face intently. "Damn," she finally whispered.

Cleo opened her eyes. "What's wrong?"

"You and Max." Sylvia waved her hand meaningfully. "The two of you."

"What about us?"

Sylvia groaned. "You fell for him, didn't you? I knew something was happening. I could feel it. We all felt it. Thank goodness he wasn't around long enough to seduce you."

Cleo said nothing.

Sylvia cleared her throat. "I said, thank goodness he wasn't around long enough to seduce you."

Cleo swallowed the last of her coffee.

"That bastard," Sylvia muttered into the stark silence.

Cleo put her cup down on the desk. "He's not a bastard."

"Yes, he is. This makes me so mad. I liked Max. Sammy liked him. Andromeda liked him. Trisha liked him. Even Daystar liked him. Why did he have to be such a bastard?"

"He'll be back," Cleo said evenly. But deep inside she could feel the cold wind that was chilling her bones.

Sylvia was right. Facts were facts. Max had come to the inn in search of his precious inheritance from Jason. Last night he had at last appeared convinced that Cleo didn't know what had happened to the Luttrell paintings. This morning Max was gone. The conclusion was obvious.

But she could not quite bring herself to accept the obvious.

"Poor Trisha," Sylvia said wearily. "I think she was really beginning to hope that Max meant it when he said he would find Benjy."

"He did mean it," Cleo insisted. The man who had made love to her last night was not a liar.

The inn door swung open, interrupting Sylvia's next disgusted comment. Cleo glanced through the office window and saw a tall, blond, elegantly slim woman stride into the lobby. The woman moved with the singular air of confidence and muted disdain that indicated the sort of wealth and social standing that reached back more than one or two generations.

"Uh-oh," Cleo said. "Something tells me that, yes, indeed, once again our humble little inn has been mistaken for a five-star hotel in the south of France."

Sylvia grinned reluctantly. "Boy, is she in for a disappointment. She looks like she just stepped out of *Vogue*, doesn't she? That little silk suit must have cost a bundle. I'll handle her, if you like."

"No, that's all right." Cleo swung her silver shoes down onto the floor and rose from the chair. "I need something to take my mind off Max."

She put on her most polished innkeeper's smile and went out to the front desk. "May I help you?"

The woman raked Cleo with an assessing glance. She did not appear to be impressed

232

with what she saw. "I'm looking for Max Fortune."

Cleo sucked in a small, startled breath. "You and everyone else." So much for distracting herself with non-Max thoughts. "I'm afraid he's not here at the moment. We're expecting him this evening."

"I'll wait."

"*Late* this evening," Cleo said carefully. *Like maybe never,* she added silently.

"In that case," the woman said, obviously annoyed, "perhaps you'd better give me a room for the night. I don't intend to sit out here in your quaint little lobby for the next few hours."

"Certainly." Cleo whipped out a registration card. "If you would just fill this out for me, I'll get you checked in immediately. Will you be using a credit card?"

Without a word the woman reached into a discreetly expensive black leather bag and produced a credit card that looked as if it had been stamped out of solid gold. She handed it to Cleo.

Cleo glanced at the card. *Kimberly Curzon-Winston.* She took another look at the middle name. "Curzon?"

"Yes." Kimberly scrawled her name on the registration form.

Cleo swallowed. "Any relation to Jason Curzon?"

Kimberly frowned. "His niece. You knew my uncle?"

"Sort of." Cleo smiled wryly. "But not as well as I thought, apparently. He seems to have had a much more interesting family background than we realized."

"I can't imagine how you came to know Jason Curzon, but I suppose it doesn't really matter." Kimberly put down the pen. "You said Max Fortune would be returning late this evening?"

"As far as we know." Cleo crossed her fingers behind her back and smiled bravely. He would return, she told herself. He had to return.

"Would you mind telling me where he is at the moment?" Kimberly's patience was obviously wearing thin.

Cleo glanced at the tall clock. "Right at this moment he's probably in a little town called Garnly."

Kimberly looked startled. "Why on earth did he go there?"

"A family matter," Cleo said smoothly.

"That's nonsense." Kimberly's eyes were cold. "I've known Max for several years. He doesn't have any family."

"He does now," Cleo said, "although I'm not sure he realizes it. Look, Ms. Winston . . ."

"Curzon-Winston."

"Ms. Curzon-Winston," Cleo repeated obediently, "perhaps I can help you."

"I doubt it."

"The thing is," Cleo said politely, "Max works for me. If something is wrong, I should know about it."

"What did you say?"

"I said, Max works for me."

A strange expression appeared in Kimberly's blue eyes. "We are talking about the same Max Fortune, aren't we? Tall. Black hair. Rather fierce-looking. Uses a cane?"

"That's our Max," Cleo agreed.

"Then he couldn't possibly work for you. He's a vice president with Curzon International." Kimberly's smile was glacial. "Max Fortune works for me."

"I didn't know what to do." Ben gazed despondently down at his half-finished burger. "It really took me by surprise, you know? I screwed up one time, and Trisha got pregnant."

"It happens," Max said. "Only takes once."

"Shit, you ever had a woman tell you that she's pregnant and you're the father?"

"No." Max reflected briefly again on how he would feel if Cleo told him she was pregnant with his baby. But that would never happen. He had been careful last night. He was

235

always careful about such matters. After all, he had a reputation for not screwing up. "I can see that it would be something of a shock."

"You can say that again. I told Trisha I needed a little time to think things through." Ben ran his fingers through his hair. "I got to figure out what to do, you know?"

"Yes."

Ben raised haunted eyes and gazed helplessly at Max. "I don't remember anything about my own dad. He left when I was a baby. How am I supposed to know what to do with a kid? I don't know anything about being a father."

"You remember Jason Curzon?"

Ben frowned. "Sure. He was a neat old guy. Helped me out with the plumbing at the inn. I liked Jason."

"So did I," Max said quietly. "Jason used to say that a man learns most things by doing them. When it comes to figuring out how to be a father, men like you and me have to depend upon on-the-job training."

Ben's expression was bleak. "I already made enough mistakes in my life."

"You know how to hold down a job, don't you? Everyone at the inn says you're a hard worker."

"Well, sure. Work's one thing. Raisin' a kid is another."

"The way I look at it," Max said, "a lot of the same rules apply."

Ben stared at him. "You think so?"

"Yes." Max looked out the window and wondered when the rain would stop. "Look, the most important thing about holding down a job is to show up for work on a regular basis. Seems to me the same thing applies to being a father. You get points for just being around."

"Yeah?" Ben slitted his eyes. "What do you know about being a father?"

"Not much," Max admitted.

"So maybe you shouldn't be giving me advice," Ben said belligerently.

"Maybe not."

A long silence descended on the booth.

Ben scowled. "Is that all you got to say?"

"No," Max said. "There was one other thing I wanted to discuss."

"What's that?"

"I was wondering if you could give me a couple of hints on how to handle the leaking pipe in room two-fifteen. I've tried everything I can think of, and the sucker just keeps on dripping on the floor of the sink cabinet. It's getting worse."

Ben blinked in obvious alarm. "Those pipes under the sink in two-fifteen are just about rusted out. You got to treat 'em with kid gloves. One wrong move, and the whole dang thing is gonna go."

"Ms. Robbins?" The urbane man on the other side of the front desk smiled aloofly. His hair was a distinguished silver-gray, and his gray suit was the last word in sophisticated tailoring. His eyes were ice cold.

Cleo eyed him warily. "I'm Cleo Robbins. Can I help you?"

"I sincerely hope so," the man said in a smooth tone that held just the barest hint of condescending amusement. "Allow me to introduce myself. My name is Garrison Spark."

"I was afraid of that." Cleo took the card that Spark handed to her. It felt heavy and rich and ever so tasteful in her hand.

"I would like to talk to you about five very valuable pictures."

"Sorry." Cleo tossed the card into the wastebasket. "Can't help you. For the last time, I know nothing about the Luttrells."

Spark smiled coolly. "I sincerely doubt that you know much about Max Fortune, either. If you did, you would be extremely cautious. The man is dangerous, Ms. Robbins."

"Look, Mr. Spark, I'm getting a little bored with this hunt-the-missing-picture game. Jason Curzon did not leave those paintings here at the inn. Believe me, if he had, I would have run across them by now."

Spark looked even more amused. "The question in my mind is not whether Curzon left those paintings here, but rather how much do you want for them?"

"What?" Cleo stared at him in amazement. "I just told you that I don't know where they are. And if I did know, I would give them to Max before I gave them to you. He's got first dibs."

"I see the clever Mr. Fortune has charmed his way into your good graces." Spark shook his head ruefully. "Either that or he has played on your sympathies with a hard-luck story. I fear I must tell you quite frankly that giving the pictures to Max Fortune would be an extremely foolish thing to do."

"Why?" Cleo shot back.

"Because he has no legal or moral claim to them. He's after them simply because they are brilliant works that he wishes to add to his collection. I should warn you, Ms. Robbins, that Fortune will stop at nothing when it comes to obtaining a painting he desires for his private collection. He can be quite ruthless."

"What about you, Mr. Spark? How far will you go?"

Spark's eyes mirrored reluctant respect. "I can be just as tenacious as Fortune, my dear, but I tend to take a rather different approach."

"What approach?"

"I shall be quite happy to pay you a fair price for the Luttrells."

"Really?" Cleo eyed him skeptically. "Max says they're worth a quarter of a million."

Spark chuckled indulgently. "Fortune always did have a flair for exaggeration. Fifty thousand is a much more realistic estimate. Although I'll grant you that in five years the figure could be much higher. However, five years is a long time to wait, isn't it? I am prepared to give you twenty-five thousand for those paintings today."

"Forget it."

"You're a hard bargainer, Ms. Robbins. Very well, make it thirty."

"Don't you ever give up?"

"No," Spark said. "I don't. And neither does Max Fortune. How much has he offered?"

"He hasn't offered a cent," Cleo said honestly.

"He will," Spark said. "Unless, of course, he can talk you out of them for nothing. He's not above trying that tactic. Presumably you will not allow him to do so, however. Call me when he makes his final offer. I will top it."

"There will be no final offer, Mr. Spark,

because there are no Luttrells laying around Robbins' Nest Inn. In case you hadn't noticed, I prefer a different sort of art."

Spark glanced disparagingly at Jason's seascapes. "So I see."

"It's all in the eye of the beholder, isn't it, Mr. Spark?"

Spark turned back to Cleo. "Ms. Robbins, if you are by any chance holding out because you believe that you can sell the paintings yourself on the open market, allow me to disabuse you of that notion. It takes contacts to sell that kind of art. I have those contacts. You do not. Please keep that in mind when you make your decision."

Spark turned on his heel and walked out.

The lights of Robbins' Nest Inn glowed with welcoming warmth through the sleeting rain. Max studied them as they drew closer. He was aware of a strange sense of unreality. If he used his imagination, he could almost make believe he really was returning home after a long, exhausting, but successful journey. Home to a hot meal, a loving family, and a woman who would fly straight into his arms the instant she realized he had arrived.

But that kind of unrealistic imagination was not his strongest suit. He was far better at envisioning the logical, pragmatic consequences of failure. And there was no getting around the fact that he was returning as a failure. Ben was not with him, and there was no guarantee that he would return on his own in the near future.

Max slowed the Jaguar as he turned into the inn's parking lot. He was not eager for what awaited him. But at least he was packed and ready to leave, as always. The difference this time was that he would be leaving something important behind him.

The inn's lot was nearly full. Max glanced curiously at the vehicles that filled it. This was Thursday. By rights it should have been a slow night, but there was a surprising flurry of activity going on in the pouring rain. Men hurried back and forth between the parked cars and the lobby entrance, transporting bags and suitcases.

Max finally found room for the Jag behind the kitchen. He parked, got out, and made his way toward the back door with a sense of bleak inevitability.

The fragrant aroma of fresh bread and a curry-spiced stew enveloped him as he opened the kitchen door. Max allowed himself a moment to savor the warmth. Almost like coming home.

Andromeda, intent on a pan full of steaming vegetables, looked up as the back door opened.

A welcoming smile lit her eyes.

"Max, you're home. Thank goodness. We're in a real panic here. A bunch of men who are supposed to be engaging in something called a Warriors' Journey on the beach got rained out. They all showed up here about an hour ago."

"Hi, Max." Daystar brushed flour from her fingers. "How was the drive?"

Trisha walked into the kitchen through the swinging door that opened onto the dining room. Max steeled himself against the hope in her eyes. Better to get this over with quickly, he decided.

"I'm sorry, Trisha," he said into the thick silence that had suddenly descended on the kitchen. "Ben's not with me."

Trisha's eyes glistened with tears. She nodded, as if she had already guessed the truth. "You saw him? He's okay?"

"Yes. He's fine." Max sought for something more to say. "He was worried about you."

"But not worried enough to come home."

"Cleo's right." Max gripped the handle of his cane. "He's scared."

Trisha's smile was watery but real. "He's not the only one, but I'm luckier than he is. At least I've got family around me. He's all alone out there."

"Yes." Max waited for her to blame him for his failure.

"Thanks for driving all that way to talk to him." Trisha crossed the room and put her arms briefly around Max. "If anyone could have talked him into coming home, it was you." She hugged him quickly and stepped back. "You're a good friend, Max."

He searched her eyes and found no sign of rejection. "I don't know what Ben's going to do," he warned, just in case Trisha had not fully understood that he had screwed up.

"Well, it's up to Ben, isn't it?" Andromeda said calmly. "You spoke to him and let him know that his family wants him to come back. Now we'll just have to wait and see what he decides to do. In the meantime, we've got an inn to run."

"Max needs a cup of tea to warm him up before he leaps into the fray," Daystar declared. "He must be chilled to the bone after that drive."

"I'll get you a cup, Max," Trisha said. "Sit down."

Max glanced back toward the door. The Jaguar with his packed carryall in the trunk was waiting outside.

Sylvia pushed open the kitchen door. "Everything okay in here? Looks like we're going to need dinner for twenty tonight. Mr. Quinton, the chief honcho of this bunch, said all his guys want red meat, can you believe it? I told him we don't serve red meat." She stopped short when she saw Max. Her slow smile was filled with satisfaction. "Well, I'll be darned. You did come back. How was the drive?"

"Wet. What made you think I wasn't coming back?" Max asked.

"Sammy came rushing downstairs right after you left this morning and informed us that all your things were gone," Sylvia said dryly. "Some of us naturally assumed that you had no intention of returning."

"I'm here." Max started toward the kitchen nook where Trisha had set a cup of tea for him. "But I didn't bring Ben with me."

Sylvia sighed. "Can't say I'm surprised. But it was worth a shot. Thanks, Max. You went above and beyond the call of duty on this one. I'll bet you could use a shot of whiskey rather than a cup of tea. George keeps a bottle behind the front desk."

Max looked at Trisha. "Tea will do fine."

The kitchen door banged open again, and Sammy dashed into the room. He skidded to a halt, his eyes widening when he saw Max. "Hi, Max." He dashed forward and seized Max's leg in a quick hug. "I was afraid you wouldn't come back."

Cleo appeared in the open doorway. "What's going on? I could use a little help with this crowd of manly males out here. They're milling around like so many bulls in a china shop. I think one of them is toting a spear —" She broke off when she saw Max. Her eyes glowed with sudden joy. "*Max.* You're home."

He stopped beside the nook and folded both hands over the hawk on his cane. "Hello, Cleo. I couldn't talk Ben into returning with me."

"Oh, Max." Cleo flew across the room toward him. "I was so afraid you weren't coming back."

At the last instant Max realized she intended to throw herself into his arms. He hastily put the cane aside and braced himself.

Cleo landed squarely against his chest. His arms closed around her as she burrowed against him. She was warm and soft, and the scent of her filled his head. Memories of the previous night flared in his mind, sending waves of heat through his body.

"Let's save the mush for later," Sylvia said, sounding amused. "We've got twenty hungry warriors to feed and shelter."

"Right." Cleo raised her head. The laughter faded from her eyes. "Good heavens, I almost forgot. There's someone here to see you, Max."

He released her reluctantly, still struggling to shift gears in his mind. He had spent the past few hours convinced that he would not be staying at the inn any longer than it took to announce his failure. Now he was having to adjust to the notion that no one was blaming him or rejecting him for the fact that Ben had not returned.

Max frowned at Cleo. "Who wants to see me?"

"Kimberly Curzon-Winston. She says Jason was her uncle."

"Damn."

"That's not all she says." Cleo pushed her glasses more firmly into place on her nose and eyed Max with speculation. "She says you work for her. I told her she was wrong."

The possessiveness in Cleo's voice made Max smile. "Did you?"

"Yes. I told her you work for me. What's going on here, Max?"

Max picked up the teacup and swallowed the contents. "Just what you said. I work for you."

"But you used to work for Ms. Curzon-Winston?"

"No," Max said flatly. "I told you, I worked for Jason. When he died, I resigned my position with Curzon International."

"I see." Cleo's eyes gleamed behind the

247

lenses of her glasses. "Well, then, that settles it, doesn't it? Who gets to tell Ms. Curzon-Winston that you are no longer her employee?"

"I'll tell her."

"Good idea. Oh, by the way, your old pal Garrison Spark showed up today, too. Never a dull moment around here."

Max went still. "What did Spark want?"

"What do you think he wanted?" Cleo raised her brows. "He offered me a measly thirty grand for the Luttrells. I told him the same thing I told you. I don't have the stupid paintings, and if I did have them, I'd give them to you."

Max stared at her. He couldn't think of anything to say. The sound of raised masculine voices from the lobby caught his attention. He picked up his cane. "I think we'd better get your unexpected arrivals settled."

"Right. I just hope they don't start shooting arrows or tossing their spears around. This is a respectable establishment." Cleo whirled and rushed to the door. "Sylvia, give me a hand with the front desk. Trisha, call George and tell him we need him to come in early tonight. Then give Andromeda a hand here in the kitchen. Max, there's a leaking shower head in one-ten. Can you take a look at it?"

"Yes," Max said.

"I'll call George," Trisha said. She gave Max a quick, misty smile. "Thanks again, Max."

It was the first time in his life that anyone had thanked him for just trying, Max reflected. He nodded at Trisha, unable to think of anything to say.

He left the kitchen wondering what kind of tools one needed to fix a leaking shower head.

"What in hell is going on around here, Max?" Kimberly paced the shadowed solarium, the only place in the inn that wasn't overrun by warriors.

Max stretched out his legs and absently rubbed his thigh. Kimberly was as stunningly beautiful as ever, he thought, but he experienced absolutely no reaction to her now. Whatever he had once felt for her had died three years ago.

"What does it look like?" Max said quietly. "I've found a new job."

She shot him a disgusted look. "Come off it, Max. You and I have known each other too long to play games. Why did you leave Curzon?"

"Let's just say that I felt like a change."

"If you wanted more money, all you had to do was ask. For God's sake, you know that." The heels of Kimberly's gray suede pumps clicked loudly on the tiles, betraying the tension that was evident in every line of her body. "If this is some kind of ploy to get the seat on the board that Uncle Jason promised you, I assure you, you didn't need to stage this dramatic little scene."

Max arched a brow. "Come off it, Kim. We both know your father would never allow anyone but a member of the family to sit on the board."

Kimberly flushed. "I know my father has a thing about that, but I might be able to talk him into reconsidering his decision. He wants you back at Curzon. He'll do just about anything to get you back, Max."

"Forget it. Things have changed. I don't give a damn about the seat on the board. Not any longer." Max listened to his own words with silent amazement. At one time he would have seized the offer with both hands. A seat on the board would have meant that the Curzons as a group had really accepted him. It would have been the next best thing to belonging to the family.

"What are you trying to do?" Kimberly asked tightly. "Why the shock tactics? What's your agenda? Just tell me, Max. We can come to terms."

"I don't have an agenda. At least not one

that concerns Curzon."

She shot him a quick, suspicious glance. "Don't tell me you've decided to go with Global Village Properties? If that's the case, I can guarantee you we'll match whatever offer they make. You know as well as I do that Curzon can't afford to have you go work for our chief competitor. You know too much."

"I'm not going with Global Village."

"What is it then? You can't be serious about working for that odd little innkeeper in the tacky running shoes."

Max smiled slightly. "Why not? The pay's good."

"Don't be ridiculous. She can't possibly pay you anything close to what you were earning at Curzon." Kimberly swept out a hand to indicate all of Robbins' Nest Inn. "We both know you could buy this place with less than one year's salary. Not to mention bonuses. How much is she paying you?"

"Minimum wage."

Kimberly stared at him. "I don't believe you."

"It's not such a bad deal. I've got my own room in the attic and three hot meals a day. I also get to keep all the tips I make in the lounge. Some guy left me a ten-dollar bill last weekend."

"You sleep in the attic? You're working for

tips? This is insane. Why are you doing this to me?" Kimberly came to a halt in front of him. "You know Curzon needs you. I need you."

Max rested his head against the back of the wicker chair. "You don't need me, Kim. Neither does the company. In a few months you'll realize that you and your family can get along just fine without me."

"We've all depended on you for years. You know that, Max."

"Dennison is probably a little nervous at the moment. After all, this is a transitional period. But he's got you." Max narrowed his eyes faintly. "You've got what it takes to handle the company, Kim."

"You know my father would never turn Curzon over to me," Kimberly said bitterly. "I'm not the son he always wanted, and I never will be."

Max said nothing. There was nothing to say. Kimberly was right. Her father, Dennison Curzon, intended to take the reins of Curzon International and prove that he had the same talent his brother had had. It was unfortunate for all concerned that he was not the brilliant corporate strategist that Jason had been.

The only one in the family who could lead Curzon International into the future was Kimberly, and they all knew that her father was highly unlikely to entrust her with the task. Dennison believed the job required a man.

It was probably going to turn into an unholy mess, but Max figured that was the Curzons' problem now.

Kimberly watched Max for a moment. Then she turned away and walked to the fountain. She stood looking down at the bubbling water, her head bowed. "I think I should tell you something, Max."

"What?"

"Roarke and I are having problems. I'm thinking of leaving him."

Max eyed her classic profile. "Why?"

"Does it matter?"

Max shrugged. "No."

Kimberly touched the blue tiles that formed the highest pool on the fountain. "I made a mistake three years ago, Max. I allowed my father to talk me out of marrying you."

"He didn't have to talk very hard. You started having doubts right after I put the engagement ring on your finger."

"I was a fool."

"Let's not get melodramatic about this. I'm in no mood for it." Max reached for his cane. "It's been a long day, and I'm tired."

Something bright gleamed in the open doorway on the other side of the room. Max turned his head and saw Cleo standing in the shadows. The light from the hall reflected off her metallic sneakers. He could not see the expression on her face.

"Max?" She took a step into the room. "I've been looking for you. I think we'd better close down the lounge. This is a rather strange crowd. All those men who arrived earlier are sitting around telling each other about their divorces. Some of them are starting to cry. It's very depressing for the other guests."

"I'll take care of it." Max rose from the chair, grateful for the interruption.

Kimberly looked at him in open astonishment. Then she swung around to confront Cleo. "I don't believe this. Will somebody please tell me what's going on?"

"I need Max," Cleo said quietly.

"Do you really?" Kimberly gave her a scathing look as she started toward the door. "The real question here is why does Max need you? A word of warning, Ms. Robbins. Max Fortune is not playing bellhop and bartender without a damn good reason."

"Is that so?" Cleo angled her chin. "And what would you know about his reasons for doing anything?"

"A great deal." Kimberly made to brush past her. "Max and I go back a long way together. Or hasn't he told you about us?"

"What's there to tell?" Cleo challenged.

Max swore softly.

Kimberly smiled coldly. "I think I'll let Max give you the details, Ms. Robbins. You might start by asking him how he got that limp."

9

Half an hour later, with all the inn's guests safely tucked in their rooms and George in command at the front desk, Max went up the stairs with Cleo. He was aware that some part of him was still waiting for the other shoe to drop.

"Sheesh." Cleo pushed hair out of her eyes. "No offense to the male of the species, but I'll be glad when Mr. Tobias Quinton's gang of manly warriors checks out. It's unnerving having a bunch of men around who are trying to get in touch with their emotions."

"We can kick them out tomorrow morning," Max suggested. "Tell them you have another group checking in or something."

"Yeah, but I don't have another group checking in," Cleo said glumly. "In fact, we're going to be fairly empty this weekend. There's no getting around the fact that Mr. Quinton and his crowd are paying customers. I suppose we can put up with them for a while."

"Spoken like a dedicated innkeeper," Max said as they reached the third floor.

He hesitated, waiting to see if she would invite him down the hall to her room or put her hand in his and let him lead her up to the attic. She did neither.

"Well, good night, Max." Cleo gave him a bright little smile, but her eyes were wary. "You must be exhausted after that long drive. I'll see you in the morning."

She stood on tiptoe and brushed her mouth against his cheek. Then she turned and went down the hall alone to her tower room.

Max did not move for a long while. He just stood there, staring after her until she disappeared. A dark, seething desire twisted his insides, but that was not the worst part. The worst part was that he did not know what Cleo was thinking.

She had not said a word to him about Kimberly since the confrontation in the solarium. He could not tell if she was angry or hurt or simply cautious. He knew she had questions. He could feel them simmering inside her.

In the meantime he had a big question of his own, and there was only one way to get it answered. Max tightened his grip on his cane and went down the hall to Cleo's room.

He came to a halt in front of her door and lifted his hand to knock. He paused, gathering his courage. Asking his question of Cleo was going to be just as hard as returning to the inn without Ben Atkins in tow. Perhaps harder. Max knocked twice on the door and waited.

It seemed to take forever before Cleo slowly opened the door and peered out through the crack. The hall light glinted on the lenses of her glasses, concealing the expression in her eyes.

"Is something wrong?" she asked politely.

"I would like to clarify the sleeping arrangements," Max said with great care.

Her brows snapped together in a frown of concern. "Is there a problem with one of the room assignments?"

"Yes," Max said evenly. "Mine."

Cleo's fingers clenched abruptly around the edge of the door. She looked as if she needed to hold on to it in order to keep from collapsing. "Yours?"

"I was just wondering where I'm supposed to sleep tonight."

Cleo stared at him. "Where do you want to sleep tonight?"

"Here." Max wedged the toe of his shoe into the narrow opening between the door and

257

its frame. "With you."

"Oh."

He braced his hand against the door frame. "Is that all you can say?"

Cleo flushed a vivid shade of pink. "I wasn't sure what you wanted to do. I mean, I didn't know how you were feeling about the situation. I thought you might need a little time to get in touch with your emotions."

"You're starting to sound like Tobias Quinton."

Cleo smiled weakly. "I am, aren't I? Well? Are you in touch with your feelings?"

"I know what I want." Max flattened one hand against the door and pushed gently inward. He would not force his way into her bedroom, he told himself. He would just lean a little and see if she leaned back. If she didn't, he would have the answer to his question.

"*Max.*"

The door gave way abruptly as Cleo released her grip on it and stepped aside. Max realized at the last instant that he was leaning a lot more heavily against the door than he had intended. He lost his balance. His bad leg started to give way. He almost fell into the room.

He was saved from sprawling ignominiously on the floor by the counter force exerted when Cleo slammed into his arms. He staggered once and managed to get a firm grip on both

Cleo and his cane. He steadied himself as she hugged him very tightly.

"I didn't know what to think this morning when I realized you had packed all your things," Cleo said into his chest. "And then when that Kimberly Curzon-Winston person showed up and told me that you worked for her, things got more confusing."

"I know. It's all right. I've been just as confused today." Max caught her chin on the edge of his hand, tipped up her face, and kissed her. Hard.

Cleo put her arms around his neck and returned the kiss with sweet fervor. Without lifting his mouth from hers, Max eased her back against the edge of the bed. They collapsed together on top of the old-fashioned quilt.

This was what it meant to come home, Max thought.

An hour later Cleo stirred in the darkness. "Max?"

"Umm?" He barely heard her. He was drifting on the edge of sleep, his body satiated, his mind at ease. Cleo was cradled against him, her lushly curved derriere pressed against his thighs. The peaceful feeling that consumed him was so unique that he wanted to savor it until he fell asleep.

"Were you and Kimberly lovers?"

"Hell." Max was suddenly wide awake. "What did you say?"

"Nothing important." Max opened his eyes, folded one arm behind his head, and contemplated the frilly canopy overhead with a brooding glare.

"So what about you and Kimberly?"

"We were engaged for a while."

"Engaged." Cleo shot straight up into a sitting position. "Are you telling me you almost married her?"

"It was a very short engagement." Max gave her a cautious glance and saw that she was glowering down at him.

"How short?" Cleo demanded.

"Uh, six weeks, I think." Five weeks and four days. Not that he had been counting at the time.

Five weeks and four days of thinking that he had finally muscled his way into the inner circle of the Curzon family. Five weeks and four days of believing he had made a secure, permanent place for himself in Jason's world.

"You think? Can't you remember?"

Max groaned. "It was three years ago, Cleo."

"What happened?"

"Nothing happened. We got disengaged, that's all."

"Did you change your mind?"

Max yawned. "She changed hers," he said before he stopped to think. As soon as the words were out of his mouth, he knew he'd made a grave tactical error. "I mean, it was a mutual decision."

But it was too late. Cleo pounced. "She's the one who called off the engagement? Not you?"

"We decided we weren't meant for each other," Max said.

"Why not?"

"There were a lot of reasons," Max said.

"What reasons?"

Max began to feel hunted. Instinctively he drew a line, just as he always did when someone tried to apply pressure. "Stop pushing, Cleo. My relationship with Kimberly was finished three years ago."

"But you've been working for her all this time?"

"I told you, I worked for Jason, not Kimberly. Now I work for you."

"Hmm." Cleo considered that. "Why did she call off the engagement?"

Max drummed his fingers lightly on the bed. "She decided that we came from two different worlds. She was right."

"Which two different worlds?"

"She came from old money, good schools,

and a long line of socially acceptable ancestors. She was the heiress to Curzon International. I came from nothing. The only money I have is what I earned working for Jason. Her father did not approve of me. Hell, Kimberly didn't approve of me, herself. Not really."

"So she married somebody named Winston?"

"Roarke Winston."

"Let me guess," Cleo said. "Old money, good schools, a long line of socially acceptable ancestors?"

"Right. He's in charge of his family's business empire."

"What did Kimberly mean when she said I should ask you about your leg?"

Max gave Cleo another sidelong glance. He had a feeling she was going to prove tenacious. It figured. That quality went right along with the other Girl Scout attributes. "We got engaged shortly after I injured my leg. While I was in the hospital recovering, as a matter of fact. Kimberly was" — he searched for the correct word — "somewhat emotional at the time."

"She was worried about you?"

"I think she was feeling a little guilty."

Cleo frowned. "Why? Did she have something to do with your accident?"

"In a way. She had insisted on flying down

to a potential hotel site in South America. I was already on the scene and had decided that it wasn't a good location. I advised her not to come, but she wanted to check it out for herself."

"What happened?"

Max shrugged. "I picked her up at the airport. On the way back into town we were stopped by a bunch of guerrillas who had gotten word that a member of the Curzon family was expected. They were planning to kidnap her and use her as a bargaining chip in their ongoing battle with the local government."

"My God." Cleo was shocked. "What did you do?"

Max slanted her a strange glance. "When I worked for Jason I spent a lot of time in places where the potential for that kind of thing existed. I routinely carried a gun. Shots were exchanged when I ran the roadblock. One of the shells came through the door of the car and hit my leg."

"That's how you got hurt?" Cleo's voice rose to a squeak. "Rescuing Kimberly?"

"Yes."

Cleo clutched his arm. "You could have been killed."

"Look, Cleo, this is ancient history, and I don't think there's much point discussing it."

"But you could have been killed," she whispered again. Her nails dug into his arm.

Max heard the old horror buried in her barely controlled voice. He realized she was no longer concerned about his relationship with Kimberly, but was thinking about her parents' death and her own past.

"It's all right, Cleo." He rolled onto his side and pulled her into his arms. "Take it easy. I'm here."

She curled into his warmth and clung to him. "I'm okay."

"Good." He stroked her back soothingly. "It's late. Try to get some sleep."

She relaxed slightly against him. "You said that your engagement only lasted six weeks?"

"Give or take a few days." He strove to sound disinterested. "I've forgotten the exact length of time."

"And now Kimberly's married to someone else."

"Yes."

"She wants you back, Max." Cleo's voice was bleak. "I can tell."

Max smiled into her hair. "Only for business reasons. Her father thinks the company needs me."

"Does it?"

"I don't particularly care if it does or it doesn't. I don't want the job."

"You're sure?"

"I'm sure." He kissed her throat. "I've got another job."

Cleo looked up at him through her lashes. "I'll bet Curzon International pays a heck of a lot better than Robbins' Nest Inn."

"That all depends on how you look at it." Max kissed the sweet, scented curve of her breast and laced his fingers through the soft thatch of hair between her legs. "I'm satisfied with what I'm getting here."

"Are you?" Cleo put her hand on his shoulder. "Max, do you still love her?"

Max was startled by the question. He had never thought about loving Kimberly. He had never thought about loving anyone. "No."

"You're sure?"

"I'm sure."

"You say that awfully easily."

"It's easy to say." Max took one nipple into his mouth. It was as firm and ripe as a raspberry. The taste of it sent a shudder of excitement through him. Sexual tension seized his insides.

"Why is it easy to say? Didn't you love her three years ago?"

"Cleo . . ."

"I just wondered," she said softly. "I know how strong love can be because my parents were deeply in love. It's not the kind of thing a man like you could dismiss easily if he had experienced it."

That stopped him. He raised his head. "A man like me?"

Cleo stroked his cheek with gentle fingertips. "You're like one of those paintings you say you collect. Very deep. Lots of layers. I think that if you ever fell in love you would stay in love for a very long time. Forever, probably."

"I'm not a work of art. Don't romanticize me, Cleo." Max caught her fingers and held them against his chest. "I don't know anything about that kind of love. I don't think it really exists."

"My parents had it." She smiled. "It's the kind of love I want for myself."

Max got a sinking feeling in the pit of his stomach. "You could spend your whole life looking for it and never be satisfied with what you find."

"That's what my therapist said." She stirred against him. "So you really weren't in love with Kimberly?"

"I think it's a safe bet that the kind of feeling Kimberly and I had for each other was nothing like the bond you say your parents had." He slid his leg aggressively between Cleo's warm thighs. He could feel her responding to him, and the knowledge reassured him. Cleo might have an unrealistic view of love, but her body had a very pragmatic reaction to his. He intended to nurture that reaction until it was more important to her than the search for an elusive, mythical grand passion.

"I don't understand." Cleo braced her hands against his shoulders and searched his face. "What sort of feeling did you have for Kimberly?"

Max tried to contain his impatience. He was thoroughly aroused, and Cleo was warm and sultry and ready for him. "Cleo, it's a little hard to explain. Kimberly represented a lot of things I thought I wanted at the time. I guess I thought that if I got her, I'd get those other things, too. I was wrong. She did us both a favor when she broke off the engagement."

"What things did you want?" Cleo whispered.

"It doesn't matter. I don't want them any longer."

"Are you certain of that?"

"Yes," Max said. He moistened the tip of his finger with his tongue and then reached down to touch the taut little bud hidden between her legs.

Cleo flinched in reaction and then lifted herself against his hand with a soft moan. He cupped her gently and eased one finger into her damp heat. She was burning for him. He couldn't wait to lose himself in her again.

"What do you want now?" Cleo asked.

"You."

She sighed in soft surrender and brushed her hands across his shoulder. "I want you, too."

A few minutes later when he buried himself deep inside her, Max realized he had spoken a greater truth than he had realized. He wanted Cleo in a way he had never wanted any other woman in his life. He did not question the need; he simply accepted it.

The distant thuds brought Cleo up out of a dreamless sleep. She lay quietly for a moment, trying to identify the sounds. They stopped after a moment.

She concluded that George, or perhaps one of the guests, had walked down the hall outside her room.

Cleo yawned and tried to turn on her side. She realized she could not move because Max was pinning her legs to the bed. He had one muscled thigh thrown over her calves.

In addition to being trapped, she was much too warm. The heat from Max's body made the quilt superfluous. Sharing a bed with Max was a very strange experience, Cleo thought. It was like sleeping with a blast furnace.

The thuds started up again. They reverberated softly through the walls in a primitive, unrelenting, extremely irritating rhythm.

Thump. Thump. Thump.

Cleo came fully awake in a hurry. She jack-knifed into a sitting position.

"Good lord, Max. Someone's drumming down there."

"What's wrong?" Max asked from the depths of the pillow.

"Don't you hear it? Someone's got a drum downstairs." Cleo pushed aside the quilt and struggled to get herself free of Max. "He'll wake up everyone in the whole inn."

Cleo managed to get out of the bed. She raced to the closet and reached for a pair of jeans and a shirt.

"Hold on, Cleo. I'll go down with you." Max got out of bed, yawning.

The distant murmur of men's voices mingled with the drumming. Cleo listened intently and then yelped in disbelief.

"They've started chanting." She grabbed her glasses and pushed them onto her nose. "It must be some of the men from Mr. Quinton's Warriors' Journey group. That does it, I'm going to throw them all out. I don't care if it is raining cats and dogs."

"If you throw them out, you'll have a hard time collecting for the rooms," Max reminded her as he zipped up his trousers.

"Right now all I care about is getting that damned drumming stopped." Cleo was at the door. "I knew I should never have taken them in tonight. I didn't like the looks of that Tobias Quinton from the start. I'm too darn soft-hearted, that's my problem."

She yanked open the door and raced out into the hall, aware that Max was following more slowly behind her.

The drumming was a lot louder when she reached the second floor, louder still when she got to the first floor. It seemed to be coming from the solarium.

Cleo went to the front desk. George was nowhere in sight. Assuming he had already gone to investigate the drumming, Cleo started to turn toward the solarium. Then she heard the snores emanating from her office.

"George?"

"Your ever vigilant night clerk is sound asleep," Max observed as he came up behind her.

"For heaven's sake." Cleo ducked into the office and saw that George was, indeed, sprawled in her chair, eyes closed, mouth agape. His feet were propped on her desk.

"Forget it," Max advised. "He wouldn't be much help, anyway."

"I suppose you're right." Cleo squared her shoulders and stalked past him. "I'll just have to take care of this myself."

"Cleo, maybe you'd better let me handle this."

"I've been running this inn for three years." Cleo turned the corner and went down the hall to the solarium. The drumming and the chanting got louder.

"You've got me to help out around here now, remember?"

"That doesn't mean I can't deal with a few rude guests." Cleo stopped in front of the French doors that opened into the solarium. The doors were closed, but through the glass panes she could see that the lights were off inside the room. An orange glow from the fireplace told her that Quinton and his crowd had built a fire on the hearth. "Of all the nerve."

"I think you'd better let me go in there first," Max said. He started to step around her, reaching for the doorknob.

"Nonsense." Cleo threw open the doors.

The thunder of a drum and the roar of masculine voices lifted in a primitive chant boomed out of the solarium. In the light of the leaping flames Cleo could just barely make out the shapes of several men seated on the floor. They formed a half circle in front of the fire.

A majestic, white-maned figure sat in their midst. He had the drum in front of him. His arm was raised to strike the next blow.

"That will be quite enough, Mr. Quinton." Cleo swept out her hand and hit all the switches on the wall in one slashing blow. The solarium was abruptly flooded with light.

Twenty stark naked men turned to gaze at her in stony-faced disapproval.

Cleo stared back in stunned amazement. Not one of the men was wearing a single stitch of clothing.

Cleo was speechless. She swung around and found Max standing directly behind her.

"I told you to let me go in first," Max said. His eyes were gleaming with amusement.

Cleo finally found her voice. "Do something."

"You bet, boss." Max moved aside so that she could step past him into the hall. "I think it would probably be best if you went back upstairs. I'll get the warriors back to their tents."

"Yes, leave us, woman," Quinton intoned in a deep, graveled voice. "This is a matter for men."

"She's just like my ex-wife," one of the participants called out. "Diane never let me have any fun, either."

"This is a time for men to come together," Quinton chanted. He thumped the drum. "This is a time of male power and strength.

272

A gathering time for warriors."

Cleo glared at Max. "I don't want them put back in their rooms. I want them out of here, do you understand? Immediately!"

"Think of the income you'd be losing if you throw them out tonight, Cleo."

"I don't care how much profit I lose. I want them off the premises."

"You are welcome to join us," Quinton said to Max. "This is a place and a time for men."

"Thank you," Max said very civilly.

"Max," Cleo hissed, "I swear, if you take off your clothes and start chanting in front of the fire, I am going to throttle you."

Max's mouth curved. "Is that right?"

Quinton rose to his feet. He held the drum discreetly in front of himself. "Don't let her intimidate you," he said to Max. "You are a man. It's time to get in touch with your own maleness. You must reach down inside yourself and discover the strength of the warrior who resides within you."

Cleo swung around once more and confronted her unwanted guest. "I do not want to hear another word out of you, Mr. Quinton. I took you in tonight out of the goodness of my heart when you and your group showed up on my doorstep. You begged me for shelter, and this is the thanks I get."

"We were not begging for shelter," one of

the seated men said in a disgruntled tone. "We could have spent the night on the beach."

"Then why didn't you?" Cleo demanded.

"Because we didn't feel like it," one of the other men declared.

"No kidding? What's the matter?" Cleo asked. "Were all you macho, manly warriors afraid of a little rain?"

Max's hands descended firmly on Cleo's shoulders. "I think this is degenerating into a farce." He turned her around and marched her out of the door. "Take yourself off, boss. I'll handle this."

"You do that. I'll go make sure we've got all their credit card numbers before they leave tonight. We're billing them for a full night's lodging. And breakfast, too, even though they won't be here to eat it."

Max smiled. "Good night, Cleo."

Cleo ground her teeth and started back down the hall. Behind her Quinton began to beat his drum. She could not recall when she had been so incensed. She rounded the corner and stormed into the lobby. She was just in the mood to chew George out for dereliction of duty.

A familiar figure came out of the office. He had a key in his hand.

"Hi, Cleo," Ben said sheepishly. He held up the key. "George was asleep, so I helped myself. I was going to go on upstairs to my room. What are you doing up?"

Cleo instantly forgot about Tobias Quinton and the nude warriors in the solarium. She stared at Ben in delight.

"Benjy — I mean, *Ben* — you're home!"

"Yeah."

"It's so good to see you again." Cleo ran forward and hugged him. "We've been so worried about you."

"Sorry for getting in so late. I just sort of decided to get into my car and start driving." Ben hugged her back a little awkwardly. "I probably should have waited until morning, huh?"

"Absolutely not." Cleo released him and stepped back. "This is your home. You were right to come straight here. Wait until Trisha finds out you're back."

"Yeah." Ben looked down at the key in his hand. "You think she'll be mad at me? I didn't mean to hurt her. I just needed to think things over, you know?"

Cleo smiled. "She's going to be very happy to see you, Ben. She knows that you got scared when she told you about the baby."

Ben flushed. "Yeah. Well, I guess she was probably even more scared. Max said that it was easier to be scared together than alone."

Cleo tilted her head slightly to one side.

"Max said that?"

Ben nodded. "He said Trisha needs me. He said the baby is going to need me, too, even though I don't know nothin' about being a father."

"He's right. Ben, I'm so glad you came home."

"Is that you, Ben?" Max called impatiently from the hallway behind Cleo.

"Yes, sir." Ben's voice held an unmistakable edge of respect. He glanced past Cleo to where Max was standing in the shadows. "I'm back."

"So I see." Max's eyes gleamed with silent approval. "Good timing. I was about to wake George and ask him to give me a hand, but something tells me you'll be more useful than George."

Ben straightened his shoulders. "What do you want me to do?"

"Cover my back while a guy named Tobias Quinton and I play a couple of hands of poker. I don't think there will be any cheating, but you can never tell."

Cleo snapped out of her short-lived good mood. "Poker? What are you talking about?"

"Relax, Cleo." Max smiled blandly. "Quinton and I have reached an agreement. We're going to settle this matter in a manly fashion. If I win, the warriors will go peacefully upstairs to bed."

Cleo was outraged. "What happens if you lose?"

"Then they get to drum and chant until dawn."

Cleo was flabbergasted. "This is insane. You might lose."

"Don't worry." Max winked solemnly. "I won't lose. Trust me."

Cleo wanted to scream. "Who came up with this stupid idea?"

"I did," Max said.

"Oh, my God." Cleo sagged against the front desk. "I don't believe this."

"Relax, Cleo," Max advised. "This is a male thing. I wouldn't expect a woman to understand it."

10

It was pleasant being a family hero, Max reflected the next morning after the breakfast rush. Trisha thought he walked on water because Ben was back. Ben seemed to be in the process of turning him into a role model. Andromeda and the rest of the Cosmic Harmony crowd thought he'd finessed the situation with Quinton's group of rained-out warriors brilliantly. Sammy thought he was great simply because he was back.

The only one who was still grumbling was Cleo.

She stalked into the kitchen shortly after the dining room had been cleared. Most of the staff were drinking coffee or tea and nibbling on the latest version of Daystar's muffins.

Cleo came to a halt in the middle of the floor and stood facing everyone with her hands on her hips. Her expression was a cross between surly and triumphant.

"That's the last of them," she announced. "Tobias Quinton and his bunch are finally gone. As I live and breathe, it is my most profound wish to never see a manly warrior male for the rest of my natural life."

Max met Ben's eyes. Neither said a word. They both turned to look at Cleo.

Max cleared his throat politely. "Just out of curiosity, how do you classify Ben and me? Wimpy weenies?"

Cleo had the decency to blush. "Don't be ridiculous. You know what I mean."

"Does this mean I'm not getting a drum for Christmas?" Max asked.

Sylvia, Andromeda, and the others burst into laughter. Cleo endured the reaction stoically. She went over to the counter to pour herself a cup of tea.

"Go ahead, laugh," she muttered. "But I'm here to tell you that it's just the sheerest good luck that Max and Ben were able to get those characters off to bed last night. What if Max had lost that stupid card game?"

"How could I lose at cards with a name like Fortune?" Max asked equably.

Andromeda was immediately intrigued. "Of course, Max. There's probably some harmonic connection between the name you were given at birth and your luck. Do you always win when you play?"

Ben grinned. "I'll bet he always wins when he feels the way he did last night. I watched him. Cleo had nothing to worry about. Tobias Quinton never had a chance."

Cleo gave Max a sharp glance over the rim of her mug. "Did you cheat, Max?"

"There are some things we manly macho men do not discuss in front of females," Max said with lofty disdain. "It's a male thing, you know."

Cleo shuddered. "Speaking of male things, I certainly hope I never see another collection like the ones displayed in the solarium last night."

Everyone fixed Cleo with deeply inquiring looks.

Max recalled the ring of nude men sitting

in front of the fire. He smiled politely at Cleo. "Disappointed, were you?"

Cleo gave him a goaded look. "Let's just say that none of them compared to the strikingly superior specimen I have recently been privileged to view in a private showing."

Max choked on his coffee. "Glad to hear that."

Sammy tugged on Cleo's jeans. "What's a male thing?" he asked with the persistence only a five-year-old can muster.

Cleo glanced down and smiled benignly. "Sometimes, it doesn't amount to much, dear. But occasionally it can be a work of art."

"Oh." Disappointed by the answer, Sammy went over to the counter to help himself to another muffin.

Everyone else started to grin. Cleo turned pink again and helped herself to more tea.

Yes, there was a lot to be said for being a hero, Max thought. But the best part was learning last night that he didn't really have to do anything except come home in order to get the job.

At midmorning Cleo halted in the middle of her walk and watched as Kimberly strode toward her across the rocky beach.

Today Kimberly looked tastefully stylish in expensive penny loafers, heather gray trousers, and a houndstooth jacket. Her blond hair was in an elegant chignon. Cleo was suddenly very aware that her own hair was a windblown tangle.

"Good morning, Ms. Curzon-Winston," Cleo said, determined to be polite. "I thought you'd left."

Kimberly stopped in front of her. Her eyes were cool and watchful. "I wanted to talk to you before I go."

Cleo folded her arms across her chest. "About Max?"

"Yes."

Cleo gave her a quizzical look. "There isn't much to say, is there?"

"I want to know what's going on between you two."

"Why?"

Kimberly's mouth tightened. "Because Max is acting very strangely. Completely out of character, as a matter of fact. He's up to something, and I want to know what it is."

"I really don't think I owe you any explanations," Cleo said as gently as possible. "My relationship with Max is personal."

Kimberly looked briefly amused. "Relationship? With Max Fortune? Trust me, Ms. Robbins, Max doesn't know the meaning of the word *relationship*. He's a robot. A very brilliant, very clever, extremely useful robot, but a robot, nonetheless."

Cleo was stunned. "That's not true."

"I've known him a lot longer than you have, Ms. Robbins. Did he tell you that we were engaged for a time?"

"Yes."

"Did he tell you that he got that limp saving my life?"

Cleo tightened her arms across her chest. "He told me."

Kimberly looked out at the cloudy horizon. "He asked me to marry him while he was lying in a hospital bed. He was well aware that I was feeling guilty. It was my fault he'd been shot, and both of us knew it. He used that knowledge in a very cold-blooded way to push me into an engagement."

"Why would he do that?"

Kimberly shrugged. "Because he wanted me and he wanted Curzon International. I'll admit I was physically attracted to him. I tried to tell myself at first that he loved me, but I knew all along that he was just using me to get what he wanted. When Max wants something, he does whatever it takes to get it."

"I think you're wrong," Cleo said.

"Am I?" Kimberly's mouth twisted. "You haven't seen him in action the way I have. Max has a certain reputation."

"What sort of reputation?"

"Once he's made up his mind that he wants something, he's almost unstoppable. Whenever Uncle Jason needed a business deal pulled out of the fire or had a problem at one of the hotels, he sent Max in to handle it. Max never failed. As far as he was concerned, whatever Uncle Jason wanted, Uncle Jason got."

"Max was very close to your uncle," Cleo said stiffly.

"Max isn't close to anyone. Not in the way you mean." Kimberly smiled bitterly. "He used Uncle Jason, just as he uses everyone else. Max deliberately set out to make himself indispensable to Curzon. As usual, he succeeded."

"If Max is so ruthless, why do you want him back?"

"Curzon International needs him." Kimberly's gaze was grim. "At least my father seems to think it does."

"What do you think?" Cleo asked quietly.

Kimberly looked out over the cold sea. "I think Max would be extremely useful to Curzon, but I also think he would be dangerous. If we pay the price he'll probably demand in exchange for his return, we'll be taking an enormous risk."

Cleo studied her intently. "What do you think Max wants from you?"

"A seat on the Curzon board. Uncle Jason

promised that he'd get it eventually. But Jason died before he could force the rest of us to accept someone on the board who was not a member of the family."

"Max doesn't seem to want to go back," Cleo said cautiously. "He thinks you and your father can run the company without him."

Kimberly gave a short, brittle laugh. "That's not what my father believes. He says we need Max. At least for a couple of years."

Cleo looked down at the toes of her silver sneakers and then raised her eyes to meet Kimberly's. "How do you feel about it?"

Kimberly shot her a swift, unreadable glance. "I think that my father is in charge of Curzon, and if he wants Max back, I'll do my damnedest to get him back. There, Ms. Robbins, I've put my cards on the table. You know exactly where I stand."

"You just want to use Max. You're no different than you say he is."

Kimberly mouthed a disgusted exclamation. "You don't understand, do you? Max relates to people in one of two ways. He either wants something from them, or he uses them to get something else that he wants."

Cleo stared at her. "Did you ever love him, Kimberly?"

Kimberly hesitated. "I will be perfectly blunt. There was no possibility of loving Max.

He and I were attracted to each other from the moment we met. But physical desire is the limit of what Max can feel for a woman."

"Are you sure of that?"

Kimberly smiled coldly. "Very sure. I was surprised to learn that he's involved with you. Max is as discriminating in his taste in women as he is in his taste in art. Quite frankly, you're not his type."

"And you are?"

"Yes." There was no arrogance or challenge in Kimberly's voice. She made the statement with simple certainty. "Uncle Jason turned Max into a very sophisticated connoisseur of art. Max picked up the technique, and he applies it to everything he wants, including women. He has the finely honed instincts of an extremely selective collector."

"If you don't believe that he's genuinely interested in me, what do you think he wants from me?" Cleo asked.

"I don't know yet. But I suppose you'll find out soon enough. We all will."

"What's that supposed to mean?"

Kimberly turned her head, her eyes hard with warning. "Just that Max obviously has his own reasons both for working for you and for seducing you. My advice is that you bear that in mind."

"What do you want me to do?" Cleo smiled

bleakly. "Fire him?"

"That might not be a bad place to start. You're in over your head, Ms. Robbins." Kimberly turned and walked off down the beach.

"The thing about hardware stores," Ben said to Max as they walked into Harmony Cove Hardware the following afternoon, "is that you got to know what you want before you walk through the door."

"Why is that?" Max glanced around curiously. He had never spent much time in hardware stores. Hardware stares were for men who had real homes of their own. Mansions didn't count. You called someone else in to do repairs in a house such as the one he owned in Seattle. He'd rarely had occasion to fix a leaking faucet, paint a bedroom, or put up wallpaper until he'd moved into Robbins' Nest Inn.

"Because if you don't know what you want and stay focused on it, you get sidetracked." Ben paused beside a display of gleaming steel wrenches. He picked one up and fingered it lovingly.

"Do we need a wrench for this job?" Max picked up one of the wrenches and examined it with interest.

"Nope." Ben put the wrench down. "But

you see what I mean? It's easy to get side-tracked. There's so much really great stuff in a hardware store."

"These are nice." Max paused beside a counter full of shiny power drills. He hefted one, testing the weight and feel of it in his hand.

Ben peered at it with admiration. "Real nice. Look at the price on that sucker."

Max glanced at the price tag. "Probably worth every penny."

"Yeah." Ben grinned. "Think I could convince Trisha that I need one to fix up the baby's room?"

"You could try." Max put the drill back down on the counter.

"Something I've been meaning to ask you," Ben said as he examined a neat arrangement of nails.

"What's that?" Max looked at a rack of colorful screwdrivers.

"You planning on sticking around the inn for a while?" Ben concentrated intently on the nails.

"Yes," Max said. "I'm planning on sticking around until someone throws me out."

"Yeah. Well, okay," Ben said. "That's all I wanted to ask. Hey, will you look at those clamps. I've been meaning to get one for my workbench down in the basement."

Max continued to study the screwdrivers. "I could use one of these."

"You never know when you're going to need a screwdriver handy." Ben picked up a clamp. "They're busy planning the wedding, you know. Trisha says that even though we're going to get married right away, the family wants to do it up real formal. Tuxes for the guys and a fancy gown for her."

"I know." Max had heard the discussions in the kitchen that morning.

Cleo, Andromeda, Daystar, and Sylvia intended to pull out all the stops for Ben and Trisha's wedding. It had already been decided that the event would take place in less than two weeks at Cosmic Harmony. Daystar had pointed out in her usual pragmatic fashion that under the circumstances, there was not a lot of time to waste.

"I've never worn a tux," Ben said hesitantly. "Didn't go to a senior prom or anything. I don't even know where to get one."

"Nothing to it," Max assured him. He selected one of the screwdrivers and took it down from the rack.

"You sure?"

"I'm sure," said Max. "Don't worry about it. I'll show you how it's done."

Ben nodded, looking vastly relieved. "Okay." He flashed Max a quick, searching glance. "So what do you think about being my best man or whatever it is they call it?"

Max slowly put down the screwdriver he had been examining. He looked at Ben. "I'd be honored."

Ben turned beet red. "Yeah, well, it probably isn't that big a deal to you. But thanks."

"You're wrong," Max said. "It's a very big deal. I've never been anyone's best man."

Ben smiled, and the two men returned to their shopping.

An hour later Max reluctantly walked out of the hardware store with Ben. He had a shiny new screwdriver in a paper sack.

"We didn't do too bad," Ben said cheerfully as they strolled toward the Jaguar with their purchases. "Been needing that clamp for a long time. And you can't have too many needle-nose pliers lying around. They're always disappearing. Hell of a sale on those toilet float balls. I wonder if we should have picked up more than three."

"Damn," Max said, as he came to a halt beside the Jaguar. "We forgot the washers for the faucet in one-oh-three."

Ben groaned. "I told you that hardware stores were dangerous. You wait here. I'll go back and get them." He tossed the sack to Max and hurried back toward the store.

Max leaned against the Jaguar's fender to

wait. It had finally stopped raining for a while, but a heavy fog was condensing just offshore. It would soon be moving inland. In another hour the roads would be shrouded in a heavy cloak of gray mist. Driving would be hazardous.

Max hoped Ben would not get captivated by a display of power tools. He wanted to be home by the fire when the fog settled in over Harmony Cove this evening.

Home by the fire. Hell, he was turning into a regular home-and-hearth kind of guy. What have you done to me, Jason? Max asked silently. Did you know what would happen when you sent me out here in search of those Luttrells?

Two men got out of a nondescript Ford that was parked across the street. One was slightly taller than the other. He was also a few years older, with thinning hair and a slight paunch. The younger one wore GQ glasses and had a mouthful of very white teeth that had clearly been labored over by an orthodontist. Both men were out of place in casual Harmony Cove. Their business suits, expensive ties, and highly polished wing tips identified them as outsiders as clearly as the fact that they were coming straight toward Max.

"Max Fortune?" The older man stuck out his hand. "Phillip Sand. This is my associate,

Hamilton Turner. We represent some people who would very much like to get you on our team."

"Global Village Properties," Max said.

Turner smiled, displaying his beautiful teeth. "How did you guess?"

"I wondered when you'd get around to talking to me." Max glanced toward the entrance of Harmony Cove Hardware. There was no sign of Ben.

"Why don't we have a cup of coffee while you wait for your friend?" Sand suggested smoothly.

Max shrugged. "Why not?"

Cleo sat quietly, her legs folded tailor-fashion, her hands resting on her knees. She gazed into the large yellow crystal, willing her mind to focus. She was the only one in the meditation room at Cosmic Harmony this afternoon.

She was not sure why she had felt the need to seek out the refuge again today. There had been no nightmares recently. But around three o'clock, she had realized that she was feeling unsettled and restless.

The sensation had not disappeared after she had fixed herself a cup of Andromeda's tea, so Cleo had gotten into her Toyota and driven the mile and a half around the cove to the

Cosmic Harmony Retreat.

Now, gazing calmly into the crystal, Cleo acknowledged to herself what she had not wanted to confront earlier. The truth was that the conversation with Kimberly had bothered her more than she had been willing to admit.

He has the finely honed instincts of an extremely selective collector.

Max obviously has his own reasons both for working for you and for seducing you.

Physical desire is the limit of what Max can feel for a woman.

Cleo closed her eyes and drew a slow, deep breath into the pit of her stomach. Kimberly was wrong about Max. She had to be wrong about him. Max had been Jason's friend, and Jason had been a kind, compassionate man.

Max was patient with Sammy. Whatever he had said to Ben had been responsible for making the younger man want to come home to Trisha and the others.

And when Max made love, Cleo reminded herself, he gave as much as he took. Perhaps more. Cleo knew her experience was extremely limited, but instinct told her that Max was a very generous lover.

Her instinct also told her that in bed, at least, he needed her in a way he would probably never be able to put into words.

Cleo opened her eyes again and stared at

the light inside the yellow crystal. Sex wasn't all Max needed from her. He was hungry for other things as well, the same kind of things she had grown up with and that she had deliberately set out to recreate after the death of her parents.

Max needed a family. Whether he knew it or not, he wanted one. Surely that was why he was hanging around Robbins' Nest Inn even though he knew the Luttrell paintings were not there.

He's a robot. A very clever, very brilliant, extremely useful robot, but a robot nonetheless.

"No," Cleo whispered. Her hands closed into small fists. Max was no robot. But she suspected Kimberly had been right when she implied that Max didn't know much about relationships.

Cleo blinked, setting herself free from the gentle thrall of meditation. She took another slow, deep breath and uncoiled from the position she had been holding for the past half hour.

As always she was a little stiff after sitting still for so long. She went to the bank of floor-to-ceiling windows and looked out, startled to see how thick the fog had become.

It was time to go home. Preparations would be starting for the evening meal, and with any luck, there would be a smattering of new guests checking in for the night. Heavy fog sometimes induced cautious travelers to spend the night at the first available inn rather than drive on to their destinations.

A woman dressed in a Cosmic Harmony gown and wearing the familiar necklace waved to Cleo as she walked up the path toward what had once been the main lodge of the old resort.

"Better hurry, Cleo. That fog is going to get worse before it gets better."

Cleo lifted a hand in acknowledgment. "I'm on my way, Nebula. Don't worry about Andromeda and the others. They can stay the night at the inn if the fog doesn't clear up later."

"Of course, dear. Have a good evening."

Cleo nodded at a small group of women who were hurrying from the indoor pool back to the lodge. They waved back. Some were familiar faces, others were visitors who had come to spend a few days at the retreat.

By the time Cleo reached the parking lot, the fog had partially obscured the trees that lined both sides of the road. Luckily there was rarely any traffic on the narrow strip of pavement that led from the retreat back to the inn.

Cleo turned on the lights and eased the Toyota out of the small parking lot. The heavy mist ebbed and swirled in front of her, revealing and then concealing the white line. By the time Cleo was halfway back to the inn, she could barely see the road at all. The fog had not been so heavy along this stretch of coastline since mid-January. She slowed the Toyota to a snail's pace.

The Toyota began to slow still further of its own accord.

Cleo pressed her foot down on the throttle. Nothing happened. She glanced down at the gauges in concern. With a shock, she saw that she was out of gas.

But that wasn't possible, she thought, annoyed. She had filled the tank just last week. Someone else had either borrowed her car or siphoned the gas out of it.

"Damn."

It was going to be a cold walk home.

A few minutes later, bundled up in her hunter green parka, flashlight in hand, car keys in her pocket, she got out of the Toyota and started to walk along the edge of the road. There was less than a mile to go, she assured herself.

The fog had become an icy gray shroud. It blanketed everything with an eerie stillness. Cleo kept to the far edge of the pavement and listened intently for the sounds of automobile engines. Anyone approaching in a car would be unable to see her until he was on top of her. The safest thing to do would be to get off the road entirely if she heard a car coming.

All she heard was the cold, relentless silence.

The gray mist grew heavier. The early night of a Northwest winter was closing in quickly. In another half hour it would be dark.

Cleo concentrated intently on listening for an approaching car. What she heard was the soft echo of footsteps on the pavement behind her.

She stopped and whirled around. The fog formed an impenetrable gray wall behind her.

"Is someone there?"

The footsteps stopped.

"Who is it?" Cleo dug out the small flashlight she had brought with her and aimed it into the dense mist. The beam did not penetrate more than a few feet. It revealed nothing.

Wondering if she had been mistaken, Cleo turned around and started walking more quickly down the road. She kept the flashlight on, even though it didn't do much good. Something about the light was reassuring.

She had not gone more than a few yards when she heard the ring of footsteps on pavement again. Cleo halted once more and turned around.

"Who's there?"

The footsteps ceased.

A chill that had nothing to do with the weather shot down Cleo's spine. She was suddenly acutely aware of the fact that the flashlight beam made her location more visible in the fog. She flicked the switch, dousing the light.

The dark mist closed in on her. So did the footsteps.

Cleo did not question her next move. She reacted instinctively. She started to run.

When she heard the muted thuds of her own soft-soled sneakers hitting the pavement, another wave of fear went through her. *Idiot,* she thought. Now she was announcing her location by sound.

She stopped and listened. The footsteps behind her were louder. Whoever it was would burst through the fog any minute.

She spun around and plunged into the trees beside the road. The soft, damp earth absorbed the impact of her shoes. Whoever was playing the cat-and-mouse game on the road would be unable to find her by sound alone.

Cleo worked her way carefully through the trees. She knew she had to be careful about straying too far from the road. If she lost her bearings in this gray soup, she could end up wandering around in the forest until she succumbed to hypothermia.

She stilled as the footsteps drew relentlessly closer on the road. Afraid to move farther into the undergrowth, she crouched down behind a thick fir and pulled the hood of the parka down over her face. She was very glad the coat was dark green rather than a vivid orange or red.

She prayed she was overreacting.

She prayed the footsteps would continue on down the road.

The taste of panic was in her mouth. She recognized it immediately even though she had not felt anything this intense outside of her nightmares for nearly four years.

The footsteps were directly opposite to her now. They paused for a moment.

Cleo stopped breathing.

A few seconds later the stalker continued on down the road.

Cleo did not take a deep breath until she could no longer hear them.

Several minutes passed before she eased back the hood of the parka. She allowed a little more time to creep past before she risked getting to her feet.

She did not dare switch on the flashlight as she made her way back toward the road. For an instant she thought she had gone in the wrong direction. The pavement was not where it was supposed to be.

Then she felt the graveled shoulder beneath her shoes. Relief poured through her, leaving her weak and jittery.

When she reached the blacktop, Cleo stopped and listened intently again. The growling purr of a sophisticated automobile engine sounded in the distance. The driver was moving slowly along the road, either out of respect for the blinding fog or because he was searching for someone.

Cleo started to retreat back into the woods, but at the last minute she hesitated. There was something familiar about the muted roar of that particular car engine.

A few seconds later Max's green Jaguar emerged from the fog like a sleek beast of prey. The low beams of the headlights sliced through the thick mist.

Cleo switched on the flashlight and waved it about wildly. The light bounced around, dancing on the gray fog. "Max, stop," she yelled. "It's me."

The Jaguar halted swiftly. The door on the driver's side slammed open and Max got out, cane in hand. Cleo could not see the expression on his face, but she could hear the steel in his voice.

"Cleo. For God's sake, what do you think you're doing?"

"Walking home." Cleo ran toward him. "Max, I've never been so glad to see anyone in my whole life. I was so scared."

She threw herself against his chest and clung to him like moss on a log. Max grunted under the impact, but he kept his balance with one hand on the top of the car door. He wrapped his other arm around her and pulled her close.

"What's wrong?" he asked harshly. "Are you all right?"

"Someone was following me. At least, I think he was." Cleo realized she sounded breathless and unnerved. "I could hear footsteps in the fog. I think they were footsteps. They sort of echoed. And there was no other sound and . . . oh, God, Max, I'm not sure if I really did hear them. But I hid in the woods, anyway. And then you came along."

His arm tightened around her. "Are you sure you're all right?"

"Yes, yes, I'm fine. Just a little shaky." Cleo made a valiant effort to pull herself together. "I'm sorry, I'm acting like an idiot, aren't I?"

"No. You're acting like someone who's had a bad scare."

Cleo straightened, but she couldn't bring herself to pull away from the comforting warmth of his arm. She found a hankie in her pocket and blew into it. Then she took a deep breath.

"The car ran out of gas," Cleo said in what she thought was a firm, controlled voice. "Only it shouldn't have, because I had just filled the tank. I started walking home. Then I heard the footsteps. I called out. No one answered. I got off the road until whoever it was had passed. That's really all there was to it. I don't know why I freaked."

Max cut through the rambling explanation. "Where's your car?"

"Back there somewhere. Not far." Cleo waved vaguely to indicate the road behind her. "I think some kid must have siphoned the gas out of my tank or something."

"We'll worry about your car later. Right now I want to get you home. Sylvia, Trisha, and the others are starting to get worried." Max opened the Jaguar's door and ushered her into the warmth.

"I'm sorry everyone's upset," Cleo mumbled as she relaxed into the warmth of the front seat. She reached for her seatbelt. "I really do feel sort of stupid. I'm sure my imagination just got the better of me."

"Maybe." Max got in beside her and started the engine. He put the Jaguar in gear and eased it back onto the road.

"Aren't you going to turn around and drive back to the inn?" Cleo asked.

"I want to make sure your car is far enough

off the road. We don't want anyone hitting it in this fog."

Cleo didn't argue.

A short distance down the road, the Jaguar's headlights picked up the ghostly shape of the Toyota wreathed in fog.

"Let me have your keys."

"What are you going to do?" Cleo asked as she handed him the keys. "You can't start it. There's no gas."

"I just want to take a quick look. I'll be right back."

"Is this another one of those male things?"

Max closed the door without deigning to answer. Cleo sat watching as he went over to the Toyota, opened the door, and got behind the wheel. She waited for the engine to sputter to life and then die, but Max made no move to start the car. He just sat behind the wheel for what seemed like a very long time. She could not tell what he was doing.

Cleo was about to get out of the Jaguar to see what was keeping him, when the Toyota door opened again. She saw that he had a piece of paper in his hand. The uneasiness stirred back to life within her.

Cold air and tendrils of fog swirled into the Jaguar when Max opened the door.

"I found this on the driver's seat." His eyes were grimly intent as he handed the piece of paper to Cleo. "I assume it wasn't there when you left the car to start walking back to the inn."

Cleo read the typewritten message on the piece of paper:

The first Cleopatra was a whore. She died the death she deserved.

11

"O'Reilly, I don't want to hear any more about the lack of results." Max's voice was low and harsh as he spoke into the phone. He was sitting at the small desk in the attic room. His cane was propped against the back of the chair. "I know you didn't find anything interesting when you ran those names through your computers. I'm telling you that we need a whole new angle on this thing."

There was a short, taut silence as Max listened to whatever his friend was saying on the other end.

Cleo sat in the middle of Max's bed, her arms wrapped around her knees. She was still fully dressed and feeling chilled, although the room was pleasantly warm. Max had hustled her straight upstairs to his room the minute they had reached the inn. On the way through the lobby he had told Sylvia, Ben, Trisha, and the others that he would explain everything later. Cleo was starting to fret because she knew the family was downstairs worrying.

"That's right, for all intents and purposes the note sounded like a death threat," Max said. His jaw tightened as Cleo shuddered. "No, I don't know of anything going on out here that would push some local crazy over the edge. Yes, I'm going to keep an eye on her. No, she's not going to go anywhere alone from now on."

Cleo opened her mouth to protest that statement, but Max only looked more grimly determined, so she shut it again.

"Yes, I think the case needs a little more in-depth work, myself," Max said, not bothering to hide his sarcasm. "And I don't want it put on the back burner. I want top-of-the-line service. All right. We'll see you sometime tomorrow. Make it before noon, O'Reilly."

He hung up the phone and regarded Cleo with brooding eyes.

Cleo moistened her lower lip. "What did Mr. O'Reilly say?"

"He said, and I quote, 'You always want top-of-the-line service, you son of a bitch.'"

"Oh." Cleo smiled ruefully. "I'll bet you always get it, too. There was no need to be rude to Mr. O'Reilly. I'm sure he's doing his best."

"I wasn't rude, I was firm. He's turned up absolutely nothing so far."

"He found Ben."

"That has nothing to do with this other matter." Max paused thoughtfully. "At least, I don't think it does."

Cleo straightened her spine, alarmed by the tone of his voice. "Of course it doesn't. How could it?"

"Damned if I know. None of this makes any sense at the moment." Max grabbed his cane and got to his feet. "Come on, we're going downstairs to let the others know what's happening."

"Max, I told you, I don't want everyone worrying about this."

"Too bad. They're going to have to worry about it. I'm going to see to it that everybody worries."

Cleo frowned. "I think we should keep this between ourselves."

"I want everyone in the family to know what's going on so that everyone can keep an eye on you."

"I'll feel like a prisoner."

"That's the whole idea." Max crossed the

room, reached down, and caught her hand in his. He yanked her lightly up off the bed. "Let's go."

"I would like to remind you that I'm the one in charge around here." Cleo went to the door and threw it open with a defiant flourish. It was much easier to feel defiant when you were once again feeling quite safe, she discovered. "I don't recall giving you permission to run things."

"It must have slipped your mind." Max herded her out of the room. "You've been busy lately."

"Max, this is not a joke."

"Christ, Cleo, you don't have to tell me that. You gave me a hell of a scare today. By the way, don't worry about me being in charge for a while around here. I'm good at running things."

"That's what Kimberly said."

"Speaking of Kimberly, when did she leave?"

"Right after we had a cozy little chat on the beach."

"What did you two talk about?" Max urged her down the second flight of stairs.

"You, for the most part."

"Sounds dull."

"I assure you, Max, you are never dull."

They had reached the first floor. Sylvia

looked up from behind the desk. She glanced first at Max's set face and then gave Cleo a concerned look.

"Everything okay?" she asked.

"No," Max said. "Everything is not okay. Call the others. I want everyone in the kitchen in five minutes."

Cleo rolled her eyes. "Honestly, Max. You're carrying this a little too far."

But Sylvia was already hurrying around the edge of the desk. "I'll find everyone."

Cleo threw Max a disgusted look as Sylvia dashed down the hall. "No one around here jumps for me like that."

"It's the difference between our two different management styles," Max explained. "You operate with what is generally called the consensus style."

"What do you call your style?" Cleo shoved open the kitchen door. "A dictatorship?"

"Don't knock it. It works."

"Where did you learn it?"

"From Jason."

"I don't believe it," Cleo declared. "I think it comes naturally to you."

One by one the others gathered in the kitchen. Sammy clung to his mother's hand, his eyes widening as he realized how serious the grown-ups were behaving.

"I don't think we should include Sammy

in this," Cleo whispered uneasily to Max. "He'll be scared."

"He's part of the family," Max said. "He already knows something is going on, and if we don't tell him what it is, and that it's under control, he'll be frightened. This way he'll feel included, and he'll know that action is being taken. That should reassure him."

"Since when did you become an authority on child psychology?" Cleo asked.

Max looked at her. "I was a child once, myself."

"I find that extremely difficult to believe."

"I'm not surprised. So do I."

Cleo watched the expressions on her friends' faces as they gathered around the nook table. Andromeda, Daystar, Trisha, Ben, Sylvia, and little Sammy all glanced first at her with deep concern. They then turned and looked expectantly at Max.

Max wrapped both of his hands around the handle of the hawk-headed cane. He regarded the family with a considering gaze.

"Someone has been threatening Cleo because of the book she wrote," he said.

Everyone stared at Cleo.

"Good heavens, I don't believe it," Andromeda said softly. "Cleo? Are you all right?"

"Yes, Andromeda," Cleo said soothingly.

"I'm fine. Max is making a big production out of this."

Ben put his arm around Trisha and frowned at Max. "What's going on?" he asked.

"Did someone hurt Cleo?" Sammy demanded anxiously.

Max looked down at him. "No," he said quietly. "And no one is going to hurt her. We are all going to keep an eye on her."

"Even you?" Sammy asked.

"Especially me," Max said.

Cleo listened with a growing sense of unreality as Max gave everyone a quick, concise summary of events. They all paid close attention. It was obvious that they were looking to Max for leadership in this crisis. No one questioned his authority.

It occurred to Cleo that somewhere along the line Max had become a very important part of the family. Today he had even begun to challenge her own role as the head of the clan. She realized that she would have to make some adjustments if Max stayed on at Robbins' Nest Inn.

In a flash of rueful insight Cleo suddenly understood why Kimberly and her family had refused to give Max a seat on the Curzon board. He would have ended up running the company in short order.

Forming a partnership with Max was going

309

to be an interesting challenge, Cleo thought.

She watched, impressed in spite of herself, as Max took complete control of the situation in the kitchen and managed to reassure everyone, including Sammy.

"O'Reilly will arrive tomorrow," Max concluded. "He's a first-class private investigator. He'll want to interview everyone, including all of us."

"But we don't know anything about these strange incidents," Andromeda said unhappily. "What can we tell him?"

"Just answer his questions," Max instructed. "O'Reilly knows how to do his job. In the meantime, we all have a job to do, too. From now on, Cleo is not going to leave the inn alone. Clear? I want someone with her any time she steps foot outside the inn's front door."

Cleo roused herself for another weak protest. "Max, that's taking things too far. I'll be careful, I promise."

"The way you were this afternoon?" he asked bluntly.

Cleo glared at him. "I didn't know the situation was going to get this bad."

"Exactly." Max turned back to the others and surveyed them with the air of a commander sending troops into battle. "Is everyone straight about this? Cleo does not leave the inn alone."

"Got it," Ben said. "We'll keep an eye on her."

Sylvia nodded. "Don't worry, we'll make sure she's never alone."

"What happens if she goes outside by herself?" Sammy demanded.

Max raised a brow. "If you see Cleo disobeying orders, you come and tell me right away. Understand?"

"Will you make her go into her room for a time out?" Sammy inquired with grave interest. "That's what Mommy does to me when she gets mad at me."

"I might do just that," Max said. "Only I think I'll make her go to my room instead of her own room."

For some reason that sent Sammy off into a gale of giggles.

"Sheesh," Cleo muttered. "I'm going to go crazy."

Trisha smiled at her. "Don't worry, we won't let you go crazy alone."

The blood was everywhere. So much blood. It had soaked into the carpets and spattered against the walls. It had saturated her mother's dress and pooled beneath her father's head. Too much blood. The smell of it made her sick to her stomach. The sight of it drove her to the edge of sanity.

Cleo opened her mouth to scream and discov-

ered that she was voiceless. She struggled to escape the evil room and realized she could not move. She was trapped.

"Cleo. Cleo, wake up. You're dreaming."

Max's voice cut through the gossamer strands of horror that had been used to weave Cleo's nightmare. She opened her eyes and saw him looming over her. He had his hands on her shoulders, pinning her against the pillows.

Reality emerged from the whirling mist of red that clouded her mind. She was safe in the attic room with Max. She was not alone.

For the first time, she was not alone when she awoke from the dream.

"Max?"

"It's all right, Cleo. I'm here."

"Oh, God." She closed her eyes and took several deep breaths, just as she did when she was meditating. "Sorry. I don't get the dreams very often, but when I do, they make me a little wild."

"What dreams?" Max released his grip on her shoulders, but he did not move away from her. He remained where he was, half covering her with his warm, comforting weight.

"I don't like to talk about them. I tried that with the therapist. But talking about them only makes them seem worse." Cleo shud-

312

dered beneath Max's weight. The heat and strength of him enfolded her in a snug, secure haven. She was not alone tonight. Max was with her.

She made a soft little sound and closed her arms around his neck. Then she turned her face into his bare shoulder and let the tears fall.

Max said nothing. He simply held her close and let her cry until the storm had passed. When it was all over, he kept her cradled against him. His hand moved slowly along her arm.

"Your parents?" he asked at last.

"Yes." Cleo hesitated. "I was the one who found them. Sometimes I dream about it."

"Jesus, Cleo." Max continued to stroke her gently. "I'm so damned sorry."

"It's been four years. But the dreams, when they come, are just as bad as ever. My therapist said I might have them occasionally for the rest of my life, especially if I'm under stress."

"Which you are right now, thanks to whoever is leaving those notes around." Max's voice was gritty with suppressed anger. "I'm looking forward to getting my hands on the bastard."

"Max?"

"Yes?"

"Thanks for coming after me this afternoon."

"Next time you get into the car, check the gas gauge."

Cleo smiled wryly. "My father used to do that."

"What? Check the gas gauge?"

"No, lecture me or my mother after the crisis was past. It was as if he was angry at us for having gotten into trouble in the first place. I remember my mother had her purse snatched once. Afterward Dad chewed her out something fierce for not being more careful."

"He was mad at himself, not her," Max said quietly. "He hadn't been able to protect her, and it scared him."

"That's what Mom said."

"When men get scared, they usually get mad," Max said.

"A male thing?"

Max smiled faintly into the shadows. "Probably."

Cleo snuggled closer. "Max, there's something I've been wanting to ask you."

"I hope this is not about my relationship with Kimberly," he warned. "Because I really don't want to talk about that anymore."

"It's not about that." Cleo wrinkled her nose. "I told you, Kimberly and I have already had a long discussion on that subject."

"Why do women always have to get together and talk about their relationships with men?" Max asked, disgusted.

"Who knows? It's a female thing, I guess. Are you going to lie there and tell me men never talk about their relationships with women?"

"Never," Max said. "I think it's against the code or something."

"Like heck it is. Never mind. What I want to know is, why did you pack your things and put them in your car before you left to find Ben yesterday?"

Max was very still. "I didn't think I'd be staying here unless I brought Ben back with me."

That was not the answer Cleo had been expecting. She turned on her side and levered herself up on her elbow to look down at Max. In the shadows it was difficult to read his expression. "What do you mean? What did Ben have to do with whether or not you stayed with us?"

Max looked up at her, his gaze shuttered. "Coming back without Ben meant I'd failed."

"So?"

Max threaded his fingers lightly through her hair. "I knew how much everyone had counted on my being able to convince Ben to come back. I knew the odds were against it, even if the rest of you didn't. I figured I'd never pull it off."

"So?"

Max shrugged. "I wasn't sure how you and the rest of the family would feel about me if I screwed up that badly."

Cleo was horrified. "Are you telling me you thought we wouldn't want you to stay with us just because you weren't able to bring Ben back?"

Max gave her an unreadable look. "It's been my experience that people only want you around as long as you can do something for them."

"Of all the ridiculous things to say." Cleo was stricken by a sudden thought. "Is that how things worked at Curzon International?"

"That's how things have worked most of my life. Curzon was no exception."

"I can't believe Jason ran his business that way."

"I hate to shatter your illusions about Jason Curzon. But I can guarantee that he didn't run Curzon International with a sweet, gentle, consensus style of management. He was one tough son of a bitch."

"Jason would have given people a second chance. I know he would have."

Max's mouth curved slightly. "Sometimes,

if there were extenuating circumstances, and if he needed whoever had screwed up badly enough to keep him around. But second chances were rare at Curzon. And there was no such thing as a third chance."

"You got along with him."

"I made it a point not to screw up when it came to getting things done for Jason."

Cleo touched his arm. "Are you saying that you think Jason would have kicked you out if you'd failed him in some way?"

Max hesitated. "Let's just say I didn't want to put it to the test."

Cleo framed his face with her palms. "That's awful. How could you live with that kind of constant pressure to perform?"

Max was genuinely amused by her concern. "I'm used to it. The flip side is that I don't screw up very often."

Cleo shook her head wonderingly. "No, I don't suppose you do. But you thought you had when you came home without Ben, didn't you?"

"Yes."

Cleo smiled sadly. "I'm sorry you felt that way. I had no idea you believed your welcome here was contingent on whether or not you brought Ben home. But I've got to admit I'm a little relieved to hear your explanation."

Max searched her face. "Why?"

"Because I'd come to my own conclusion about why you'd packed your bag before you left."

"What conclusion was that?" Max asked.

Cleo ducked her head and kissed his mouth lightly. "Promise you won't laugh?"

"I promise."

"I thought it was just barely possible that you weren't coming back because you'd finally realized I didn't know where those Luttrell paintings were."

Max's gaze turned fierce. "What the hell are you saying?"

"I thought maybe the paintings were all you cared about." Cleo smiled tremulously. "It crossed my mind, Max, that you might have just possibly seduced me primarily to see if you could get me to tell you where I'd stashed your Luttrells. Your old pal, Garrison Spark, didn't help matters when he told me you were quite capable of using that kind of tactic."

Max's fingers tightened abruptly around her waist. His dark lashes veiled his eyes. "You believed that?"

Cleo felt herself growing warm, but she did not lower her gaze. "After you made love to me you asked me about the paintings one last time. Don't you remember? You said something like 'You really don't know where the Luttrells are, do you?'"

"Cleo, I told you I'd come back."

"I know," she admitted.

"But you didn't believe me?"

"I didn't know what to believe. All I could do was cross my fingers and hope you'd return, with or without Ben."

Max watched her intently. "Cleo, what if I told you that it did occur to me that seducing you might be the easiest way to see if you were telling the truth about the Luttrells?"

She grinned. "I'd say you were teasing me."

"You think so?"

"Yep." She touched the edge of his mouth with her fingertip. "We both know you didn't seduce me just to find out where the paintings are. If that was all you wanted from me, you would never have tracked Ben down and talked to him. And you would never have come back here to the inn. Right?"

Max's hand closed tightly around hers. He brushed his mouth across the inside of her wrist in an incredibly gentle, almost reverent kiss. "I guess you're right."

"And before you say anything more, let me remind you that you've got no business lecturing me about my lack of faith in you."

"No?"

"No." Cleo folded her arms on top of his chest. "You displayed the same lack of faith in me and the rest of the family. I can't believe you didn't know we'd want you to come back regardless of whether or not you were successful. We like you because you're you, Max, not because you have a reputation for never screwing up."

"Hardly ever screwing up." Max brought her face close to his and kissed her with rough passion. When he released her, his eyes were gleaming, hard and fierce.

Cleo smiled slowly. "I guess we've both learned something about each other from all this, haven't we?"

Max's answering smile was laced with lazy sensuality. "Well, I'm convinced that you aren't hiding my Luttrells. I knew the first night I met you that you were either one of the most formidable opponents I had ever encountered or . . . Never mind."

"What do you mean, never mind?" Cleo said. "Finish the sentence."

"Or you were one of the nicest, sweetest, most innocent women I had ever met," Max concluded smoothly.

Cleo glowered at him. "That's not what you originally intended to say, was it? What did you really think that first night? That if I wasn't extremely shrewd, I was probably not too bright? Is that what you thought?"

"I can't even remember what I thought that first night. Too much has happened." Max rolled her over onto her back and sat up beside her. He opened the drawer next to the bed and reached inside.

"What are you doing?" Cleo asked, straining to focus on whatever it was he was removing from the drawer. "What's that? It looks like a scarf."

"That's exactly what it is." Max shook out the large square of yellow and blue silk.

"What are you going to do with it?"

"I'm going to try something I read about in chapter five of *The Mirror.*" Max took hold of opposite corners of the scarf and stretched the fabric into a taut, narrow rope.

Cleo's eyes widened even as the first tremors of excitement flowed through her. "Max, you wouldn't."

Max's eyes gleamed with warm, sexy amusement. "Relax, Cleo. I rarely screw up, remember?"

"Yes, I know, but *Max.*" Cleo was suddenly hot all over.

Max slowly eased the hem of her chaste, flower-printed flannel gown up to her waist. Then he slid the strip of yellow and blue silk beneath her buttocks and drew it up between her thighs as if it were a thong-style bikini. He gently pulled it taut.

"*Max.*" Cleo could feel the strip of silk working its way into the moist, heated folds of her feminine flesh. She grabbed fistfuls of the sheet in both hands.

Max tightened the scarf slowly until it was gliding over the delicate bud hidden in the triangle of dark hair. The sensation left Cleo gasping. The feeling was one of tantalizing torment, just as she had imagined it would be when she had written the scene in *The Mirror*.

When Max embellished the original version and used his mouth to dampen the silk between her legs, Cleo came apart in his hands.

She knew Max was watching her in rapt fascination as she surrendered to the climax. For some reason that only made the final sweet convulsions all the more exquisitely exciting.

Max opened one eye a long time later to find Cleo sitting up in bed, leaning over him. She had a speculative expression on her face as she shook out the yellow and blue scarf.

"What do you think you're going to do with that?" he asked with sleepy unconcern.

"Experiment. You never know. Someday I might write a sequel to *The Mirror*." Cleo started to drape the silk square over him. "From a man's point of view."

Max started to smile. Then he sucked in a deep breath as his recently satisfied body reacted to the sensual touch of the silk. "Sounds interesting."

"Yes, I think it will be."

The phone rang just as Cleo was starting to do some truly creative things with the length of silk. Max swore as he reached for the receiver beside the bed.

"Fortune here."

"Max?" George sounded wide awake for once. "This is me. George. At the front desk."

"What's wrong, George?"

Cleo halted the process of tying the narrowed scarf into a bow around an extremely rigid portion of Max's anatomy. She leaned across him to fumble for her glasses on the nightstand.

Max groaned as her soft stomach pressed against his decorated manhood.

"There's a guy down here says he knows you, Max. Says he wants to talk to you right away. He's threatening to tear the place apart if you don't get down here."

Max sat up against the pillows. "Who is it?"

"He says his name is Roarke Winston."

"Hell, that's all I needed. I'll be right down." Max tossed the phone back into its cradle. He reached for the cane he had propped against the wall.

"What's wrong?" Cleo demanded. She was already off the bed, searching for her jeans.

"Winston's here." Max got out of bed and

went to the closet.

"Kimberly's husband?"

"Right." Max started to pull on his trousers and stopped when he noticed that the silk scarf was still tied around him in a wispy, languid bow. He cautiously removed it.

"What's he doing here?" Cleo swiftly buttoned her oxford cloth shirt.

"How the hell should I know? Maybe he's looking for Kimberly." Max tossed the scarf aside with genuine regret.

"Why ask for you?"

Max cocked a brow as he led the way to the door. "Damned if I know. We'll find out soon enough."

He went down the two flights of stairs with Cleo hard on his heels. When he walked into the lobby, he knew there was going to be trouble.

Roarke Winston, patrician-featured, well-dressed, and normally brimming with the subtle arrogance that came from old money and solid family connections, was in a towering rage.

He swung around as Max entered the room. "Fortune, you son of a bitch. Where's my wife?"

"I don't know," Max said calmly. "She's not here."

"You're lying." Roarke started forward, his

hands clenched at his sides. His handsome face was mottled with fury. "She's here. I know she is. You talked her into coming here with you, didn't you? You're sleeping with my wife, you bastard."

"Take it easy, Winston," Max said.

"What made you think I'd let you get away with having an affair with my wife?" Roarke closed the distance between himself and Max with long, swift strides.

"Stop it," Cleo yelped in alarm. "Max isn't having an affair with Kimberly."

"The hell he isn't." Roarke's voice rose. "He's wanted to get his hands on Curzon from the start. He figures seducing Kim is one way to do it."

"That's not true," Cleo said. She turned toward the front desk and glared at George. "You're the night desk man, George. Do something."

George gazed at her helplessly and then banged the bell that sat on the front desk. Apparently pleased with that decisive maneuver, he banged it again.

"Oh, for heaven's sake," Cleo muttered.

Roarke came to a halt less than two feet away from Max. "You don't love her. You never did love her. You're just trying to use her. I'll be damned if I'll let you do it."

He swung wildly.

"No," Cleo shouted. "Don't hit him. He didn't do anything."

She leaped in front of Max just as Roarke's fist came crashing toward its target. At the last instant, Max realized that the blow was going to strike Cleo.

He grabbed Cleo's shoulder and spun her aside, out of the path of Roarke's fist. Unfortunately the maneuver did not give him time to use the cane in self-defense. Instead it took him straight into the path of the punch.

Cleo stumbled and fell. In an effort to avoid hitting her, Roarke obviously tried to pull his punch at the last second. But it was too late. His fist clipped the side of Max's jaw.

Max staggered, lost his balance, and sprawled back against the front desk. As he slid gracefully to the floor, he saw Cleo reach for the vase that sat on the corner stand. She grabbed it with both hands and took aim at Roarke's head.

Max didn't know whether to laugh or curse. He was not accustomed to having anyone leap to his defense. It was a pleasant novelty, but enough was enough. If things went any further, someone was going to get hurt.

"Put the vase down, Cleo." Max sat on the floor, propped against the desk in what he hoped was a suitably dramatic fashion. He groaned and gingerly fingered the side of his jaw. "I quit, Winston. You're the winner."

Roarke stood over him, breathing heavily. "Bastard."

"Don't you dare touch him," Cleo said to Roarke. "Get away from him." She set the vase down on the stand and dashed across the room to Max's side. "He's not sleeping with your wife."

"How do you know?" Roarke demanded.

"Because he's sleeping with me." Cleo touched Max's face with gentle, questing fingers. "Isn't that right, Max?"

"Right," said Max.

The sound of running footsteps overhead made everyone, including George, look toward the staircase.

Ben came thundering down the stairs first. His hair was tousled, and his shirt was unbuttoned. He was trying to fasten his jeans. Trisha was right behind him. She was tying the belt of her robe as she hurried down the steps.

Sylvia and Sammy brought up the rear. Both were in their nightclothes. Sammy was yawning.

"What's going on down here?" Ben scanned the lobby scene quickly. "Cleo? Max? Are you guys okay?"

"No," Cleo said.

"Yes," Max said, overriding her. "Allow me to introduce Roarke Winston. He's Kimberly's husband. He was under the mistaken impression that I was spending the night with his wife."

Ben glared at Roarke. "No way, man. Max isn't messin' around with your wife. He and Cleo are like a couple, y'know?"

"Is that right?" Roarke asked with cold disbelief.

"Damn right," Ben said authoritatively. "In fact, they're going to get married."

"Uh, Ben," Cleo began carefully.

Ben ignored her. "Isn't that right, Max?"

Max knew a turning point when he saw one. "Right."

12

"Okay, so maybe we jumped the gun a little," Ben said.

"We?" Max eyed the pipe joint that was less than four inches above his head. He was not in a good mood, and his bad attitude this morning had nothing whatsoever to do with the fact that he was sprawled on his back beneath the bathroom sink in room one-oh-one.

"So I kind of rushed the announcement," Ben admitted.

"You think so?" A drop of water from the leaking pipe fitting hit Max on the forehead. "Dammit."

"Give me a break, Max, I had to think fast last night. That guy Winston was really pissed. He looked like he was going to take the place apart."

"Hand me the other wrench."

"Look, I know you got clipped, but you weren't really hurt." Ben stooped down and thrust a wrench into Max's hand. "Besides, I'll bet you walked right into Winston's punch."

"I did not walk into it. Hand me a rag."

"You sure?" Ben crouched down on his haunches and handed Max a scrap of an old inn towel that was frayed and torn. "He's no fighter. He's too soft. You can't tell me he took you with a sucker punch."

"I was unable to duck because I was too busy trying to shove Cleo out of the way," Max said with great dignity. He wiped the dripping joint with the rag and adjusted the new wrench.

"Yeah? Is that how it happened?" Ben frowned at the pipe joint. "I thought maybe you deliberately took the punch so Cleo would feel sorry for you and fuss and stuff. Which she did."

"Not for long." Max took a grip on the wrench handle and tightened the pipe fitting with ruthless force.

The fact that Cleo had not hovered very long last night after discovering that he was unhurt was one of the chief reasons for Max's foul temper this morning.

She had not only failed to play the ministering angel for more than a few brief minutes, she had not returned to his room after the uproar had died down. Nor had she invited him to hers.

Cleo had recovered her professional innkeeper aplomb almost immediately. She had risen from Max's fallen body, checked the confused Winston into one of the inn's best rooms, and sent everyone back to bed. She had then retired to her own bedroom without so much as a good-night kiss for Max.

"Take it easy or you'll strip the threads," Ben warned.

"You want to take over?"

"No, that's okay. I've fixed a lot of leaking pipes. I know how it's done. You're supposed to be getting experience, remember?"

"You're supposed to be giving helpful advice, remember?"

"Hey, you're doin' okay, man. A real natural. Anyhow, about last night."

"What about it?" Max surveyed the pipe

fitting. Another drop of water oozed out of the metal joint.

"Well, I know we all kind of rushed things by making that big announcement about you and Cleo getting married."

"Yes." Max gave the wrench another twist. "You did."

"But it's not like you aren't planning to marry her, or anything like that," Ben pointed out earnestly.

"Is that right?"

Ben scowled. "What the hell's that supposed to mean?"

"Maybe it means I want to take off for a few days and go work in a gas station while I think things over." Max wiped the joint again. It looked dry.

"Come on, Max, that was a cheap shot. We both know you aren't going to take off the way I did. You aren't spooked."

"No, but I think Cleo is. Turn on the water."

"Huh?"

"I said, turn on the water."

"I heard that." Ben got to his feet and turned on the faucet. Water gushed into the sink. "What did you mean about Cleo being spooked?"

"You saw her last night." Max watched to see if the joint was going to start dripping again. "After she figured out that I wasn't dying, she did a damn good job of pretending I didn't exist. She couldn't wait to send everyone, including me, off to bed."

"I guess she was a little embarrassed." Ben turned off the faucet. "You guys hadn't announced anything yet."

"We hadn't announced anything because there wasn't anything to announce. I think this thing is fixed. For your information, Cleo and I have not discussed marriage."

"You sure?"

"Yes, I'm sure. It's not leaking at all now." Max was aware of a pleasing sense of satisfaction. He was getting good at this plumbing business. "Dry as the Sahara." He started to work himself out from the tight confines of the sink cabinet.

"Shit, Max, will you stop talking about the damn pipe?" Ben's face was tight with worry. "Why haven't you asked Cleo to marry you? We all know you're sleeping with her."

"What's that got to do with it?" Max flattened one palm on the countertop and levered himself to his feet. He winced at the twinge in his thigh.

"What do you mean?" Ben demanded. "You know damn well what I'm talking about. We've all known Cleo for a long time. As far as any one in the family knows, you're the first guy she's ever been serious about."

"What makes you think she's serious about me?" Max turned on the faucet full force again and leaned down to study the pipe connection under the sink. There was no sign of moisture around the fittings.

He realized it was probably idiotic to take so much satisfaction out of the knowledge that he had repaired the leak, but he couldn't help it. Nothing like a little immediate, short-term gratification to take a man's mind off bigger problems, he thought.

"Don't give me that," Ben said. "Cleo wouldn't be sleeping with you if she weren't serious about you. Come on, Max, quit jerking my chain. You're going to marry her, aren't you?"

"Yes." Max turned off the faucet and wiped his hands on the rag. "But first I've got to talk her into it, which might be a lot harder than you seem to think."

"Why?" Ben looked baffled.

"Because you and the others put her under a lot of pressure last night when you made your big announcement," Max said with a patience he did not feel. "She was just getting used to me. She was nowhere near ready to talk about marriage. Now the whole family is acting like it's a fait accompli."

"What's a fait accompli?"

"A done deal."

"Oh." Ben frowned. "You think she's really upset?"

"As I said, she's feeling pressured. People do weird things when they're under pressure."

Ben looked suitably alarmed. "Like what?"

"Like dig in their heels and make life difficult for the people they think are trying to pressure them."

Ben nodded in sober comprehension. "But you can handle her, can't you?"

"First I've got to get her to start talking to me again." Max tossed the wet rag into the tool kit.

Ben brightened. "That shouldn't be any problem. Cleo likes to talk."

Trisha whisked dirty plates and glasses off one of the dining room tables and stacked them in a plastic tub. "Do you want to talk about it, Cleo?"

"No." Cleo bundled up a tablecloth and the used napkins from another table. The familiar routine of clearing the dining room after the small breakfast crowd had departed was doing nothing to soothe her nerves this morning. She had spent a sleepless night, and she felt as if she were walking an invisible tightrope.

"We know you're a little upset, Cleo," Sylvia said from the other side of the empty dining room. Dishes clattered cheerfully as she removed them from a table. "But I'm sure you'll feel better if you talk about it."

"What is there to say?" Cleo jerked another tablecloth off a table with enough force to make it snap in the air. "I have been humiliated, embarrassed, and generally mortified beyond belief."

Andromeda appeared in the doorway. "Now, dear, there's no need to be so agitated. We all know how you feel about Max."

Cleo scanned the expectant faces of her friends. "You do? Well, that's just ducky. I'm glad somebody does, because I don't."

Sylvia smiled gently. "Cleo, let's get real here. You're sleeping with him."

"So what?" Cleo said.

Trisha exchanged a glance with the others. "Between us, we've known you for over three years, Cleo. This is the first time any of us has seen you really interested in a man."

Andromeda smiled serenely. "This is definitely the first time you've had an affair during the whole time I've been acquainted with you, dear."

Sylvia dropped another stack of plates into the bin. "Admit it, Cleo, Max is something special."

"That doesn't mean he wants to marry me," Cleo muttered.

Trisha glanced at her, astonished. "What are you talking about? He said he was going to marry you. I heard him myself."

"So did I," Sylvia said quickly.

"I am so sorry I missed the big scene." Andromeda sighed. "It sounds wonderfully romantic."

Cleo whirled around, her arms full of dirty tablecloths. "It was not romantic. It was a disaster. Max was lying there on the floor, injured. Roarke Winston had accused him of sleeping with Kimberly and was getting ready to hit him again. All George could do was slam the desk bell like a crazy person. Things were in complete chaos."

"And that's when Ben and the others arrived?" Andromeda asked cheerfully.

"Yes." Cleo dumped the dirty tablecloths into a pile. "And that's when Ben, in his infinite wisdom, announced that Max was going to marry me."

"And Max agreed," Andromeda concluded happily.

"It was not like he had a lot of choice under the circumstances," Cleo said. "The man was under enormous pressure. After all, Roarke Winston was threatening to beat him to a pulp."

Andromeda looked thoughtful. "Somehow I don't think pressure bothers Max too much."

Sylvia nodded. "Andromeda's right. Max wouldn't say something like that, regardless of the circumstances, unless he meant it."

"I agree," Trisha said.

Cleo felt trapped. "I don't care if he did mean it." She picked up the basket of dirty tablecloths. "Just because Max agreed to marry me doesn't mean I intend to marry him."

Andromeda frowned. "Whatever are you talking about, dear?"

Cleo lifted her chin. "Don't you understand? There are two things wrong with this situation. First, Max has never asked me to marry him. Two, I'm not at all sure I would marry him even if he did ask me."

Sylvia, Trisha, and Andromeda stared at her. In the ensuing shocked silence, Daystar emerged from the kitchen. She stood, hands on hips, and eyed Cleo speculatively.

"Why wouldn't you want to marry him?" Daystar asked bluntly. "It's as plain as the nose on your face that you love him."

"That does not mean that Max Fortune is good husband material," Cleo said through gritted teeth.

"I disagree," Andromeda said calmly. "I'll admit I had a few qualms about him at first, but that was only because we didn't know much about him."

337

"Well, now we know a lot more about him, don't we?" Cleo retorted. "And a lot of what we've learned lately makes me have real doubts about marrying the man."

"Cleo, Max loves you," Sylvia said quietly.

Cleo tightened her grip on the basket of dirty tablecloths. "Don't be too sure of that. To be perfectly frank, I'm not sure Max knows how to love."

"Oh, dear," Andromeda murmured. "Whatever do you mean?"

Cleo sighed. "Max knows how to collect the things he wants, and I think that he does want me. At least for the moment. But wanting isn't the same thing as loving, and I have no wish to become a part of Max Fortune's collection of fine art."

Trisha stared at her. "Cleo, I'm sure you're wrong."

"Am I? I'm the one who's been sleeping with him. I know him better than any of you, and I'm here to tell you that Max has never once said anything about love. Kimberly Curzon-Winston may be right. He may not know the meaning of the word *relationship*."

"How would Ms. Curzon-Winston know anything about Max?" Sylvia demanded.

"Because she was engaged to him at one time."

They all stared at her in amazement.

Satisfied with the effects of her small bombshell, Cleo headed for the swinging door. When she reached it, she turned around and backed through it.

She collided with Roarke Winston, who was on his way out of the kitchen into the dining room. The impact sent the tablecloths in the bin flying in a variety of directions.

"Excuse me." Roarke disentangled himself from a tablecloth. He smiled ruefully. "I seem fated to crash into you, Ms. Robbins. Sooner or later, I'm going to do some damage."

"Don't be ridiculous. And please call me Cleo." She quickly collected the fallen tablecloths. "What were you doing in the kitchen, Mr. Winston? Or should that be Curzon-Winston?"

Roarke's eyes darkened with annoyance. "No, it damn well is not Curzon-Winston. My wife can call herself anything she likes, but my name is just plain Winston. I'd rather you called me Roarke. And the answer to your question, Cleo, is that I went in there looking for you. Someone said you were helping to clear the dining room. I was on my way to find you."

"I see. What can I do for you?" Cleo put down the bin of tablecloths.

Roarke glanced at the ring of interested faces behind Cleo. He lowered his voice. "I wanted to apologize to you for that damned farce I conducted last night in your lobby."

"Forget it. No harm done."

"I promise you I don't generally go around making a fool of myself on a regular basis. But I've been under a lot of stress lately."

"Haven't we all?" Cleo was aware of Sylvia, Daystar, Trisha, and Andromeda listening intently as they stacked dishes. She appealed to them with a silent look.

They took the hint and, one by one, quietly vanished back through the swinging door into the kitchen.

"I suppose so." Roarke's face turned red. "As I said, I just wanted to apologize."

Cleo took pity on him. "Don't worry about it." She opened the linen cupboard and removed a stack of clean tablecloths. "I understand how you must have felt."

"Do you?" Roarke's eyes were bleak.

"Yes," Cleo said gently. "I think so." She smiled. "As long as you're just standing around, why don't you give me a hand with these?"

"What?" Roarke glanced at the stack of tablecloths. "Oh, sure." He smiled. "Not exactly my line of work, but I think I can handle it."

"I don't need any more hotel industry experts around," Cleo muttered. "I've had enough of them lately."

Roarke slanted her a strange glance. "Just between you and me, you're marrying one of the best. Max Fortune is one hell of an expert. Dennison Curzon will do anything to get him back. As you've already discovered, the son of a bitch will even stoop to using Kim."

Cleo hesitated. "Kimberly was anxious to convince Max to return. She told me her father insisted on it."

"He did. As the new chairman of the board of Curzon International, Dennison is having a great time throwing his weight around. For years he lived in Jason's shadow. Now he's determined to show everyone he's even better at running a hotel empire than his brother was."

"Why does he want Max to come back?"

Roarke unfolded another tablecloth and arranged it neatly on a table. "Because the truth is, Dennison is not the natural leader that Jason was. He hasn't got the talent to run Curzon International, and deep down I think he knows it."

"He thinks he can use Max to help run the company?"

Roarke nodded. "He's decided that Jason's secret weapon was Max Fortune. Dennison figures that if he can persuade Fortune to come back, everything will be like it was before, except that Dennison will be in charge this time."

Cleo glanced at Roarke. "Where does Kimberly fit into all this?"

Roarke's jaw set in rigid lines as he whipped open another tablecloth. "My wife has spent most of her life trying to please her father. She's still struggling to be the son Dennison never had. I knew it was a problem when I married her, but I thought we could work it out. Now she feels torn, and part of me is afraid she's going to choose Daddy instead of me."

"One of these days," Max said coldly from the hall doorway, "Kim is going to have to figure out that she can never please Dennison, no matter what she does. Or whom she marries."

Cleo spun around, startled. It was the first time all morning that she had come face to face with Max. He looked even more fierce than he usually did. "Max, I'm warning you, I don't want any more scenes."

Max's brows rose. "I'm not the one who started that scene last night."

"Nor do I want to see any finger-pointing," she added primly.

"Too bad," Roarke said. "I was just getting ready to put in my two cents' worth."

Max smiled without any trace of genuine

humor. "Maybe Winston and I had better finish this discussion in private. What do you say, Winston?"

"Not a chance." Roarke snapped open another tablecloth. "I'm not going to volunteer to step outside so that you can beat my brains out."

Cleo was horrified. "Max wouldn't do anything like that."

"No?" Roarke looked distinctly skeptical.

"Of course not." Max gave Roarke a dangerously polite smile. "What I want to discuss is the possibility of getting all you Winstons and Curzons and Curzon-Winstons out of my life on a permanent basis."

"What a strange coincidence. I've got exactly the same goal." Roarke eyed him. "How do you plan to accomplish it?"

"I think it could be arranged if Kim challenged Dennison Curzon for control of the board."

Roarke's jaw dropped. "Are you crazy? Kim could never pull that off."

"She could with your help. You're on the board. Jason appointed you a member the day you married Kimberly."

"Yes, but you know as well as I do that I'm only on the board because I'm one of the family through marriage. It was understood from the start that I'm not supposed to actively interfere with Curzon operations."

"Jason's gone, and the situation has changed," Max said. "We all know that Dennison hasn't got what it takes. Left to his own devices, he'll probably drive Curzon into the ground within three years. Kimberly knows that, too."

Roarke's expression was grim. "She knows it, but she's still trying to please her Daddy."

"She only thinks she wants to please Dennison. What she really wants to do is prove she's as good as any son he might have had."

Roarke eyed him thoughtfully. "Is that a fact? You're a shrink?"

"No, but I hung around the Curzon family for twelve years. I know them all fairly well. If Kim takes a good hard look at the situation, I think she'll realize that what she really wants to do is show him that she's capable of running Curzon International just as well as the son Dennison always wanted and never got," Max said softly.

Roarke folded his arms across his chest and watched Max with the respect and wariness of one predator sizing up another.

Cleo was fascinated.

"What makes you an authority on Kim? Your famous six-week engagement?" Roarke asked finally.

"Try to be objective, Winston. Why do you

think Kim let herself get talked into getting engaged to me three years ago?" Max showed no sign of emotion. He sounded as if he were talking about an excruciatingly boring incident in the past.

"I've often wondered what she saw in you," Roarke said dryly. "You're not exactly her type."

"I'm aware of that," Max said.

"You were, however, Jason's best friend and confidant. You knew more about the inner workings of Curzon management than anyone else in the whole damn company, including the Curzons."

"That was as far as it went. I wasn't quite good enough to become a member of the family."

"Hell." Roarke gave him an unconcealed look of surprise. "Do you think the Curzons are crazy? If they'd made you a member of the family and put you on the board, you'd have taken complete control of the company in about one month."

Max said nothing. Cleo noticed, however, that no denial sprang instantly to his lips. With a chill she realized that Roarke was right, and Kimberly's fears were not entirely groundless. In one way, Max would have been a serious threat to the Curzons if he had gotten a seat on the board. He would have taken control of the company. His talents and aggressive instincts would have made that outcome inevitable.

What the Curzons had not understood, Cleo thought, was that, as a member of the family, Max would have been one-hundred percent on their side — more of a Curzon, in fact, than any of the rest of them. He would have used his power to protect the family and its holdings.

Cleo knew in that moment of shattering insight that Max cared far more about belonging to a family than he did about making money or running a company.

"Don't give me any bullshit," Roarke said into the sudden silence. "We both know that the only reason you wanted to marry Kim was so that you could get your hands on Curzon."

Max continued to gaze at him impassively. "You're entitled to your own opinion, of course."

Roarke appeared almost amused. "Damn right I am. I know that all you ever wanted from Kim was the chance to control Curzon International. Hell, I don't even blame you, if you want to know the truth."

"No?"

Roarke lifted one shoulder in a negligent shrug. "For all intents and purposes, you were second-in-command for years. Everyone knows it was you who helped Jason turn Curzon into what it is today."

"Thank you," Max said. "I'll assume that's a compliment."

Roarke smiled briefly. "Hey, I'm not arguing that you had a right to try to grab the whole shooting match when the opportunity arose. But don't expect me to approve of the way you tried to use Kim to get what you wanted."

"I think," Max said, "that we're going down a dead-end road as far as this topic of conversation goes. Why don't we get back to our original subject?"

"You want me to help Kim pull a coup and unseat her father? Nice idea, but it's pure fantasy."

"I disagree. Nothing says you're limited to the role of a rubber-stamper on the Curzon board. You can take action. I never noticed you having any problem controlling your own board of directors."

"Damn it, I don't particularly want to get involved with running Curzon. I've got my hands full with my own company."

"This would be a very short-term arrangement. Help Kim take control of the board. Once she's been elected CEO, you can retreat gracefully from active management and let her take over completely. You can start rubber-stamping her projects the same way you used to rubber-stamp Jason's."

Roarke rubbed his jaw. "Kim's brilliant and gutsy. She's got what it takes to run Curzon, doesn't she?"

"Once she's no longer worried about trying to placate Dennison, she'll do fine. She doesn't need me. What she needs is help taking the company away from her father. You can be the one to give her what she wants most in the world." Max paused and smiled slightly. "Think how grateful she'll be."

Roarke narrowed his eyes. "She'd never go up against her old man."

"I think you could convince her to do it," Max said.

Roarke looked briefly intrigued. Then he shook his head. "I don't know. Even if I could talk her into trying to stage a coup, I doubt we could pull it off. Kim would have me on her side, but that still leaves a couple of cousins and her aunt. They'd follow Dennison because they're used to taking orders from his brother."

"You can handle the cousins, and that's all you need," Max said quietly. "If you and Kim show a united front, they'll start taking their lead from you two, rather than Dennison."

Roarke considered that for a moment. "Maybe. It just might work. I don't want to look a gift horse in the mouth or anything, but would you mind telling me what's in this for you, Fortune? What do you want for being so damn helpful?"

"All I want is your guarantee that you and Kim and everybody else with the last names of Curzon or Winston will quit showing up here at the inn at unexpected and inconvenient moments," Max said softly.

"I think I'm getting the picture." Roarke looked at Cleo, and then he met Max's eyes. "You want us out of your way."

"Yes," Max said. "I do. And I'd really appreciate it if you'd start the process immediately."

Roarke slanted another glance at Cleo and smiled. "I can take a hint. It's a long drive back to Seattle. Guess I'd better get started."

13

"That was a cozy little scene I walked in on just now," Max growled as the door of the dining room swung closed behind Roarke. He gave the stack of folded tablecloths that Roarke had left behind a disgusted glance. "Thinking of taking on additional help?"

"Why not? Hotshot executive material is all over the place these days. I might as well take advantage of some of it." Cleo concentrated on spreading another cloth on a table.

Max sat down at one of the tables in the far corner near the window. He propped his cane beside his chair and watched Cleo with brooding eyes. "We have to talk."

"About what?"

"Last night would probably be a good place to start," Max said.

"I've got a better idea. Let's talk about this morning, instead."

Max's eyes darkened. "What about this morning?"

"Did you really try to marry Kimberly in order to get your hands on Curzon International?" Cleo asked in what she hoped was a tone of mild curiosity.

There was a long silence from the table in the corner. "What do you think?" Max finally asked.

Cleo threw him a glare as she whipped open another tablecloth. She looked away quickly because his eyes were burning with an emotion she could not define.

"I think you must have had a very good reason for asking her to marry you," Cleo said in a subdued voice. "Either you were in love with her, which everyone including you seems to seriously doubt, or you wanted something from her. What was it, Max?"

"It's been three years since the engagement ended." Max absently rubbed his thigh. "I believe I've forgotten what it was that convinced me I wanted to marry her."

"Don't give me that." Cleo approached his table with the last of the unfolded cloths. "You told me that she represented a lot of things you wanted. What were those things, Max?"

He looked at her. "Whatever they were, they don't matter any more."

"You don't want Curzon International?"

"No."

"You don't want Kimberly Curzon-Winston?"

"No." Max watched Cleo unfold the last tablecloth. "I want you."

"Hmm." So much for trying to get him to put his quest into words. She understood, then, that his need for a family of his own was an inchoate longing that he probably did not even fully comprehend himself, let alone want to analyze.

The risk here was excruciatingly clear, Cleo thought. She was in danger of playing the same role in Max's life as Kimberly had played. He did not love her, at least not in the way Cleo wanted to be loved. What Max really wanted were all the things that came with her.

"Why did you insist on going back to your own room last night, Cleo?"

"I wanted to think."

"About us?"

"I suppose so." Cleo refused to be drawn. She did not trust her own mood this morning. She was edgy and unsettled. There were moments when she thought she could see all the way to Max's shadowed soul. But there were other times when he seemed more of an enigma than ever.

Max leaned forward, his expression intent. "Cleo, let's get out of here for a couple of days. We need to be alone together for a while."

She shot him a quick, wary glance. "Why?"

"So that we can talk, damn it."

"We're talking now."

"But not for long." Max glanced toward the door. "Sooner or later someone will interrupt us. You can bet on it. It's damned tough to find any privacy around here, isn't it?"

"Doesn't bother me," Cleo said blithely.

"I noticed. I think you're trying to hide behind the family. Don't be afraid of me, Cleo."

That annoyed her. "I'm not afraid of you."

"Then why have you been avoiding me since last night?"

"I'll give you one guess."

"Because of Ben's announcement." Max

smiled persuasively. "Don't blame him. He and everyone else here knows that you're sleeping with me, and they all know that you don't make a habit of having affairs. It's logical that they would conclude we're serious about each other."

"Are we?"

Max's smile vanished. "Yes, damn it, we are."

Cleo lost her precarious temper. "You might be interested to know that I do not blame Ben for embarrassing me last night. I blame you. You went right along with his announcement. You told everyone we were getting married."

"Under the circumstances, it seemed the gentlemanly thing to do. It would have been a lot more awkward for everyone if I'd denied it."

"I don't think you went along with the program just because it was the gentlemanly thing to do," Cleo stormed. "I think you saw Ben's announcement as an extremely convenient opportunity to prevent poor Roarke Winston from beating you to a pulp. You used me."

Max's jaw tightened ominously. "You really believe that?"

Cleo fiddled a bit with her glasses. "Yes, I do."

"You really have an attitude problem this morning, don't you?"

"You think so?" Cleo tilted her head to one side and narrowed her eyes. "Actually, I thought I was behaving with remarkable restraint, given the circumstances."

"That's not how I see it," Max said.

"Too bad." Cleo frowned sharply as she saw his hand move on his thigh. "Why are you massaging your leg? Is it bothering you this morning?"

"Forget my leg. Look, Cleo, I understand that you're feeling as if you've been backed into a corner. I realize we hadn't actually talked about marriage."

"Oh, good." Cleo gave him a bright, brittle smile. "For a while there I thought I was just getting forgetful. It happens when someone is under stress, you know."

"Stop being so waspish. I'm trying to have a rational conversation here."

"In that case you'd better find someone else to have it with," Cleo said. "I'm not feeling very rational at the moment."

"Damn it, Cleo —" Without any warning Max slammed his palm flat against the table in a small explosion of violence that graphically communicated his own anger.

The sharp crack of sound startled Cleo. She jumped and took a step back as Max started to rise from his chair. The dining room door burst open.

"Cleo?" Sylvia's voice was laced with concern. "What's going on here?"

"I knew someone would come in at the wrong moment." Max dropped back into his chair with an air of resigned martyrdom. "No privacy at all."

"That's family life," Cleo said sweetly.

She swung around to face the door. Sylvia stood there, gazing anxiously at the pair near the window. She was not alone. Sammy was with her and so was a very large stranger.

The newcomer was a mountain of a man with the endearingly homely face and sad eyes of a basset hound. He wore a loud green and orange plaid sport coat and a pair of brown polyester slacks. His tie was studded with red polka dots.

"Are you mad at Cleo, Uncle Max? You look mad." Sammy scampered over to Max's chair and gazed up at him with worried eyes.

"Cleo and I were having a private discussion," Max said. "It was a very serious talk."

Cleo raised her brows at the gruff reassurance in his voice. "Don't let him fool you, Sammy. He's mad at me."

Already satisfied by Max's response, Sammy giggled. "But not really, really mad, I bet."

"No." Max scowled at Cleo. "Not really, really mad."

"He's right, Sammy," the stranger said in

a deep, rumbling voice that matched his size, "I've known Max for quite a while now, and I can say for sure that when Fortune's really, *really* mad, no one can even tell until it's too late."

Sammy looked at the man in the doorway. "So if he just looks mad, what does that mean?"

"It means he's feeling a tad grumpy." The man sauntered into the dining room. "Probably hasn't had his morning coffee." He looked at Max. "Hi, Max."

"About time you got here, O'Reilly." Max glanced briefly at the polka-dot tie his friend was wearing. "Where did you get that tie?"

"Bought it from some guy who sells them off the back of a truck in an alley between Third and Fourth avenues in downtown Seattle," O'Reilly said proudly. "Heck of a deal. I'll introduce you to him next time you're in town."

"Don't bother."

"We can't all afford to buy our clothes in Europe," O'Reilly said easily.

"I like O'Reilly's tie," Sammy said. "It's nice. Mommy thinks so, too, don't you, Mommy?"

Cleo was astonished to see the faint blush that warmed Sylvia's cheeks.

"Stunning," Sylvia murmured.

O'Reilly grinned at her. The smile transformed his face. "I'm glad someone around here has good taste." He turned back to Cleo. "Allow me to introduce myself. I'm O'Reilly. Compton O'Reilly of O'Reilly Investigations."

"I'm pleased to meet you," Cleo said politely.

"Presumably Max has told you all about me. How brilliant I am. How resourceful and clever. How fearless, tireless, and tenacious, et cetera, et cetera."

Cleo smiled reluctantly. "Max said you were very good at what you do."

A strange twinge of fear went through her as she acknowledged the introduction to Compton O'Reilly. It loosed a flock of butterflies in her stomach and made her feel light-headed.

The arrival of a private investigator brought home the reality of what was happening. Max was taking the recent troubling incidents very seriously. The realization that he was doing so made them suddenly all the more disturbing.

"That's Max for you," O'Reilly said. "Always the master of the understatement. When he says I'm good at what I do, he really means I'm terrific."

Max looked at Cleo. "Did I tell you how

modest he was?"

It was Sylvia who answered. "I think Mr. O'Reilly's modesty is self-evident."

O'Reilly grinned at her again. "Thank you, ma'am."

Sylvia turned slightly more pink. She looked at Sammy. "Why don't you come with me, dear? We'll see if we can find Mr. O'Reilly a cup of coffee in the kitchen."

"And some cookies," Sammy said eagerly.

"Now that's one of the better ideas I've heard today," O'Reilly murmured. "I prefer chocolate chip, if you've got them."

Sammy clapped his hands in delight. "So do I."

"Great minds move in the same paths," O'Reilly said. He looked pleased.

"We'll be back in a few minutes," Sylvia promised as she took Sammy's hand.

O'Reilly watched the pair disappear through the swinging doors into the kitchen. Then he turned and gave Max a slow, perusing examination.

"What the heck have you gotten yourself into out here, Max, old buddy? And what's this I hear about you being engaged?"

"Rumors." Cleo cleared her throat. "Rumors, innuendoes, and lies."

"Is that right?" O'Reilly stuck his hands in his pants pockets and regarded her with a gravely interested expression. "Nothing to all those rumors, innuendoes, and lies?"

"Of course not." Cleo ignored Max's annoyed gaze. "Max, here, hasn't even bothered to ask me to marry him, so how could there possibly be a real engagement?"

O'Reilly nodded. "Good point."

"Damn it to hell." Max pinned Cleo with a fierce look. "Is that what's made you so prickly this morning? The fact that I haven't formally asked you to marry me?"

Cleo did not deign to answer that. She gave O'Reilly a bland smile. "Ignore him. He's got an attitude problem today."

"Max always has an attitude," O'Reilly said. "Can't you tell by the way he dresses?"

A short while later, fortified with several cookies and a cup of coffee, O'Reilly glanced down at his notebook. He leaned back in the fanback wicker chair and contemplated Max and Cleo, who were seated across from him in the solarium.

"The bottom line here is that there aren't any obvious suspects. As far as you know, you don't have any enemies. No one's got a grudge against you?"

Cleo shuddered. O'Reilly seemed nice enough, but she was still having qualms about getting a private investigator involved in the situation. "Not that I know of. I haven't had any run-ins with anyone, unless you count Tobias Quinton."

"Who's Tobias Quinton?"

Max shifted slightly. "Forget him. He's not a factor in this."

O'Reilly gave him a level look. "You're sure?"

"I'm sure. Just a slightly disgruntled inn guest. Stayed one night and left the next morning," Max explained.

O'Reilly turned back to Cleo. "Pardon the personal questions, but I need to know the answers. Any possibility you've got an ex-boyfriend who might have become a little too possessive? Especially now that Max is in the picture? Max sometimes makes enemies, I'm sorry to say."

"I wasn't in the picture when the incidents started," Max pointed out. "Nolan Hildebrand was. But he and Cleo had nothing more than a casual dating relationship."

O'Reilly peered at him from beneath bushy brows. "You're positive about that?"

"He wasn't sleeping with her, if that's what you want to know," Max said coolly. "And before you ask, the answer is, yes, I'm sure of that."

"*Max.*" Cleo felt herself turn bright red. "I can answer Mr. O'Reilly's questions on my

360

own." She gave O'Reilly an embarrassed smile. "Nolan and I really were just friends, although I have reason to believe that he might have been thinking of marriage."

"That sounds as if things were more than just friendly between the two of you," O'Reilly said quietly.

"Well, I never actually knew for certain that he had marriage in mind," Cleo said, feeling unaccountably reckless, "because he never actually *asked* me, you see. He had been making certain *assumptions,* apparently. Just like someone else I could name."

"Cleo." Max's voice was laced with dark warning.

"The first I knew of Nolan's plans," Cleo continued, "was when he sort of casually tossed the concept of marriage at me one morning when he was under a lot of stress." She glared at Max. "Men tend to do that a lot around me, too."

"Ignore her, O'Reilly," Max advised. "She's in a bad mood today for some reason."

"Uh-huh." O'Reilly looked at Cleo. "Maybe we ought to talk a little more about Nolan Hildebrand."

Cleo shrugged. "As I told you, there isn't much to talk about. He was very upset when he found out I'd written *The Mirror*, but only because he felt that it disqualified me from being the wife of a future senator."

"He wasn't weird about it, then?" O'Reilly asked. "He didn't act like he had been assigned some holy mission to rid the world of people who write sexy books?"

Cleo blushed again, but she kept her voice cool. "No, just annoyed at having wasted time dating me. Trust me, the only thing Nolan is obsessed with is launching his political career."

"What about this Adrian Forrester you mentioned?" O'Reilly asked.

Cleo wrinkled her nose. "Forget Adrian. My relationship with him was even more casual than the one I had with Nolan."

O'Reilly smiled briefly. "Okay. That will do it for now. Once I've had a chance to talk to your staff and take a look around Harmony Cove, I'll probably have more questions, but I've got a few other angles to check first."

Cleo, weary from the long, intensive session, straightened in alarm. "Wait, what do you mean? You can't run around Harmony Cove asking questions about me and my book."

"Why not?" O'Reilly asked.

"Because no one here knows I wrote it," Cleo said impatiently. "I told you I did it under a pen name. Only the family knows I'm the author."

"That's not true, Cleo," Max said quietly.

362

"Nolan Hildebrand knows, and whoever is staging these incidents knows. It probably won't be long before a lot of other people discover you're the author of *The Mirror*."

Cleo laced her fingers together very tightly. "I didn't want outsiders to know about *The Mirror*. It's such a personal book."

"Max is right," O'Reilly said. "I'm afraid the secret is out. There's not much point trying to keep your identity hidden any longer. It's to your benefit right now to go public."

"Why?" she demanded.

"In a small town like Harmony Cove news travels fast," O'Reilly explained. "Sure, people will talk about the book. But they'll also talk about the fact that someone is threatening you. That process could turn up some new information."

Max looked thoughtful. "He's right, Cleo. You're well liked in town. That won't change when people find out you wrote *The Mirror*. Most of the people in Harmony Cove are going to be angry on your behalf about the threats that have been made. It's possible that someone knows more than he or she realizes."

"People will be alert for strangers or unusual actions. That will provide some protection for you." O'Reilly smiled reassuringly at Cleo. "I'll talk to your police chief first. We'll get him in our corner and go from there."

363

Cleo bit her lip, aware that it was useless to argue in the face of such relentless masculine logic. Max and O'Reilly simply didn't understand. They couldn't know how much she dreaded the invasion of privacy she would face once her secret was widely known. It was one thing to be known as a writer of romantic-suspense; it was quite another to be known as the author of something as deeply personal and intimate as *The Mirror*.

She flopped back onto the wicker lounge chair and glared at the bubbling fountain. "I'm not sure it's worth all this fuss. Maybe the incidents are nothing more than someone's idea of a practical joke."

"That note we found in your car was more than a joke," Max said. "And whoever followed you through the fog was either trying to frighten you or worse. I want this business stopped before it goes any farther."

Cleo saw the unshakable intent in his eyes and knew there was no point staging a protest. Besides, she was getting scared herself. She turned back to O'Reilly. "You really think it has to be someone here in Harmony Cove? You said that none of the people who were here the weekend of the motivational seminar looked suspicious?"

"I didn't turn up any red flags when I ran the names of your guests through my usual computer checks," O'Reilly said. "But that doesn't mean one of them isn't nuttier than a fruitcake. However, I don't think we'll find our rabid book critic in that crowd. After all, according to what you told me, the incidents started before any of them arrived at the inn."

"There was the anonymous letter that came through your publisher last month," Max reminded Cleo. "Someone put a copy of the book in Hildebrand's mailbox while the motivational seminar group was at the inn, but none of that crowd was around when that jerk stalked you in the fog."

"I suppose you're right. It must be someone here in Harmony Cove. My God, that's a strange thought." Cleo wrapped her arms beneath her breasts and hugged herself. "To think that it's someone I *know*."

"It often is in cases like this," O'Reilly said.

Max looked at Cleo. "I think the best thing for us to do is get you out of town for a couple of days while O'Reilly starts asking his questions."

Cleo glanced up sharply. "Leave town? I can't do that. I've got a business to run."

"You're not heavily booked this week," Max said. "Sylvia, Andromeda, and the others can handle things for a couple of nights."

He was right, but Cleo did not want to admit it. "I'd rather stay here."

Cleo watched, annoyed, as O'Reilly exchanged man-to-man glances with Max. Then the detective smiled at her. "Might be easier if you took off for a couple of days. It would give me a chance to break the news to everyone about *The Mirror* and what's been happening to you. By the time you get back, the initial uproar will have had a chance to die down. Your friends here at the inn can field the first round of curiosity seekers for you."

Cleo stirred uneasily. Logically speaking, she knew that the hubbub that would ensue when O'Reilly started asking his questions would be relatively mild compared to what she had gone through four years earlier. At least the gossip would focus on her sex life, she thought ruefully, not death and destruction.

But then there would be all those questions about the obsessed critic who was pestering her. Patty Loftins at the beauty shop would probably read *The Mirror* and speculate to her customers on what the stalker would do next. The pimply-faced kid who worked at the drugstore would watch to see if she bought any birth control supplies the next time she shopped for shampoo. Chuck, the gas station attendant, would wonder if she practiced any of the techniques in *The Mirror* when she went out on a date. He'd probably ask her out the next time she stopped in to fill her tank. Cleo winced at the thought.

"Maybe it wouldn't hurt to leave town for a day or two," Cleo said.

"We'll go to Seattle for a couple of days," Max said, as if everything was settled.

"Seattle?" She slanted him a wary glance.

Max achieved a remarkably earnest expression. "It will give you a real change of scene. O'Reilly will keep an eye on the family for you."

"No problem," O'Reilly said cheerfully. "As long as your kitchen keeps pumping out chocolate chip cookies, I'll be happy to hang around forever."

Max glanced casually at his watch. "We can leave in an hour."

Cleo scowled at him. She knew perfectly well what he was doing. The tendrils of his willpower were forming an invisible net around her, dragging her slowly but inevitably in the direction he wanted her to go. Max was a difficult man to resist when he put his mind to getting what he wanted. In fact, according to Kimberly, he was unstoppable.

"Well . . . ," Cleo said hesitantly.

"Let's get you packed." Max gripped his cane and levered himself to his feet. He looked at O'Reilly. "You've got my number in Seattle. Call me if you learn anything."

"Right." O'Reilly stuffed his notebook into his pocket and rose from the wicker chair. "I'll start talking to the staff here at the inn this afternoon. We'll see where it goes from there."

"Hold it a minute." Cleo held up a hand. "I think we'd better discuss your fee before we go any farther, O'Reilly."

"Fee?" O'Reilly looked as though he were unfamiliar with the concept.

"Yes, fee." Cleo frowned. "I hired a private investigator once. The man spent months on the project. He sent me a bill for nearly fifteen thousand dollars and never turned up a single useful piece of information. I don't want a repeat of that experience."

Max and O'Reilly stared at her as if she'd just announced that she was from Saturn. Max recovered first.

"Why in hell did you hire a private investigator?" he demanded.

Cleo watched the water froth in the fountain. "I wanted someone besides the police to look into the deaths of my parents."

"You told me the cops said it was a case of murder-suicide," Max said very quietly. "Your father killed your mother and turned the gun on himself."

Cleo continued to stare at the fountain. She

was intensely aware of O'Reilly's silent, questioning gaze. "I also told you that I've had a hard time accepting that conclusion. Last summer I decided to hire someone to look through the old records of the case and see if there was any reason to think something had been mishandled or overlooked."

"Mind telling me who you hired?" O'Reilly asked in a neutral tone. "Professional curiosity. I might know him."

"His name was Harold Eberson. He had an office in Seattle."

"Yeah." O'Reilly nodded. "I've heard of him. Did he turn up anything for you?"

Cleo put her hands between her knees and pressed them together. "No. He strung me along for a couple of months. He told me he had found a few odd things about the case that he was checking out. But it was all a scam."

"Scam?" O'Reilly repeated.

Cleo nodded, embarrassed at the memory of her own gullibility. "I kept paying his bills until one day they just stopped coming. I called his office to ask what was happening. I got a recording saying the number was no longer in service."

O'Reilly glanced at Max and then looked back at Cleo. "Eberson died in a car accident in October. The reason you never heard any more from him was that no one took over his business. He worked alone. When he died, the business died, too."

"Was he a con man?" Cleo asked bitterly. "How badly did I get taken?"

"Eberson was a small-time operator." O'Reilly shrugged. "If he billed you for fifteen grand, I think it's safe to say you were probably the biggest client he ever had."

Cleo frowned. "But do you think he deliberately ripped me off?"

O'Reilly met her eyes. "I never heard that he was crooked. He just wasn't very big-time. Probably didn't have a head for the business side of things."

"I see." Cleo felt stiff. She started to rub the back of her neck.

Max put his hand on her shoulder and squeezed gently. His thumb moved across the tense muscles. The strength in his fingers felt very good. Cleo could feel the warmth in his hand seeping into her.

"Let's get out of here, Cleo," Max said.

"What about O'Reilly's fee?" she said stubbornly. "I think I need a contract or something. I told you, I don't want another fifteen-thousand-dollar surprise."

"I'll take the same deal you gave Max, here," O'Reilly said. "Minimum wage plus tips and room and board while I'm here."

Cleo wrinkled her nose. "He told you about that?"

"Yeah."

Cleo gave Max a disgusted look. "I suppose you thought it was all very funny, Mr. Hot-shot hotel executive."

"No," said Max. "I thought it was the best deal I'd been offered in a long, long time."

14

The old brick mansion had never seemed so cold. Max checked the thermostat before he went downstairs into the wine cellar to find his best California Cabernet. It was a cold night, but the house should have been comfortably warm. The temperature was set at seventy-four degrees. Max frowned and nudged the setting up to seventy-six. It occurred to him that his attic room at the inn had never seemed chilly.

He knew it was not the mansion that was cool, it was him. It was a familiar sensation. He had felt like this several times before in his life. The first occasion was when a social worker had explained to him that he was going to live with a very nice family. The last time had been when Jason had died.

Tonight was another turning point. He could sense it. A fine tension had set all his nerve endings on red alert.

This time the feeling was the worst it had ever been. This time there was too much at stake. Always before he had been able to walk away from what he knew he could not possess. He did not know how he would walk away from Cleo if she refused his offer of marriage.

On his way back to the kitchen he paused to glance uneasily into the vast living room. Cleo stood with her back to him in front of the broad expanse of windows that overlooked the city and Elliott Bay. She was studying the lights of the downtown high-rises, which gleamed like bright jewels in the rain.

Max watched her, aware of a deep sense of longing inside himself. She had been far too quiet during the drive from the coast. He had made several attempts to start a conversation, only to have each effort flounder.

Cleo had been polite since they left the inn, but she seemed to be off somewhere in a world of her own. Max could not tell what she was thinking, and that fact was making him extremely edgy.

He carried the Cabernet into the kitchen and uncorked it carefully. Long ago Jason had explained to him that a good Cab had to be treated with reverence.

Max experienced a few qualms about his choice of wine as he poured the ruby-colored liquid into two glasses. Maybe he should have chosen champagne, instead. His mouth curved wryly as he realized that, despite Jason's teaching, there were still times when he was unsure of the proper thing to do.

"What are you smiling about?" Cleo asked from the kitchen doorway.

Startled by the question after several hours of near-silence, Max managed to screw up the deft little twisting movement that was designed to prevent the wine bottle from dripping. Two blood-red drops splashed on the polished granite countertop. He looked at them as he set down the bottle.

"I was just thinking that there's one hell of a difference between being born into money and having to battle your way into it," he said. He reached for a paper towel to wipe up the small drops of wine.

"What's the difference?" Cleo asked, her gaze unreadable.

Max shrugged. "A sense of assurance. The certainty that you always know the right thing to do or wear or serve." He handed her one of the glasses. "When you're born into money, you absorb that kind of confidence from the cradle. When you fight your way into it, you never really acquire it."

"I suppose you're right." Cleo delicately tasted her wine. Apparently satisfied, she took a swallow. "On the other hand, when you become successful the hard way, you have the confidence that comes from knowing you earned it."

Max met her eyes. "It's not quite the same thing."

"No, it's a much more impressive sort of assurance. It's the kind of deep-rooted arrogance that comes from knowing that if you lost everything tomorrow and had to start over, you could make your way to the top again. You radiate that kind of confidence, Max."

"That's different. I wasn't talking about that kind of assurance."

"Why not? It's much more interesting than the other kind," Cleo said coolly. "In fact, it can be downright intimidating at times. It's probably most intimidating to someone who comes from a background of wealth. When you're born into money, deep down you don't really know for certain if you could make it on your own. But, Max, you know you can. You've proved it to yourself and the world."

Max smiled. "But the guy who was born with a silver spoon in his mouth wouldn't have to worry about whether to serve champagne or a good Cabernet in a situation like this.

He'd know the answer."

"Oh, dear." Cleo's eyes sparkled behind the lenses of her glasses. "Were you suffering a great deal of angst over the matter?"

"Don't worry, I wasn't going to let it ruin my whole evening."

"Because you knew I wouldn't particularly care whether you served champagne or Cabernet or diet cola, right?"

"Right." Max came to a decision. Glass in one hand, cane in the other, he went toward the door. "Come on, I want to show you something."

"What?" She got out of his way and then turned to follow him.

"Come with me." He went down the dark, paneled hallway to the steel door that guarded his treasures. He thrust the glass into Cleo's hand. "Hold this for a minute."

She took the glass and watched curiously as he punched in the code that opened the door. "What's in there?"

"Some things that are important to me." Max opened the door. The lights came on automatically, revealing a stairwell.

Cleo studied the stairs with interest. "Say, you aren't going to do anything real weird to me down there, are you?"

"That depends on what you consider real weird."

Max led the way down the stairs and opened the second steel door at the bottom. Another bank of lights came up as the barrier swung open to reveal his gallery. Max heard Cleo suck in her breath as she stepped into the chamber.

"My God, Max. Is this stuff all genuine?"

The question irritated him. "Hell, yes. Do you think I'd bother to collect fakes?"

She shot him an odd glance. "No, I guess not." She drew a finger along the top of the room's single chair. "Nice chair."

"It's an original," Max said dryly. "English. Early nineteenth century."

"Naturally." She walked to the center of the chamber and turned slowly in a circle, examining the masterpieces of modern art that were hung on the white walls. "I don't see a single picture with a dog or a horse in it."

He couldn't tell if she was teasing him or not. "No seascapes, either."

She looked at him. "I'll give you a couple of the seascapes that Jason painted. You can hang them in your room at the inn next to Sammy's picture."

"Thank you," Max said. "I'd like that."

Cleo paused as she spotted the blank space on the north wall. "Why isn't there anything there?"

"That's where I'm going to hang the Luttrells when I find them."

"Oh, yes. I forgot." Cleo walked over to the bookcase and scanned the shelves. She read the titles on the spines of several leather-bound volumes. "Gosh. Real Latin. Real old. Real impressive. I'll bet the local libraries hope you remember them in your will."

"I did," Max said.

Cleo stopped short when she came to a series of narrow, tattered books. "What's this? *Dr. Seuss? The Hardy Boys?* Max, what are these doing in here?"

"They were the first things I ever collected."

Cleo glanced at him, her eyes gentle. "I see."

"Cleo, will you marry me?"

She went still.

Max realized he suddenly could not breathe.

"Where do you intend to put me?" Cleo asked softly.

A rush of bewildered anger swept through Max. "What the hell are you talking about?"

"I was just wondering where you would hang me in your gallery. I'm not sure I would fit in here, Max." Cleo walked slowly around the room, peering at his collection. "I'm not a very good example of modern art. I might work better in someone's butterfly collection or maybe an exhibit of carnival glass."

"I said I wanted to marry you, not collect you," Max whispered savagely. He put his wine glass down carefully on the small inlaid table near the Sheraton chair. He was afraid that if he kept the fragile crystal in his hand he would snap the stem. He was gripping the carved hawk on his cane so tightly that the muscles in his wrist ached.

"Is there a difference in your mind?" Cleo asked.

"Yes, damn it. Cleo, you said you were angry this morning because I hadn't asked you properly. I'm trying to do it right."

"It wasn't just that you hadn't asked."

"Cleo."

Max took a step toward her and stopped abruptly when he saw her move back a pace. *She was going to refuse.* Anguish ripped through him. He felt more pain than he had ever known in his life. He could feel it gnawing at his vitals, eating him alive. This was worse than when Jason had died.

Cleo's eyes were wide and luminous. When he took another step toward her, she held up a hand as if she were warding off the devil himself.

"Max, why do you want to marry me?"

"Because I want you." The words were torn from him, leaving a raw, gaping wound. He wondered if he would bleed to death right there on the Oriental rug.

Cleo's gaze seared Max's soul for a moment longer, and then, with a small, soft cry, she went into his arms.

"All right," she said into his shirt. "I'll marry you."

Max felt the wound inside him start to close. He was going to survive, after all. He let the cane fall to the rug as he folded Cleo tightly against him. The volatile emotions that had been raging through him were transmuted into a wild, desperate hunger.

He needed her more than he had ever needed anything in his life.

As if she sensed his need, Cleo raised her face to his. Max kissed her heavily. When he felt her response, he groaned and pulled her down onto the rug.

"Max."

He tugged at her clothing, pulling off her shirt and yanking open the fastening of her jeans. He managed to get the denims off together with her silver shoes. Then he fumbled awkwardly with the zipper of his trousers. He didn't even bother trying to take them off. He knew he wouldn't be able to manage the task.

Cleo reached up for him, parting her legs and opening her mouth for him. He fell on top of her like a starving man on a feast.

A moment later he was where he needed to be, deep inside Cleo. She was warm and soft and snug, and he was home.

Cleo opened her eyes and looked up at the canvases that peered down at her like so many dark, tormented eyes. Max's taste in art definitely did not tend toward the sweet or sentimental.

The pictures that hung on the walls of his secret lair exhibited the same riveting combination of savagery and civilized polish that he did. And they were just as complicated and enigmatic as he was.

Cleo knew that, for better or worse, she had just allowed herself to be collected by Max Fortune.

The only things in this room that gave her hope were the inexpensive copies of the children's books that she had discovered amid the valuable tomes in his bookcase. She smiled.

"Cold?" Max sat up slowly. His eyes darkened with satisfaction as he moved his hand possessively along the curve of her thigh.

"A little." Cleo looked up at him. "It's chilly in here."

"The room is climate controlled."

Cleo sat up and reached for her shirt. "To protect the canvases and the books?"

"Yes." Max watched her closely. "Cleo, I

want to be married immediately."

She paused in the act of buttoning her shirt. "What's the rush?"

"You know damn well what the rush is." Max used the cane to get to his feet. He reached down to catch hold of her hand. "I don't want you changing your mind."

"I've got news for you, Max." Cleo allowed herself to be pulled to her feet. "You won't be allowed to marry me in some hurried little ceremony at the courthouse. The family won't stand for it. Sylvia, Andromeda, and the others will want it done right. And we can't preempt Trisha and Ben's wedding. It wouldn't be fair to steal the limelight from them."

Max zipped up his trousers. "I was afraid you'd say that."

Cleo made a face at him as she finished dressing. She was vastly relieved to see that his expression was once again one of general irritation. He was no longer wearing the stark, cold mask he'd worn an hour ago when he had asked her to marry him.

She could deal with Max's irritation, Cleo thought. She could handle anything except that terrible, bleak look that had been in his eyes when she'd hesitated to give him the answer he wanted. She'd seen that look in her own eyes often enough in the mirror during the months following her parents' death. It was the look of a person who has lost every-thing that mattered.

But Max hadn't lost his dreams, Cleo thought. After all, the man had read Dr. Seuss and The Hardy Boys. He couldn't be all ice and iron.

"Cleo? You have a strange expression on your face. What are you thinking about?"

"Dinner," she said.

Max relaxed visibly. "I almost forgot about dinner. I think I've suddenly developed an appetite."

"Me, too. You can fix the scallops. I'll make the salad."

"I meant what I said, Cleo." Max's fingers closed gently but very firmly around her wrist. He brought her palm to his mouth and kissed it. "I want us to be married as soon as possible."

She touched his cheek lightly with her fingertips. She knew he was thinking of how Kimberly had reneged on the engagement six weeks after Max had asked her to marry him.

"It's all right, Max. I'm not going to change my mind."

He veiled his glittering eyes with his lashes. "Word of honor?"

"Word of honor."

Cleo waited until after dinner to call home.

Max lounged beside her on the sofa, his eyes on the night-shrouded city, as she dialed the number.

"Robbins' Nest Inn."

"Sylvia? It's me."

"What a surprise," Sylvia chuckled. "Hang on a second." Sylvia cupped her hand over the receiver. "I win," she hissed to someone in the background.

"What's going on? Are you busy?" Cleo asked quickly. "I can call back later if you've got people checking in."

"Nope, we're not busy," Sylvia said cheerfully. "I just had a small bet on with O'Reilly that you'd be unable to resist checking on us this evening. He bet that Max would be keeping you too busy to call. I said that nothing, not even a proper proposal of marriage, could keep you from fretting about how things were going out here."

Cleo shot a quick glance at Max. "Well, you were right."

"About you fretting? That's no big revelation."

"No," Cleo said softly. "About the proper proposal."

"Aha." Sylvia's voice held great satisfaction. "I knew it. And you said yes, right?"

"Right."

"That makes it all nice and official then,"

Sylvia crowed. "We'll start making plans for the wedding as soon as we get Trisha and Ben married off. I'm sure Sammy will want to be in this ceremony, too. O'Reilly can give the bride away."

"O'Reilly?"

"Sure. He's going to practice on Trisha."

Somewhere along the line, Cleo realized, O'Reilly had become a member of the wedding party. At this rate he was going to become one of the family, just like Max. "Okay."

"Don't worry, Cleo. Andromeda, Daystar, and I will take care of everything."

"Thank you." Cleo didn't know what else to say. "Uh, so how are things going there?"

"Believe it or not, we're managing to scrape along without you. Had a few new reservations for the weekend. Oh, by the way, good old Herbert T. called to book another corporate seminar."

"I thought Mr. Valence was annoyed with us because we lost power the last time he used the inn. Remember how upset he got when he couldn't show his video?" Cleo could still hear Valence's angry protest. *I've got a reputation for flawless performance.*

"He says that in spite of the electrical difficulties, our inn still makes a good background for his seminars. I booked him for the weekend after next. A group of fifteen from some computer firm this time."

"Good," Cleo said. "That will give us a nice crowd. Jason was right when he suggested we start promoting the inn for corporate retreats and seminars."

"Yes, he was. Hey, I'm sure you've got better things to do than chat with the home office. Say hello to Max. We'll see you both in a couple of days."

Cleo hung up the phone and looked at Max. "They're doing just fine without us."

"Don't worry," Max said. "They couldn't get by for long on their own."

"You're sure?"

He smiled. He put his arm around her shoulders and drew her down onto the couch. "I'm sure. I, on the other hand, can't get by for more than a few minutes without you."

The dream came as a shock in the middle of the night. Blood-spattered walls whirled around Cleo, closing in on her. She tried to scream, but, as always, no sound emerged from her horror-constricted throat. She could not move her arms. Her legs were pinned by some heavy object.

"*Cleo.* Wake up. Wake up, damn it."

Cleo awoke drenched in sweat. Max was crushing her against him. He was holding her tightly, trapping her with the weight of his body as if he could hold her back from the invisible tentacles that reached out for her.

"I'm okay," she whispered. Little wonder she had been unable to move in her dream, she thought wryly. She couldn't move in real life, either. Max's grip was so fierce she could barely breathe.

"The dream again?" Max released her slowly, his eyes shadowed in the darkness.

"Yes. That's the second time in a week." Cleo rubbed her eyes. "I wonder what's happening."

"Stress. Tension. Worry." Max massaged her shoulders. "There's plenty of explanation for the bad dreams you've had lately."

"Do you ever get nightmares?"

"Everyone gets nightmares occasionally."

She relaxed against his chest. Max's hands were warm and strong and comforting. "What are yours like?"

"Some of them are hanging on the walls of my gallery downstairs," he said calmly.

Cleo shuddered. There were a lot of private, secret places in Max Fortune.

"Cleo?"

"Hmm?" She was feeling drowsy again. The last traces of her dream had already retreated to the dark recesses of her mind. Max was good at banishing nightmares, Cleo reflected.

"We could get married the week after

Trisha and Ben have their wedding. Your family can arrange to have another reception that soon, can't they?"

She was torn between laughter and exasperation. He was not going to stop pushing until she had set a date. "I've already told you that I'll marry you. Do we have to pick the day and time tonight?"

"I'd like to get the details nailed down."

"Okay, okay. One week is a little fast. We've got the inn to run, you know. How about two weeks after Trisha and Ben's reception?" She felt the exultant relief sweep through him. "We may have to delay the honeymoon for a while," Cleo warned. "I've got a couple of small conventions scheduled next month."

Max's fingers tightened around her shoulders. "I don't give a damn about the honeymoon."

Cleo chuckled. "Thanks a lot."

"You know what I mean. I just want to get everything settled."

Cleo lifted her head and kissed Max lightly on the mouth. He fell back onto the pillow and pulled her down on top of him.

"There's just one thing you should know, Max." Cleo touched the tip of her tongue to the corner of his mouth.

"What's that?"

"It's not *my* family that is going to arrange our wedding reception. It's *our* family."

"You're right. Our family." Max twisted his fingers in Cleo's hair and dragged her face down to his.

"What do you want to do today?" Max asked the next morning. He watched contentedly as Cleo made waffles in the gleaming iron positioned on a table in the breakfast room.

"I don't care. I don't get to Seattle very often any more. I guess I'd like to do the usual tourist things. Visit the Pike Place Market. Do some shopping. Take in a few good bookstores."

"I've got a better idea. Why don't we shop for a ring?" Max glanced out the window. The downtown high-rises sparkled after the night's rain. "It looks like it's going to be clear for a while. I know a couple of good jewelers."

Cleo smiled ruefully. "It shouldn't take long to find a ring. We'll do the other stuff later." She popped out a waffle and dropped it onto a plate.

The doorbell chimed.

Max looked irritated. He seized his cane and got to his feet. "Whoever that is, I'll get rid of him."

Cleo poured maple syrup on the waffle and listened to Max make his way down the hall.

Max's house was awfully big for one person, she thought. It took forever just to get to the front door. The mansion needed a butler. She wondered why he had bought such a place. Maybe he had been under the impression that if he spent enough money, he could buy a home. Cleo wondered how long it had taken him to discover his mistake.

Cleo heard Kimberly's voice just as she forked up a bite of waffle. She stifled a small groan of dismay when she heard the other woman's high heels on the terrazzo floor of the hall. So much for Max's being able to get rid of his unexpected caller.

"Max, I have to talk to you," Kimberly said in a cool, businesslike tone as she came down the hall. "This is extremely important."

"How did you know I was in town?"

"I called Robbins' Nest Inn. I was told you were here with Cleo. Max, you can't put me off. This is absolutely critical. I've talked to Roarke. He told me you suggested that he and I try to take over the Curzon board. Were you serious?"

"Why not? Looks like the logical move."

"Roarke seems convinced it could be done," Kimberly said slowly.

"The two of you can do it together."

"But my father —"

Max cut her off abruptly. "The only way

you're going to prove to your father that you're as good as the son he never had is to take Curzon from him."

"Do you really think so?" Kimberly asked. "Yes."

Kimberly hesitated. "That isn't the only thing I want to talk to you about. Max, give me five minutes. That's all I'm asking."

"All right," Max said impatiently. His cane thudded softly on the tile as he led Kimberly into the breakfast room. "Five minutes, but no more. Cleo and I have things to do today."

"Such as?" Kimberly asked dryly.

"Such as shop for a ring," Max said. "Cleo and I are engaged."

"Well, isn't that interesting," Kimberly murmured. She looked at Cleo. "I can't say I'm surprised."

"Thank you," Cleo said around a mouthful of waffle. "I think."

"Max was always very good at arranging advantageous engagements for himself," Kimberly said.

"If you're going to make cracks like that, Kim," Max said calmly, "you can leave now."

Kimberly looked at him. "What's the matter, haven't you told her why you've gotten yourself engaged to her?"

Max sat down and regarded Kimberly with cobra eyes. "Say whatever it is you came here to say and then leave."

Kimberly walked over to the sideboard and helped herself to a cup of coffee with the ease of a woman who was familiar with her surroundings. She smiled bleakly at Cleo.

"Has he told you yet that he's negotiating with an outfit called Global Village Properties?" Kimberly asked. "They've offered him the same deal Curzon has, but Max wants more. He wants the CEO position."

"No," Cleo said. She looked at Max. "He didn't mention that."

"Damn," Max said. "I knew I shouldn't have opened the door this morning."

15

Cleo forked up another bite of waffle and ate it in silence. She was aware of Max's gaze on her as Kimberly talked.

"It's all true," Kimberly said not unkindly to Cleo. "My sources tell me that Max recently met with Turner and Sand, two point men for Global Village Properties."

Cleo glanced at Max. "Is that right?"

"Yes," Max said. His eyes did not leave her face.

Kimberly looked grimly satisfied. She started to pace the breakfast room with the elegant, restless stride of a racehorse that had been penned for too long. Cleo wondered how she could stand wearing high heels all day.

"I only know of one meeting," Kimberly said. "But that doesn't mean he hasn't been negotiating with them since he left Curzon last month. I'm told that they made him a very generous offer."

Cleo glanced at Max. "Did they make you an offer?"

"Yes," Max said.

Kimberly shot him a knowing glance. "The rumor I heard is that the offer included a vice presidency and a seat on the Global Village board. But as I said, Max wants the CEO slot. So he's told them that he's going independent unless they can make it worth his while not to do so."

"What's that supposed to mean?" Cleo asked curiously.

"It means he's allowing everyone to believe he's going into business on his own."

"Unless he receives a better offer from Global Village? Is that what you're saying?" Cleo watched Kimberly carefully.

Kimberly gave a sigh that held a trace of genuine sympathy. "Try not to feel too bad about it, Cleo. Max has a reputation for getting the job done and for using whatever means he thinks are necessary to do it. People who are far more savvy about business than you will ever be have gotten ground to dust beneath his chariot wheels."

"A colorful image." Cleo ignored Max's silent, brooding stare and kept her attention on Kimberly.

Kimberly looked briefly disconcerted. She flicked a quick, searching glance at Max and then frowned at Cleo. "The point I'm trying to make here is that Max is using you to add an element of realism to the picture he's painting for Global Village. Getting engaged to you will convince everyone he's serious about going independent."

"And that will make Global Village surrender to his demands?" Cleo asked.

Kimberly shrugged. "Probably. They want him very badly."

Cleo looked at Max. "Nice to be wanted, isn't it?"

"Depends on who wants you." Max's gaze was unwavering.

Kimberly stopped pacing for a moment. "I wondered why Max turned down my father's offer to come back to Curzon. Now I know why. The CEO slot at Global Village probably looks a good deal more tempting. Max likes to be in charge. At Curzon he'd always be battling the family for control. But at Global Village he can be the one in command."

Cleo used a linen napkin to blot a drop of syrup from the corner of her mouth. When that didn't do the trick, she used the tip of her tongue. "When did you first talk to Global Village, Max?"

"The day I went into town with Ben to get some stuff at the hardware store." His eyes willed her to believe him.

Cleo took a deep breath. "That would be about a week after you had accepted my offer of employment."

"Yes."

"What did you say to them?"

"That I wasn't interested in any position at Global Village," Max said quietly.

"Not even the CEO slot?" Cleo asked.

"No. Not even the CEO slot."

Cleo smiled tremulously. "I guess that means you're still working for me, doesn't it?"

"Yes." Max's eyes were brilliant with an emotion that was not reflected in his voice. "I'm still working for you. I have no plans to quit."

"I thought so," Cleo said. "Well, that settles that little problem, doesn't it? Stop worrying, Kimberly. Max isn't going to work for the competition."

She got up to pour herself a cup of coffee.

She wanted to make the action look as nonchalant as Kimberly had earlier, but that plan went out the window when she had to hunt for a cup.

"Second cupboard on the left," Kimberly said coldly.

Cleo set her teeth. "Thank you."

"I can't figure you out." Kimberly eyed her warily. "Originally I thought you were just naive and rather unsophisticated. But right now I'm starting to wonder if there's more to you than meets the eye."

"You mean you're wondering if I'm as dumb as I look?" Cleo asked innocently. "Max had a problem with that in the beginning, too. I wonder what it is about me that gives that impression? Do you think it's the sneakers?" She glanced down at the silver sneakers she was wearing. "Maybe I should do something about my image."

"What sort of game are you playing, Cleo? Do you really think you can control Max?" Kimberly's gaze was bright with speculation. "If you're planning to use him to build an empire for you, I'd advise caution. If Max creates an empire, you can bet he'll be the one who owns and runs it. In the end you'll be left with nothing."

Cleo blew on her coffee. "I'm not trying to build an empire. I'm just trying to run an inn. Good help is hard to find. I was lucky to get Max."

"Don't give me that. We both know you can't possibly afford him."

"All I know is that the offer I made to him was accepted." Cleo looked at Max. "Wasn't it?"

Max smiled faintly for the first time since Kimberly had arrived. His eyes were gleaming. "Yes."

Kimberly scowled at Cleo. "Damn it, what's going on here? There's no way you could match an offer from Global Village or Curzon International."

"You're wrong," Cleo said softly. "Robbins' Nest Inn has something to offer Max that neither you nor Global Village can possibly match."

Kimberly's smile was laced with scorn. "And just what would that be, Cleo? You? Do you really think that Max would walk away from a CEO slot or a vice presidency with corporations like Global Village or Curzon for you or any other woman?"

"No," Cleo said. "Not just for me alone. But I think he'd do it for what comes along with me."

"Robbins' Nest Inn?"

"No," Cleo said. "A family."

"You're out of your mind." Kimberly stared

at her in astonishment. "What would Max want with a family?"

"For one thing," Cleo said, "he won't have to worry about the occasional screwup."

"What are you talking about?" Kimberly looked at her blankly.

Cleo took a sip of coffee. "With us Max knows that even if he fails to live up to his amazing reputation once in a while, we'll still want him around. He's one of us whether he screws up or not."

Kimberly's mouth opened on a soundless exclamation. When she could not find the words she sought, she turned to Max.

"All right," she said, "I give up. I can't figure out what's going on here, but it's obvious you've got things in the palm of your hand, as usual. I assume that sooner or later we'll all find out what your agenda is, Max."

"There's no hidden agenda," Max said quietly. "Cleo told you the truth. I'm working for her. I'm not open to outside offers. You may congratulate me on my engagement, and then you may leave."

Kimberly gave him a disgusted look. "Congratulations." She turned around and walked to the door.

Silence descended on the breakfast room. Max looked at Cleo. "Thanks."

"For what?"

"For everything."

"Sure." Cleo ladled up another spoonful of batter. "Want a waffle?"

"Among other things," Max said. His glance went to the pot of honey that sat in the middle of the table.

Cleo gave him a severe frown. "Don't get any ideas. That scene with the honey in *The Mirror* was pure fantasy."

"My specialty is turning fantasy into reality."

"Forget it. Too sticky."

"Let me worry about the technical details." Max smiled slowly. He picked up the pot of honey.

Cleo forgot about the next waffle.

A cold rain began to fall just as Max and Cleo emerged from an antiquarian bookshop in Pioneer Square. Cleo flicked open her umbrella. Her silver sneakers were getting soaked.

"It's pouring. Let's go back to your place," she suggested.

"I've got a better idea." Max took the umbrella from her and held it aloft so that it shielded both of them. When his fingers brushed against hers he glanced with approval at the emerald ring he had put on her finger an hour earlier. "There's an interesting little gallery around the corner. We can get out of the rain for a while in there."

"I'll bet this gallery doesn't hang any nice pictures of dogs or horses or seascapes," Cleo muttered. They had already been in three other galleries, and none of them had featured the sort of art she liked. All the owners knew Max on sight.

"The day this place hangs a picture of a spaniel will be the day I stop buying art here." Max took a possessive grip on Cleo's arm and shepherded her into the white-walled gallery.

Cleo studied the collection of mostly dark, mostly bleak, mostly gray and brown paintings with an unimpressed eye. She wrinkled her nose at Max. "I really don't understand what you see in this stuff."

Max took in the paintings on display with a single, sweeping glance. "If it's any consolation, I don't see anything at all in this batch."

"Good." Cleo grinned. "There's hope for you yet."

A shining, bald head popped up from behind the counter. "Max, my friend." A heavyset middle-aged man dressed entirely in black smiled widely. "Long time, no see. Where have you been? I've left half a dozen messages with your office telling you to call me as soon as possible. Did you get them?"

"No," Max said. "I'm no longer working for Curzon. Walter, I'd like you to meet my fiancée, Cleo Robbins. Cleo, this is Walter Stickley. He owns this gallery."

"How do you do?" Cleo said.

"My pleasure." Walter's eyes lit with curiosity. He glanced at Max. "Engaged, did you say?"

"Yes."

"Congratulations. And you say you've left Curzon?"

"That's right. I'm with another firm now."

"That explains why I haven't been able to reach you. I'm glad you decided to drop in today." Walter rubbed his palms together. "I was just about to start making a few phone calls to other clients."

"What have you got to show me?" Max gave the paintings on display another dismissing glance. "I don't see anything very interesting here."

Walter chuckled. "You know I always keep the good stuff in the back room. Follow me."

He came out from behind the counter and led the way down a short hall to a closed door. He opened it and waved Cleo and Max inside.

Cleo took a quick look at the large canvas leaning against the wall and rolled her eyes. This picture was bleaker, more savage, and admittedly more interesting than the ones that were hanging in the outer room, but she didn't like it any better than she had the others.

"Yuk," Cleo said.

Walter shot her a scathing glance. "Philistine."

"She likes pictures of dogs and horses," Max said absently. He was staring at the painting with rapt attention.

"And seascapes," Cleo added. "I'm very fond of seascapes."

"I don't carry that sort of thing," Walter said stiffly.

"I noticed." Cleo watched Max. "You okay, Max? You look a little strange." She wondered uneasily if he were looking into one of his own nightmares.

"I'm fine," Max said softly. "Who's the artist, Walter? I don't recognize the style."

"A recent discovery of mine," Walter said smugly. "His name is David Verrier. What do you think?"

"I'll take it. Can you get it delivered this afternoon? I'm leaving town tomorrow."

"No problem." Walter rubbed his hands together and chortled knowingly. "Thought you'd like it. Five years from now Verrier is going to be worth a mint."

"Yes," Max said. He was still gazing into the painting. "Call me as soon as you get anything else from him. I'll leave you my new number."

"Of course," Walter said happily. "Yours will be the first name on my list."

"Mine will be the only name on your list," Max said.

Walter cleared his throat. "Uh, yes. The only name. But see here, Max. Verrier needs a chance to gain some exposure. You can't grab everything he does and lock it up before the art world has an opportunity to see his work. I want to be able to give him some shows. He deserves the recognition."

Max did not look pleased, but he nodded reluctantly. "All right. You can show his pictures. But I get first crack at whatever he produces."

"It's a deal."

Cleo tipped her head to one side and studied the canvas from a different angle. When that didn't make it any more cheerful, she walked to another corner of the room and peered at it from there. Then she crouched down and tried again from another vantage point.

"Okay, Max, tell me what you see in that picture," she said. "It looks like the bottom of a bucket of black paint to me."

Walter cringed. "Did you say you're going to marry this . . . this *person*, Max?"

"Yes." Max finally tore his gaze away from

the picture. He smiled. "She doesn't know much about art, but she knows what she likes."

"I see." Walter's eyes glittered. "By the way, Max, there are rumors floating around."

"Rumors about what?" Max asked without any real show of interest.

"About five Amos Luttrell paintings that have recently disappeared," Walter said softly. "You wouldn't know anything about them, would you?"

"I know that they belong to me," Max said.

"Uh, yes. I suspected you'd say something like that." Walter pursed his lips. "But there appears to be some question of ownership."

Max's mouth curved in a humorless smile. "There's no question at all about who owns the Luttrells, Walter."

Walter cleared his throat. "The story I heard involves Garrison Spark. Word is, he's on the trail of the Luttrells. He's got a client who will pay a quarter of a million for them. He's also got a bill of sale from Jason Curzon. He claims it predates the will."

"The bill of sale, if it exists, is a forgery." Max's eyes met Walter's. "We both know it wouldn't be the first forgery Spark has handled, don't we?"

Walter smiled wryly. "Point taken."

The following afternoon Cleo sat beside

403

Max in the Jaguar and watched with trepidation as Harmony Cove came into sight. "I wonder if the city council will have roadblocks up at the entrance to town to prevent me from coming back."

"Relax, Cleo. No one's going to be upset about the fact that you wrote a book."

"Nolan was."

"Nolan's an ass."

"Yes, well, I'm afraid he's not the only ass in Harmony Cove." Cleo twisted the ring on her finger. She was very conscious of its weight. "By now I suppose O'Reilly has talked to everyone."

"Probably. O'Reilly is very thorough."

"I don't know if this was such a good idea, Max."

He slanted her a sidelong glance. "You think letting that stalker get closer and closer is a better idea?"

"Well, no, but I have to live here in Harmony Cove after this is all over. I don't want people staring at me. I had my fill of curiosity seekers after my parents died."

"I'll keep the curiosity seekers at bay," Max promised softly.

She saw the grim line of his jaw and knew he meant every word. Cleo relaxed slightly. With Max by her side no one was going to give her too much trouble. "I may have to give you a raise."

"I'll take it out in Daystar's cornbread muffins."

Max slowed the Jaguar as they drove through Harmony Cove's block-long downtown district. A woman waved at them from the entrance to the grocery store.

Cleo waved back. "At least Mrs. Gibson doesn't look like she wants to paint a large red A on my forehead."

"Who's Mrs. Gibson?"

"She owns the little bookshop on the corner."

Max smiled. "She's probably ordered several copies of *The Mirror* in anticipation of the rush."

"Oh, geez, Max. This is going to be awful." Cleo fiddled nervously with the car phone.

"Put down the phone and stop panicking." Max slowed the Jaguar still further and turned into the grocery store parking lot.

"What are you doing?" Cleo yelped in alarm.

"We're going to get the worst of this over with in a hurry so you'll stop working yourself up into a lather."

"Max, I don't need anything at the grocery store."

"We'll find something." Max slid the Jaguar neatly into one of the parking spaces and opened the door on his side.

Cleo made no move to unfasten her seatbelt. Max walked around to her side of the car and opened the door.

"Come on, Cleo. This isn't going to be that bad."

"I don't want to deal with this yet."

"You're going to have to deal with it sometime."

"I know. But I don't want to do it today," Cleo insisted.

"Get out of the car, Cleo," Max said gently, "or I will peel you out of there and carry you inside the damn grocery store."

She looked at him with mute defiance. Max's expression was even more stubborn than her own. She knew he was right. Sooner or later she was going to have to face the people of Harmony Cove.

"All right, let's get this over with." Cleo unbuckled the seatbelt and exploded out of the car. She stormed past Max.

"That's my brave Cleopatra," Max muttered.

Already halfway to the door, Cleo stopped and glanced back over her shoulder. She scowled when she realized that she had left Max behind in the dust.

"I'm not going in there alone," she said.

"Then you'll have to slow down a bit." Max

reached her side and took her arm. "I don't run except in cases of acute emergency and this is not one of those cases."

"You can move fast enough when you want to," Cleo grumbled. "I've seen you go up and down the stairs at the inn as rapidly as any of the rest of us. Max, are you sure we have to do this?"

"I can't believe you're this nervous about it." Max pushed open the glass door of the grocery store and shoved her gently ahead of him. "You're here for milk."

"We don't need milk. We get a dairy delivery twice a week at the inn," Cleo muttered.

"Today you need milk."

Cleo felt the eyes as soon as she stepped into the familiar surroundings of the store. Everyone from the stock boy to the counter clerk looked at her as if they had never seen her before in their lives. They all waved enthusiastically.

Cleo ducked her head and hurried toward the dairy case.

The young man stocking milk and cottage cheese smiled tentatively at her. "Hi, Ms. Robbins."

"Hi, Tom. How are you today?" Thankful for Max's reassuring presence, Cleo opened the glass door and yanked out a quart of skim.

"Fine. I heard someone was pestering you

on account of you wrote a book. Is that true?"

Cleo's fingers trembled around the carton of milk. "Yes."

"Real sorry to hear someone's bothering you. Hope they catch him."

"Thank you, Tom."

"Say, I was, uh, wondering." Tom cast a surreptitious look up and down the aisle and sidled closer.

Cleo steeled herself. "What were you wondering, Tom?"

"About the book you wrote."

Cleo's stomach tightened. "Yes?"

"I, uh, I've been thinking about writing a book myself."

Cleo blinked. "You have?"

Tom nodded urgently and turned a bright shade of red. "Yeah, it's science fiction, y'know?"

"I see," Cleo said uncertainly. "That's great. Good luck with it."

Tom brightened at the encouragement. "It's an alternate world story, see. There's a lot of stuff in it that's similar to our world, but the basic laws of science are different. More like magic, y'know."

"Uh-huh." Cleo took a step back.

Tom eagerly closed the space between them. "My main character is this guy from our world who finds himself stranded in this alternate world. At first he thinks he's dreaming. Then he realizes he's trapped there. He has to learn how to survive or he'll get killed."

"Very clever," Cleo said weakly. She retreated another step.

Tom followed. "He's a computer nerd on earth, so when he's caught in this weird world run by magic, he's really confused for a while."

It dawned on Cleo that Tom the stock boy had no interest at all in *The Mirror*. Convinced he had found a soul mate, he was going to regale her with the plot of his entire book right there in front of the dairy case.

"And then he meets this character who's like a sorcerer, y'know . . ."

"Interesting," Cleo said. She inched back down the aisle, aware of Max's silent amusement. Tom followed her every step of the way.

"Then there's this other sorcerer who's like crazy, y'know? He's discovered some new law of magic. I haven't quite decided what that's going to be yet, but whatever it is, it threatens the whole alternate world . . ."

"That's absolutely fascinating," Cleo said. She glanced at her watch. "I'd love to hear the rest, but I've really got to run."

"Huh?" Engrossed in his tale, Tom frowned, puzzled. "Oh, sure. Look, maybe I could stop by the inn sometime and tell you the rest?"

"We'll see." Cleo turned and fled toward the checkout counter. She did not look back to see if Max was following.

The gray-haired woman at the checkout counter smiled broadly. "Oh, hello, Cleo. Heard someone's been making a nuisance of himself because you wrote a book. I didn't know you were a writer."

"I've only had one book published so far," Cleo muttered. She set the milk down on the counter.

"That's all right, dear, I'm sure you'll write some more. You know, I haven't read a book in years. Just never had the time, what with TV and all. Milk?"

"Yes, please, Ernestine."

"Thought you got dairy deliveries out there at the inn."

Cleo groped for an explanation as Max arrived at the counter. "Ran short."

"Oh." Ernestine whisked the milk through the checkout routine. "You know you and I should get together one of these days."

"We should?"

Ernestine beamed. "I could tell you all about my family history. You could write a book about it. I'm sure people would want to read it. Some real fascinating stuff in my family's history. Did I ever tell you that one of my

410

relatives came out West on a wagon train?"

"I don't believe you ever mentioned it, Ernestine."

"That was Sarah Hill Montrose, I believe." Ernestine assumed a contemplative look. "Her story would make a terrific book. Then there was my great-grandfather, Morton Montrose. He used to farm over in Eastern Washington. Raised turkeys, too. Used to tell the funniest stories about those birds. Dumb as bricks, they are."

"Is that right?" Cleo looked at her milk, which was standing forgotten on the counter.

"Eugene Montrose, that's my grandfather, was probably the most interesting of the lot. He fished."

"You don't say. Could I please have my milk, Ernestine?"

"What's that?" Ernestine glanced down at the milk. "Oh, yes. The milk. Here, I'll put it in a bag for you." She stuffed the milk into a sack.

"Thanks." Cleo snatched up the milk, aware that Max's eyes were brilliant with laughter. "See you around, Ernestine."

"Just let me know when you've got time to write that book about my family," Ernestine said cheerfully. "I've got lots of old newspaper clippings and photos and such."

"I'll let you know if I ever get a free minute," Cleo promised. "But I'm pretty busy these days."

She was halfway out the door, with Max still following faithfully behind her, when another familiar figure loomed in her path. Cleo was forced to come to a halt. She clutched the milk close and smiled weakly.

"Hello, Adrian."

Adrian Forrester glowered at her from beneath dark brows. He had a large manila envelope in his hand. "Heard you had a book published."

"Yes, I did." Cleo glanced uneasily at the envelope he was holding. She was afraid she knew what was inside. She'd received her share of rejections before she'd sold *The Mirror*.

"I suppose you had an agent?" Adrian demanded.

"Well, no, I didn't, although I'm thinking of getting one for the next book."

"Know someone in publishing?"

"Uh, no. I didn't know anyone, Adrian. I just sent the manuscript off to a lot of different publishers, and someone finally bought it."

"So you just got lucky."

"Right," Cleo said. "I just got lucky."

"It's because you're writing women's stuff," Adrian said in an aggrieved tone. "That's why they published you instead of me. New York is only interested in women's books these days. Romance, self-help, glitz, erotica. It's all aimed at women. Hell, even the mystery market is skewed toward women."

"What about all the thrillers and science fiction and horror stuff that's published?"

"They're putting relationships in them, too." Adrian looked at her as if it were all her fault.

"Gosh, I don't really think . . ."

"Do you know what this rejection letter says?" Adrian waved his manuscript aloft. "It says they're not interested in hard-boiled detective mysteries featuring male protagonists. The editor suggests I turn my hero into a female private eye."

"Gee, Adrian, I can't imagine why the editor would suggest a thing like that. Unless, of course, it's because a lot of women like to read and are willing to spend their money on books that feature stories they enjoy."

Adrian's glare would have frozen lava. "I'll tell you something. If they weren't putting out books like yours, they'd be publishing my stuff."

Cleo's temper overcame the last vestiges of her fear of being identified as the author of *The Mirror.* "You think so?" she asked.

Max apparently recognized the dangerous sweetness of her tone and finally bestirred himself to intervene. "I think we'd better be on our way, Cleo. The family will be waiting." He took her arm and started toward the Jaguar.

Cleo dug in her heels. "Wait a second. I want to give Adrian some publishing advice."

Max grinned. "I don't think Forrester wants your advice, do you, Forrester?" He wrapped an arm around Cleo and dragged her toward the car.

"She just got lucky," Adrian snarled.

"You think so? Well, maybe it was more than luck," Cleo shouted as Max stuffed her into the front seat of the Jaguar. "Maybe I write better than you do. Maybe my book was better than yours. Did you ever think about that possibility?"

"It's because it was a woman's book," Adrian yelled. "That's the only reason it got published. The women's market is taking over, I tell you."

"So get a sex change operation," Cleo yelled back.

"Good Lord," Max muttered as he slammed the car door shut, "I've created a monster."

16

"You can stop laughing now," Cleo muttered as Max drove along the bluffs toward Robbins' Nest Inn.

Max glanced at her, unable to suppress his grin. She was sitting with her arms folded in a gesture of complete disgust, her gaze fixed on the winding road.

"Sorry," Max said.

"You're not the least bit sorry. I can tell."

"Come on, Cleo, admit the whole thing was funny. You've been terrified of what everyone in town would think when they found out you wrote *The Mirror*. But being discovered wasn't so bad, was it?"

"I don't think any of them even bothered to read it." She sounded disgruntled.

"I'd say that's a fairly safe assumption. If our recent unscientific survey holds true, we can assume that the vast majority of the people you meet will never actually read your books. But they'll want to talk to you about publishing. People are fascinated with publishing."

"You mean they'll want to tell me the plots

415

of their own books or suggest I write their family's history or complain because I got published instead of them."

"Yes."

Cleo started to smile. "It was sort of funny, wasn't it?"

"Very," Max said softly. "Especially the look on Forrester's face."

"When I think about the way he used to drone on and on about his own book and how it was going to take the publishing world by storm —" Cleo broke off and started to grin.

She burst first into giggles and then into full-blown laughter.

Max watched her out of the corner of his eye and smiled to himself. "I'm not saying you won't get the occasional critic," he cautioned. "But I think you can handle it if someone comes up to you and tells you he thinks your book was trash."

"The way Nolan did?" Cleo's mouth twisted wryly. "Yes, I think so. I've been anxious about having people pry into my private life, but the truth is, all that most of them really wanted to talk about was themselves. This isn't anything like what happened to me after my parents died."

"Of course not."

"I guess I'd let my imagination run away with me."

"You do have a first-class imagination," Max conceded.

The laughter died in Cleo's eyes. "I just wish the stalker was a product of my imagination."

Max watched the road. "So do I."

Cleo turned to him with an expression of intrigued speculation. "Hey, you don't suppose Adrian is the stalker, after all, do you? Maybe his jealousy has gotten the better of him. Maybe he's trying to punish me because I got published and he didn't."

Max shook his head with grim certainty. "No. It's obvious Adrian only recently found out that you'd published *The Mirror*. The incidents started over a month ago. He'd never have been able to keep his jealousy under wraps this long."

Cleo lounged back in the seat. "I'm not so sure about that. Maybe he knew all along and just pretended that he didn't."

Max took one hand off the wheel and reached out briefly to touch her leg. "We'll find out who's trying to scare you, Cleo."

"I hope so."

Max put his hand back on the wheel and drove in silence for a while. There was less than a mile to go until they reached the inn. He and Cleo would be home soon.

Home.

In spite of his concern about the incidents

that had been plaguing Cleo, Max was aware of the pleasant sense of anticipation that was simmering deep inside him.

For the first time in his life he felt like he belonged somewhere. Best of all, he had a woman who wanted him, a woman who had waited her whole life for him.

"What are you thinking about, Max?" Cleo asked softly.

"I was wondering if Ben took care of that dripping shower head in two-sixteen."

Cleo smiled.

The early darkness of a winter night was descending on the coast. Heavy clouds overhead promised more rain before dawn. Max drove around the last bend in the road and saw the lights of Robbins' Nest Inn blazing in the distance.

"Cleo?"

"Hmmm?" Cleo was studying the mostly empty parking lot with an innkeeper's professional frown of concern.

"I want us to have a baby."

She jerked her gaze away from the lot. "A what?"

"A baby." A baby would make everything more secure, Max thought. It would be another bond linking him to Cleo and her friends.

"Why?"

Max hesitated. "Why does anyone want a baby?"

"There are a lot of reasons why someone might want a baby. Not all of them are good reasons. Why do you want one?"

"Is this a test?" Max asked.

"Probably."

He felt the tension in his jaw as he searched for a way to put his certainty into words. "It's time." He concentrated. "I'm going to be thirty-five next month. I've got a secure income from the investments I've made over the past few years. I've got a stable life-style now that I'm working for you. And I've got you."

"I'm not sure those reasons are good enough," Cleo said quietly.

Fear surged through him. His fingers clenched around the steering wheel. "What the hell is that supposed to mean?"

Cleo bristled. "Having a baby is a major decision. There are a lot of things to consider. We're talking about a serious commitment."

"You and I have already made a serious commitment."

"I know, but still . . ."

"What's the risk?" Max asked swiftly, sensing a weak point. "Are you afraid I'm going to walk out on you in a year or so, the way Sylvia's husband did to her and Sammy?"

419

Cleo turned her head to gaze at him with perceptive eyes. "No." Her voice was very soft and very certain. "No, I don't think you would walk out on your family."

"You think I'd make a lousy father, is that it? Look, I know a man with my kind of background probably doesn't seem like a good bet as a father. But I think I could handle the basics. You once told me you didn't have to jump out of a plane in order to figure out what it would do to your insides."

"What do you think are the basics of fatherhood?" Cleo asked with genuine curiosity.

Max flashed her a quick glance. "Being there. Sticking around to do the job."

"Where did you learn that?" Cleo asked.

"From my own father," Max said roughly.

"He spent a lot of time with you?"

"No," Max said. "I never met him. He left before I was born."

"Oh." There was a wealth of understanding in her voice.

"My strategy for being a father is to do just the opposite of everything that was done to me when I was growing up."

Cleo touched his thigh. "Max, I think you'd make a terrific father."

Relief washed over him. He had pushed hard and won again. "You do?"

"Yes." She gazed through the windshield

420

at the warm lights of the inn. "I do."

"Then it's settled." Max turned the Jaguar into the parking lot. "We'll get started right away."

"Could we wait until after dinner?" Cleo asked. "I'm sure the family will have a lot of questions, and Ben and Trisha will probably want to talk about their wedding plans. I'd like to have a chance to go through the new bookings, and maybe O'Reilly will have some news for us."

Max smiled ruefully. "If you insist, I guess we can wait until after dinner."

Everything was going to be okay, he thought. So why did he feel this disturbing sense of unease beneath the satisfaction he was experiencing, he wondered.

But even as he asked the question, he knew the answer. He was still on dangerous ground. After all, he knew better than anyone else that he had pushed Cleo into the engagement just as he had once pushed Kimberly. And now he had pushed Cleo into another commitment. Maybe he was pushing too hard in his effort to force his way into her life. He knew that he didn't have a good track record when it came to this kind of thing. It was the one area in which he always screwed up.

He probably should have held back, Max thought, suddenly worried about his own successful pressure tactics. Something was wrong.

The things he wanted most in life always seemed to elude him just as he was reaching for them.

Three hours later Max watched, amused, as O'Reilly put his feet up on a wicker footstool in the solarium and lounged contentedly in one of the fanback chairs.

"Playing pasha?" Max asked.

O'Reilly looked at him with knowing eyes. "I think I've finally figured out why you changed jobs, Max. Just be careful you don't put on weight eating chocolate chip cookies."

"I'll work it off. There's always something that needs doing around an old place like this."

"Yeah. Found that out fast. I helped Ben with a couple of leaking faucets while you were gone. Ben thinks you leap tall buildings in a single bound, by the way."

"I don't know why," Max said. "I haven't leaped any lately."

"I guess we all have to find our heroes where we can." O'Reilly grinned. "Sammy supervised the plumbing repairs."

"Sammy's good at supervision."

O'Reilly looked pleased. "He's a great little kid, isn't he?"

"Yes."

"Smart as a whip," O'Reilly said.

"Talented, too," Max said, remembering the crayon drawing that was hanging in the attic.

"What kind of a father would run off and leave Sammy and a fine woman like Sylvia on their own?" O'Reilly asked.

"A real jerk of a father."

"Some guys don't know when they've got it made, do they?" O'Reilly mused.

"No," Max said. "Some guys don't."

O'Reilly gave him a level look. "But some guys, guys like you and me, for instance, are a little brighter. We know a good thing when we see it."

Max's attention was caught by the unfamiliar undercurrent he thought he detected in O'Reilly's voice. He had known the other man for a long time. Since the death of O'Reilly's wife and child, it had been rare to hear any emotion other than unrelenting, completely superficial amusement in his voice.

"Yes," Max said. "Some of us know a good thing when we see it." He glanced toward the French doors as they opened. Ben walked into the room. "Come on in, Ben. We've been waiting for you."

"What's up?" Ben glanced at Max and then at O'Reilly. "You said we needed to have a strategy session?"

"Right. Sit down." Max waved him to a seat. "I figure this is something the three of us should discuss before we talk to the rest of the family. I don't want everyone worrying unnecessarily."

O'Reilly chuckled. "Translated, that means Max thinks this is a job for the men of the household. I'm warning you, the ladies will have a fit if they find out we're making plans behind their backs."

"Gotcha." Ben dropped down on a nearby seat, obviously proud to be included in the strategy session. "I take it we're going to talk about what you found out while Cleo and Max were gone?"

"I've got my notes here somewhere." O'Reilly rummaged around in his pants pockets and pulled out a small notebook. "I'd better bring Max up to speed first."

Max watched him intently. "Anything interesting?"

"Nothing for certain, but when you lay it all out some intriguing questions arise."

Before Max could ask what those questions were, the French doors opened again.

"What's going on in here?" Cleo demanded from the doorway. Trisha and Sylvia hovered to one side, looking half irritated and half anxious. Andromeda and Daystar were standing just behind Cleo.

Max looked at the phalanx of women and swore softly.

"So much for trying to have a war council with just us guys," O'Reilly said dryly. "Come on in, ladies."

"Thank you." Cleo stalked into the room. The others followed with determined expressions. "We intended to do just that."

"Who's watching the front desk?" Max asked.

"George is on duty," Sylvia said. "He'll keep an eye on the handful of guests in the lounge." She sat down next to O'Reilly. "Don't worry, gentlemen, everything is under control. Now, what are you up to in here?"

"I was merely about to give my report," O'Reilly said mildly. "Such as it is."

"You said earlier that you hadn't turned up much." Cleo sat down next to Max. "What's to report?"

O'Reilly flipped open his notebook. "The way I see this, there are three possible explanations for the incidents. The first is the one you and Max came up with, which is that we're dealing with a deranged critic out to punish you for writing *The Mirror*."

Max looked up, frowning. "You don't sound like you think that's the most likely explanation."

"I don't think it is," O'Reilly said. "Mostly

because as near as I can tell, no one in town had read the book until I started asking questions about it two days ago. The local bookshop didn't even have it in stock."

"It was a rather small print run," Cleo said apologetically.

"What about the possibility that it's someone from out of town who's read the book and tracked Cleo down?" Trisha asked.

O'Reilly shook his head. "The only place a stranger could be staying here in Harmony Cove is at this inn, Cosmic Harmony, or the motel on the other side of town. None of those establishments have had any repeat customers in the past couple of months."

Ben considered that. "So there was no one person who kept showing up around here each time there was an incident, is that it?"

"That's it," O'Reilly said. "Now, I'm not saying someone couldn't have snuck into town and staged the incidents, but he would have had to know his way around. He would also have had to know something about Cleo. The fact that she was dating Nolan Hildebrand, for example. The time of night she usually goes upstairs to bed. Which room is hers. The fact that she often visits Cosmic Harmony. That kind of thing."

"Good heavens," Andromeda said uneasily. "It sounds like someone has researched Cleo."

"Exactly," O'Reilly said. "That kind of detail can only be learned by studying a person's routine over a period of time."

"All of which means that whoever is doing this knows a great deal about what goes on around here." Max picked up his cane and got to his feet. He ignored the protesting twinge in his thigh as he walked to the window.

It was raining outside, but Max felt warm and comfortable and replete. It had been a pleasant homecoming. Andromeda and Daystar had fixed a special meal of clam chowder, barley salad, and homemade bread. There had been new drawings by Sammy to admire on the refrigerator door. Everyone had exclaimed over Cleo's ring and had instantly begun making plans for the future. It was a future that included Max.

A man could get used to this kind of life real fast, Max thought. But a smart man would never take it for granted. He prided himself on being a smart man.

"Like I said," O'Reilly continued, "it could be a complete stranger, but whoever it is has spent time in and around Harmony Cove. My gut feeling is that someone would have noticed him in a small town like this. Trust me. When we find out who's behind the incidents, the first words out of everyone's mouth will be

427

'But he seemed like such a nice guy.'"

"Or girl," Cleo murmured.

O'Reilly nodded. "Or girl."

Max braced both hands on the cane. "All right, what's the next possibility?"

O'Reilly glanced down at his notes. "There's a clear connection between the start of these incidents and the death of Jason Curzon."

Cleo and the others went very still.

"Damn." Max gazed out into the rain. "You're right, O'Reilly."

"I usually am," O'Reilly murmured.

"I should have seen that for myself," Max said, disgusted.

"What on earth are you saying?" Andromeda asked anxiously. "How could Jason's death have anything to do with this?"

"Because he left a quarter of a million dollars worth of art unaccounted for," Max said grimly. "And everyone seems to think Cleo knows where the paintings are."

"Everyone meaning you and Garrison Spark?" O'Reilly asked dryly.

Max set his back teeth. "I know Cleo doesn't know where the Luttrells are. But Spark still believes she does. He's already tried to talk her into turning them over to him for a fraction of what they're worth."

"You wouldn't believe how many people

428

think I'm not real bright," Cleo said. "My theory is that my choice in foot attire gives the wrong impression."

O'Reilly ignored her. "You think maybe these incidents are part of some sort of elaborate ploy to terrorize Cleo into producing the paintings, Max?"

"It's a possibility," Max said. "As you pointed out, the timing fits. They started shortly after Jason died."

O'Reilly hesitated. "Then why hasn't she received any notes warning her to sell or else?"

Cleo held up a hand for attention. "Maybe Mr. Spark or whoever is behind this wants to get me really spooked first. When I'm totally traumatized and scared to death, he'll zing me with a demand to turn over the Luttrells."

"Maybe," O'Reilly agreed. He didn't look convinced. He tapped his notebook with the tip of his pen. "Something else I wanted to mention while we're on the subject of the paintings. Nolan Hildebrand has to be counted as a suspect."

"Nolan?" Cleo's eyes widened. "Are you crazy? Nolan wouldn't stage those incidents."

"You can't be sure of that," Max said. "He tried to get you to help him find the paintings so that he could collect Spark's finder's fee, remember?"

Cleo grimaced. "Yes, but I just don't see Nolan as the sort who would concoct all those stagy incidents. Besides, he was genuinely shocked when he found out I'd written *The Mirror*. I know he was. He couldn't have known about it earlier."

"His shock could have been an act," Max said. "He might have been trying to deflect suspicion from himself."

"I don't know." Cleo's expression was dubious. "Nolan just isn't that convoluted in his thinking processes, if you know what I mean."

"You mean he's simpleminded?" Daystar asked bluntly.

Cleo scowled. "Not quite. I just don't see him as the type to put together a real devious scheme like this."

"Maybe," O'Reilly said. "Maybe not. I still think we have to consider him as a possibility."

Cleo threw up her hands in surrender. "Okay, okay. Nolan is a suspect. In that case, you might as well add Adrian Forrester to the list. The same logic applies. But I want you all to know that I'm going on record with my own private, personal opinion that neither one of them is behind the incidents."

Max looked at her. "You were willing enough to consider Forrester as a suspect earlier."

Cleo sighed. "I know, but I was annoyed

with him at the time. I've had a chance to calm down, and I have to admit that I really can't see him doing this kind of thing."

Max considered that. He had to allow for the possibility that she was right. Cleo could see into people the way he could see into paintings. He should know. She had looked into him and seen what he had wanted most in the world. And she had given it to him.

A twinge went through his thigh. Max stirred, changing position slightly. The long drive from Seattle was taking its toll. He pushed the old, familiar ache to the back of his mind and concentrated on the problem at hand as he walked to the fountain.

"If Spark is behind these incidents," he said quietly, "I think we can squelch the problem fairly easily."

Everyone stared at him.

"How?" Sylvia asked.

"I'll call him tomorrow and arrange a meeting." Max gazed into the turquoise blue fountain. "I'll tell him to forget the Luttrells. I'll also tell him that I want him to vanish."

O'Reilly eyed him in cool appraisal. "We're talking about a quarter of a million bucks here. What makes you think Spark will back out of the scene quietly when there's that kind of money involved?"

"He'll go," Max said.

431

No one said a word. They all sat in tense silence, staring at him. Max felt their silent questions hammering at him, but he did not volunteer an explanation of just how he would get rid of Spark.

"Okay," O'Reilly finally said in a brisk, businesslike voice, "that takes care of the Spark angle. Which leaves us with a third possible explanation to consider."

Max met O'Reilly's eyes. "I think I like this one the least."

Cleo frowned. "You haven't even heard it yet."

O'Reilly smiled wryly. "Max has a very analytical brain. He's already figured out that the third possibility is a rather nasty one."

"What is it?" Trisha asked uneasily.

Max looked down into the bubbling fountain water. "That there is something in Cleo's past that has triggered someone into coming after her."

"Shit," Ben whispered, awed. He looked at Max. "Are you serious?"

"Yes." Max looked at Cleo, then continued. "I know we talked about this possibility briefly and then let it drop. I didn't want you worrying about it. But it looks like we need to look into it further."

"What is there to look into?" Cleo asked. "I've already told you that I don't have any strange, obsessive men in my past. Nothing bizarre has ever occurred in my life except for the deaths of my parents."

"Your parents died in a very unusual manner," Max said quietly.

"Yes, but there was a logical explanation for it," Cleo reminded him. Her eyes turned bleak. "At least according to the authorities there was a logical explanation."

O'Reilly glanced at Max. Then he turned to Cleo. "I think this is as good a time as any to tell you that I did a little checking into the death of that investigator you hired last summer."

Cleo's gaze swung to O'Reilly. "You looked into Mr. Eberson's death? Why?"

"Because you mentioned that he was working on your case at the time, and because I am a very thorough investigator myself," O'Reilly said.

"Well?" Cleo waited expectantly. "Was there anything strange about his car accident?"

"Not officially. The records indicate that it was an accident. But when I phoned the insurance salesman who took over Eberson's office space, he mentioned that he'd had to wait quite a while before he could move in."

Max watched O'Reilly's face closely. "Why?"

"Because there was some fire damage that

had to be repaired first." O'Reilly closed his notebook with a snap. "It seems that there was a small blaze caused by faulty wiring in the office. It completely destroyed Eberson's files."

"Is that so?" Max asked softly.

Cleo wrapped her arms around her knees. Her eyes were huge with worry as she gazed at O'Reilly. "What are you saying? Do you think that Eberson had uncovered something about my parents' death that may have gotten him killed?"

O'Reilly held up a hand. "Cleo, I will tell you honestly that I don't know where this is going to lead. It could very well be a dead end. In fact, in all likelihood, it is a dead end. But it's something that needs to be checked out."

"What are you going to do?" Ben asked.

"I'm going to resume the investigation that was dropped when Eberson died," O'Reilly said. "Now that Max is here to keep an eye on all of you, I'm going to Seattle to start looking into the background surrounding the death of Cleo's parents."

Max saw Cleo go absolutely rigid.

"I'm not sure that's a good idea," she whispered. "What if there is some crazy person out there?"

"Then we'd better find out who he is,

hadn't we?" O'Reilly asked calmly. "Before he does any more damage."

Sylvia shifted uneasily in her chair. "I don't want you to take any risks, O'Reilly."

Max noted the very personal note of concern in Sylvia's voice.

O'Reilly beamed reassuringly. "Hey, I'm good at this. It's what I do."

"Sylvia's right," Cleo said quickly. "If there's something dangerous going on here we should call in the police."

"There's no point doing that at this stage," O'Reilly said. "We haven't got enough to go on. Like I said, we're probably chasing a dead-end lead. I just want to be sure we've covered all the bases."

Andromeda frowned. "You still think Spark is the most likely suspect, don't you?"

"That's exactly what I think," O'Reilly said. "The timing of the incidents and the amount of money involved make that the most likely possibility."

"I don't like this," Cleo whispered. "I'm getting a weird feeling."

"What kind of feeling?" Trisha asked.

"I don't know. It's just weird."

Max reached down to take her hand and pull her to her feet. "I think it's time we all went to bed." She didn't resist when he tugged her up off the chair, but the coldness in her fingers worried him.

Trisha looked at O'Reilly. "You're going to leave in the morning?"

"Afraid so." O'Reilly glanced at Sylvia.

"But you'll be coming back, won't you?" Trisha asked. "You said you'd be here for the wedding on Friday."

"Wouldn't miss it for the world," O'Reilly said. "I'll definitely be back on Friday. With my best suit."

"God help us," Max muttered.

Andromeda beetled her brows at him. "I'm sure O'Reilly's best suit is very nice."

"It's green, and it's made out of polyester," Max said. "Need I say more?"

17

The following night, Cleo put her hands behind her head and gazed up at the shadowed ceiling of the attic. "I'm going with you tomorrow when you talk to Spark."

"No," Max said from the other side of the bed. "For the last time, I don't want you there."

The argument had been festering since four o'clock that afternoon, when Cleo had discovered that Max had made arrangements to talk to Garrison Spark the next day. She had immediately announced her intentions of confronting Spark with Max. Max had put his foot down with a forcefulness that had not only startled her; it had hurt her.

"Max, this is all happening because of me. I have a right to be there with you when you talk to Spark."

"Cleo, stop pushing. I told you, I'm going to handle this."

She sat up in bed, exasperated to the point of anger. "Why are you being so bloody-minded about it? Give me one good reason why I shouldn't be there."

"You don't know anything about handling someone like Spark."

"And you do?"

"Yes."

"What makes you an expert?" she snapped.

"I told you, I once worked for Spark. I know how he thinks. I also know how he operates."

"So?" Cleo challenged.

"So I don't want you anywhere around when I talk to him about what's been happening."

"I'm not an idiot, Max. I won't mess up your plans, whatever they are."

"I never said you were an idiot."

"I am also not as naive as everyone seems

to think." Cleo paused suddenly. "Max, does it strike you that we're having our first major quarrel?"

"We're not quarreling."

"Sure sounds like a quarrel to me."

"We are not quarreling, damn it."

Cleo was taken aback by the fierce insistence in his voice. "Okay, so we're having a heated discussion. Whatever you want to call it, I think the time has come for you and me to clear up a little communication problem we seem to have developed."

"What communication problem?" he asked warily.

Cleo took a breath. "You once noted that you and I have different styles of management. Well, those two styles have just collided, and they will probably do so again in the future. We need to learn how to deal with each other when that happens."

"Damn. The last thing I need tonight is a conversation like this."

"Tough. We're having it." Cleo touched his shoulder. "I think you and I need to get something settled here, Max. You can't walk into this family and just start throwing your weight around the way you apparently did when you worked for Curzon International. If you and I are going to make this relationship work, we're going to have to learn to work as a team."

Max did not move. The new tension radiating from him was palpable. "What's that supposed to mean?"

Cleo watched him uneasily. She had the feeling that she had accidentally stepped into a minefield. "I'm just trying to talk about our mutual problem."

Max moved without any warning. He shoved the covers aside and sat up on the edge of the bed. He reached for his cane and got to his feet. "Are you telling me that if we don't do things your way, our relationship, as you call it, is over?"

"*Max.*" Cleo clutched the sheet to her breast. "For heaven's sake, I never said that. I just said we needed to iron out some of our communication problems."

"*Communication problems* sounds like code for *I'm having second thoughts about marrying you, Max.*"

"That's not true," Cleo retorted. "We're having a little trouble relating to each other, that's all."

"Don't give me a lot of pop-psych communication theory." Max looked down at her with dangerous eyes. "Just cut to the bottom line."

"There is no bottom line." Cleo was bewildered by his reaction. "I'm only trying to tell you that you can't expect me to meekly step aside and let you take over running the family and everything else in sight. Good grief, no wonder Kimberly was afraid to give you a seat on the board. She knew you'd take over Curzon if you got half a chance."

Max looked as if she'd slapped him. His hand clenched around the handle of his cane. "Is that what you think I'm trying to do? Take control of your family and your inn?"

Cleo was horrified. "Of course not." She scrambled to a kneeling position in the center of the bed. "Max, you're getting this all wrong."

"Is that right? What part am I getting wrong? It all sounds very clear to me. You think I'm taking over, and unless I handle things the way you want them handled, you're going to back out of the marriage. Did I miss anything?"

"I am not going to back out of the marriage. Will you please stop putting words in my mouth?"

"I'm using the words you used."

Cleo lost her temper. "What on earth is the problem here? Why don't you want me with you tomorrow when you talk to Spark?"

"Because I don't want you there. Isn't that reason enough?"

"No, damn it, it's not."

Max moved to the window and stood looking out into the darkness. "It's all the reason you're going to get. And if that's not good enough, you'll have to make your own decision about what to do next."

The bleakness in his voice was Cleo's undoing. His words echoed with a cold, aloof loneliness that tore at her heart. She wondered how many times in his life Max had waited for others to make the decisions that would send him down the road to the next temporary home.

With a soft exclamation of pain that was as deep as his own, Cleo leaped off the bed and ran across the room to where he stood at the window. She threw her arms around him and leaned her head against his bare chest.

"Max, I've got news for you. It doesn't work like that now."

He touched her hair with a hesitant hand. "What do you mean?"

Cleo raised her head to meet his eyes. She framed his hard jaw between her palms. "You don't get kicked out of this family just because you are occasionally as stubborn as a mule and have an annoying tendency to govern by fiat."

"I don't?" He searched her face with eyes that mirrored both grim acceptance of his fate and a tiny flame of hope.

"No." Cleo stood on tiptoe and kissed him

lightly on the mouth. "You're one of us now. It doesn't matter if you occasionally screw up, remember?"

Max's eyes were more enigmatic than Cleo had ever seen them. "You're sure?"

"I'm sure." Cleo grinned. "Of course, in return, you have to learn to accommodate some of my little foibles, which may tend to irritate you now and again. For instance, I am not going to give up on this matter of going with you when you confront Spark. But that's family life for you. A little give and take. What the heck. Nothing's perfect."

There was no answering amusement in Max's expression. "Cleo . . ."

"Yes?"

"Never mind."

Max pulled her against him and held her so tightly Cleo thought her ribs might crack. But they didn't.

After a while Max led her back to bed.

A long time later Max stirred and rolled reluctantly off of Cleo. "You can come with me tomorrow," he said.

Cleo wondered why he sounded like a gambler who had just bet everything on a long shot.

The meeting had been arranged on neutral

territory. Spark had suggested that Max meet him at a small motel located forty miles from Harmony Cove. Max had agreed.

He had thought about the meeting most of the night, but he was still not fully prepared for the flood of memories that assailed him when Spark opened the door of his small motel suite. No matter how he sliced it, Max thought, there was no getting around the fact that he owed Spark a great deal.

It was Spark, after all, who had first made it possible for Max to indulge his grand passion for fine art. It was Spark who had allowed him to handle some of the most brilliant paintings that had been produced by West Coast artists in the past twenty years. It was Spark who had provided Max with the opportunity to meet Jason Curzon.

"Well, well, well." Spark's expression was one of cool, half-amused appraisal. "It's been a long time, Fortune. You seem to have done rather well for yourself. Hard to believe that once upon a time you made a living running errands for me."

Spark had changed little during the past twelve years, Max thought. He looked as polished and sophisticated as ever. He still had the supercilious curl of the lip and that expression of bored condescension that was so useful for intimidating timorous collectors.

"There's no point wasting time reminiscing," Max said. He tightened his grip on Cleo's arm. "You've met my fiancée, I believe."

"Fiancée?" Spark's smile was rueful. "I'm sorry. I hadn't realized you had actually made the mistake of falling in love with Fortune, my dear. What a pity. Do come in."

Cleo glared at him as she walked into the room. "We're here to discuss the paintings, Mr. Spark. I suggest we skip the small talk."

"Ah, yes. The Luttrells." Spark motioned Max and Cleo to chairs and then sat down himself. He crossed one leg languidly over the other. "I must admit to being rather startled when I got your call yesterday, Max. May I assume that you are ready to deal?"

"There is no deal," Max said. "If and when the Luttrells are found, they belong to me. I have no intention of selling them."

"I have a bill of sale from Jason Curzon." Spark's eyes were speculative. "It clearly shows that he sold the Luttrells to me shortly before he died."

"That bill of sale is as phony as the Maraston you sold to that collector down in Portland last year," Max said calmly.

Spark's eyes narrowed. "You can't prove that painting was a forgery."

Max smiled faintly. "Sure I can. I own the original."

A flash of annoyance appeared in Spark's eyes. It vanished almost instantly. "You're lying."

Max shook his head with weary patience. "No, Spark, I'm not lying. We both know that I never bluff. I picked up the original three years ago. It's been hanging in my vault ever since. If you insist on producing your bill of sale, I'll contact the Portland collector and suggest he have his Maraston examined by an expert."

"You're the leading authority on Maraston's work."

"Exactly." Max shrugged. "I'll be only too happy to volunteer my expertise in this instance. I imagine the Portland collector will be very grateful. I think it would be safe to say that he'll probably want his money back from you. He will undoubtedly never buy anything from you again, and neither will any one else who hears the story, which I imagine would spread like wildfire in certain circles."

"Bastard," Spark said, but he sounded more resigned than outraged.

Spark was, at heart, a businessman, Max reflected. He knew when to cut his losses. "I'm surprised you're still peddling the occasional forgery. I would have thought you'd have given up that sideline by now. After all, you do just fine handling the real thing. What's the matter? Still can't resist a quick buck?"

"Some of us never change, do we, Fortune?" Spark's answering smile was tinged with poison. "I see you're still as much of an opportunist as ever. I'm amazed that you've stooped to seducing nice young women in order to get what you want, however. Even in the old days you had some rather irritating standards."

The standards hadn't been all that high, Max reflected. The arrangement he'd had with Spark was a simple one. In exchange for being allowed to handle the art he craved more than food, Max had agreed not to voice his opinions to Spark's clients.

Unless those clients asked for his opinion.

Jason Curzon was the only one who had ever asked Spark's rough-edged errand runner and odd-job man for an opinion.

Out of the corner of his eye, Max watched Cleo's expression. His insides were twisted into a cold knot of anticipation. He had known what would happen if he brought Cleo with him to this confrontation. That was why he had fought so hard to keep her away from the meeting.

But in the end she had destroyed his defense in her own gentle fashion. At some point last night Max had realized he would have to take his chances. He did not know how she would react to this glimpse into his less-than-savory past, but he accepted the fact that his fate was in her hands.

"Do we understand each other, Spark?" Max asked quietly.

"I think so." Spark turned to Cleo. "Did your fiancé ever tell you precisely what he did for a living when he worked for me, Ms. Robbins?"

Cleo shot a quick glance at Max. "He said he did odd jobs for you."

"That he did." Spark looked pleased. "Some very odd jobs. His duties included picking up extremely valuable works of art from certain sources that were, shall we say, less than reputable. Fortune carried a gun when he worked for me, Ms. Robbins. That should tell you something of the nature of his responsibilities."

Cleo frowned. "I imagine that transporting expensive art requires some security precautions."

"Oh, yes, yes, indeed." Spark chuckled. "Especially when some of that art was purchased from collectors who had ties to the underworld. And then there were the occasions when Max delivered paintings which had rather cloudy provenances."

"You mean they were fakes?" Cleo demanded.

"Excellent fakes, Ms. Robbins." Spark contrived to look offended. "Max can tell you that when I deal in forgeries, I make certain I deal in only first-class forgeries. Ninety-nine percent of the time no one can tell the difference between a good Spark forgery and the original."

"Except Max?" Cleo asked.

Spark sighed. "Unfortunately, yes. Max has what amounts to a preternatural talent for telling the real from the fake. At times it was an extremely useful skill. At other times, it was rather annoying."

"You mean you used Max's talent to make certain you didn't get burned yourself," Cleo concluded. "But you worried that when you burned others, he might spill the beans?"

"Precisely, Ms. Robbins." Spark's eyes glittered. "To my knowledge, however, he experienced an attack of integrity only once during the course of our association. That was when he delivered a certain painting to Jason Curzon. In retrospect I'm inclined to believe that it was not integrity but sheer opportunism that overcame him. Max saw a chance to better himself, didn't you, Max?"

Max kept his gaze steady. "We had a deal, Spark. I told you I wouldn't lie about a painting if one of your clients asked my opinion. Jason asked."

"And shortly thereafter Max resigned his position as my odd-job man to accept a more lucrative offer with Curzon." Spark smiled thinly at Cleo. "Once again I advise you to be cautious around Fortune, Ms. Robbins. Once he has his hands on those Luttrells, he'll be gone."

"That's enough, Spark. I think we understand each other, don't we?" Max got to his feet.

Spark lifted one shoulder in an elegant shrug. "We always did understand each other rather well, Fortune."

"One more thing. Make sure that you notify Nolan Hildebrand that you are no longer in the market for the Luttrells."

"If you insist."

Max folded his hands on top of the hawk and looked at Cleo. The deep sense of foreboding was eating him alive. "Let's go, Cleo."

Without a word, she rose from the chair and walked toward the door. Max followed.

"Fortune," Spark murmured softly behind him.

Max glanced back over his shoulder. "What is it, Spark?"

"I urge you to reconsider. I have a client who will pay a quarter of a million for those Luttrells. I'll split it with you, fifty-fifty. Think about it."

"They're not for sale," Max said.

"I was afraid you'd say that." Spark raised a hand. "Take yourself off. I trust we won't run into each other again any time soon."

"That will be just fine with me. By the way, you probably ought to know that my attorney has a sealed letter which is only to be opened if I suffer an unfortunate accident. The letter contains a short list of the more prominent forgeries that are presently hanging on the walls of some of your clients' homes."

"You always were an ungrateful wretch." Spark's mouth twisted wryly. "Never fear. I shall light candles for your continued good health."

"Thank you. The deal we made still stands, as far as I'm concerned, Spark. You stay out of my way, and I'll stay out of yours."

Spark looked at him. "It's going to be interesting to see how you adjust to married life."

Cleo turned at the door. "He's going to do just fine, Mr. Spark."

Max saw the warmth in her eyes. The tension inside him evaporated at last. It was going to be all right. Cleo was not going to hold his past against him.

Max followed her out into the hall and closed the door of Spark's room. Without a word he took Cleo's arm. Together they walked out of the motel and into the cold, misty rain.

"Well, that's that," Cleo said as Max opened the door of the Jaguar. "What do you think?"

"About Spark?" Max watched her intently. "I think the same thing I thought before. He's not the one behind the incidents. But if I'm wrong and he is the one who's been harassing you, or if he put Hildebrand up to doing it, it will stop now."

"You're sure?"

"Yes. Spark and I understand each other. He knows I'll destroy him if he gets in my way. But he also knows that I'll leave him alone if he leaves me alone."

Cleo shuddered. "Why on earth did you go to work for that man in the first place?"

"I needed a job."

Max shut her door and went around the nose of the Jaguar. He got in behind the wheel and turned to look at Cleo. He didn't know what to say.

Cleo looked thoughtful. "I think I know now why you didn't want me to come along with you this morning."

"I used to pride myself on never screwing up," Max said quietly. "But now when I look back, it seems to me my whole life was a screwup."

"Nah," Cleo said. "You're just feeling a little depressed this morning. You'll get over it."

"You think so?"

"I'm sure of it," Cleo said. She leaned across the seat and kissed him.

"I give up." Ben grimaced at his image in the mirror. "I can't figure out how to tie this stupid bow tie. I've never tied one of these things before in my life."

"Hang on a second, I'll get to you as soon as I've finished with Sammy." Max concentrated on adjusting Sammy's tie. "Hold your chin up, kid. That's it."

Sammy lifted his chin obediently as Max tied the black bow tie that complemented his tiny tuxedo. "Can I take Lucky Ducky?"

"You won't have any place to put him during the ceremony. You're supposed to be guarding the rings, remember?" Max finished his task and surveyed his work with a critical eye.

Sammy was wearing a perfect miniature version of the black and white formal attire that he and Ben were wearing. Max was well aware that this was the first time either Ben or Sammy had been exposed to the fine art of wearing a tux. He had told them it was never too soon to start.

"You look good, kid." Max nodded once,

satisfied with the effect. "Your mom isn't going to recognize you."

Sammy studied himself in the mirror. "I look just like you and Ben, huh, Max?"

"You sure do." Max picked up the little black jacket and stuffed Sammy's arms gently into it. He straightened the tiny cummerbund. "Now, whatever you do, don't get any dirt on this outfit until after the ceremony, understand?"

"Sure, Max. I'll be careful. Do you think O'Reilly will be here in time?" Sammy looked worried. He had been fretting about O'Reilly's belated arrival for the past hour.

"He said he'd be here," Max reminded him. "If O'Reilly says something, you can count on it."

The truth was, Max was beginning to fret a bit, himself, although he had no intention of revealing the fact. O'Reilly was normally close to compulsive when it came to matters of punctuality. There was no denying he was pushing the limits today. Max glanced at his watch for the fourth time in the past twenty minutes. The ceremony at Cosmic Harmony was scheduled to begin in an hour.

Ben fiddled with the ends of his tie. "Maybe he had a flat tire." His eyes met Max's in the mirror, reflecting a trace of the unease Max was feeling.

"Could be," Max agreed. "But he's got a car phone. He'd have called if he were going to be late. Here, let me take care of that tie. If you keep fooling with it, we'll have to get it ironed again."

"I don't know why we had to get all gussied up like this," Ben muttered. "Waste of time. I feel like an idiot in this suit."

"It'll be worth it when you see the look in Trisha's eyes. Women are suckers for men in tuxes."

"Yeah?" Ben looked intrigued by that notion. "You really think Trisha will like it?"

"Trust me." Max took charge of the black tie, expertly shaping a perfect bow. "She's going to be swept off her feet."

Ben fingered his starched white shirt. "I'm not sure about these little pleats. You don't think they look like something a girl would wear, do you?"

"Men have been wearing little pleats like this for nearly two hundred years. You're in good company."

"You sure I don't look like a waiter in a fancy restaurant?" Ben asked doubtfully.

"You look like James Bond," Max assured him.

Ben scowled. "I'd rather look like you," he said gruffly. "That way I'd know I don't look like an idiot. You always look like you're supposed to look, y'know?" He groped for words. "You always look right."

Max felt a peculiar twist of emotion. He could not recall anyone ever wanting to emulate him. "Just remember to wear the clothes with an attitude that says you're a lot sharper than they are."

"If you say so." Ben watched in the mirror as Max worked on the tie. "Where'd you learn to do this?"

"Jason taught me."

Old memories swept through Max as he finished the bow and adjusted the points of Ben's collar. Twelve years ago he had been as dubious about the whole process of wearing a tux as Ben was today. Jason had tied the tie for him and had even had to show him how to wear the cuff links.

There was something satisfying about handing on the manly art of dressing for a formal occasion to another young man who was just as rough and unsophisticated as he had once been, Max thought.

"There, that does it. Let's take a look." He stepped back to survey his work. "Perfect. You look like you've been wearing tuxes for years."

Ben studied himself in the mirror. A pleased expression gleamed in his eyes. He straightened his shoulders. "I look older or something, don't I?"

"Cool," Sammy proclaimed. "You look cool, Ben."

"Yeah, I do, don't I?" Ben tugged on the jacket of the tuxedo.

"Just like Max," Sammy said. He picked up Lucky Ducky and tucked the plastic duck under his arm.

"So, I guess we're ready, huh?" Ben turned away from the mirror. There was a slight but definite swagger in his step.

Sammy was instantly alarmed. "We can't go anywhere until O'Reilly gets here."

"We'll wait for O'Reilly," Max assured him. "Go to the window and keep an eye out for him, Sammy."

"Okay." Sammy raced for the window.

Max looked at Ben. "There's one more thing we've got to take care of before we leave for Cosmic Harmony." Max reached into the pocket of his jacket and drew out an airline ticket folder.

"What's that?" Ben asked, momentarily distracted.

"Your honeymoon trip." Max opened the lapel of Ben's jacket and stuffed the ticket folder into the inside pocket. "You're going to Hawaii for a week. It's a gift from the family."

Ben's jaw dropped. "*Hawaii*. I thought me and Trisha were going to Seattle."

"There's been a change in plans. You're driving to Seattle this afternoon, but instead of checking into a hotel downtown, you're going to the airport." Max's mouth curved. "You'll stay the night at a hotel there. Your plane leaves at seven tomorrow morning."

"*Hawaii.*" Ben looked dazed. "But we can't afford to go to Hawaii."

"Like I said, it's a gift from the family." Max briefly checked his own reflection in the mirror and tweaked the bow of his tie. "Now pay attention, Ben. When you reach Honolulu, there will be a limo waiting. The driver will have a card that has your name on it."

"A limo. Holy shit. Trisha won't believe this."

"It's all been paid for in advance. You don't even tip the driver, got that?"

"Yeah, sure. No tip."

"The limo will take you to the Curzon Paradise. It's right on the beach. You'll have one of the honeymoon suites."

"A honeymoon suite?" Ben was clearly overwhelmed. "But that must cost a bundle."

It did, Max reflected, but he had no intention of telling Ben that. "The manager of the hotel is a friend of mine," he said easily. "He owes me a favor." What he owed Max was his job, but that was not important. In any event, Max was paying full price for the

457

suite. Now that he was no longer working for Curzon, he wanted no favors from the corporation. "You sign for everything, got that?"

"Everything?"

"The hotel bill, the meals you eat in the hotel, the snorkeling equipment, and the Hawaiian dress you're going to buy for Trisha. Everything."

"Damn, I can't hardly believe this," Ben said. "Does Trisha know?"

Max smiled and slowly shook his head. "No. You'll get to tell her all about it on the way to the airport this afternoon."

"She's gonna freak," Ben said. "She's gonna be so happy."

"That's the whole point," Max said.

"Shit, Max. This is something else." Ben stared at him. "I don't know how to thank you."

"I told you this was a gift from the family, not just me. And if you want to thank us you can do it by taking good care of Trisha and the baby."

"I will," Ben vowed.

"And by getting back here as soon as the honeymoon's over, so that you can rescue me from whatever home repair disaster I happen to be involved in at the time."

Ben grinned. "Don't worry, I'm not gonna abandon you to the plumbing. Hot damn, this is too much. *Hawaii.* Man, I hope I don't screw up at the airport or make a fool out of myself in that fancy hotel."

Max put a hand on his shoulder. "Listen to me, my friend, I am going to give you some words of wisdom that I want you to remember for the rest of your life."

Ben sobered and looked at Max with an intent expression. "I'm listening."

"It is okay to screw up once in a while," Max said. "Got that?"

"Yeah." Ben started to grin again, but his eyes stayed serious for a moment longer. "I think I can remember that."

"He's here, he's here!" Sammy shouted. "I see O'Reilly! He's just getting out of his car."

"Wearing his green suit?" Max asked.

"Nope. He's got a tux on, just like us. And he's carrying a big present all wrapped in shiny paper."

"We're all set, then," Max said. "Let's go." He picked up his black jacket and shrugged into it. Then he turned to take one last look at Ben and Sammy. He smiled slightly. "We're going to wow the ladies, my friends."

Ben and Sammy exchanged grins.

O'Reilly was pacing back and forth in the lobby and glancing nervously at his watch when Max, Ben, and Sammy arrived downstairs a few minutes later. George, who had come in early to cover the office while the family went to the wedding, smiled.

"What kept you?" Max asked O'Reilly.

"Tell you later," O'Reilly said quietly.

"Hi, O'Reilly." Sammy ran up to O'Reilly and stopped short right in front of him. "I was afraid you weren't coming."

O'Reilly went down on his haunches in front of Sammy. He grinned. "I told you I'd be here, didn't I?"

"Uh-huh." Sammy's eyes reflected his enormous relief. "Ben said maybe your car broke or something."

"Nope, I just had some business to take care of. Hey, let me look at you, kid. Aren't you all spiffed up? I can see Max has been at work. He's the only guy I know who actually knows how to tie a bow tie. Mine is pretied."

"Max says I have to look good on account of I'm supposed to guard the rings," Sammy explained.

"A very important job," O'Reilly said. He got to his feet and nodded at Ben. "So this is the big day. You ready?"

"Ready as I'll ever be," Ben said, but his eyes were eager. "The family is sending me and Trisha to Hawaii. Can you believe it?"

O'Reilly slanted a glance at Max. "Yeah, I can believe it." He handed his gift to Ben.

460

"This is for you and Trisha."

"Hey, thanks." Ben gave the package to George. "Put this with the others, okay? Trisha says we'll open the presents when we get back."

"Will do," George said. He stashed the gift behind the desk. Then he regarded Ben with approval from beneath his bushy brows. "Best of luck to you, Ben."

"Yeah, well thanks." Ben looked at Max. "I guess this is it, huh?"

"This is it." Max took one last assessing look at his charges. He frowned briefly when he saw that Sammy had a smudge on the tip of his nose. "How did you get that?" he asked as he grabbed a tissue from the box behind the front desk.

"I dunno." Sammy stood still while Max rubbed off the smudge. "Maybe from Lucky Ducky."

"Right. I should have known." Max tossed the tissue into a small trash can behind the desk. "Everyone in the car."

Sammy raced out the front door. Ben followed at a slightly slower but no less enthusiastic pace.

Max waited until they were out of earshot before he looked at O'Reilly. "How serious?"

"I wish to hell I knew the answer to that," O'Reilly said. "I'll give you the whole story

461

later. In the meantime, I don't think Cleo should be left alone for even a few minutes."

Max's insides froze. "Christ, O'Reilly, you can't just drop that on me and then say you'll tell me the rest later."

"It's a long story. I don't want to talk about it in front of Ben and Sammy."

"It has something to do with the death of her parents, doesn't it?"

"Maybe. I just don't have all the answers yet, Max. I'm sorry."

"Goddamn it to hell." Max took a savage grip on his cane and went toward the Jaguar.

"Would you believe this is the first wedding I've been to since my own?" O'Reilly asked an hour and a half later as he stood with Max near the buffet table.

"That's two more weddings than I've attended." Max bit into an exquisite salmon canapé that he had just plucked from the table.

"Could have fooled me," O'Reilly said. "You looked like you knew just what you were doing when you took up the position of best man."

"It's the clothes." Max swallowed the canapé. "A man who wears the right clothes for the job always looks like he knows what he's doing, and that's half the battle."

"That sounds like one of Jason Curzon's bits of wisdom."

"It is."

Max scanned the crowd, searching for Cleo. She stood with a group that included a number of townspeople as well as Andromeda and Daystar. Cleo's hair was swept up in a chignon that was more tightly secured than the usual careless knot she wore. The style was decorated with a row of yellow roses that were a beautiful contrast to the deep red highlights in her dark mane.

She looked achingly feminine in her low-necked, tight-waisted yellow gown, Max thought. But, then, the sight of her always made him ache. He wondered if the need for her would ever diminish. He doubted it. He suspected it would only intensify over the years.

The women of Cosmic Harmony had turned the graceful old resort lodge into a fantasy extravaganza done in yellow and white. All the stops had been pulled out for the wedding. In the center of the room a glowing Trisha, dressed in a floor-length creamy white gown and a tiny hat and veil, stood near Ben. Ben looked as if he had just been crowned king of the world. He caught Max's eye and grinned.

Sammy was dashing here and there in the

crowd and helping himself to everything that looked like it contained sugar.

"The kid's going to be overstimulated tonight," O'Reilly observed. "Where the hell do they get so much energy at that age?"

Max turned his head at the wistful tone in O'Reilly's voice. "Damned if I know. Let's have the whole story, O'Reilly. Take it from the top."

O'Reilly stuffed a canapé into his mouth. "I took a second look at everything I could find that dealt with the death of Cleo's parents. She's been right about one thing all along; her father wasn't the kind who suddenly ups and shoots his wife and then himself."

"That's what everyone always says after it happens. *He seemed like such a nice man.*"

"Yeah, I know, but in this case, Cleo has a point. Neither Mr. nor Mrs. Robbins had a history of violent outbursts. Neither appeared to suffer from depression or suicidal tendencies. There had been no recent financial reverses for them. Neither had been diagnosed with a fatal illness."

"In other words, no obvious motivating factors." Max watched Cleo. "No wonder she hasn't been able to buy the story the authorities gave her. She knew them too well to believe it."

O'Reilly scowled thoughtfully. "I think

there's a real possibility that there was something else going on, and when Eberson started looking into the situation, he triggered a response."

"From someone who did not want the situation investigated?"

"Yeah. Maybe. I just don't know yet, Max."

"Had Robbins recently fired someone who might have been crazy enough to murder him in retaliation?"

O'Reilly shrugged. "He was a businessman, owned a good-sized electronics firm. He had fired a few people over the years. Part of the job. But I couldn't find any evidence to indicate that any of them were deranged or had made threats. The police probably checked that angle at the time, too."

"Anything else?"

"The only other thing I turned up was that Robbins had testified for the prosecution at a murder trial two years before he was killed. I don't know if there was any connection, but I do know that the guy was convicted and sent to prison."

"A long shot."

"I know, but it's all I've got at the moment." O'Reilly glanced at the buffet table. A strange expression lit his eyes. "What the hell is that thing floating in the punch bowl?"

Max followed his gaze. "That's Lucky

Ducky. He can swim anywhere. You wouldn't believe some of the places he turns up."

"No kidding?"

"No kidding. I suppose I'd better get the duck out of the punch before someone notices." Max started toward the large crystal bowl.

"Max?" Cleo called.

He stopped and turned around. "Right here, Cleo."

"Oh, there you are." Cleo emerged from the crowd looking cheerfully harried. "I've been looking all over for you and O'Reilly. The photographer is ready to take the next batch of pictures. Come on, let's go before Sammy runs off again."

"Photos?" Max looked at her, bemused. "Of O'Reilly and me?"

"Of course. And the rest of us, too." Cleo smiled brilliantly as she took his hand. "The photographer has finished the portraits of the wedding couple. We're ready to do the family photos now."

"Family photos?" Max looked at O'Reilly.

"Don't mind him," O'Reilly said to Cleo. "Max isn't used to being included in pictures of a family."

"Well, he'd better get used to it," Cleo said dryly. "Daystar is thinking about taking up photography as a hobby."

"You sure you want me in the shot?" O'Reilly asked.

"Sammy and Sylvia insisted," Cleo said.

"Yeah?" O'Reilly looked inordinately pleased.

"Yeah," Cleo said. She grinned.

Ten minutes later Max found himself standing together with Cleo, Andromeda, Daystar, Sylvia, O'Reilly, and Sammy. They formed a tight, warm circle around Ben and Trisha.

"Big smiles, everyone," the photographer ordered unnecessarily.

"Wait," Sammy yelped. "I forgot Lucky Ducky."

"He's in the punch bowl," Max said. "You stay here. I'll get him."

A short while later the photographer finally snapped the picture. The family portrait was complete with a rubber duck.

18

"I trust you have my usual room ready for me, Ms. Robbins?" Herbert T. Valence asked bursquely as he filled out the registration slip in his precise handwriting. "I don't care to be shifted around from room to room."

"Yes, I know, Mr. Valence. Two-ten is ready for you." Cleo maintained her best professional smile as she handed the key to Valence. "And you may use the parlor for your seminars, just as you have in the past."

Valence clicked his pen five times before replacing it neatly in his jacket pocket. "I hope there won't be any problems with the electricity this time."

"Let's keep our fingers crossed that we won't get any severe storms this weekend," Cleo said with determined cheeriness.

"I don't believe in luck," Valence said. "I've already checked the forecast, and it's supposed to be clear most of the weekend."

"Wonderful. Well, it looks like you've got a nice crowd this time. We've checked in fifteen people who say they're here for your workshop."

"Fifteen is the ideal number of people for my seminar. I can't guarantee results if I'm forced to deal with a larger crowd. And I am known for getting results. I have a reputation to maintain, you know."

"Yes, Mr. Valence. So you've said." Cleo told herself that it was worth putting up with Valence's odd little ways because of the business he brought to the inn. But occasionally she wearied of his cold, inflexible personality and small, obsessive mannerisms. "I hope you enjoy your stay."

Valence frowned as he turned away from the desk. "I am not here to enjoy myself, Ms. Robbins. I am here to conduct business."

Cleo wrinkled her nose at his back as he walked briskly toward the stairs. "You know something, Sylvia? I think Mr. Valence is getting worse. He seems awfully tense tonight."

Sylvia stuck her head out of the office and smiled. "Think of the money."

"I know. Maybe he's just overmotivated. Does it strike you that Max and Herbert T. Valence have something in common?"

"Like what?"

"A reputation."

Sylvia chuckled. "You've got a point. But there's a big difference between Max and Herbert T."

"What's that?"

"You love one, and you're not particularly fond of the other."

Cleo froze. Then she spun around. "What did you say?"

"You heard me. You love Max."

Cleo looked at her anxiously. "Is it that obvious?"

"You've given him everything he wanted, including yourself. You're a generous woman, Cleo, but you've never been that generous

469

with any other man. You've always protected yourself on some level. Except with Max."

"I knew he was different the minute I saw him. He was the man in the mirror," Cleo whispered. "The one in my book."

"I had a hunch that was exactly who he was."

Cleo ran her fingertips along the polished edge of the front desk. "I've become part of his collection."

"Fair's fair, isn't it? You've made Max a part of your family."

Cleo hesitated. "I'll tell you something I haven't told anyone else. Sometimes I'm a little afraid, Sylvia."

"Afraid of Max? I don't believe it. You can trust Max with your life, and you know it."

"That's not what I mean." Cleo gripped the edge of the desk. "I'm afraid that he won't let himself love me. He knows how to go after what he wants, and he knows how to hang on to it. But he's been protecting himself for a lot longer than I've been protecting myself. He's got it down to an art. You should pardon the expression."

"Have you told him that you love him?"

"No," Cleo shook her head quickly. "I didn't want to push him. I guess I've been waiting for him to wake up one morning and realize he's in love with me. But sometimes

I'm not sure he'd recognize love if it whapped him in the face. Men can be so dense sometimes."

"You may have to make the first move, Cleo. I'm not sure Max can." Sylvia ducked her head into the office.

Cleo stared at one of the three seascapes left on the lobby walls. The other two were now upstairs in the attic.

But she did not see Jason's foamy seascapes when she gazed at the nearest painting. Instead she looked into the phantom mirror where her deepest secrets were hidden. The figure in the silvery reflection was no longer a mysterious shadow. He was Max, the man she had been waiting for all her life. He had walked into her life and set her free.

But Cleo knew that she had not yet returned the favor. Max was still trapped in the mirror. She had not yet succeeded in freeing him.

Cleo and Max did not climb the stairs to the attic room until nearly midnight.

Cleo was exhausted. The crowd that had checked in for Valence's seminar had been more motivated to party than to study the five steps to success and prosperity. They were still making a lot of noise downstairs in the lounge, but George had assured her he could handle the situation.

471

"Any more groups like this one and Mr. Valence can take his show on down the road." Cleo flopped on the edge of the bed, pulled off her silver shoes, and removed the clip from her hair.

"I think this bunch is already fairly well motivated." Max watched her shake her hair free. He smiled the faint, enigmatic, utterly sensual smile of the man in the mirror. "And so am I."

"You've had a hard day."

"The hardest part is yet to come." He made his way across the room. When he was standing directly in front of her, he set aside his cane and framed her face with his hands. "But I think I'll rise to the occasion."

"Since when did you become the master of the double entendre?"

"Since I read chapter fifteen." Max eased her onto her back and came down on top of her. "Funniest chapter in *The Mirror*."

"I'm glad you enjoyed it." He was warm and heavy and deliciously male. Cleo felt her tiredness slip away. It was replaced by a sense of deep anticipation.

Max looked down at her. His eyes darkened. "I enjoy everything about you, Cleo." His mouth covered hers.

She smiled slowly beneath his kiss. Then, rousing herself slightly, she pushed him gently

472

off of her and got to her feet. She took off her glasses and put them down on the side table. Feeling wonderfully wicked, she started to unbutton her oxford cloth shirt.

"Did you read chapter sixteen, by any chance?" she asked.

"Another one of my favorites." Max rolled onto his back and folded his arms behind his head. The faint smile edging his mouth was full of lazy, seductive challenge. "Going to act it out for me?"

"If you like."

"I like." His voice was husky with desire. "Go slow. I don't want to miss a single word of the story."

Emboldened by the sensual encouragement that she saw in his eyes, Cleo slowly finished undoing her shirt. She let the edges hang over her breasts, concealing and revealing.

"Don't forget the mirror," Max said softly.

Cleo walked over to the mirror and looked at her slightly blurred reflection. Her hair was flowing free and wild around her shoulders. Her eyes were shadowed and mysterious. She looked intriguing and exotic, she thought.

She was the fantasy, but she was also the creator of the fantasy. She was both seducer and seduced. A sense of her own power as a woman flowed through her.

Max did not stir on the bed. Cleo knew

he was watching her as she watched herself in the mirror, willing her to plunge them both deeper into the world behind the silvered glass.

Her fingers trembled a little as she undid the fastenings of her jeans. She eased the denim slowly down over her hips, leaving her filmy panties in place.

Her eyes never left the mirror as she stepped out of the jeans. Her shirttails fell to the top of her thighs, barely covering the curve of her buttocks. She could see the dark thatch of curling hair through the silk of her panties and knew that Max saw it, too. She sensed the smoldering wildfire of his desire and knew a sweet, singing joy that she could create this reaction in him. It gave her a heady sense of feminine power and at the same time made her feel infinitely generous.

"I'm on my knees," Max assured her softly.

She met his gaze in the mirror and knew that the power she was feeling was inextricably linked to the power in him. It could not be savored to the fullest unless it was in the presence of an equal and opposite force.

Max radiated his own power, and she was as bound by it as he was by the power in her.

"So am I," she whispered.

Max's mouth curved in a smile that made

Cleo's knees weak. "That should make it even more interesting."

It also created a bond between herself and Max that was unlike anything she had ever known. She wondered if Max felt the strength of the connection.

Cleo raised her hands and removed her shirt with a gentle shrug. It pooled on the floor at her feet. She saw the rosy crests of her own breasts in the mirror and felt the heat of Max's gaze.

"Imagine that I'm touching you," Max said.

Cleo met his eyes in the glass. "But you aren't touching me."

"Look into the mirror and pretend that I'm standing right behind you. My hands are on your breasts. I can feel your nipples beneath my palms. They're small and firm, like raspberries."

"Raspberries?"

"Raspberries and cream. Very sweet," Max said. "Very fresh. I want to taste them. Can you feel my tongue on you?"

A wave of heat flowed through Cleo. Her nipples became hard and full. She closed her eyes, but the sensation only intensified. "Yes. I can feel your mouth on me."

"What does it feel like?"

Cleo concentrated. "Hot. Wet. Powerful."

"You make me powerful, Cleopatra. Where

do you want me to touch you next?"

"Lower." Cleo opened her eyes again and stared at her slightly unfocused image. "I want your hands to go lower."

"There, between your legs?"

"Yes." She shuddered as she felt the coiling, tensing sensation radiating up through her.

"You feel so good, Cleo. Soft and warm." Max paused, as if he were actually exploring her with his fingers. "You're getting wet for me, aren't you?"

"Yes." Cleo felt the dampness between her thighs. She looked into the mirror with a knowing expression. "You're getting hard for me, aren't you?"

"I'm going out of my mind," Max said. "Put your hands on top of my fingers."

"Where are your fingers now?"

"Wherever you want them to be."

"Here," Cleo whispered. She brushed her fingers lightly over her silken panties. Then she drew them up across her belly. Slowly and deliberately she cupped her breasts and offered them to the man in the mirror.

"I think I've had about all the fantasy I can handle tonight," Max muttered. "I don't know about you, but I need the real thing very badly."

"So do I." Shivering with her need and excitement, Cleo turned away from the mirror and walked over to the bed. "There's something that I've been meaning to tell you, Max."

He looked up at her with eyes that were dark with soul-shattering desire. "What's that?"

"I love you."

Without a word, Max reached up and pulled her down on top of him. He captured her head in his hands and crushed her mouth against his own.

Cleo awoke hours later, aware that she was alone in the bed. She turned her head on the pillow and saw Max across the room. He loomed near the window, a ghostly shadow silhouetted against the blackness of the night. She knew from the angle of his body that he had both hands folded on top of the hawk on his cane.

"Max?"

"It's all right, Cleo. I'm just doing some thinking. Go back to sleep."

"I can't sleep with you prowling around the room," she grumbled. "Is something wrong?"

Max was silent for a moment. "I don't know."

She had never heard that tone in his voice. Cleo sat up quickly. "What is it, Max?"

"Remember the feeling you said you had

477

that day when someone stalked you in the fog?"

"I remember it," she said. "I believe it's called a sense of impending disaster."

"It's also called having the sensation that someone just walked across your grave."

"My God, Max." Cleo was unnerved. "Is that how you feel right now?"

"Yes."

She wondered gloomily if her declaration of love earlier had caused this disturbing air of unease around him. He had never responded to her confession, although he had made love to her with an intensity that had shocked her senses.

It had been a risk. She had realized that at the time. Max was not accustomed to love, she reminded herself. There had been no way of knowing how he would react to being told that he was loved.

Cleo tortured herself on the altar of *perhaps*.

Perhaps being loved made Max feel trapped. Perhaps he did not want that kind of pressure. Perhaps he was ambivalent about being the one who was loved. Perhaps all he really wanted was to belong to the Robbins' Nest Inn family. Perhaps he only wanted Cleo because she could give him a home.

Perhaps he didn't really love her at all in the way she wanted to be loved.

478

Perhaps she had been the one who had screwed up tonight.

Cleo rested her chin on her updrawn knees. "What do you want to do?"

"I don't know. I've felt like this once or twice before in my life. There was trouble every time." Max turned away from the window. "I think I'll give O'Reilly a call."

"Now?" Cleo squinted at the clock. She was so relieved that he didn't seem to be dwelling on her unwelcome declaration of love that she had trouble following the conversation. "It's two in the morning."

"I know." Max reached for the phone, apparently having no trouble seeing its dark shape in the shadows. He picked up the receiver and then froze.

"Max?"

He put the receiver slowly back into the cradle and stared out across the cove. "Christ."

"Max, what is it?" Cleo scrambled out of bed and went to stand beside him. She squinted when she saw the strange orange glow in the distance. "What on earth is that?"

"Cosmic Harmony," Max said. "It's on fire." He turned abruptly away from the desk.

"Oh, my God." Panic welled up in Cleo. "Andromeda and Daystar and the others will be asleep. We've got to get to them." She whirled around, scrabbling about frantically for her glasses.

"Calm down, Cleo." Max was halfway across the room, heading toward the closet. "First, make sure the fire department is on its way."

"Yes. Yes, of course." Cleo grabbed the phone and realized she couldn't see well enough to punch out the emergency number. She fumbled with the light switch and finally found it. She pushed her glasses onto her nose with shaking fingers and stabbed at the phone.

"Forget it," Max said as he pulled on his shirt. "They've already got the word. Hear the sirens?"

Cleo listened to the shrill howl in the distance. "Thank God. Max, we've got to get over there."

"I'll go. You stay here." Max was already dressed. He yanked up his zipper.

"No, I'll come with you." She grabbed her jeans.

Max looked at her, eyes grim. "I want you to stay here."

"Why?"

"Because something is wrong."

"I know something is wrong. Cosmic Harmony is on fire." Cleo had her jeans on and was frantically trying to button her shirt. She realized she was shaking so much that she could barely find the buttonholes.

Max unlocked his leather carryall and removed an object from inside. Cleo froze when she saw that it was a revolver.

"Where did you get that?" she whispered as she watched him load it.

"I've been keeping it handy since that day someone stalked you in the fog." Max looked up. "Don't worry, I'll get rid of it when this is all over. I don't want to keep a gun in the house any more than you do."

"Oh, Max." Cleo shivered.

He moved to stand in front of her. He caught hold of her shoulder with one hand. "Listen to me, Cleo. I want you to stay here at the inn. Do you understand me? You'll be safe here. There are people downstairs. George is here. Sylvia is in her room. There are plenty of lights on in the place. *I want you here.*"

She stared at him, momentarily stunned by the implications of what he was saying. "You're worried about me? But it's Cosmic Harmony that's in trouble."

"I don't like this, Cleo. A fire at Cosmic Harmony at this particular time is too damn weird. I want you where I know you'll be safe while I check out what's happening on the other side of the cove." He released her and went to the door.

"But, Max . . ." Cleo raced after him.

"Stay here, Cleo." Max opened the door.

She instinctively reacted to the command in his voice. For an instant she was immobilized. By the time she could move a few seconds later, Max was already out in the hall. He closed the door in her face.

She heard the familiar squeak of the hall floorboard, and then he was gone.

Cleo made up her mind. She would go downstairs and awaken Sylvia. Together they could discuss the wisdom of going to Cosmic Harmony.

The phone rang on the desk.

Cleo jumped. She paused, her hand on the doorknob, and glanced at the instrument as if it had come alive. It rang again, an urgent summons that sent a thrill of fear down her spine. Reluctantly she went toward it and picked it up.

"Hello?"

"Cleo? It's O'Reilly. I'm on the car phone. I'm on my way to the inn."

"O'Reilly." Cleo felt weak with relief. "Max was just about to call you."

"That doesn't surprise me. Sometimes that guy is downright psychic when it comes to trouble. Is he there?"

"No, he just left. He's on his way to Cosmic Harmony. There's a fire over there."

"Damn it to hell," O'Reilly muttered. "You sure?"

"We can see the flames from here."

"Cleo, listen to me." O'Reilly's voice was suddenly cold and tense. "You stay put, do you hear me?"

Cleo grimaced. "That's what Max just said. Give me one good reason."

"Because something has finally turned up, and I don't like it at all."

"What is this all about, O'Reilly? I'm already scared enough tonight."

"Cleo, did you know your father was a witness at a murder trial two years before he died?"

"Sure, I knew about it." Cleo's fingers clenched around the phone. "He saw a man leaving a building where the police said a murder had been committed. He identified the man on the stand. What has that got to do with anything?"

"That man's name was Emile Wynn. He was a professional hit man. A couple of small-time hoods gave evidence against him, but it was your father's testimony linking him to the scene of the crime that tipped the case in the prosecution's favor. Wynn went to prison."

"I know. O'Reilly, what is this all about? Please hurry. I want to go see what's happening at Cosmic Harmony."

"Three months before your father and mother died, Wynn was released on a technicality."

"What?" Cleo stared at the flames on the other side of the cove. "We were never told about that."

"It wasn't exactly news. Happens every day. At any rate, Wynn disappeared almost immediately. The authorities believed that he had left the country. It was a logical assumption. But I'm beginning to think that Wynn may have changed his identity instead."

Cleo sank down onto the chair. "You think he may have killed my parents out of revenge?"

"It's a real possibility. Cleo, there were a couple of things about Wynn that were noted at the trial. The first was that he had a reputation, and that reputation meant everything to him. He was a fanatic about it."

Cleo rubbed her temple, trying to think. "What sort of reputation?"

"He never failed, and he never left any evidence. He was a professional, and he was obsessive about it."

"Sort of like Max," Cleo whispered.

"Max? What the hell are you talking about?"

"He never screws up."

"Yeah, well, Wynn screwed up that last time, and your father saw him. Now your father is dead. It's possible that Wynn killed him and then murdered your mother simply because she was on the scene at the time."

Cleo squeezed her eyes shut. She felt sick to her stomach. "No witnesses."

"Right. Wynn never left witnesses. Listen, Cleo, this is all conjecture at this point, but I think you may have triggered Wynn back into action when you hired Eberson last summer."

"No," Cleo said softly. "Oh, no."

"I think Eberson did some digging around and came up with some of the same conclusions that I've come up with. He may have been careless and accidentally alerted Wynn to the fact that someone was looking into the case again. Wynn may have decided that his new identity was at risk."

"You think Wynn killed Mr. Eberson, too?"

"I think it's a real possibility. Cleo, do you understand what I'm saying here?" O'Reilly asked tightly. "If I'm right, then you're Wynn's target now. Don't leave the inn."

"But what has all this got to do with the threats I've received concerning my book?"

"Wynn was noted for being very thorough. He did his research carefully. He preferred to make his jobs look like accidents or, as in the case of your father, suicide. He had a reputation for going to a lot of trouble to set up

485

the scene of the hit."

"You think he did some checking on me, found out I'd written *The Mirror*, and decided to set up the scenario that would make people think I was murdered by a deranged reader?"

"He probably knows how much Cosmic Harmony means to you. I don't like the sound of this fire. A little too coincidental."

"That's what Max said."

"Max is on his way to the cove now?"

"Yes."

"Good. You stay put, Cleo. Don't step foot outside the inn until he gets back."

Cleo gave up trying to argue. "All right. I'll go downstairs and wake Sylvia. She and I and Sammy will circle the wagons and wait for the men to do their thing."

"I'll be there in another hour or so." O'Reilly paused briefly. "Tell Sylvia I'm on my way, will you?"

"She'll be waiting for you. We'll all be waiting."

"That's nice to know," O'Reilly said. "Been a long time since I had anyone waiting for me. Listen, I've got to get off the phone now. I'm going to call your police chief. I want to let him know what's going on."

"We've only got a one-man force, O'Reilly. Harry will be out at Cosmic Harmony right now."

"Hell, that's the trouble with small towns. Okay, sit tight. Max and I will handle everything."

Cleo put down the phone.

Her parents had been killed. Murdered. Shot by a cold-blooded hit man.

But all she felt was relief.

As horrible as the truth was, it was infinitely preferable to the explanation that the authorities had insisted upon all these years. Her father had not gone mad and killed her mother and himself. Her parents' love for each other had not been tainted by a foul sickness in her father's mind. The bond between them had been pure and clean, wholesome and steadfast. Just like her love for Max.

In spite of the situation, Cleo felt as if a dark weight had been lifted from her soul.

She rose slowly and started for the door. She wanted to talk to Sylvia.

The flames in the distance caught her attention once more. She paused to glance out the window. It was impossible to tell if it was the main lodge that was on fire or one of the smaller buildings.

The hall floorboard squeaked.

Cleo went perfectly still.

I have a reputation to maintain.

Her own words to Sylvia a few hours earlier came back to her. *Does it strike you that Max and Herbert T. Valence have something in common?*

A reputation.

A reputation.

Cleo leaped for the door. It opened before she could lock it. Herbert T. Valence stepped into the room. He had a pistol in his hand. There was something odd about the shape of the barrel, Cleo realized. Perhaps that was what a silencer looked like.

"Well, Ms. Robbins." Valence smiled his thin, humorless little smile. "We meet properly at last. Allow me to introduce myself. My real name is Emile Wynn. Perhaps you've heard of me. Your father ruined me professionally."

Cleo tried to speak and realized that she could not find her voice. She took a deep breath, the same kind she took when she meditated. She had to say something, anything, in order to break the paralysis.

"You bastard." Her voice was only a squeak. But rage swept through her without warning, driving out the fear. *"You killed my parents."*

Valence frowned as he closed the door behind himself. "I had no choice. Your father's testimony destroyed my reputation. I could not rest until he had paid for it. A man's reputation is everything, Ms. Robbins."

"My mother . . ." Cleo began in a choked voice.

"Had to go, too, I'm afraid. I plan my little dramas with exquisite care, and I had determined that a murder-suicide seemed most appropriate for that particular situation."

"You've come after me because you knew I'd find you sooner or later," Cleo said.

Valence looked at her with a strangely troubled gaze. "You hired a second-rate investigator last summer. He was a very unprofessional sort, Ms. Robbins. I realized almost immediately that he was nosing around, and I took appropriate steps. But I also knew then that I had to do something about you."

"In other words, you knew I might decide to hire someone else, and next time I might get my money's worth." Cleo took a step back.

Valence did not appear to know that O'Reilly had already learned who he was. Whatever happened here tonight, she must not betray O'Reilly or Max. Valence would surely go after them next.

"Unfortunately it became clear that you were going to be a nuisance, Ms. Robbins." Valence followed her movement with the pistol. "But I must confess that one thing puzzled me. If you had suspicions about your parents' death, why did you wait nearly four years before you hired an investigator?"

"It took me all that time to recover to a point where I could deal with it." Cleo had never known such primitive rage. It consumed her. She was no longer afraid of Valence. "You destroyed my family, you stupid, crazy little man."

"Don't call me crazy." Valence's eyes glittered with an evil light. "Those idiot psychiatrists in prison called me crazy. But they were wrong. You're all wrong. I was a professional with a perfect track record. I never made mistakes. I never failed. Your father destroyed my reputation."

"He didn't destroy it. You screwed up."

"Don't say that." Valence took another step forward. "It's not true. I never screw up, as you so crudely put it, Ms. Robbins."

Cleo edged back toward the mirror. The only defense she could think of at the moment was to keep him talking. The man was insane. It occurred to her that a genuinely professional hit man would have killed her by now. "You're going to try to make people think I was murdered by some deranged person who hated my book, aren't you?"

Valence scowled. "Even if I did not have my personal reasons for terminating you, you deserve to be punished for writing *The Mirror*."

He was even nuttier than she had first thought, Cleo decided. "Why do you say that?"

"You are the author of a pornographic novel, Ms. Robbins," Valence chided with the outrage of an evangelist. "You're no better than a whore. You write filth, and every decent person knows it."

"Decent person?" She looked at him in disbelief. "You consider yourself a decent person?"

"I am a clean man, Ms. Robbins." Valence's fingers flexed around the grip of the pistol. "My mother made certain that I did not dirty myself in the gutter of sexuality. I am proud to say that I have not had carnal knowledge of a woman since she showed me how obscene the act was."

"Let me guess. You're the product of a dysfunctional family, right?" Cleo did not know if taunting Valence would keep him talking or push him over the edge, but she couldn't think of anything else to do.

"My mother was a pure woman," Valence said savagely. "And she kept me pure."

"By keeping you for herself? I'll bet those prison shrinks had a field day with that, didn't they?"

"Shut up," Valence snarled. "You created a work of filth. No one will think it strange that some clean person took it upon himself to punish you."

Cleo realized with shock that Valence believed what he was saying. "You've got a lot of nerve condemning me for writing erotica. You're a hit man, for God's sake. What does that make you?"

"It makes me a professional." Valence drew a length of red ribbon from his jacket pocket. "A professional with only one stain upon my spotless reputation. But I will soon rub out that stain."

He started toward her. Cleo saw the glint of the wire entwined in the ribbon. She knew that he was going to put it around her neck. The same way the man in the mirror put the ribbon around the throat of the woman in *The Mirror*.

Valence was going to strangle her with the scarlet ribbon.

She opened her mouth to scream, knowing Valence would probably shoot her before she could make herself heard. Perhaps if she made enough of a racket before she died he would not escape undetected.

At that instant the lights flickered and went out.

"Goddamn it," Valence shouted in intense agitation. "Don't move. I'm warning you."

Cleo ignored him and dove for the floor.

Valence was as blind as she was, and she knew the room far better than he did. She crawled toward the door, knowing it would take several seconds for Valence's eyes to adjust to the sudden darkness.

A soft, hissing sound overhead told her that Valence had fired the silenced pistol. The bullet splintered wood.

At the same instant the floorboard outside the door squeaked. A draft of air from the hallway told her that someone had opened the door and entered the room. She looked up and thought she could see a dark shadow moving against the deeper shadows of the attic.

Max.

Her hand touched the base of the mirror stand.

Another soft, hissing sigh seared the air in the room. Cleo surged to her feet, grabbed the mirror and its frame, and hurled it toward the spot where she knew Valence was standing.

The mirror struck something solid and fell to the floor. Glass shattered. Valence cried out, revealing his location.

The bright rays of the powerful flashlight that Cleo always kept behind the front desk snapped into life. They pinned Valence in a beam of blinding light.

"Get away from me," Valence screamed. He

held out one hand as if in supplication, aimed the pistol toward the source of the light, and pulled the trigger.

The crack of an unsilenced revolver shot rang out at the same instant. Valence slumped to the floor, motionless.

The flashlight fell to the floor, its beam still illuminating Valence's body.

"Max," Cleo shouted as she dashed across the room. "Max, answer me."

"Shit," Max said. "The same damn leg."

19

Valence was dead, but the following morning Max decided he was still pissed at him and would be for a long time. Every time Max felt the lancing pain from the new stitches in his thigh, he was reminded of how close he had come to losing Cleo. Rage and fear had surged through him last night as he had made his way up the stairs to the attic. The damned cane had never felt so clumsy in his hand. Trying to manage the revolver and the flashlight had been a difficult task. He had never resented his bad leg so much.

But Cleo was safe now, and Max intended

to keep her that way even if he had to put a leash on her.

Ensconced in a bed in the local community hospital, Max studied the ring of anxious faces gathered around him. He was still not accustomed to having people fuss over him, he reflected. He wondered if he would ever get to the point where he would take such concern on his behalf for granted. He doubted it. When you had spent most of your life looking for something, you weren't likely to treat it casually when you finally stumbled into it.

The whole family, with the exception of Ben and Trisha, who were still blissfully unaware of events, was hovering at Max's bedside. Cleo had insisted on spending what was left of the night in a chair in his hospital room. The others, who had been sent home by the staff a few hours earlier, had crowded back in right after breakfast.

The nurses had already complained twice that there was no room for them to carry out their duties. The doctor, a smiling woman in her mid-fifties, had told Max that it looked like he was in good hands.

"Does your leg hurt real, real bad?" Sammy clutched Lucky Ducky and gazed at Max with wide-eyed concern.

Max considered the matter closely. Getting shot had been a definite screw-up. When he'd gotten a fix on Valence's location, thanks to Cleo, he'd switched on the flashlight with the intention of blinding Valence.

Knowing that Valence would fire toward the beam of light, Max had taken pains to hold the light well off to the side while he aimed his own weapon. Unfortunately, crazy as he was in some ways, Valence had still been enough of a cool-headed professional to shoot to the left of the light. Most people, after all, were right-handed. It was a safe bet that whoever had entered the room would be holding a gun in his right hand and the flash-light in his left. If that person was thinking, he would be holding the flashlight as far from his body as possible.

Valence had been right on all counts. Max had taken the bullet in his left thigh. He would have another scar two inches away from the first one. The doctor had assured him that it was only a flesh wound. Unfortunately, that didn't make the stitches any more comfortable.

"It doesn't hurt real, real bad," Max said. "Just sort of bad."

"Hey, could have been worse." O'Reilly grinned. "Could have been the other leg this time, and then you would have had to use two canes."

"You're a real ray of sunshine, O'Reilly."

As it was Max knew he was going to be on crutches for a while. He looked at Cleo, who was standing at the head of the bed. She had such a fierce grip on his hand that the ring on her finger was leaving an imprint on his skin. It felt good. "You're sure you're okay?"

"For the hundredth time, I'm okay." She leaned down and kissed his cheek. "Thanks to you."

"You're a hero, Max," Andromeda told him proudly. She poured some of her special tea out of a thermos she had brought with her. "The local newspaper wants to do a feature on how you rescued Cleo from that horrid Mr. Valence."

Max grimaced as he took the mug of tea from Andromeda. "I don't want to talk to any reporters."

"It's just Bertie Jennings from the *Harmony Cove Herald*," Daystar assured him. "Don't worry. I've already told him that he can't talk to you until you're back on your feet."

"Thanks." Max scowled. "Maybe by that time he won't want to do the story." A thought occurred to him. "How much damage did the fire do?"

"The meditation center is gone, but the lodge is fine. So are the guest quarters," Daystar said. "We're in good shape considering what might have happened. But, then,

O'Reilly says that destroying Cosmic Harmony was not really Valence's goal. He just wanted to use the fire as a means of causing confusion."

"Valence set the fire using timed fuses so that he could get back to the inn before the blaze started," O'Reilly explained.

"Poor Nolan," Cleo said. "To think we once suspected him of being behind the incidents."

Max did not like the sound of "*poor* Nolan," but he nobly chose to ignore the reference. He could afford to be generous, he told himself. He had Cleo. All Hildebrand had was a budding career in politics, to which he was more than welcome as far as Max was concerned.

"Valence knew a fire at Cosmic Harmony would create chaos not just there but also at the inn," Sylvia said.

"He'd stayed at the inn often enough to know how important Cosmic Harmony was to me," Cleo agreed.

"He obviously figured one of two things would happen when the fire was discovered," Max said. "The first possibility was that Cleo would rush to the scene. If that happened, he no doubt intended to follow and try to get at her in the confusion and darkness while everyone concentrated on the fire."

"The other possibility was that you would

leave her safely behind at the inn while you went to see what was happening," O'Reilly concluded.

Max swore softly. "It was a logical plan. Either way Cleo would be vulnerable for the first time since that day Valence had stalked her in the fog."

"He must have realized that Max was keeping an eye on you, Cleo, because of the incidents that had been occurring," Sylvia said. "It was no secret, especially after O'Reilly started talking to people in town about them."

"That's right," Daystar said. "Valence knew he would somehow have to separate Max and Cleo. Trying to get at Cleo while Max was protecting her would have complicated things no end for him."

"He was very proud of his research and planning," Cleo whispered. "And absolutely obsessive about his reputation."

Max felt the shudder that went through her. He tightened his grip on her hand. She smiled tremulously at him. The love in her eyes was bright and clear, and he knew it would last him his whole life.

No one had ever looked at him the way Cleo did. Last night when she had told him that she loved him, he had been so shaken by his good fortune that he had been unable to sort out his emotions. He had only known that he wanted her more than ever, that he had to protect her. She was the most important thing in his world.

This morning when he had awakened to find Cleo sitting beside his bed, he had taken one look at her and finally understood what had happened to him.

"When did it hit you that the fire might be a diversion?" Andromeda asked.

Max pulled his thoughts back to the subject at hand. "When I was about a quarter of a mile down the road. I turned around and drove straight back to the inn. But I had a feeling that something had really gone bad. I started to call Cleo on the car phone, but O'Reilly called me first."

"He was just pulling back into the parking lot when I reached him," O'Reilly said. "I told him what I had told Cleo about a psychotic killer who had a thing about his reputation and who always planned his hits with military precision. The last thing I heard Max say before he hung up was that he knew who the guy was."

"I came to the same conclusion Cleo did," Max said quietly. "Valence was the obvious suspect. He'd been in and out of Harmony Cove all winter giving his damn seminars. He'd had plenty of opportunity to see how things worked at the inn. Plenty of time to set things up."

"We didn't think of him when we drew up that list of guests who had been at the inn the night the ribbon was left on my pillow," Cleo said ruefully.

Max exchanged glances with O'Reilly. "I put him on the list," he said.

"You did?" Cleo was startled.

O'Reilly made a face. "Valence was on the list, and I checked him out, but there were no red flags. The guy had a nice, clean background. Everything was in order." He held up his hands. "What can I say? Valence was a pro."

Max looked at Cleo. "All I could think of was that I had left you alone. I knew that group of seminar attendees had all had too much to drink and were probably sound asleep. When I reached the lobby, George was also asleep, just as he had been when I'd left. I went to Valence's room, and it was empty."

"So he came to my room," Sylvia said. "He woke me up and told me to run down to the basement and throw the main circuit breaker while he climbed the stairs to the attic."

"I was hoping that having the lights go out without warning would throw Valence off stride for at least a few seconds," Max explained. "I recalled how he'd reacted that time when he lost power during one of his seminars."

"I remember that," Sylvia said thoughtfully. "He really got upset, didn't he? It disrupted his carefully orchestrated seminar."

"Earlier this evening when he checked in, he made a point of saying that there were no storms expected this weekend," Cleo mused. "He probably had planned everything so that there would be no rain to put out the fire too quickly at Cosmic Harmony or cause a power failure."

"A real thorough kind of guy," O'Reilly mused. He put his arm around Sylvia. "But not real flexible."

"I think that Valence had gotten so crazy that every little alteration in his schedule threw him into a turmoil," Cleo said.

A commotion out in the hall made Max and everyone else in the crowded room glance toward the door.

"I'm afraid you can't go in there, sir," a nurse said in a loud, authoritative voice. "Mr. Fortune already has far too many visitors."

"I came all this way to see Fortune, and I damn well intend to see him," a man answered in a voice that was louder and more commanding. "I have business with him."

"But he's been seriously injured," the nurse said.

"He's used to it."

"Just what I needed," Max muttered as a familiar figure came through the door. "Another well-wisher. What the hell do you want, Dennison? I'm not supposed to have any visitors. Just family."

Dennison Curzon had the same autocratic attitude Jason had had. He also had the same silver hair and the strongly etched features that characterized the rest of the Curzon family. But his eyes lacked the penetrating, analytical intelligence that had characterized Jason's gaze.

Dennison swept the faces of the small group gathered around Max and dismissed them all. He glowered at Max.

"What's going on here, Fortune? I hear you've gotten yourself shot again."

"I'm recovering nicely, thank you," Max said. "Dennison Curzon, meet the family."

"Family?" Dennison's forehead furrowed in confusion and annoyance. "What family? You don't have a family."

"He does now," Cleo said quietly. She kept her grip on Max's hand as she surveyed Denison with a curious, searching look. "Jason was your brother?"

"Yes, he was." Dennison switched his attention briefly to her. "Who are you?"

"My fiancée," Max said before Cleo could respond. "Congratulate me, Dennison. Cleo and I are going to be married."

Dennison ignored the announcement and, with typical Curzon single-mindedness, zeroed in on his main target. "Listen, Max, we've got to talk." He cast an irritated glance at Cleo and the others. "Do you think we could have some privacy around here?"

"No," Cleo said.

Nobody made a move toward the door.

Max grinned at Dennison. "Guess not."

"What the hell?" Dennison took a closer look at Cleo. "Who did you say you were?"

"I told you, she's my fiancée," Max said.

"I am also Max's employer," Cleo said crisply.

"The hell you are." Dennison stared at her. "Fortune works for Curzon International."

"No, he doesn't," Cleo said. "Not anymore."

"He works for Cleo," Sammy announced.

Dennison scowled. "Now, see here, I am Dennison Curzon of Curzon International. Max Fortune has worked for my company for twelve years."

"I believed he resigned when your brother died," Cleo murmured. "He now works for me."

"Quite right," Daystar said in her no-nonsense way. "Max has been on the payroll of Robbins' Nest Inn for some time now. He's doing an excellent job."

"Yes, indeed. He's one of the family," Andromeda said.

"Bullshit." Dennison looked at Max. "I don't know what game you're playing here, Fortune, but I need you at Curzon. My daughter and that damned husband of hers took over my board of directors yesterday."

"Kim will do a good job with Curzon," Max said. "She's got what it takes. My advice is don't fight her."

"I'll fight anyone who tries to take over my company. I've waited all these years to take command, and I'm going to do it. I want you in my corner. Let's cut the bullshit, Fortune. Name your price."

"For what?" Max asked.

"For coming back to Curzon as my personal troubleshooter." Dennison narrowed his eyes. "I'll give you the same deal my brother did plus a ten percent increase in salary and bonuses. In return I want your guarantee that you report to me and to me alone."

"I've already got a job," Max said.

"All right." Dennison's expression was taut. "If you come back, I'll consider giving you that seat on the board that Jason wanted you to have."

"No, thanks. I seem to have developed an

aptitude for plumbing and home repairs," Max said.

"You heard him," Cleo said. "He doesn't want to work for you. Mr. Curzon, I think you had better leave. Max has had a very rough night, and he needs his rest." She turned to Max. "Don't you need your rest?"

"I need my rest," Max said equably.

"He needs his rest," Sylvia said.

Andromeda and Daystar nodded in agreement.

O'Reilly looked as though he was going to explode with laughter at any second.

Dennison rounded on Cleo. "Don't you dare try to kick me out of here, young lady. Max Fortune belongs to me."

"He most certainly does not." Cleo released Max's hand and took a step toward Dennison. "He belongs to me. And to the rest of us." She looked around at the others. "Isn't that right?"

"Oh, yes," Andromeda murmured. "No question about it."

"He's one of the family," Sammy said loudly. "You can't have him."

Daystar glowered at Dennison. "I'm afraid you're wasting your time and ours with all this nonsense, Mr. Curzon. Why don't you leave?"

"Nonsense? You call this nonsense?" Dennison turned on her with an air of appalled outrage. "Are you out of your mind, lady? Curzon is a multinational corporation. Do you have any idea how much Fortune can earn in a year working for me?"

"No," Daystar said honestly. "But I don't see that it matters."

"Believe me, it matters," Dennison snarled. "Curzon has made Fortune a wealthy man. He can become even wealthier if he comes back to work for me."

"Piffle," Andromeda said. "Max already has a perfectly good job at Robbins' Nest Inn. Isn't that right, Max?"

"Right," said Max.

Dennison looked at him. "This is a joke, isn't it?"

O'Reilly grinned. "Face it, Curzon, it's not a joke. You can't match the benefits that Max has found in his new job."

"Can't match them?" Dennison glared at O'Reilly. "I can pay Fortune enough in one year to enable him to buy that damned inn."

"The man hasn't got a clue," O'Reilly said cheerfully.

Sammy clung very tightly to Lucky Ducky as he gazed up at Dennison. "Go away."

"Yes," Cleo said. "Go away."

"Drive carefully," Andromeda said brightly.

"You're becoming a pest, Mr. Curzon,"

Daystar said. "I do wish you would take your-self off."

Dennison looked at Max with disbelief and desperation. "Think about this, Fortune. There's a good chance I can talk Kimberly into leaving Winston. I don't think she's been all that happy with him lately. You and my daughter would make a hell of a combina-tion."

"You didn't think so three years ago," Max said. "And you know something? You were right. I owe you for talking Kimberly out of the engagement. In exchange, I'm going to give you some good advice. Don't get in her way now. She'll be the best thing that's ever happened to Curzon International."

"She's taking over, don't you understand?"

"I understand," Max said. "And you're all going to get even richer with her at the helm. If you behave yourself, maybe she'll give you some grandkids."

"That sounds lovely." Andromeda smiled kindly at Dennison. "Wouldn't you love some grandchildren?"

Dennison stared at her and then looked at Max with a baffled expression. "You're seri-ous about this, aren't you? You aren't just playing a game in order to jack up your price?"

"I'm serious, all right," Max said. "You couldn't meet my price in a million years. Go away, Dennison."

Cleo scowled at him. "You are becoming extremely offensive, Mr. Curzon. Only family is supposed to be in this room until the regular visiting hours. Please leave, or I will summon someone from the hospital staff to deal with you."

Dennison gave her one last bewildered glare, and then he turned around and stomped out of the room.

An acute silence descended.

"I want to go home," Max said.

Cleo awoke at dawn the next morning. It wasn't the gray, wet light of the new day that had brought her up out of her slumbers. It was the knowledge that Max was not in bed beside her.

Worried, Cleo sat up abruptly. "Max?"

There was no sign of him. Cleo glanced across the attic room and saw that his crutches were missing. She frowned. Max was still getting accustomed to using the crutches. She didn't like the idea of his navigating the stairs without her assistance.

She heard the floorboard squeak on the other side of the door just as she was about to push aside the covers and go in search of the invalid.

The attic door opened softly, and Max maneuvered himself cautiously into the room. He was wearing a pair of trousers and nothing else. Andromeda had opened the seam on the left pant leg to accommodate the bandage on Max's thigh.

Max concentrated intently, his attention on the floor as he angled the crutches into position. The stem of a white rose was clenched between his teeth.

Cleo stared at the rose, a great joy welling up inside her. *Red for seduction; white for love.*

"Max?" she breathed, hardly daring to believe what she was seeing.

Max looked up quickly. "You're supposed to be asleep," he mumbled around the rose stem.

Cleo smiled brilliantly. She recalled the last chapter of her book very clearly. The man in the mirror, freed at last, had awakened the narrator with a single white rose. Seduction had been transformed into love.

"I'd rather be awake for this, if you don't mind," Cleo whispered.

Max started across the room. His eyes never left Cleo. "I don't mind."

Out of the corner of her eye, Cleo saw something yellow. She glanced down and noticed that Sammy had left Lucky Ducky lying on the floor after paying a visit to Max's bedside last night.

Cleo's eyes widened in alarm as she saw Max's right crutch come down on top of the toy.

"Max, *look out.*"

It was too late. The crutch skittered off the rounded edges of the rubber duck and went out from under Max.

"Hell." Max made a valiant effort to steady himself with the left crutch, but it was hopeless.

Max unclenched his teeth from around the stem of the rose and let it fall.

"That damned duck," Max said as he crashed to the floor.

With a cry of dismay, Cleo leaped out of bed and rushed to his side. "Are you all right? Max, Max, speak to me."

Flat on his back, Max glared at her. "Everything's just ducky."

"Do you think your stitches have come undone?" Cleo bent over his bandaged thigh. "Maybe we should get you to the clinic."

"Forget the leg. Cleo, I love you."

Cleo's hand rested on his leg. Tears misted her eyes. "I'm so glad."

She threw herself down on top of him, careful not to hurt his injured thigh. Max's arms closed tightly around her, holding her close.

"I should have known right from the start,"

Max said into Cleo's hair.

"It's not your fault you didn't recognize love when you found it," Cleo said against his chest. "You haven't had enough of it to know it when you see it."

"I know it now," Max said, his voice laced with raw wonder. He abruptly went very still.

"Max?" Cleo raised her head and looked down at him in concern. "Are you sure you're all right?"

Max started to smile. "Look up, Cleo."

"At what?"

"At Jason's seascapes."

Cleo craned her head and stared up at the two seascapes hanging on the wall. "What about them?"

"There's something strange about the frames. I never noticed it when I looked at the pictures before, but from this perspective you can see that the frames are too wide." Max levered himself up into a sitting position and reached for one of the fallen crutches.

"What are you doing?"

"Help me get one of those things off the wall."

"I'll handle it." Cleo got to her feet and hefted one of the seascapes. She took it down off the wall and carried it across the room to the bed.

Max made his way over to the desk, opened

one of the drawers, and removed the screwdriver he had bought at the Harmony Cove hardware store. "Ben was right. You never know when you're going to need a good screwdriver."

Max crossed the room to the bed, sat down beside the seascape, and went to work on the back of the frame with the screwdriver.

Cleo watched, fascinated. "Max, do you really think that Jason . . . ?"

"Hid the Luttrells behind his seascapes?" Max's mouth curved with satisfaction as he undid the last of the screws. "Yes."

He lifted the back of the frame and set it aside. Then, with great reverence, he removed a white, flat board out of the frame. There was a note attached to it. Max opened it.

Now that you've found this one, Max, you know where to find the others. I never could paint worth a damn, and I figured that sooner or later you'd wonder why I had bothered with these lousy seascapes. The Luttrells are only a portion of your inheritance, son. I trust you found the rest of it at Robbins' Nest Inn. How does it feel to have a family of your own?

Love,
Jason

513

Max turned the board over. Cleo looked at the canvas that was fastened to the other side.

It was a dark, elegantly savage painting full of swirling shapes and abstract tension, and yet it was not entirely bleak. Even to Cleo's untrained eye, it was a work of art perfectly suited to Max. The painting seemed to radiate both the potential for despair and the possibility of love.

Cleo smiled softly. "Good old Lucky Ducky. I wonder why Jason went to the trouble of hiding the paintings if he wanted you to have them."

Max glanced up from the Luttrell. His eyes were brilliant. "Jason wanted me to find something else first. Something that was a lot more important than any painting."

"Did you?" Cleo asked.

"Yes," Max said with absolute certainty. He smiled, his love for her plain to read in his eyes. "I did."